The Best Science-Fiction
Stories and Novels
Ninth Series

THE BEST SCIENCE - FICTION
STORIES AND NOVELS
Ninth Series

Edited by T. E. DIKTY

WITH *The Science-Fiction Year,* by T. E. DIKTY

AND *The Science-Fiction Book Index,* by EARL KEMP

Chicago: 1958

To
Judy
for
5 years
and the 3

COPYRIGHT 1958 BY T. E. DIKTY

Designed by PUBLICATION ASSOCIATES

Published simultaneously in Canada by
George J. McLeod, Ltd., Toronto

Library of Congress Catalog Card Number: 49–10461

Contents

Acknowledgments

The following acknowledgments are gratefully made for permission to reprint copyrighted material:

2066: ELECTION DAY, by Michael Shaara: Copyright, 1956, by Street & Smith Publications, Inc. Reprinted by permission of Harry Altshuler and *Astounding Science Fiction.*

THE MILE-LONG SPACESHIP, by Kate Wilhelm: Copyright, 1957, by Street & Smith Publications, Inc. Reprinted by permission of the author and *Astounding Science Fiction.*

THE LAST VICTORY, by Tom Godwin: Copyright, 1957, by Quinn Publishing Company, Inc. Reprinted by permission of T. W. Raines and *IF—Worlds of Science Fiction.*

CALL ME JOE, by Poul Anderson: Copyright, 1957, by Street & Smith Publications, Inc. Reprinted by permission of Scott Meredith and *Astounding Science Fiction.*

DIDN'T HE RAMBLE, by Chad Oliver: Copyright, 1957, by Fantasy House, Inc. Reprinted by permission of Willis Kingsley Wing and *The Magazine of Fantasy and Science Fiction.*

THE QUEEN'S MESSENGER, by John J. McGuire: Copyright, 1957, by Street & Smith Publications, Inc. Reprinted by permission of the author and *Astounding Science Fiction.*

THE OTHER PEOPLE, by Leigh Brackett: Copyright, 1956, by Fantasy House, Inc., where it originally appeared under the title "The Queer Ones." Reprinted by permission of the author and *Venture Science Fiction.*

INTO YOUR TENT I'LL CREEP, by Eric Frank Russell: Copyright, 1957, by Street & Smith Publications, Inc. Reprinted by permission of Scott Meredith and *Astounding Science Fiction.*

NOR DUST CORRUPT, by James McConnell: Copyright, 1956, by Quinn Publishing Company, Inc. Reprinted by permission of Harry Altshuler and *IF—Worlds of Science Fiction.*

NIGHTSOUND, by Algis J. Budrys: Copyright, 1956, by Renown Publications, Inc. where it originally appeared under the title "The Attic Voice." Reprinted by permission of Scott Meredith and *Satellite Science Fiction.*

THE TUNESMITH, by Lloyd Biggle, Jr.: Copyright, 1957, by Quinn Publishing Company, Inc. Reprinted by permission of Harry Altshuler and *IF—Worlds of Science Fiction.*

HUNTING MACHINE, by Carol Emshwiller: Copyright, 1957, by Columbia Publications, Inc. Reprinted by permission of Harry Altshuler and *Science Fiction Stories.*

In addition the publishers would like to acknowledge the assistance of the following people: Mr. Harry Altshuler, Mr. Anthony Boucher, Mr. John W. Campbell, Jr., Mr. Oscar J. Friend, Mrs. Leigh Brackett Hamilton, Miss Cylvia Kleinman, Mr. Arthur P. Lawler, Mr. Robert W. Lowndes, Mr. Robert Mills and Mr. James L. Quinn.

The

Science-Fiction

Year

by T. E. DIKTY

People who tried to keep up with the world in 1956–57, to quote the Red Queen in *Through the Looking Glass,* had to run as hard as they could just to stand still. Science had progressed at a dizzying rate during the year. By the end of 1957 few people would have bet against the human race hitting the moon with a rocket within a few weeks or months. Two satellites had already been launched in orbits around the earth and one of them contained a living creature—a small dog. How long would it be until there was a manned station whizzing around the world a thousand miles overhead? It looked like it might be far sooner than anybody, including science-fiction fans, had thought possible.

As if anticipating the great strides in science, science-fiction itself had recovered completely from the sharp recession of 1955 and was enjoying a modest boom. Complete figures, partly compiled from science-fiction's indispensable newspaper, *Science Fiction Times,* showed that the hobbyist who purchased every issue of the science-fiction magazines published during 1956 invested $38.80 in 112 issues of 18 different titles—a slight increase in cost and number of issues over 1955. For 1957, preliminary figures showed an even larger total: $55.95 for 160 issues of 25 different titles.

New titles started in 1956–57 included *Science Fiction Adventures,* a companion magazine to *Infinity* and, like that magazine, also edited by Larry Shaw, an old-time fan. *Venture* saw publication as a companion to *Fantasy and Science Fiction* with Robert Mills, managing editor of Mercury Publications, as its editor. The Ziff-Davis Publishing Co. started two magazines: *Dream Worlds* and *Amazing Stories Science Fiction Novels*. *Dream Worlds* saw numerous delays during 1957 and *Amazing Stories Science Fiction Novels* saw only one issue; it was temporarily suspended with the collapse of the American News Co. and resulting unsettled conditions in the distributing industry. Last entry of the year in the magazine sweepstakes was a quarterly, published by Ballantine Books and edited by Frederik Pohl. Title: *Star Science Fiction*.

New publishers in the field started *Space Science Fiction,* a bi-monthly and *Saturn,* edited by an old-timer in the field, Donald A. Wollheim, editor of the Ace double-novels pocketbook line. An old title—but a new publisher and really a new magazine—was *Super Science Fiction,* a bi-monthly which made news later in the year when it cut its pages to 112 to become the smallest magazine offered at 35¢. *IF* magazine published a "one-shot" titled *The First World of IF* and priced at 50¢. Pines Publications got back in the field rather briefly with a magazine-format anthology carrying the old and honorable title of *Wonder Stories*.

The last of the 25¢ magazines, *Science Fiction Quarterly,* increased its number of pages and upped its price to 35¢. *Future Science Fiction* switched from an occasional issue to full-fledged quarterly publication and was due to go bi-monthly with the first 1958 issue. Ziff-Davis switched *Fantastic Science Fiction* to a monthly, and *Infinity* and *Science Fiction Adventures* were slated for monthly publication during 1957.

There were some soft spots in the picture, however. *Science Fiction Stories,* which had announced monthly publication at the start of 1957, still had not gone monthly by year's end and, in fact, had cut back from 144 pages to 128. A few other titles in the field had also cut pages or suffered delays in publication; enough so that veteran editors in the field viewed the "boom" with a good deal of caution.

At the end of the year Leo Margulies, publisher of *Satellite Science Fiction* (and what a stroke of foresight *that* title was!) revealed that he had gained control of the old all-fiction men's magazine *Short Stories,* as well as the original science-fiction and fantasy magazine, *Weird Tales*. *Short Stories* appeared under the Margulies imprint in late 1957; plans for *Weird Tales* were still tentative but the chances for its being revived seemed very good.

One major event in publishing had yet, at this writing, to be assessed as being good or bad for the science-fiction field. The American News Company, distributor of a number of science-fiction magazines as well as many large circulation "slicks," withdrew from the distributing field. All of its science-fiction clients were able to make contact with other distributors, but for a period of several months newsstand conditions were chaotic to say the least.

Some magazines failed to appear in several of the nation's larger cities. To complicate the picture, many publishers found that checks from ANC were delayed, resulting in a "capital" squeeze. Turbulent distributing conditions meant, of course, fewer newsstand sales and consequent loss of revenue for publishers who could ill afford it. These conditions, plus attempts by wholesalers, retailers, and major distributors to increase their percentage of the take, were bound to trim already thin profit margins of many magazine publishers. To top it off, one figure in the distributing industry frankly stated it was uneconomical to distribute magazines with newsstand sales of less than 100,000 copies per issue. This, unfortunately, would include all the science-fiction magazines.

On the bright side of the picture were preliminary reports from some publishers who found their sales going up, possibly due to more efficient distribution by the independents. How would the distribution picture finally shape up? At year's end, nobody knew for sure.

Editorial changes during the year included the departure of Sam Merwin, Jr., from *Satellite Science Fiction* to the West Coast where he settled down as editor of a string of men's magazines. Succeeding Merwin was Frank Belknap Long, Jr., long well-known in the science-fiction field. B. G. Davis, veteran president of the Ziff-Davis Publishing Co., resigned from that company to form a new company of his own. His first magazine purchase: *Ellery Queen's Mystery Magazine*.

Overseas, the science-fiction picture was a little spottier than it was in the U.S. In England, the field suffered a blow when *Authentic Science Fiction* folded, effective with the October, 1957, issue. It had been one of England's major science-fiction magazines and had seen 85 issues before its demise. Brightening the picture slightly was the fact that *Nebula* had switched to monthly publication.

In Mexico, the American publication *Fantasy and Science Fiction* started a Spanish language edition titled *Ciencia y Fantasia*. The first Austrian science-fiction magazine appeared, entitled *Uranus*. Germany experienced a minor science-fiction boom but Australia saw *Science Fiction Monthly* and the *Science Fiction Library* cease publication. Reports also trickled out from behind the Iron Curtain that science-fiction was not exactly unknown in the various people's republics. Russia reportedly pirated Ray Bradbury's famous story "Fahrenheit 451."

Quality-wise, science-fiction was at least on a par with previous years, though some of the biggest news in the field was made by names with an unfamiliar ring to the regular science-fiction audience. No stranger at all to the field, however, was Alfred Bester who came close to equaling the success of his *The Demolished Man* with his four-part serial in *Galaxy* titled *The Stars My Destination* (October, November, December, 1956, January, 1957). Originally published in hardcover in England (Sidgwick and Jackson, 12&6) under the title *Tiger, Tiger!*, it was later reprinted in softcover in the U.S. (Signet, 35¢) under the magazine title. The story of the vengeance of one Gully Foyle, it had all the sweep and imagination (and odd typography!) of the author's first science-fiction novel.

Robert A. Heinlein, the old master, was in fine form during 1956–57 with two novels first serialized in magazines and later issued in book form. *The Door Into Summer* (*Fantasy and Science Fiction*, October, November, December, 1956; Doubleday, $2.95) concerned an engineer who finally did some plain and fancy time traveling to even the score with an old partner (why the vengeance theme in science-fiction?). Heinlein's insight into the minds of both cats and engineers was well worth the price of admission.

One of the most adult stories of the year was another Heinlein novel, supposedly a "juvenile." *Citizen of the Galaxy* (*Astounding Science Fiction*, September, October, November, December, 1957; Scribner's, $2.95) was the story of a small boy named Thorby sold into slavery on a distant planet and of the part he finally plays in ridding the galaxy of slavery. Perhaps the plot could be criticized as corny, but the Heinlein gift for narration still made it one of the more powerful novels of the year.

The hardcover book field, though far from being as overinflated as it was in the boom years of the early '50's, was doing considerably better than in the previous two years.

There were 70 original hardcover books issued in 1956; 1955 saw the publication of 67. For 1957, the total was even higher, 80. There were 5 anthologies in 1956, and again in 1957, an increase over 1955 when 3 anthologies were published. Juveniles numbered 18 in 1956 and 9 in 1957. One-author collections accounted for 7 in 1956 and 13 in 1957—novels in 1956 with 40 and in 1957 with 53.

The two novels to make the biggest splash in the field were sold to the general public without the label "science-fiction" attached. John Christopher's *No Blade of Grass* (Simon and Schuster, $2.95), originally *The Death of Grass* (Michael Joseph, 1956), appeared in the States first as a 7-part serial in *The Saturday Evening Post*. After the Simon and Schuster edition, it was sold to the movies for a reported $100,000. The book details what happened when a blight began to destroy all the grasses in the world, including the grass grains such as wheat, oats, barley, etc. John Christopher is not a complete stranger to regular science-fiction readers, having written a number of tales for magazines, chiefly in England.

The other book to make quite a splash in the general book field was *On the Beach* (Morrow, $3.95) by Nevil Shute. The book takes place after the next war, when the world's population is slowly dying of radioactive fallout. The book covers the last days of the last survivors. Grim as it was, the book found enough of a popular audience to become a bestseller and to be serialized in a large number of metropolitan dailies.

In 1957, several major publishers were edging back into a field they had hastily abandoned in 1955, while others were trying science-fiction for the first time. Simon and Schuster contributed a collection of stories by Clifford D. Simak, titled *Strangers in the Universe* ($3.50), and Rinehart issued *Jules Verne: Master of Science Fiction* ($3.00), an anthology of the old master edited by I. O. Evans, and Jack Finney's *The Third Level* ($3.00), a collection not to be missed by any science-fiction enthusiast.

In 1956 the J. B. Lippincott Co. successfully launched a series of books, many of which were basically science-fiction although labeled as "Novels of Menace." Starting with Frank M. Robinson's *The Power*, the series had included books by Charles Eric Maine and for early release in 1958 had scheduled one by Richard Matheson. Also on the Lippincott list for '58 release was a novel by Walter M. Miller, Jr. This last book was essentially a reworking of Miller's "Canticle" stories, originally published in *Fantasy and Science Fiction*.

Other publishers starting science-fiction lines included both Avalon and Roy Publishers. Martin Greenberg and his Gnome Press, of course, were well-represented during both 1956 and 1957. One of the newer publishers in the field was Advent: Publishers of Chicago which broke into the publishing business with one of the most unusual—and on the surface of it, least likely to succeed—projects in publishing history—a book of book reviews. The book, titled *In Search of Wonder* was authored by Damon Knight, one of the most perceptive critics in the field of science-fiction. A credit to both the publisher, the author and the audience, this volume surprised the skeptics by actually making money.

Other books worth mentioning are Bradbury's *Dandelion Wine* (Doubleday, $3.95), the somewhat autobiographical story of a young boy growing up on the Illinois prairies. Non-science-fiction, the book was an immediate critical success and gave increased stature to a writer who "came up from the ranks" in science-fiction. Also to be noted was Lester del Rey's rewritten version of *Nerves* (Ballantine, $2.00 and 35¢), a story of a not-so-distant tomorrow when atomic power plants are fairly familiar buildings on the horizon.

If it took anything more to convince skeptics that science-fiction has matured in a literary sense, the Modern Library added the clincher when it published a volume titled *Famous Science Fiction Stories* ($2.95). This was a retitling of *Adventures in Time and Space* edited by Raymond J. Healy and J. Francis McComas and generally agreed to be one of the most outstanding anthologies of all time.

Oddest literary note of the Science Fiction Year: the discovery by Sam Moskowitz of a story titled *The Vengeance of Nitocris* by one Thomas Lanier Williams, who at the time he wrote it was 14 years old. Mr. Williams' writing abilities have matured considerably since then. He's better known to the literary public today as Tennessee Williams.

Science-fiction in softcovers increased again in 1956 over 1955. Reflecting the healthy trend of 1955, paperback anthologies continued to decline while both original and reprint novels showed an up-swing in 1957. Reprint paperbacks numbered 41 in 1956, 52 in 1957 (50 in 1955) and originals 32 in 1956, 31 in 1957 (25 in 1955).

It is with a sense of sadness that we realize science-fiction is no longer young and, like most fields of endeavor, has acquired a lengthy necrology. Deaths in the field during the past two years include many who quite literally made science-fiction what it is today. F. Orlin Tremaine, who died in October, 1956, from a series of heart attacks, was influential in preparing the way for today's "modern" science-fiction. When Street and Smith purchased *Astounding Stories* in 1933, it was Tremaine who made it into the Number 1 magazine in the field with his "thought variant" stories. It was also

Tremaine who later appointed John W. Campbell, Jr., as the magazine's editor.

The ranks of science-fiction authors were thinned with the passing of two members of the "old guard." Bob Olsen, author of some 30 stories published in the Gernsback era of science-fiction and best known for his "fourth-dimension" stories in the old *Amazing*, died at the age of 72. Ray Cummings, another giant in the early days of magazine science-fiction and one-time personal secretary to Thomas Edison, also passed away, leaving behind fond memories of novels like *The Girl in the Golden Atom* and *The Man Who Mastered Time*. Another figure, well known to the general literary public as well as fantasy enthusiasts, was Lord Dunsany, who died at the age of 79.

No artist was ever more completely identified with an author as was J. Allen St. John with Edgar Rice Burroughs. The man who breathed artistic life into Tarzan, Korak the Killer, John Carter, and a hundred other Burroughs characters was in his 80's when he died in May, 1957.

Bela Lugosi, who scared the pants off many of us when we were younger and who was best remembered for his role as Count Dracula, died in California this past year as did James Whale, the producer of the early Frankenstein movies.

That figures of the stature of Lugosi and Whale would be sadly missed was all too apparent after viewing the annual Hollywood offerings. However, the movies, while producing their usual quota of cellulosic corn, also turned out a few films actually worth seeing. Perhaps the best of the lot, although an imperfect best, was *The Incredible Shrinking Man*, based on a story and scripted by Richard Matheson. One of the major talents in the science-fiction field, Matheson turned out a creditable script about a young man dusted with radioactive fallout which makes him start shrinking at, as we recall, the rate of a tenth of an inch per day. Eventually, of course, he is pursued by the family tabby and duels with a horrendous spider. Unfortunately, this is the type of movie that should have ended with the Hero Winning Over All Odds. Instead, Matheson leaves us with a mouthful of message.

A movie that had all the necessary ingredients but somehow failed to make the grade was *1984*, scripted rather faithfully after the novel of the same name. Edmond O'Brien and Jan Sterling were good in the lead roles but somehow the movie failed to jell.

Hollywood also turned out its usual monster movies, and it's a sad commentary to report the bulk of them did well at the box-office.

I Was a Teenage Werewolf, a coldly logical attempt to capitalize on the two biggest box-office fads, was coining money as predictably as grain ripens in the fall. And with the success of *The Shrinking Man,* it doesn't take a Univac to predict that the local theaters will shortly be filled with Things that shrink, grow to ungodly sizes, or maybe shoot out sideways.

Not to be overlooked in a review of the visual medium was Gore Vidal's *Visit to a Small Planet.* A huge success on TV, Vidal later enlarged it into a full-scale—and successful—Broadway play. The play, of course, owed much to the acting of Cyril Ritchard as Kreton, the visitor from another planet.

Regular readers of "The Science Fiction Year" know that the science-fiction field has a large and active fan following, a number of whom sooner or later trickle into professional ranks. Perhaps the best known of fan activities is the holding of both regional and "world" conventions.

The 1956 convention held in New York achieved an almost record attendance with 1,120 fans, professionals, readers, and souvenir hunters registering for the event. Held at the Biltmore Hotel, the convention ran for four days. The Guest of Honor was Arthur C. Clarke, popular science-fiction and science writer and former president of the British Interplanetary Society.

One of the high points of the convention was a speech by Al Capp, creator of "Li'l Abner" and "Long Sam." Other speakers at the convention included Robert Bloch, science-fiction's perennial toastmaster, Isaac Asimov, Anthony Boucher, editor of *Fantasy and Science Fiction,* and John W. Campbell, Jr., editor of *Astounding Science Fiction.* Winners of the convention's annual merit awards, dubbed "Hugos," were Robert A. Heinlein for his novel *Double Star,* Murray Leinster for his novelette *Exploration Team,* and Arthur C. Clarke for his short story *The Star. Astounding Science Fiction* was voted the best magazine and Robert Silverberg the most promising new author.

The 1957 convention in London was rated a "howling success" by those who attended, despite a much smaller number present (268) than at the New York shindig. A number of American fans chartered a plane and flew over to make the convention a truly "world" convention. The Guest of Honor was John W. Campbell, Jr., whose magazine again won the award as the best of the year. Voted as the site for the 1958 world science-fiction convention: Southgate (Los Angeles), California.

Regional conventions were not to be ignored during 1957, particularly since the world convention was held in London and the bulk of American science-fiction convention goers were not in a position to take a trip over the Big Pond. The biggest of the small conventions was the Westercon, held on the Pacific Coast over the 4th of July weekend. About 500 people attended. At the Midwestcon, a smaller crowd of 150 gathered at the North Plaza Motel in Cincinnati.

In trying to cover science news for 1956–57, there is only one place to begin and literally only one story to cover. All other science news fades into insignificance beside it. For 1957 was the year in which science donned seven-league boots and made strides that shook the world. Much to the dismay of the West, however, it was Russian science that wore the boots.

On July 29, 1955, President Eisenhower announced to the world that the U.S. intended to launch a small, metal moon designed to circle the globe in an orbit some 300 miles up. The Russians announced similar plans a day later, claiming that their satellite would be up within 18 months and would be heavier than the U.S. version. The Soviets later announced—on June 1, 1957—that they had finished working on a rocket motor for their satellite. *Tass*, the official Russian news agency, announced on September 17, 1957, that the Russians would launch their satellite "shortly."

October 4, 1957, the Russians *did* launch a satellite—in Russian, a *sputnik*—that was 22.8 inches in diameter and weighed 184.3 pounds. Its elliptical orbit had a peak altitude of 560 miles. Speed of the satellite was close to 18,000 miles an hour, and it circled the earth once every 96.2 minutes. For exactly three weeks (as Russian scientists had predicted), radio transmitters aboard the satellite emitted short "beeps" at frequencies of 40.002 and 20.005 megacycles and then went dead. Estimates were that the satellite—trailed by the bulkier third stage—would stay up at least until the end of the year.

Some scientists speculated that the initial weight of the Russian satellite rocket was 100 tons or more. In contrast, the American "Vanguard" rocket weighs 11 tons and the satellite itself 22 pounds. The Russian success in launching so heavy a satellite lent credence to their claim that they had successfully test fired a 5,000-mile-range intercontinental ballistic missile in August.

Some American scientists claimed that the U.S. could have launched a satellite earlier than the Russians if a variation of the Army's Redstone rocket had been used. (One such variation, the

Jupiter C rocket, had risen to an altitude of 640 miles in a firing in 1956). While congratulating the Russians for a scientific achievement of the first magnitude, scientists and engineers in the U.S. urged that more steam, money and talent be put into our own rocket program. One engineer, G. Harry Stine, better known in science-fiction circles as "Lee Corey," was quoted as saying, "Either we catch up or we're dead." Stine, who was working for the Glenn L. Martin Company, a prime contractor on the Vanguard Project, was promptly fired.

Shortly after launching of the first sputnik, the United States laid claim to the altitude record with a successful firing of Project Farside. This was a multi-stage rocket suspended from a balloon which carried it to a height of 20 miles. Once above most of the earth's turbulent atmosphere, the rocket was fired. The last stage reportedly rose as high as 4,000 miles.

While the world was still reeling from the success of the Russian's first satellite launching, the Soviets fired still another into the heavens. The second satellite was launched on November 3, almost a month to the day after the first one. If American scientists were surprised at the weight of the first Russian moon, they were stupified at the weight of the second—1,120 pounds (though some scientists speculated that this might have been the weight of the entire third stage of the rocket). Even more astonishing was the maximum height of the orbit—1,056 miles—and the fact that the satellite contained a small, living dog, named Laika (in Russian, "little barker"). The second satellite was immediately nicknamed "muttnik" by the western world. From data radioed back the first few days she was up, there was no doubt but that Laika was alive and healthy—an optimistic sign for man's own eventual trip into outer space.

In astronomy, some of the results were now in of last year's close look at the planet Mars. Dr. R. S. Richardson claimed that he had seen some of the famed Martian canals. So far, confirmation has not come in from other scientists who participated in the study.

Is there life on Mars? Probably no one will know for sure until Man actually lands on the red planet. However, scientists at the Air Force School of Aviation Medicine, Randolph Air Force Base, Texas, have made bacteria grow and reproduce in a Mars-like atmosphere duplicated in laboratory bottles. What's a Mars-like atmosphere? Mostly nitrogen under a pressure equal to that of the Earth's atmosphere 10 miles up, the faintest trace of water, and temperatures ranging from 70 degrees Fahrenheit to 95 below zero. The temperature changes were simulated by keeping the bottles in a very cold refrigerator during the night and then letting them warm up during the day.

And astronomers now believe that the Milky Way Galaxy is half again as big as they formerly thought. (Time and a half for Kimball Kinnison?)

The field of theoretical physics was "cracked wide open" when Dr. T. D. Lee of Columbia and Dr. C. N. Yang of the Institute for Advanced Study, Princeton, upset the "principle of parity" governing the way meson particles disintegrate. For their work in this field the young scientists received the Nobel Prize in Physics for 1957.

That Neanderthal Man was actually a varied race and one that may have interbred with modern man was the most important conclusion from the discovery of Shanidar Man, a variation of Neanderthal, by Dr. Ralph S. Solecki of the Smithsonian Institution. The bones were found in a cave in northern Iraq. The skull of Shanidar Man—who had been crushed in a rockfall—showed an important difference from the skulls of Neanderthal Man found in France. The brow ridge, instead of being a continuous bulge above the eyes, is broken between the eyes, a modern trait. It's interesting to note that Shanidar Man is younger than a group of Neanderthals found at Mt. Carmel in Palestine. This latter group, while older, was nevertheless more advanced in modern characteristics than Shanidar.

The diamond, as the hardest material found in nature, has now been exceeded by a material made in the laboratory. The General Electric Company reported in 1957 that one of its scientists had developed a material capable of scratching diamonds and which could retain its form at temperatures where diamonds would burn up. The new material was called "borazon".

More and more reputable scientists were calling attention to the dangers of radioactive strontium-90 as a fallout hazard (remember Robert A. Heinlein's story *Solution Unsatisfactory?*). Some scientists claimed that the present "safe" radiation dose may be three to five times too high. Meanwhile, some progress has been made in developing a radiation sickness pill. The chemical used to make the pill is called AET. It's been found to be 100 per cent effective for mice exposed to deadly doses of radiation and is also supposed to be effective in monkeys. It's currently being tested on human beings.

Solid fuels were coming into greater use for many of the smaller rocket missiles. Their supporters claimed they were more reliable than liquid fuels, easier to store, easier to handle, and actually cheaper to produce.

Electronics, revolutionized once with the invention of the transistor, was due for another revolution with the development of the "spacistor". The spacistor was not dependent on high-quality silicon and germanium, it could amplify frequencies as high as 10,000 megacycles—40 times the vibration limit of ordinary transistors and 10 times that of the ordinary vacuum tube. Perhaps most important of all, the spacistor could operate at temperatures over 900°F. The temperature limit for transistors is 400°F.

Another new element was created by an international team of scientists from America, England and Sweden. Element Number 102 was named Nobelium.

Recall that glass, frequently used in science-fiction stories, that's as hard as steel? It's not fiction any more, it's fact. It's called Pyroceram, is harder than steel, lighter than aluminum and many times stronger than plate glass. The Corning Glass organization developed it.

In medicine, the big news was the spread of Asiatic flu—and the prompt development of a vaccine capable of immunizing most people against it. The chances of a flu epidemic the size of the 1918–19 epidemic that killed 20 million people throughout the world were slight.

There was increasing evidence that mental illness may be caused by chemical imbalances in the body. Partial proof: a group from the Tulane University School of Medicine, New Orleans, reported finding a substance in the blood of schizophrenic patients which produced psychotic symptoms in normal individuals. The blood substance is called taraxein.

High fidelity may be a mixed blessing, report some psychiatrists. Dr. H. Angus Bowes, clinical director in psychiatry, Ste. Anne's Hospital, Quebec, Canada, reports some addicts use their sets as power symbols and that others have developed compulsive urges to buy more and more records and actually suffer withdrawal symptoms when their money gives out and they have to quit.

"Inertial guidance" is not quite the same as E. E. Smith's inertialess drive, but in many respects it's almost as remarkable. It's now possible, if they use the guidance system, for aircraft, ships and missiles to operate without compasses, radio, radar, or a glimpse of the earth, sun or stars. The guidance gadget, which can fit in a coffee can, can't be jammed by enemy radar, and weather, sunspots and magnetic fields don't bother it a bit. The heart of the system is a gyroscope package that is vertically aligned at the start of the trip. Regardless of how it is carried by the vehicle thereafter, the axis of spin of the gyro remains the same.

Super plants may become possible through the use of gibberellic acid, a chemical that greatly stimulates plant growth.

Electronic devices called image converters can boost the light-gathering abilities of telescopes by a factor of ten, promising to make the 200-inch telescope at Palomar the equivalent of a 2,000-inch instrument.

So closed another year of the Age of Anxiety—or perhaps, to borrow a phrase from Robert Heinlein, 1957 should be called the Year of the Jackpot. It was certainly a year in which human history literally changed with each edition of the daily paper. At the close of the year, there was no longer any doubt that within the lifetime of most of the people reading these pages Man would set foot on the moon and the nearest planets. Humanity had taken its first toddling step into space—how long would it be before it strode among the stars?

And what of science-fiction? It was no accident that those writers called upon by the nation's press to explain to the public the significance of the Russian satellites were writers well known to science-fiction readers. For the coming year science-fiction would remain—as it has been in the past—the press agent for the Atomic Age, the sometimes frightening but always entertaining forecaster of mankind's fascinating future.

2066:

Election Day

by MICHAEL SHAARA

Early that afternoon Professor Larkin crossed the river into Washington, a thing he always did on Election Day, and sat for a long while in the Polls. It was still called the Polls, in this year 2066 A.D., although what went on inside bore no relation at all to the elections of primitive American history. The Polls was now a single enormous building which rose out of the green fields where the ancient Pentagon had once stood. There was only one of its kind in Washington, only one Polling Place in each of the forty-eight states, but since few visited the Polls nowadays, no more were needed.

In the lobby of the building, a great hall was reserved for visitors. Here you could sit and watch the many-colored lights dancing and flickering on the huge panels above, listen to the weird but strangely soothing hum and click of the vast central machine. Professor Larkin chose a deep soft chair near the long line of booths and sat down. He sat for a long while smoking his pipe, watching the people go in and out of the booths with strained, anxious looks on their faces.

Professor Larkin was a lean, boyish-faced man in his late forties. With the pipe in his hand he looked much more serious and sedate than he normally felt, and it often bothered him that people were able to guess his profession almost instantly. He had a vague idea that it was not becoming to look like a college professor, and he often tried to change his appearance—a loud tie here, a sport coat there—but it never seemed to make any difference. He remained what he was, easily identifiable, Professor Harry L. (Lloyd) Larkin, Ph.D.,

Dean of the Political Science Department at a small but competent college just outside of Washington.

It was his interest in Political Science which drew him regularly to the Polls at every election. Here he could sit and feel the flow of American history in the making, and recognize, as he did now, perennial candidates for the presidency. Smiling, he watched a little old lady dressed in pink, very tiny and very fussy, flit doggedly from booth to booth. Evidently her test marks had not been very good. She was clutching her papers tightly in a black-gloved hand, and there was a look of prim irritation on her face. But *she* knew how to run this country, by George, and one of these days *she* would be President. Harry Larkin chuckled.

But it did prove one thing. The great American dream was still intact. The tests were open to all. And anyone could still grow up to be President of the United States.

Sitting back in his chair, Harry Larkin remembered his own childhood, how the great battle had started. There were examinations for everything in those days—you could not get a job streetcleaning without taking a civil-service examination—but public office needed no qualifications at all. And first the psychologists, then the newspapers, had begun calling it a national disgrace. And, considering the caliber of some of the men who went into public office, it *was* a national disgrace. But then psychological testing came of age, really became an exact science, so that it was possible to test a man thoroughly—his knowledge, his potential, his personality. And from there it was a short but bitterly fought step to—SAM.

SAM. UNCLE SAM, as he had been called originally, the last and greatest of all electronic brains. Harry Larkin peered up in unabashed awe at the vast battery of lights which flickered above him. He knew that there was more to SAM than just this building, more than all the other forty-eight buildings put together, that SAM was actually an incredibly enormous network of electronic cells which had its heart in no one place, but its arms in all. It was an unbelievably complex analytical computer which judged a candidate far more harshly and thoroughly than the American public could ever have judged him. And crammed in its miles of memory banks lay almost every bit of knowledge mankind had yet discovered. It was frightening, many thought of it as a monster, but Harry Larkin was unworried.

The thirty years since the introduction of SAM had been thirty of

America's happiest years. In a world torn by continual war and unrest, by dictators, puppet governments, the entire world had come to know and respect the American President for what he was: the best possible man for the job. And there was no doubt that he was the best. He had competed for the job in fair examination against the cream of the country. He had to be a truly remarkable man to come out on top.

The day was long since past when just any man could handle the presidency. A full century before men had begun dying in office, cut down in their prime by the enormous pressures of the job. And that was a hundred years ago. Now the job had become infinitely more complex, and even now President Creighton lay on his bed in the White House, recovering from a stroke, an old, old man after one term of office.

Harry Larkin shuddered to think what might have happened had America not adopted the system of "the best qualified man." All over the world this afternoon men waited for word from America, the calm and trustworthy words of the new President, for there had been no leader in America since President Creighton's stroke. His words would mean more to the people, embroiled as they were in another great crisis, than the words of their own leaders. The leaders of other countries fought for power, bought it, stole it, only rarely earned it. But the American President was known the world over for his honesty, his intelligence, his desire for peace. Had he not those qualities, "old UNCLE SAM" would never have elected him.

Eventually, the afternoon nearly over, Harry Larkin rose to leave. By this time the President was probably already elected. Tomorrow the world would return to peace. Harry Larkin paused in the door once before he left, listened to the reassuring hum from the great machine. Then he went quietly home, walking quickly and briskly toward the most enormous fate on Earth.

"My name is Reddington. You know me?"

Harry Larkin smiled uncertainly into the phone.

"Why . . . yes, I believe so. You are, if I'm not mistaken, general director of the Bureau of Elections."

"Correct," the voice went on quickly, crackling in the receiver, "and you are supposed to be an authority on Political Science, right?"

"Supposed to be?" Larkin bridled. "Well, it's distinctly possible that I—"

"All right, all right," Reddington blurted. "No time for politeness.

Listen, Larkin, this is a matter of urgent national security. There will be a car at your door—probably be there when you put this phone down. I want you to get into it and hop on over here. I can't explain further. I know your devotion to the country, if it wasn't for that I would not have called you. But don't ask questions. Just come. No time. Good-by."

There was a click. Harry Larkin stood holding the phone for a long shocked moment, then he heard a pounding at the door. The housekeeper was out, but he waited automatically before going to answer it. He didn't like to be rushed, and he was confused. Urgent national security? Now what in blazes—

The man at the door was an Army major. He was accompanied by two young but very large sergeants. They identified Larkin, then escorted him politely but firmly down the steps into a staff car. Larkin could not help feeling abducted, and a completely characteristic rage began to rise in him. But he remembered what Reddington had said about national security and so sat back quietly with nothing more than an occasional grumble.

He was driven back into Washington. They took him downtown to a small but expensive apartment house he could neither identify nor remember, and escorted him briskly into an elevator. When they reached the suite upstairs they opened the door and let him in, but did not follow him. They turned and went quickly away.

Somewhat ruffled, Larkin stood for a long moment in the hall by the hat table, regarding a large rubber plant. There was a long sliding door before him, closed, but he could hear an argument going on behind it. He heard the word "SAM" mentioned many times, and once he heard a clear sentence: ". . . Government by machine. I will not tolerate it!" Before he had time to hear any more, the doors slid back. A small, square man with graying hair came out to meet him. He recognized the man instantly as Reddington.

"Larkin," the small man said, "glad you're here." The tension on his face showed also in his voice. "That makes all of us. Come in and sit down." He turned back into the large living room. Larkin followed.

"Sorry to be so abrupt," Reddington said, "but it was necessary. You will see. Here, let me introduce you around."

Larkin stopped in involuntary awe. He was used to the sight of important men, but not so many at one time, and never so close. There was Secretary Kell, of Agriculture, Wachsmuth, of Commerce, General Vines, Chief of Staff, and a battery of others so imposing that Larkin found his mouth hanging embarrassingly open. He closed it immediately.

Reddington introduced him. The men nodded one by one, but they were all deathly serious, their faces drawn, and there was now no conversation. Reddington waved him to a chair. Most of the others were standing, but Larkin sat.

Reddington sat directly facing him. There was a long moment of silence during which Larkin realized that he was being searchingly examined. He flushed, but sat calmly with his hands folded in his lap. After a while Reddington took a deep breath.

"Dr. Larkin," he said slowly, "what I am about to say to you will die with you. There must be no question of that. We cannot afford to have any word of this meeting, any word at all, reach anyone not in this room. This includes your immediate relatives, your friends, anyone—anyone at all. Before we continue, let me impress you with that fact. This is a matter of the gravest national security. Will you keep what is said here in confidence?"

"If the national interests—" Larkin began, then he said abruptly, "of course."

Reddington smiled slightly.

"Good. I believe you. I might add that just the fact of your being here, Doctor, means that you have already passed the point of no return . . . well, no matter. There is no time. I'll get to the point."

He stopped, looking around the room. Some of the other men were standing and now began to move in closer. Larkin felt increasingly nervous, but the magnitude of the event was too great for him to feel any worry. He gazed intently at Reddington.

"The Polls close tonight at eight o'clock." Reddington glanced at his watch. "It is now six-eighteen. I must be brief. Doctor, do you remember the prime directive that we gave to SAM when he was first built?"

"I think so," said Larkin slowly.

"Good. You remember then that there was one main order. SAM was directed to elect, quote, *the best qualified man.* Unquote. Regardless of any and all circumstances, religion, race, so on. The orders were clear—the best qualified man. The phrase has become world famous. But unfortunately"—he glanced up briefly at the men surrounding him—"the order was a mistake. Just whose mistake does not matter. I think perhaps the fault lies with all of us, but—it doesn't matter. What matters is this: SAM will not elect a president."

Larkin struggled to understand. Reddington leaned forward in his chair.

"Now follow me closely. We learned this only late this afternoon. We are always aware, as you no doubt know, of the relatively few people in this country who have a chance for the presidency. We know not only because they are studying for it, but because such men as these are marked from their childhood to be outstanding. We keep close watch on them, even to assigning the Secret Service to protect them from possible harm. There are only a very few. During this last election we could not find more than fifty. All of those people took the tests this morning. None of them passed."

He paused, waiting for Larkin's reaction. Larkin made no move.

"You begin to see what I'm getting at? *There is no qualified man.*"

Larkin's eyes widened. He sat bolt upright.

"Now it hits you. If none of those people this morning passed, there is no chance at all for any of the others tonight. What is left now is simply crackpots and malcontents. They are privileged to take the tests, but it means nothing. SAM is not going to select anybody. Because sometime during the last four years the presidency passed the final limit, the ultimate end of man's capabilities, and with scientific certainty we know that there is probably no man alive who is, according to SAM's directive, qualified."

"But," Larkin interrupted, "I'm not quite sure I follow. Doesn't the phrase 'elect the best qualified man' mean that we can at least take the best we've got?"

Reddington smiled wanly and shook his head.

"No. And that was our mistake. It was quite probably a psychological block, but none of us ever considered the possibility of the job surpassing human ability. Not then, thirty years ago. And we also never seemed to remember that SAM is, after all, only a machine. He takes the words to mean exactly what they say: Elect the best, comma, *qualified*, comma, man. But do you see, if there is *no* qualified man, SAM cannot possibly elect the best. So SAM will elect no one at all. Tomorrow this country will be without a president. And the result of that, more than likely, will mean a general war."

Larkin understood. He sat frozen in his chair.

"So you see our position," Reddington went on wearily. "There's nothing we can do. Re-electing President Creighton is out of the question. His stroke was permanent, he may not last the week. And there is no possibility of tampering with SAM, to change the directive. Because, as you know, SAM is foolproof, had to be. The circuits extend through all forty-eight states. To alter the machine at all requires clearing through all forty-eight entrances. We can't do that. For one thing, we haven't time. For another, we can't risk letting the world know there is no qualified man.

"For a while this afternoon, you can understand, we were stumped. What could we do? There was only one answer, we may come back to it yet. Give the presidency itself to SAM—"

A man from across the room, whom Larkin did not recognize, broke in angrily.

"Now Reddington, I told you, that is government by machine! And I will not stand—"

"What else can you *do!*" Reddington whirled, his eyes flashing, his tension exploding now into rage. "Who else knows all the answers? Who else can compute in two seconds the tax rate for Mississippi, the parity levels for wheat, the probable odds on a military engagement? Who else but SAM! And why didn't we do it long ago, just feed the problems to *him,* SAM, and not go on killing man after man, great men, *decent* men like poor Jim Creighton, who's on his back now and dying because people like you—" He broke off suddenly and bowed his head. The room was still. No one looked at Reddington. After a moment he shook his head. His voice, when he spoke, was husky.

"Gentlemen, I'm sorry. This leads nowhere." He turned back to Larkin.

Larkin had begun to feel the pressure. But the presence of these men, of Reddington's obvious profound sincerity, reassured him. Creighton had been a great president, he had surrounded himself with some of the finest men in the country. Larkin felt a surge of hope that such men as these were available for one of the most critical hours in American history. For critical it was, and Larkin knew as clearly as anyone there what the absence of a president in the morning—no deep reassurance, no words of hope—would mean. He sat waiting for Reddington to continue.

"Well, we have a plan. It may work, it may not. We may all be shot. But this is where you come in. I hope for all our sakes you're up to it."

Larkin waited.

"The plan," Reddington went on, slowly, carefully, "is this. SAM has one defect. We can't tamper with it. But we *can* fool it. Because when the brain tests a man, it does not at the same time identify him. We do the identifying ourselves. So if a man named Joe Smith takes the personality tests and another man also named Joe Smith takes the Political Science tests, the machine has no way of telling them apart. Unless our guards supply the difference SAM will mark up the results of both tests to one Joe Smith. We can clear the guards, no problem there. The first problem was to find the eight men to take the eight tests."

Larkin understood. He nodded.

"Exactly. Eight specialists," Reddington said. "General Vines will take the Military; Burden, Psychology; Wachsmuth, Economics; and so on. You, of course, will take the Political Science. We can only hope that each man will come out with a high enough score in his own field so that the combined scores of our mythical 'candidate' will be enough to qualify him. Do you follow me?"

Larkin nodded dazedly. "I think so. But—"

"It should work. It has to work."

"Yes," Larkin murmured, "I can see that. But who, who will actually wind up—"

"As president?" Reddington smiled very slightly and stood up.

"That was the most difficult question of all. At first we thought there was no solution. Because a president must be so many things— consider. A president blossoms instantaneously, from nonentity, into the most important job on earth. Every magazine, every newspaper in the country immediately goes to work on his background, digs out his life story, anecdotes, sayings, and so on. Even a very strong fraud would never survive it. So the first problem was believability. The new president must be absolutely believable. He must be a man of obvious character, of obvious intelligence, but more than that, his former life must fit the facts: he must have had both the time and the personality to prepare himself for the office.

"And you see immediately what all that means. Most businessmen are out. Their lives have been too social, they wouldn't have had the time. For the same reason all government and military personnel are also out, and we need hardly say that anyone from the Bureau of Elections would be immediately suspect. No. You see the problem. For a while we thought that the time was too short, the risk too great. But then the only solution, the only possible chance, finally occurred to us.

"The only believable person would be—a professor. Someone whose life has been serious but unhurried, devoted to learning but at the same time isolated. The only really believable person. And not a scientist, you understand, for a man like that would be much too overbalanced in one direction for our purpose. No, simply a professor, preferably in a field like Political Science, a man whose sole job for many years has been teaching, who can claim to have studied in his spare time, his summers—never really expected to pass the tests and all that, a humble man, you see—"

"Political Science," Larkin said.

Reddington watched him. The other men began to close in on him.

"Yes," Reddington said gently. "Now do you see? It is our only hope. Your name was suggested by several sources, you are young enough, your reputation is well known. We think that you would be believable. And now that I've seen you"—he looked around slowly —"I for one am willing to risk it. Gentlemen, what do you say?"

Larkin, speechless, sat listening in mounting shock while the men agreed solemnly, one by one. In the enormity of the moment he could not think at all. Dimly, he heard Reddington.

"I know. But, Doctor, there is no time. The Polls close at eight. It is now almost seven."

Larkin closed his eyes and rested his head on his hands. Above him Reddington went on inevitably.

"All right. You are thinking of what happens after. Even if we pull this off and you are accepted without question, what then? Well, it will simply be the old system all over again. You will be at least no worse off than presidents before SAM. Better even, because if worst comes to worst there is always SAM. You can feed all the bad ones to him. You will have the advice of the cabinet, of the military staff. We will help you in every way we can, some of us will sit with you on all conferences. And you know more about this than most of us, you have studied government all your life.

"But all this, what comes later is not important. Not now. If we can get through tomorrow, the next few days, all the rest will work itself out. Eventually we can get around to altering SAM. But we must have a president in the morning. You are our only hope. You can do it. We all know you can do it. At any rate there is no other way, no time. Doctor," he reached out and laid his hand on Larkin's shoulder, "shall we go to the Polls?"

It passed, as most great moments in a man's life do, with Larkin not fully understanding what was happening to him. Later he would look back to this night and realize the enormity of the decision he had made, the doubts, the sleeplessness, the responsibility and agony toward which he moved. But in that moment he thought nothing at all. Except that it was Larkin's country, Larkin's America. And Reddington was right. There was nothing else to do. He stood up.

They went to the Polls.

At 9:30 that evening, sitting alone with Reddington back at the apartment, Larkin looked at the face of the announcer on the television screen, and heard himself pronounced President-elect of the United States.

Reddington wilted in front of the screen. For a while neither man moved. They had come home alone, just as they had gone into the Polls one by one in the hope of arousing no comment. Now they sat in silence until Reddington turned off the set. He stood up and straightened his shoulders before turning to Larkin. He stretched out his hand.

"Well, may God help us," he breathed, "we did it."

Larkin took his hand. He felt suddenly weak. He sat down again, but already he could hear the phone ringing in the outer hall. Reddington smiled.

"Only a few of my closest friends are supposed to know about that phone. But every time anything big comes up—" He shrugged. "Well," he said, still smiling, "let's see how it works."

He picked up the phone and with it an entirely different manner. He became amazingly light and cheerful, as if he was feeling nothing more than the normal political good will.

"Know him? Of course I know him. Had my eye on the guy for months. Really nice guy, wait'll you meet him . . . yup, college professor, Political Science, written a couple of books . . . must know a hell of a lot more than Polly Sci, though. Probably been knocking himself out in his spare time. But those teachers, you know how it is, they don't get any pay, but all the spare time in the world . . . Married? No, not that I know of—"

Larkin noticed with wry admiration how carefully Reddington had slipped in that bit about spare time, without seeming to be making an explanation. He thought wearily to himself I hope that I don't have to do any talking myself. I'll have to do a lot of listening before I can chance any talking.

In a few moments Reddington put down the phone and came back. He had on his hat and coat.

"Had to answer a few," he said briefly, "make it seem natural. But you better get dressed."

"Dressed? Why?"

"Have you forgotten?" Reddington smiled patiently. "You're due at the White House. The Secret Service is already tearing the town apart looking for you. We were supposed to alert them. Oh, by the saints, I hope that wasn't too bad a slip."

He pursed his mouth worriedly while Larkin, still dazed, got into his coat. It was beginning now. It had already begun. He was tired but it did not matter. That he was tired would probably never matter again. He took a deep breath. Like Reddington, he straightened his shoulders.

The Secret Service picked them up halfway across town. That they knew where he was, who he was, amazed him and worried Reddington. They went through the gates of the White House and drove up before the door. It was opened for him as he put out his hand, he stepped back in a reflex action, from the sudden blinding flares of the photographer's flashbulbs. Reddington behind him took him firmly by the arm. Larkin went with him gratefully, unable to see, unable to hear anything but the roar of the crowd from behind the gates and the shouted questions of the reporters.

Inside the great front doors it was suddenly peaceful again, very quiet and pleasantly dark. He took off his hat instinctively. Luckily he had been here before, he recognized the lovely hall and felt not awed but at home. He was introduced quickly to several people whose names made no impression on him. A woman smiled. He made an effort to smile back. Reddington took him by the arm again and led him away. There were people all around him, but they were quiet and hung back. He saw the respect on their faces. It sobered him, quickened his mind.

"The president's in the Lincoln Room," Reddington whispered. "He wants to see you. How do you feel?"

"All right."

"Listen."

"Yes."

"You'll be fine. You're doing beautifully. Keep just that look on your face."

"I'm not trying to keep it there."

"You aren't?" Reddington looked at him. "Good. Very good." He paused and looked again at Larkin. Then he smiled.

"It's done it. I thought it would but I wasn't sure. But it does it every time. A man comes in here, no matter what he was before, no matter what he is when he goes out, but he feels it. Don't you feel it?"

"Yes. It's like—"

"What?"

"It's like . . . when you're in here . . . you're *responsible.*"

Reddington said nothing. But Larkin felt a warm pressure on his arm.

They paused at the door of the Lincoln Room. Two Secret Service men, standing by the door, opened it respectfully. They went on in, leaving the others outside.

Larkin looked across the room to the great, immortal bed. He felt suddenly very small, very tender. He crossed the soft carpet and looked down at the old man.

"Hi," the old man said. Larkin was startled, but he looked down at the broad weakly smiling face, saw the famous white hair and the still-twinkling eyes, and found himself smiling in return.

"Mr. President," Larkin said.

"I hear your name is Larkin." The old man's voice was surprisingly strong, but as he spoke now Larkin could see that the left side of his face was paralyzed. "Good name for a president. Indicates a certain sense of humor. Need a sense of humor. Reddington, how'd it go?"

"Good as can be expected, sir." He glanced briefly at Larkin. "The president knows. Wouldn't have done it without his O.K. Now that I think of it, it was probably he who put the Secret Service on us."

"You're doggone right," the old man said. "They may bother the by-jingo out of you, but those boys are necessary. And also, if I hadn't let them know we knew Larkin was material—" He stopped abruptly and closed his eyes, took a deep breath. After a moment he said: "Mr. Larkin?"

"Yes, sir."

"I have one or two comments. You mind?"

"Of course not, sir."

"I couldn't solve it. I just . . . didn't have time. There were so many other things to do." He stopped and again closed his eyes. "But it will be up to you, son. The presidency . . . must be preserved. What they'll start telling you now is that there's only one way out, let SAM handle it. Reddington, too," the old man opened his eyes and gazed sadly at Reddington, "he'll tell you the same thing, but don't you believe it.

"Sure, SAM knows all the answers. Ask him a question on anything, on levels of parity tax rates, on anything. And right quick SAM will compute you out an answer. So that's what they'll try to do, they'll tell you to take it easy and let SAM do it.

"Well, all right, up to a certain point. But Mr. Larkin, understand this. SAM is like a book. Like a book, he knows the answers. *But only those answers we've already found out.* We gave SAM those answers. A machine is not creative, neither is a book. Both are only the product of creative minds. Sure, SAM could hold the country together. But growth, man, there'd be no more growth! No new ideas, new solutions, change, progress, development! And America *must* grow, must progress—"

He stopped, exhausted. Reddington bowed his head. Larkin remained idly calm. He felt a remarkable clarity in his head.

"But, Mr. President," he said slowly, "if the office is too much for one man, then all we can do is cut down on his powers—"

"Ah," the old man said faintly, "there's the rub. Cut down on what? If I sign a tax bill, I must know enough about taxes to be certain that the bill is the right one. If I endorse a police action, I must be certain that the strategy involved is militarily sound. If I consider farm prices . . . you see, you see, what will you cut? The office is responsible for its acts. It must remain responsible. You cannot take just someone else's word for things like that, you must make your own decisions. Already we sign things we know nothing about, bills for this, bills for that, on somebody's word."

"What do you suggest?"

The old man cocked an eye toward Larkin, smiled once more with half his mouth, anciently worn, only hours from death, an old, old man with his work not done, never to be done.

"Son, come here. Take my hand. Can't lift it myself."

Larkin came forward, knelt by the side of the bed. He took the cold hand, now gaunt and almost translucent, and held it gently.

"Mr. Larkin," the president said. "God be with you, boy. Do what you can. Delegate authority. Maybe cut the term in half. But keep us human, please, keep us growing, keep us alive." His voice faltered, his eyes closed. "I'm very tired. God be with you."

Larkin laid the hand gently on the bed cover. He stood for a long moment looking down. Then he turned with Reddington and left the room.

Outside he waited until they were past the Secret Service men and then turned to Reddington.

"Your plans for SAM. What do you think now?"

Reddington winced.

"I couldn't see any way out."

"But what about now? I have to know."

"I don't know. I really don't know. But . . . let me tell you something."

"Yes."

"Whatever I say to you from now on is only advice. You don't have to take it. Because understand this: however you came in here tonight you're going out the president. You were elected. Not by the people maybe, not even by SAM. But you're president by the grace of God and that's enough for me. From this moment on you'll be president to everybody in the world. We've all agreed. Never think that you're only a fraud, because you aren't. You heard what the president said. You take it from here."

Larkin looked at him for a long while. Then he nodded once briefly.

"All right," he said.

"One more thing."

"Yes?"

"I've got to say this. Tonight, this afternoon, I didn't really know what I was doing to you. I thought . . . well . . . the crisis came. But you had no time to think. That wasn't right. A man shouldn't be pushed into a thing like this without time to think. The old man just taught me something about making your own decisions. I should have let you make yours."

"It's all right."

"No, it isn't. You remember him in there. Well. That's you four years from tonight. If you live that long."

Now it was Larkin who reached out and patted Reddington on the shoulder.

"That's all right, too," he said.

Reddington said nothing. When he spoke again Larkin realized he was moved.

"We have the greatest luck, this country," he said tightly. "At all the worst times we always seem to find all the best people."

"Well," Larkin said hurriedly, "we'd better get to work. There's a speech due in the morning. And the problem of SAM. And . . . oh, I've got to be sworn in."

He turned and went off down the hall. Reddington paused a moment before following him. He was thinking that he could be watching the last human President the United States would ever have. But—once more he straightened his shoulders.

"Yes, sir," he said softly, "Mr. President."

The Mile-Long Spaceship

by KATE WILHELM

Allan Norbett shivered uncontrollably, huddling up under the spotless hospital sheet seeking warmth. He stirred fretfully as consciousness slowly returned and with it the blinding stab of pain through his head. A moan escaped his lips. Immediately a nurse was at his side, gently, firmly forcing him back on the bed.

"You must remain completely still, Mr. Norbett. You're in St. Agnes' Hospital. You suffered a fractured skull in the accident, and surgery was necessary. Your wife is outside waiting to see you. She is uninjured. Do you understand me?"

The words had been spoken slowly, very clearly, but he had grasped only fragments of them.

What accident? The ship couldn't have an accident. He'd be dead out there in space. And his wife hadn't even been there.

"What happened to the ship? How'd I get back on Earth?" The words came agonizingly, each effort cost much in pain and dizziness.

"Mr. Norbett, please calm yourself. I've rung for your doctor. He'll be here presently." The voice soothed him and a faint memory awakened. The wreck? His wife? HIS WIFE?

"Clair? Where's Clair?" Then the doctor was there and he also was soothing. Allan closed his eyes again in relief as they reassured him about Clair's safety. She would be here in a moment. The other memories receded and mingled with the anaesthetic dreams he'd had. The doctor felt his pulse and listened to his heart and studied his eyes, all the while talking.

"You are a lucky man, Mr. Norbett. That was quite a wreck you were in. Your wife was even luckier. She was thrown clear when the biwheel first hit you."

Allan remembered it all quite clearly now and momentarily wondered how he'd come out of it at all. The doctor finally finished his examination and smiled as he said, "Everything seems perfectly normal, considering the fact that you have been traipsing all over space for the last five days."

"Days?"

"Yes. The wreck was Saturday. This is Thursday. You've been under sedation quite a bit—to help you rest. There was extensive brain injury and absolute quiet was essential. Dr. Barnsdale performed a brilliant operation Saturday night."

Allan had the feeling the doctor was purposely being so loquacious to help him over the hump of the shock of awakening after almost six days. He was in no pain now while he kept his head still, but talking brought its own punishment and he was grateful to the doctor for answering unasked questions. The doctor waited by his side for a second or two, then in a professional tone he told the nurse to bring in Clair.

And again to Allan: "She can only stay a few minutes—less if you begin talking. I'll be in again this afternoon. You rest as much as possible. If the pain becomes severe, tell your nurse. She's instructed to administer a hypo only if you request it." Again he laughed jovially, "Don't let her talk you into it, though. She is really thrilled by that space yarn you've been telling and might want to put you to sleep just to hear more."

Clair's visit was very brief and very exhausting. Afterwards he rested comfortably for nearly an hour before the pain flooded his whole being.

"Nurse."

"Yes, Mr. Norbett?" Her fingers rested lightly on his wrist for a moment.

"The pain—"

"Just try to relax, sir. It will be gone soon." He didn't feel the prick of the needle in his arm. But the pain left him in layers, gradually becoming a light enough load to permit sleep. And the coldness.

Space was so cold. No winds to blow in spurts and gusts, to relieve the cold by their absence, only the steady, numbing same black, empty cold. He turned his head to look over his shoulder and already Earth was indistinguishable among the countless stars and planets. Never had man, he told himself, seen all the stars like this. They were incredibly bright and even as he viewed them, he wondered at the movement of some of them. There was a visible pulsation, sometimes almost rhythmically, other times very erratic. A star would suddenly seem to expand enormously on one side, the protuberance around it glow even more brightly, then die down only to repeat the performance over and over. Allan wished he knew more about astronomy. He had only the most rudimentary knowledge that everyone had since the first spaceship had reached Mars. He had been out of school when space travel had become possible and had never read past the newspaper for the information necessary to understand the universe and its inhabitants.

He shivered again and thought about the advantages of eyeless seeing. There was no pupil to dilate, no retina to burn or damage, no nerves to protest with pain at the brightness of the sight. It was, he decided smugly, much better to be here without his cumbersome body to hamper him. Then he suddenly remembered the ship—the mile-long spaceship. For an instant he sent his mental gaze deep into space all around him, but the ship was nowhere to be seen. He surmised it must still be millions of light-years from Earth. As he visualized it again he slowly became aware that once more he was aboard her and the stars he was seeing were on the giant wall screen.

He watched with interest as one planet after another turned a pale violet and became nearly invisible. He had grown accustomed to the crew of the ship, so paid little heed to them. Their voices were low, monotonous to his ear, never rising or speeding up or sounding indecisive. Completely expressionless, their words defied any attempt to interpret them.

"He's back," the telepath announced.

"Good. I was afraid that he might die." The navigator in charge went calmly about his duties of sighting and marking in a complex three-dimensional chart the course of the mighty ship as it ranged among the stars.

"He's recovering from his injury. He still can't receive any impulses from me." The telepath tried again and again to create a pic-

ture in the alien mind in their midst. "Futile," he said, "the differences are too great."

"Undisciplined," said the psychologist who had been waiting ever
since that first visit by the alien. "A disciplined mind can be reached
by telepathy."

"Can you see his world?" This from the astro navigator.

"Only the same intimate scenes of home-life, his work and his immediate surroundings. He is very primitive, or perhaps merely
uneducated."

"If only he knew something about astronomy." The navigator
shrugged and made a notation on his chart as two more distant
planets registered violet.

"The names he associates with stars are these," the telepath probed
deeper, "The Dipper, North Star, Mars . . . no, that is one of the
planets they have colonized." A wave of incredulity emanated from
him, felt by the others of the crew, but not expressed in his voice.
"He doesn't know the difference between single stars, clusters, constellations, only that they appear as individual stars to him, and he
thinks of them as such."

The navigator's calm voice belied the fury the others felt well
out from him. "Look at his sun, perhaps that will give us a hint." They
all knew the improbability of this. The telepath began droning what
little Allan knew about the sun when the captain appeared through
another wall screen.

He was accompanied by the ship's ethnologist, the expert who
could reconstruct entire civilizations from the broken remains of a
tool or an object of art, or less if necessary. The captain and his
companions made themselves comfortable near the star screen and
seemed immediately engrossed in the broken lines indicating the
ship's flight in the three-dimensional reproduced outer spaces.

"Is he still here?"

"Yes, sir."

"Is he aware yet that we discovered his presence among us?"

"No, sir. We have made no effort to indicate our awareness to
him."

"Very good." The captain then fell silent pondering his particular
problem as the ethnologist began adding to the growing list of facts
that were known to Allan about Earth.

They would have a complete picture of the present and the past.
As complete as the alien's mind and memory could make it. But unless they could locate his planet they might just as well go home

and view space-fiction films. This exploration trip had achieved very little real success. Only fourteen planets that could be rated good with some sub-intelligent life, several hundred fair with no intelligence and only one he could conscientiously rate excellent. This mind was of an intelligent, though as yet unadvanced humanoid race. The planet it inhabited met every requirement to be rated excellent. Of this the captain was certain.

Suddenly the telepath announced, "He's gone. He became bored watching the screen. He knows nothing about astronomy; therefore, the course loses its significance to him. He has the vague idea that we're going to a predetermined destination. The idea of an exploration, charting cruise hasn't occurred to him as yet."

"I wonder," mused the captain, "how he reconciles his conscious mind to his subconscious wandering."

The psychologist answered. "As he begins to awaken other dreams probably mingle with these memories causing them to dim at the edges, thus becoming to his mind at any rate merely another series of especially vivid well-remembered dreams. I believe much of what lies in his subconscious is dream memory rather than fact memory." The psychologist didn't smile, or indicate in any fashion the ridicule and sarcasm the others felt as he continued, "He has the memory of being always well fed. He has buried the memory of hunger so far down in his subconscious that it would take a skilled psychologist a long time to call it forth."

The telepath stirred and started to reply, then didn't. The alien's mind had been like a film, clear and easy to read. Some of the pictures had been disturbing and incomprehensible, but only through their strangeness, not because they were distorted by dream images. The psychologists never could accept anything at face value. Always probing and looking for hidden places and meanings. Just as he did when told of the world democracy existing on Earth.

"Most likely a benign dictatorship. A world couldn't be governed by a democratic government, a small area, perhaps, but not a world." Thus spoke the psychologist. But the telepath had been inside Allan's mind, and he knew it could and did work. Not only the planet Earth, but also the colonies on Mars and Venus.

The captain was still pursuing his own line of questioning.

"Has he ever shown any feeling of fear or repulsion toward us?"

"None, he accepts us as different but not to be feared because of it."

"That's because he believes we are figments of his imagination; that he can control us by awakening."

The captain ignored this explanation advanced by the psychologist. A mind intelligent enough for dreams, could feel fear in the dreams—even a captain knew that. He was beginning to get the feeling that this Earth race might prove a formidable foe when and if found.

"Has he shown any interest in the drive?"

"He assumed we use an atomic drive. He has only the scantiest knowledge of atomics, however. His people use such a drive."

"The fact that the race has atomics is another reason we must find them." This would be the third planet using atomic energy. A young race, an unknown potential. They did not have interstellar travel now, but one hundred fifty years ago they didn't have atomic energy and already they had reached their neighbor planets. It had taken three times as long for the captain's people to achieve the same success. The captain remembered the one other race located in his time that had atomics. They were exploring space in ever widening circles. True they hadn't made any startling advances yet in weapons, they had found decisive bombs and lethal rays and gases unnecessary. But they had learned fast. They had resisted the invaders with cunning and skill. Their bravery had never been questioned, but in the end the aggressors had won.

The captain felt no thrill of satisfaction in the thought. It was a fact, accomplished long ago. The conclusion had been delayed certainly, but it had also been inevitable. Only one race, one planet, one government could have the energy, and the right to the raw materials that made the space lanes thoroughfares. The slaves might ride on the masters' crafts, but might not own or operate their own. That was the law, and the captain was determined to uphold to the end that law.

And now this. One mind freed from its body and its Earth roaming the universe, divulging its secrets, all but the only one that mattered. How many millions of stars lit the way through space? And how many of them had their families of planets supporting life? The captain knew there was no answer, but still he sought ways of following the alien's mind back to his body.

Allan stirred his coffee slowly, not moving his head. This was his first meal sitting up, now at its conclusion he felt too exhausted to lift his spoon from his cup. Clair gently did it for him and held the cup to his lips.

"Tired, darling?" Her voice was a caress.

"A little." A little! All he wanted was his bed under him and Clair's voice whispering him to sleep. "I don't believe I'd even need a hypo." He was startled that he had spoken the thought, but Clair nodded, understanding.

"The doctor thinks it best to put off having anything if you can. I'll read to you and see if you can sleep." They had rediscovered the joy of reading books. Real leather-bound books instead of watching the three D set, or using the story films. Allan loved to lie quiescent, listening to the quiet voice of his wife rise and fall with the words. Often the words themselves were unimportant, but there was music in listening to Clair read them. They were beautifully articulated, falling into a pattern as rhythmic as if there were unheard drums beating the time.

He tried to remember what the sound of her voice reminded him of. Then he knew. By the very difference in tone and expression he was reminded of the crew of the mile-long spaceship in his dream. He grinned to himself at the improbability of the dream. Everyone speaking in the same metallic tone, the monotonous flight, never varying, never having any emergency to cope with.

The noises of the hospital dimmed and became obscure and then lost entirely. All was silent again as he sped toward the quiet lonesome planet he had last visited. There he had rested gazing at the stars hanging in expanding circles over him. He had first viewed the galaxy from aboard the spaceship. Interested in the spiral shape of it he had left the ship to seek it out at closer range. Here on this tiny planet the effect was startling. If he closed out all but the brightest and largest of the stars there was ring after ring of tiny glowing diamonds hanging directly above him. How many times had he come back? He couldn't remember, but suddenly he thought about the mile-long spaceship again.

"He's back," the telepath never moved from his position, before the sky screen, nor did the astro navigator. Abruptly, however, the panorama went blank and the two moved toward the screen on the opposite wall.

"Is he coming?"

"Yes. He's curious. He thinks something is wrong."

"Good." The two stepped from the screen into a large room where a group watched a film.

The navigator and the telepath seated themselves slightly behind the rest of the assemblage. The captain had been talking, he continued as before.

"Let me know what his reactions are."

"The film interests him. The dimensional effect doesn't bother him, he appears accustomed to a form of three-dimensional films."

"Very good. Tell me the instant something strikes a responsive chord."

The film was one of their educational astronomy courses for beginners. Various stars were shown singly and in their constellations and finally in their own galaxies. Novae and super novae, planets and satellites appeared. The telepath dug deep into the alien's memory, but found only an increasing interest, no memories of any one scene. Suddenly the telepath said,

"This one he thinks he has seen before. He has seen a similar galaxy from another position, one that shows the spiral directly overhead."

The captain asked, "Has this one been visible on the screen from such a position?"

"Not in detail. Only as part of the charted course." The navigator was making notes as he answered. "There are only three fixes for this particular effect. A minor white dwarf with six satellites and two main sequence stars, satellites unknown."

The captain thought deeply. Maybe only a similar galaxy, but again maybe he was familiar with this one.

The orders were given in the same tone he had used in carrying on the conversation. The alien had no way of knowing he was the helmsman guiding the huge ship through space.

The telepath followed the alien's mind as he gazed raptly at the ever-changing film. Occasionally he reported the alien's thoughts, but nothing of importance was learned. As before, the departure of the alien was abrupt.

With the telepath's announcement, "He's gone," the film flicked off and normal activity was resumed.

Later the captain called a meeting of the psychologist, the telepath, the chief navigator and the ethnologist.

"We represent the finest minds in the universe, yet when it comes to coping with one inferior intellect, we stand helpless. He flits in and out at will, telling us nothing. We are now heading light-years out of our way on what might easily prove to be a fruitless venture, merely because you," he held the telepath in his merciless gaze, "think he recognized one of the formations." The captain's anger was a formidable thing to feel, and the rest stirred uneasily. His voice, however, was the same monotone it always was as he asked, "And did you manage to plant the seeds in his mind as suggested at our last meeting?"

"That is hard to say. I couldn't tell." The telepath turned to the psychologist for confirmation.

"He wouldn't know himself until he began feeling the desire for more education. Even then it might be in the wrong direction. We can only wait and hope we have hit on the way to find his home planet through making him want to learn astro-navigation and astronomy." Soon afterward the meeting adjourned.

Allan was back at work again, with all traces of his accident relegated to the past. His life was well-ordered and full, with no time for schooling. He told himself this over and over, to no avail. For he was still telling himself this when he filled out the registration blank at the university.

"He's here again!" The telepath had almost given up expecting the alien ever again. He kept his mind locked in the other's as he recited as though from a book. "He's completely over his injury, working again, enrolled in night classes at the school in his town. He's studying atomic engineering. He's in the engine room now getting data for something they call a thesis."

Quietly the captain rolled off a list of expletives that would have done justice to one of the rawest space hands. And just as quietly, calmly, and perhaps, stoically, he pushed the red button that began the chain reaction that would completely vaporize the mile-long ship. His last breath was spent in hoping the alien would awaken with a violent headache. He did.

The
Last
Victory

by TOM GODWIN

The transport ship, bound for Capella with Outlander colonists from Earth and Frontier Guards from Arcturus, struck the hyperspace vortex without warning. It seized her, wrenching and twisting her, and flung her across its gigantic rim at thousands of times the speed of light. She emerged into normal space in an unknown region of the galaxy, broken and driveless, but near enough a planet that she could descend by means of her antigravity plates before the last of her air was gone.

It was sunset when she settled heavily to earth on a grassy slope beside a forest, leaning at a dangerous angle with only her failing antigravity plates to hold her from falling. The dead had been disposed of in space and the living filed out of her: fifty Outlander men, women and children, eighteen ship's crewmen, and ten Frontier Guards.

The Guard officer and ship's captain came last, of equal rank and already appraising each other with cold speculation.

The howling things in the dark forest were coming closer. Thane listened as he watched Curry, the ship's captain, approach across the strip of land that separated the two camps; standing back from his fire as he waited, where he would make an uncertain target for an assassin's blaster.

No one could be seen near any of the fires in the two camps on the hill. Only the unarmed Outlanders, at their fires in the swale below, moved about without wariness. And it was not yet three hours from the landing of the ship.

Curry stopped before him, restrained anger on his arrogantly handsome face.

"You failed to report to me and turn your Frontier Guards over to my command as you were ordered," he said.

"Since your rank is no higher than mine I saw no reason to do so," Thane answered.

Curry smiled, very thinly. "Perhaps I can show you a reason."

"Perhaps. Let's have it."

"First, I want to remind you of our circumstances," Curry said. "The ship will never lift again and we're marooned here for centuries to come. You know what the reaction of the Outlanders will be."

The Outlanders were the outcasts of a society that could not tolerate individuality. Two hundred years before the complexities of civilization had combined technocracy with integration and produced Technogration. Technogration had abolished race, creed and color, nations and borders, had welded all into a common mass and prohibited all individual pursuits that did not contribute to the Common Good. The Outlanders, refusing to come under Technograte domination, lived as best they could in the deserts, plateaus and jungles that Technogration could not use. The ones on the ship had been bound for Capella Five where men accustomed to wrestling a living from hostile environments were needed. Under such circumstances Outlanders were given certain rights and freedoms. Until they were no longer needed. Then, again, they became a people without a world . . .

"For two hundred years the Outlanders have hated Technogration and wanted a world where they could set up their own archaic form of society," Curry said. "Now, those down there will think their millenium has arrived and they can refuse to recognize Technograte authority."

"I see," Thane said. "And you want my cooperation so that Technogration won't fall by the wayside?"

"Your willingness to accept a subordinate position would give me an intact force of both crewmen and Guardsmen." Curry's lips thinned. "But there will be Technogration, with or without your support. There will be no retrogression back into the Outlanders' hallowed Dark Ages."

"There is no argument—we both want Technogration," Thane said. "We only disagree over who should be in command."

"There is a slight difference in our qualifications. Your present rank was gained by your ability to kill and not by loyalty to Technogration."

"Yes, of course," Thane agreed. "We'll say that I'm a materialistic opportunist while you're a noble idealist. But it's still the same identical whip that we're both going to reach for."

"As I said, I would prefer a peaceful transfer of your Guardsmen to my command. But my crewmen outnumber them almost two to one and they are expendable if necessary." The thin smile came back, almost mocking in its confidence. "You haven't much choice but to cooperate and accept a subordinate role, have you?"

The subordinate role would be very brief; it would end with a blaster beam in the back as soon as the Guardsmen were transferred to Curry's command . . .

"Try again, Curry. I can't bite on that one."

The smile faded from Curry's face, leaving it icily cold. "That was the only opportunity you'll ever get."

The howling sounded again in the forest and Thane said:

"We understand each other, now. But the Outlanders are unarmed and it may require our full forces to hold off whatever is out there. I suggest a truce until morning."

The iciness remained on Curry's face and he did not reply at once. "Perhaps you are right. You will order your men to observe a truce for the rest of the night."

He turned back to his camp.

Thane made the rounds where his guards patrolled with their searchlights probing out into the darkness. All of Curry's men but two had been added to reinforce the guard ring around the Outlander camp; most of the crewmen along the east and south lines, leaving the more experienced Guardsmen to patrol the two lines facing the forest.

Guardsmen and crewmen patrolled in silence, watching one another with the calculating regard of men who knew they might soon be ordered to kill one another. Apparently it was obvious to all of them that two officers of equal rank was a situation that could not for long exist.

Thane's return to his camp took him through the scattered camp
fires of the Outlanders. There were not many men to be seen; most of
the survivors were women and children whom the Outlander leader
had ordered into the safer inner compartments when the ship began
breaking up.

Thane met him at the second fire; a gaunt old man with a jutting
gray beard and sharp blue eyes under bristling gray brows. He
stepped out from the fire and spoke:

"Captain Thane—I'd like to ask a question."

Thane stopped. "What is it?"

"My name is Paul Kennedy and I speak for all of us," the old man
said. "Captain Curry has locked up all arms from us—he's already
starting the regimentation for a permanent Technograte colony here
and making sure we can't object. For two hundred years Technogration has failed on Earth except to turn men into robots. Here we
could have a new chance and live like humans again."

"The question," Thane reminded him.

"You were in the Frontier Guards, where men still have to think
for themselves to survive, and we were hoping you would understand why we don't want to start another ant hill here."

He could understand—but now, after thirty years of planning and
fighting, he was only one step from the top.

"There will be Technogration," he said.

"We thought you would say that." Kennedy's expression did not
change. "We hoped we would be wrong."

An ecstatic yelping sounded suddenly from nearby and something
brown and white raced across the firelit ground with a laughing boy
in pursuit. Thane stared.

It was a dog.

He had not seen one for thirty years. Technogration prohibited
the owning of pets as an unnecessary drain upon the planned econ-
omy and as non-contributive to the Common Good.

"We knew about the regulations," Kennedy said, "but children
need pets to love and be loved by. She's going to have pups—only
she and Lornie's kitten were left." The old man's eyes watched him
closely, questioningly. "Surely, no one will object to them?"

The dog circled back and a dark haired young woman beyond another fire called to it: "Binkie—come here!"

The dog obeyed, its tail drooping a little, and the woman looked
uncertainly in Thane's direction before she disappeared back into

the shadows, the dog close behind her. The boy followed, asking, "Why did you stop us, Blanche?"

Thane watched them go, the sight of the boy and dog bringing back with unwanted vividness the memory of another Outlander boy who had played with his dog, long ago; bringing back the past that necessity had forced him to forget . . .

He put the dangerous weakness from his mind and spoke to Kennedy:

"You Outlanders were bound for a Technograte world when you left Earth. You now stand on a Technograte world. You will do as you are ordered to do. As for your pets—you may have as many as you want so far as I'm concerned."

He stepped past Kennedy and continued on through the camp. The conversation of the Outlanders froze as he drew near, letting him walk in a little sea of silence that moved along with him. It was the usual reaction to the presence of a Technograte officer.

A little girl was out beyond the last fire; her back turned to him as she knelt in the grass and worked at something. He came closer and saw she was trying to tie a white cord around the neck of a half grown kitten. It sat with resigned patience as she struggled with earnest, inexperienced fingers to tie a knot that would not fall apart. She was talking to it as she worked:

"—and maybe the things in the forest kill cats. So you'll have to stay tied up, Tommy, and close to me because you're the only kitten on this whole world—"

His shadow fell across her and she looked up. Black curls framed a startled little face and gray eyes went wide at the sight of his uniform. She seized the surprised kitten and held it protectively in her arms, the knot falling apart again on the ground.

"Please—Tommy won't ever hurt anything—"

Two women and a man were watching him from beyond the fire with frozen-faced hatred. Technograte regulations required the immediate killing of any animals found smuggled aboard a ship . . .

"I won't harm your kitten," he said. He smiled sardonically at the Outlanders beyond the fire. "My horns aren't quite that long yet."

He met Curry when he was almost back to his camp. Curry had two bodyguards with him and passed without speaking.

The hours went by and the night was like a cold October night on Earth but for the strange constellations that crept across the sky. The Outlander fires burned lower and the things in the forest became silent, as though massing for a surprise attack. Twice the wind shifted, to bring the scents from the forest, and each time he heard the dog growl uneasily while the woman tried to quiet her.

He was going down the south guard line, the western horizon touched with the light of coming moonrise, when the monsters attacked the north line.

They broke suddenly from the forest with a demoniac howl of command from their leader, a boiling wave of them. They were green, hard to see against the green grass, racing low to the ground like giant tigers, their long, serpentine necks thrust forward and eyes blazing yellow in hyena faces.

The blaster fire of the Guardsmen met them, pale blue beams that blossomed into brief incandescence when they struck. Curry's guards added their fire, their reactions slower than those of the Guardsmen. The guards along the other three lines turned to help halt the attack, the south line guards firing across the Outlander camp.

The front rank of monsters went down, with them the leader. For an instant the onslaught slowed, leaderless and uncertain, then the monster that had been behind the leader gave the commanding howl and the others surged ahead again.

At that moment, when the attention of every guard in every guard line was on the north perimeter attack, the Outlander dog broke loose from whoever had been holding her. She ignored the attack from the north and was a blur as she went through the south guard line, screaming a snarl of warning and her leash whipping in the air behind her. She vanished behind the guard line and Thane swung his searchlight.

Five monsters were almost upon the backs of the unsuspecting guards, charging without sound.

His blaster beam raked at them and two went down. The others struck three guards with their bodies, knocking them to the ground before they could fire. Then the monsters passed on, to lurch a dozen steps and fall limply to the ground. They did not even twitch after they fell.

He saw, when he reached the first one, that it was dead. So were the other two.

Yet there was not a blaster mark on them.

Then he saw another thing. One of the monsters had fallen with its jaws slackly open and its teeth were visible. They were blunt and even.

Despite their ferocious appearance, the monsters were only herbivores.

The three fallen guards were getting to their feet, apparently unharmed. Along the north perimeter the attack was over as suddenly as it had begun; the leader of the monsters lying dead against the guard line and all the others still alive fleeing wildly back into the forest. Quiet came, broken only by the growling of the dog out near the two monsters Thane had killed.

He turned his light on her, then went closer to make sure he had seen rightly.

She was fighting something on the ground, green-eyed with fury as she ripped and tore at it. But there was nothing there. Nothing.

"Binkie!"

The dark haired woman was coming toward them, wraithlike in a white sleeping garment. The dog turned away, with a last rip at the nothing it fought, and saw the three guards the monsters had knocked down. She froze, as though she saw something she could not believe.

Then, deadly with menace, a growl vibrated in her throat and she crouched to attack them.

"Binkie—*don't!*" The voice of the girl was shrill with urgency. "Come here—come here!"

The dog hesitated, then obeyed; going past the guards in a swift lope, her head turned to watch them and her teeth bared in a snarl. The girl seized the leash and girl and dog disappeared back into the Outlander camp, both of them running.

Curry loomed out of the darkness, his two bodyguards with him, and flashed his light over the fallen monsters.

"So you let three get through?" he said. He glanced to the north guard line where the searchlights of the guards showed only the dark, lifeless edge of the forest. "But no one was harmed and there's no indication that they are going to attack again."

He regarded Thane with cold thoughtfulness. "Apparently the camp is in no danger, after all."

To Thane the implication of his words was obvious: if the monsters were not a menace his cooperation was no longer needed by Curry. The three guards were Curry men and Curry had two with him. He was outnumbered six to one . . .

"Sir—"

It was one of the three guards; Bellam, the ship's pharmacist. He hurried up to Curry, the other two close behind him.

Curry swung on him, impatiently. "What is it?"

"We must combine our forces to fight a new danger. This camp is infected with rabies."

"Rabies?"

"Yes, sir," Bellam answered. "The Outlander's dog had a convulsion beyond the guard line and then almost attacked the three of us. That dog is mad."

"How do you know it was a convulsion?" Thane asked.

"You saw it yourself," Bellam answered.

He turned his head to face Thane as he spoke and Thane saw his eyes for the first time.

They were the lifeless, staring eyes of a dead man.

He flicked his light over the faces of the other two guards. They were the same; all three were like walking dead.

"Did the monsters harm you?" he asked Bellam.

Bellam hesitated, seeming to tense with suspicion. "No." The dead eyes stared into his. "What makes you ask?"

He saw that Curry had noticed nothing different about the three guards. It was typical of Curry; to him subordinates were only automatons to carry out his orders.

"We were discussing a mad dog, Thane," Curry said. "Not the health of my men." He spoke to Bellam. "As I recall, rabies was a pre-Technogration plague, often fatal."

"The bite of a rabid animal is invariably fatal, the death prolonged and painful," Bellam said. "There is no preventative or cure among the medical supplies on the ship. The dog must be killed at once, together with all other animals in the Outlander camp."

"If the dog was mad, why hasn't it bitten any of the Outlanders," Thane asked Curry. "I suggest we keep it on a leash until we know for sure."

"The dog was smuggled aboard the ship in defiance of regulations," Curry said. "It would have been destroyed before had I known about it."

He turned to Bellam, ignoring Thane. "The three of you will search the Outlander camp from end to end. Kill all animals and report to me the names of the owners."

The three departed, to begin the search at the nearer end of the camp. Thane made no further objection. He knew the Outlanders well enough to know that they would have overheard the discussion on the hill and slipped the dog out through the guard lines before that discussion ended. Outlanders could be very clever in such matters—the searchers would find no dog.

There was satisfaction on Curry's face as he turned and with his two bodyguards started back up the hill to his camp. Thane watched him go, smiling a little. Curry was making the mistake that had been fatal for so many before him; he was taking it for granted too soon that he had won.

A man came hurrying from the north guard line before Curry had gone far. He called to Curry:

"Sir, there is something you ought to know—"

Thane saw, with almost disbelief, that it was one of his own men: Gorman.

Curry waited and when Gorman reached him he said:

"When I was helping inspect the Outlander section of the ship for hidden weapons this evening I saw some small animals in storage compartment Thirteen. I think they were very young kittens. I would like to volunteer to go and kill them."

Curry said something that a vagrant breeze made inaudible then his words came clear:

"—I'll send a detail to the ship as soon as the camp is searched. You will report to my guards now for orders and help them hunt for the dog."

Gorman started back to meet the guards and Curry stood for a little while before he went on his way. Thane could imagine his feeling of pleased surprise and triumph.

Thane called to Gorman as he passed some distance in front of him.

"Were you injured in the attack?" he asked.

"No," Gorman said. Then, with the same tense suspicion that Bellam had had he asked the same question: "Why do you ask?"

"Why did you report to Curry instead of me?"

The answer came quickly, mechanically, "The animals are in his ship and they must be killed. They may be mad."

"Go help Curry's men," he said and watched Gorman go, trying to fit together the incidents that did not make sense.

Herbivores had attacked without reason. They had fallen dead, without a blaster mark on them. The Outlander dog had fought nothing and almost attacked the guards. One of his own men had gone over to the other side. And there was a sudden strange urgency to kill all animals in camp.

There was nothing he could do for the time being but wait for further developments so he waited. The moon came up, so swift in its retrograde orbit that its speed was visible and so near that it had the brilliance of a dozen Earth moons. When it had lifted clear of the horizon it flooded the land with a cold silver light that made the searchlights of the guards unnecessary and revealed the camp with metallic light-and-shadow clarity.

The search party was halfway through the camp, Gorman with them and Bellam in command. They were ransacking the possessions and temporary shelters of the Outlanders with swift efficiency, ignoring the protests of the women and their blasters leveled warningly on the men.

They found the little girl.

She was carrying her kitten ahead of them, a small, silent shadow in the moonlight, when Gorman saw her. He spoke to Bellam and Bellam's head jerked up. Then the two of them advanced on her.

She tried to run when she realized they had seen the kitten, hugging it in her arms with the white cord trailing behind her. Bellam overtook her and caught her by the shoulder, jerking her to a halt. He tore the kitten from her arms and flung it hard to the ground. It made a thin little scream of pain and the girl fought to reach it, her cry sobbing and frantic:

"Don't hurt him—"

Gorman's blaster hissed and blue flame leaped from it. Incandescence enveloped the kitten and then there was nothing where it had been but a small black hole in the ground.

Bellam and Gorman wheeled back, like mechanical men, to resume the search. The girl stood a moment, staring before her, saying something very low that sounded like, *"Tommy . . . Tommy . . ."* Then she stumbled to the little black hole and dropped to her knees beside it as though she hoped that somehow she might still find her kitten there.

He looked away, strangely disturbed. He drummed his fingers restlessly on the butt of his holstered blaster. Then he turned again to go down into the Outlander camp.

The moon was up and it was time he found the dog. Something had come out of the night with the monsters and perhaps she could tell him what it was. He could not yet believe she was mad.

The dark haired woman stood by the fire, watching the little girl and the searchers with bitter, smouldering hatred. She faced him, her breath coming fast in her anger.

"Her parents and her brother—when the ship broke up—she lost them all. Only her kitten was left to her."

"Where is the dog?" he asked.

"Find her!"

"The dog—where is she?"

"Find her," she challenged again. "Find her and kill her—if you can!"

He stepped past her and went on his way. She had told him what he wanted to know: despite her attempts not to do so she had been unable to keep from glancing toward the ship.

His route took him by the little girl. She was standing by the hole, small and barefooted in the grass, her hands holding the white cord that was black and charred on one end. She was crying, silently, as though too proud to let him see her break.

After he had passed her the vision went with him for a little way; the terrible, helpless hatred and hurt in her eyes and the moonlight gleaming coldly on her tears.

He looked back when he reached the ship. Gorman was coming, running, and the other three were turning back from the far end of the camp to hurry after Gorman.

He looked toward Curry's camp and saw Curry watching him. Curry and his men moved toward him and there were six to make a rendezvous with him.

The truce was over.

He found the dog behind the farthest tail fin, leashed to a thorny bush and almost invisible in the shadows.

She watched him as he stopped before her, her ears forward questioningly and her tail moving a little with tentative friendliness. He spoke to her and her reply was a low bark, her tail whipping with delight. She thought he had come to release her . . .

He had known dogs well as a boy and he knew the one before him was not mad.

He heard Gorman's feet plodding fast through the grass and he waited with his blaster in his hand.

Gorman came around the tail fin, panting, his own blaster in his hand. The dog went rigid at the sight of him, a growl in her throat, and Gorman's blaster swung toward her.

"*Hold it!*" he ordered.

Gorman paused, and the dead eyes looked into his. "There the mad dog is—we must kill it."

"We can kill it later if it's mad. We'll watch it a while, first."

The suspicion became like something almost tangible about Gorman and his blaster started the first movement toward Thane.

"Why?"

"I think it can see something—"

Gorman fired, so swiftly that Thane felt the heat of the beam even though he had been expecting it. Thane shot for the heart and Gorman collapsed before he could fire again. He lay still on the ground, the eyes that stared up into the sky no deader than when he had been alive.

The dog was lunging against her leash, trying to get to him. Thane stepped closer and watched the grass beside Gorman's head. A patch of it the size of his hand suddenly bent down, as from an unseen weight, and then something struck his knee.

He slapped at it as it darted up his leg and knocked it off; something that felt like a mass of cold, rubbery tentacles. He knew, then.

He stepped back, his blaster swinging aimlessly. The thing would leap again, to reach his head as it had done with Gorman, and it was invisible. There was nothing but the moonlit grass to be seen. Perhaps it was behind him, already preparing to spring . . .

The dog's snarling was a frenzied scream as she fought against her leash. He swung his blaster and its blue beam cut the leash in two.

She flashed toward him, then up, her ears laid back, her eyes blazing slits and her teeth slashing at his throat. His blaster was in line with her chest and for a brief instant he had only to press the firing stud.

He did something he had not done for thirty years; he trusted his life to another being and did not fire.

Cold tentacles whipped against his face and her teeth closed together beside his cheek with a vicious snap and gust of hot breath. She rebounded and held the thing on the ground between her paws as she tore at it; gagging a little, whining and snarling in fury and triumph.

He squatted beside her and laid his hand on her, speaking to her soothingly. She calmed a little, though her chest still pounded with the beating of her heart, and he saw the thing she had killed.

It was dead and slowly becoming visible as it changed to a color like pale milk. It resembled a huge, hairless spider.

It was a parasite; a highly intelligent parasite that could take over the mind of its host as well as the body. The parasites had had only the forest monsters as hosts, before, but with the coming of the humans they had the opportunity for hosts of a far higher order. They possessed a means of locomotion but apparently it was limited in its duration or else they would not have needed to control the leaders of the monster bands and stage the attack that would carry them to the guard lines.

The dog, with the acute sixth sense of some animals, could sense the hostile alienness of the things. She could see them—apparently the vision range of dogs went a little farther beyond that of humans. So also would that of cats but the kitten had had no chance to show by its actions what it had seen.

The dog had hated the changed men because they were alien things, no longer human. The thing that had been Bellam had used the knowledge stored in Bellam's mind to claim there was rabies in the camp and thereby enlist the support of the humans in killing their only means of detecting the parasites.

There was a pounding of feet beyond the ship as the zombies came. On the slope above him Curry was striding toward him, his bodyguards flanking him and the moonlight bright on his face.

Thane stood with the dog beside him and watched them come to kill him. Only he and the dog knew of the parasites; if they were killed the way would be open for the parasites to infiltrate the camp. In the end the new world would hold only the walking dead, down to the last Outlander child.

"Curry," he called.

He did not have to speak loudly in the still night air for Curry to hear him but Curry came on, his face hard, arrogant metal in the moonlight.

"Give me one minute, Curry, to tell you what I found."

Curry's reply was the order to his men.

"The dog is with him. Kill them both."

His blaster swung up as he spoke.

Thane dropped, firing as he went down. Curry's arrogant face dissolved into nothing and his blaster flamed aimlessly into the ground at his feet. The blaster of the swiftest guard sent its beam hissing like a snake over Thane's head, then he went down as Curry had done, the other guard falling beside him with his first and only shot licking off into the moonlight.

Then the zombies came around the tail fin, in a quick rush with their dead eyes staring and their blasters making a curtain of blue fire before them.

The dog lunged at them and a blaster beam dipped down to meet her. Bellam—his headless body was falling forward as Thane killed the zombie beside him. The blaster of the third one ripped its beam like a white-hot iron along Thane's ribs as he died. Then, within two heartbeats, it was over and the night was quiet again.

Thane returned his blaster to its holster. The dog was limping from one zombie to the other, searching for parasites, her shoulder red with blood and staining the grass.

She found none and he called her to him to look at her shoulder. It was not a serious wound but it was painful and bleeding fast and should be cared for. He took her around the ship, where the Outlander camp lay in view below. He looked again at the wound and she whimpered a little from the pain, gentle though his touch had been, then licked his hand in quick apology.

"Your job is over for now," he said. He motioned toward the camp below, where the dark haired woman was waiting. "Home, girl—go home."

She left him and went running and limping down the hill where her hurts would be cared for.

His side was burning and blood was like a warm, wet sheet down it. He made a temporary bandage of his shirt and then leaned wearily against the tail fin.

It was all over. The nature of the parasites was known and everyone could be fitted with a thin metal helmet until they were completely eliminated. They did not seem to be numerous—apparently there had been no more than ten or twelve among the scores of monsters. The dog would watch, and warn them if any more were in the vicinity.

It was all over, with Curry a motionless spot on the hillside above him and no one left to challenge him. He had come a long way from the Outlander boy on the high, cold prairie who had hated Technogration. He had been nineteen before he finally realized the futility of hating the unassailable power of Technogration and realized he must accept it and adapt it. And then carve out a niche for himself with a ruthlessness greater than any of those around him. So he had fought his way up, trampling those who would have trampled him had they been a little stronger, each step another victory in his conquest of the system that had condemned him.

And now—the last victory. There was no one to challenge him; there could be no one under the rigid discipline of Technogration.

The last victory. The security of Power to the end of his life.

That was Technogration.

Dawn touched the sky, softening the moon's hard light. As though the coming of day was a signal, the ship trembled and there was the whisper of dislodged soil as the tail fin lifted a fraction of an inch. The antigravity plates were almost exhausted—the ship would fall within minutes.

Down in the Outlander camp the children were gathering around the dog as the dark haired woman bandaged her shoulder. A voice came to him, treble and joyous, "Binkie is back—Binkie is back . . ."

The little girl sat to one side, so small and alone that he almost failed to see her. She watched the children crowd up to pet their dog but she did not move to join them. Only her hands moved, caressing the white cord that was charred on one end.

He felt the triumph and satisfaction become like something turned bitter around the edges and draining away.

Technogration was planning and fighting and killing until at last a man reached the top and no one dared oppose him; Technogration was control of a world and the seeds of an empire.

And Technogration was a child crying in the cold moonlight, was a little black hole where a kitten had screamed out with pain, with a little girl's heart that had nothing left to hold but harsh and poignant memories and a piece of burnt cord.

He ran to the boarding ramp, feeling the fiery lash of pain and hot flow of blood as the wound reopened, telling himself he was a fool who would probably die in the falling ship and would deserve it.

He stood by the gray ashes of his fire, the Guardsman's combat helmet under his arm, and watched the little girl come alone up the hill. Someone had washed the tearstains from her face and she stopped before him with her head held high and defiant, trying not to let him see she was afraid of him and almost succeeding.

"I sent for you, Lornie, to tell you I'm sorry about last night."

He saw she did not believe him. Her face was like a little carving of cold, unforgiving stone and she did not answer him.

He set the helmet down in the grass before her. Six tiny kittens lay inside it, red and white and gray fluffs of fur, their pink mouths questing hungrily.

Her eyes widened with incredulous wonder.

"Oh!"

Then the suspicion came back and she stopped the quick forward step she had taken.

"They haven't any mother and they're hungry," he said.

She did not move.

"They're yours, Lornie. To keep."

"They're—mine?" Then the doubt fled from her and she ran forward to gather them in her arms.

He left her with her head bent down over the kittens in her lap, making soft little sounds of endearment to them, her face so radiant that there was no room left for hurt or hatred on it.

Kennedy was coming, not yet knowing why he had been summoned nor that Technogration had died at dawn. He would not relinquish all his authority, of course. And he would have to remember to tell Kennedy that they were going to give him one of Binkie's pups.

The companionship of an understanding dog might be comforting in the years to come, whenever he recalled the morning he had owned a world and a bare-footed girl had taken it away from him.

Call

Me

Joe

by POUL ANDERSON

The wind came whooping out of eastern darkness, driving a lash of ammonia dust before it. In minutes, Edward Anglesey was blinded.

He clawed all four feet into the broken shards which were soil, hunched down and groped for his little smelter. The wind was an idiot bassoon in his skull. Something whipped across his back, drawing blood, a tree yanked up by the roots and spat a hundred miles. Lightning cracked, immensely far overhead where clouds boiled with night.

As if to reply, thunder toned in the ice mountains and a red gout of flame jumped and a hillside came booming down, spilling itself across the valley. The earth shivered.

Sodium explosion, thought Anglesey in the drumbeat noise. The fire and the lightning gave him enough illumination to find his apparatus. He picked up tools in muscular hands, his tail gripped the trough, and he battered his way to the tunnel and thus to his dugout.

It had walls and roof of water, frozen by sun-remoteness and compressed by tons of atmosphere jammed onto every square inch. Ventilated by a tiny smokehole, a lamp of tree oil burning in hydrogen made a dull light for the single room.

Anglesey sprawled his slate-blue form on the floor, panting. It was no use to swear at the storm. These ammonia gales often came at sunset, and there was nothing to do but wait them out. He was tired anyway.

It would be morning in five hours or so. He had hoped to cast an axhead, his first, this evening, but maybe it was better to do the job by daylight.

He pulled a decapod body off a shelf and ate the meat raw, pausing for long gulps of liquid methane from a jug. Things would improve once he had proper tools; so far, everything had been painfully grubbed and hacked to shape with teeth, claws, chance icicles, and what detestably weak and crumbling fragments remained of the spaceship. Give him a few years and he'd be living as a man should.

He sighed, stretched, and lay down to sleep.

Somewhat more than one hundred and twelve thousand miles away, Edward Anglesey took off his helmet.

He looked around, blinking. After the Jovian surface, it was always a little unreal to find himself here again, in the clean quiet orderliness of the control room.

His muscles ached. They shouldn't. He had not really been fighting a gale of several hundred miles an hour, under three gravities and a temperature of 140 Absolute. He had been here, in the almost nonexistent pull of Jupiter V, breathing oxynitrogen. It was Joe who lived down there and filled his lungs with hydrogen and helium at a pressure which could still only be estimated because it broke aneroids and deranged piezoelectrics.

Nevertheless, his body felt worn and beaten. Tension, no doubt—psychosomatics—after all, for a good many hours now he had, in a sense, been Joe, and Joe had been working hard.

With the helmet off, Anglesey held only a thread of identification. The esprojector was still tuned to Joe's brain but no longer focused on his own. Somewhere in the back of his mind, he knew an indescribable feeling of sleep. Now and then, vague forms or colors drifted in the soft black—dreams? Not impossible, that Joe's brain should dream a little when Anglesey's mind wasn't using it.

A light flickered red on the esprojector panel, and a bell whined electronic fear. Anglesey cursed. Thin fingers danced over the controls of his chair, he slewed around and shot across to the bank of dials. Yes—there—K-tube oscillating again! The circuit blew out. He wrenched the faceplate off with one hand and fumbled in a drawer with the other.

Inside his mind, he could feel the contact with Joe fading. If he once lost it entirely, he wasn't sure he could regain it. And Joe was an investment of several million dollars and quite a few highly skilled man-years.

Anglesey pulled the offending K-tube from its socket and threw it on the floor. Glass exploded. It eased his temper a bit, just enough so he could find a replacement, plug it in, switch on the current again—as the machine warmed up, once again amplifying, the Joeness in the back alleys of his brain strengthened.

Slowly, then, the man in the electric wheel chair rolled out of the room, into the hall. Let somebody else sweep up the broken tube. To hell with it. To hell with everybody.

Jan Cornelius had never been farther from Earth than some comfortable Lunar resort. He felt much put upon, that the Psionics Corporation should tap him for a thirteen-months exile. The fact that he knew as much about esprojectors and their cranky innards as any other man alive, was no excuse. Why send anyone at all? Who cared?

Obviously the Federation Science Authority did. It had seemingly given those bearded hermits a blank check on the taxpayer's account.

Thus did Cornelius grumble to himself, all the long hyperbolic path to Jupiter. Then the shifting accelerations of approach to its tiny inner satellite left him too wretched for further complaint.

And when he finally, just prior to disembarkation, went up to the greenhouse for a look at Jupiter, he said not a word. Nobody does, the first time.

Arne Viken waited patiently while Cornelius stared. *It still gets me, too,* he remembered. *By the throat. Sometimes I'm afraid to look.*

At length Cornelius turned around. He had a faintly Jovian appearance himself, being a large man with an imposing girth. "I had no idea," he whispered. "I never thought . . . I had seen pictures, but—"

Viken nodded. "Sure, Dr. Cornelius. Pictures don't convey it."

Where they stood, they could see the dark broken rock of the satellite, jumbled for a short way beyond the landing slip and then chopped off sheer. This moon was scarcely even a platform, it seemed, and cold constellations went streaming past it, around it. Jupiter lay across a fifth of that sky, softly ambrous, banded with colors, spotted with the shadows of planet-sized moons and with whirlwinds as broad as Earth. If there had been any gravity to speak of, Cornelius would have thought, instinctively, that the great planet was falling on him. As it was, he felt as if sucked upward, his hands were still sore where he had grabbed a rail to hold on.

"You live here . . . all alone . . . with this?" He spoke feebly.

"Oh, well, there are some fifty of us all told, pretty congenial," said Viken. "It's not so bad. You sign up for four-cycle hitches—four ship arrivals—and believe it or not, Dr. Cornelius, this is my third enlistment."

The newcomer forbore to inquire more deeply. There was something not quite understandable about the men on Jupiter V. They were mostly bearded, though otherwise careful to remain neat; their low-gravity movements were somehow dreamlike to watch; they hoarded their conversation, as if to stretch it through the year and month between ships. Their monkish existence had changed them— or did they take what amounted to vows of poverty, chastity, and obedience, because they had never felt quite at home on green Earth?

Thirteen months! Cornelius shuddered. It was going to be a long cold wait, and the pay and bonuses accumulating for him were scant comfort now, four hundred and eighty million miles from the sun.

"Wonderful place to do research," continued Viken. "All the facilities, hand-picked colleagues, no distractions . . . and of course—" He jerked his thumb at the planet and turned to leave.

Cornelius followed, wallowing awkwardly. "It is very interesting, no doubt," he puffed. "Fascinating. But really, Dr. Viken, to drag me way out here and make me spend a year-plus waiting for the next ship . . . to do a job which may take me a few weeks—"

"Are you sure it's that simple?" asked Viken gently. His face swiveled around, and there was something in his eyes that silenced Cornelius. "After all my time here, I've yet to see any problem, however complicated, which when you looked at it the right way didn't become still more complicated."

They went through the ship's air lock and the tube joining it to the station entrance. Nearly everything was underground. Rooms, laboratories, even halls had a degree of luxuriousness—why, there was a fireplace with a real fire in the common room! God alone knew what *that* cost!

Thinking of the huge chill emptiness where the king planet laired, and of his own year's sentence, Cornelius decided that such luxuries were, in truth, biological necessities.

Viken showed him to a pleasantly furnished chamber which would be his own. "We'll fetch your luggage soon, and unload your psionic stuff. Right now, everybody's either talking to the ship's crew or reading his mail."

Cornelius nodded absently and sat down. The chair, like all low-gee furniture, was a mere spidery skeleton, but it held his bulk comfortably enough. He felt in his tunic, hoping to bribe the other man into keeping him company for a while. "Cigar? I brought some from Amsterdam."

"Thanks." Viken accepted with disappointing casualness, crossed long thin legs and blew grayish clouds.

"Ah . . . are you in charge here?"

"Not exactly. No one is. We do have one administrator, the cook, to handle what little work of that type may come up. Don't forget, this is a research station, first, last, and always."

"What is your field, then?"

Viken frowned. "Don't question anyone else so bluntly, Dr. Cornelius," he warned. "They'd rather spin the gossip out as long as possible with each newcomer. It's a rare treat to have someone whose every last conceivable reaction hasn't been— No, no apologies to me. 'S all right. I'm a physicist, specializing in the solid state at ultrahigh pressures." He nodded at the wall. "Plenty of it to be observed—there!"

"I see." Cornelius smoked quietly for a while. Then: "I'm supposed to be the psionics expert, but frankly, at present I've no idea why your machine should misbehave as reported."

"You mean those, uh, K-tubes have a stable output on Earth?"

"And on Lunar, Mars, Venus . . . everywhere, apparently, but here." Cornelius shrugged. "Of course, psibeams are always persnickety, and sometimes you get an unwanted feedback when— No. I'll get the facts before I theorize. Who are your psimen?"

"Just Anglesey, who's not a formally trained esman at all. But he took it up after he was crippled, and showed such a natural aptitude that he was shipped out here when he volunteered. It's so hard to get anyone for Jupiter V that we aren't fussy about degrees. At that, Ed seems to be operating Joe as well as a Ps.D. could."

"Ah, yes. Your pseudojovian. I'll have to examine that angle pretty carefully too," said Cornelius. In spite of himself, he was getting interested. "Maybe the trouble comes from something in Joe's biochemistry. Who knows? I'll let you into a carefully guarded little secret, Dr. Viken: psionics is not an exact science."

"Neither is physics," grinned the other man. After a moment, he added more soberly: "Not my brand of physics, anyway. I hope to make it exact. That's why I'm here, you know. It's the reason we're all here."

Edward Anglesey was a bit of a shock, the first time. He was a head, a pair of arms, and a disconcertingly intense blue stare. The rest of him was mere detail, enclosed in a wheeled machine.

"Biophysicist originally," Viken had told Cornelius. "Studying atmospheric spores at Earth Station when he was still a young man—accident, crushed him up, nothing below his chest will ever work again. Snappish type, you have to go slow with him."

Seated on a wisp of stool in the esprojector control room, Cornelius realized that Viken had been soft-pedaling the truth.

Anglesey ate as he talked, gracelessly, letting the chair's tentacles wipe up after him. "Got to," he explained. "This stupid place is officially on Earth time, GMT. Jupiter isn't. I've got to be here whenever Joe wakes, ready to take him over."

"Couldn't you have someone spell you?" asked Cornelius.

"Bah!" Anglesey stabbed a piece of prot and waggled it at the other man. Since it was native to him, he could spit out English, the common language of the station, with unmeasured ferocity. "Look here. You ever done therapeutic esping? Not just listening in, or even communication, but actual pedagogic control?"

"No, not I. It requires a certain natural talent, like yours." Cornelius smiled. His ingratiating little phrase was swallowed without being noticed by the scored face opposite him. "I take it you mean cases like, oh, re-educating the nervous system of a palsied child?"

"Yes, yes. Good enough example. Has anyone ever tried to suppress the child's personality, take him over in the most literal sense?"

"Good God, no!"

"Even as a scientific experiment?" Anglesey grinned. "Has any esprojector operative ever poured on the juice and swamped the child's brain with his own thoughts? Come on, Cornelius, I won't snitch on you."

"Well . . . it's out of my line, you understand." The psionicist looked carefully away, found a bland meter face and screwed his eyes to that. "I have, uh, heard something about . . . well, yes, there were attempts made in some pathological cases to, uh, bull through . . . break down the patient's delusions by sheer force—"

"And it didn't work," said Anglesey. He laughed. "It *can't* work, not even on a child, let alone an adult with a fully developed personality. Why, it took a decade of refinement, didn't it, before the machine was debugged to the point where a psychiatrist could even 'listen in' without the normal variation between his pattern of thought and the patient's . . . without that variation setting up an interference scrambling the very thing he wanted to study. The machine has to make automatic compensations for the differences between individuals. We still can't bridge the differences between species.

"If someone else is willing to co-operate, you can very gently guide his thinking. And that's all. If you try to seize control of another brain, a brain with its own background of experience, its own ego— you risk your very sanity. The other brain will fight back, instinctively. A fully developed, matured, hardened human personality is just too complex for outside control. It has too many resources, too much hell the subconscious can call to its defense if its integrity is threatened. Blazes, man, we can't even master our own minds, let alone anyone else's!"

Anglesey's cracked-voice tirade broke off. He sat brooding at the instrument panel, tapping the console of his mechanical mother.

"Well?" said Cornelius after a while.

He should not, perhaps, have spoken. But he found it hard to remain mute. There was too much silence—half a billion miles of it, from here to the sun. If you closed your mouth five minutes at a time, the silence began creeping in like fog.

"Well," gibed Anglesey. "So our pseudojovian, Joe, has a physically adult brain. The only reason I can control him is that his brain has never been given a chance to develop its own ego. I *am* Joe. From the moment he was 'born' into consciousness, I have been there. The psibeam sends me all his sense data and sends him back my motor-nerve impulses. But nevertheless, he has that excellent brain, and its cells are recording every trace of experience, even as yours and mine; his synapses have assumed the topography which is my 'personality pattern.'

"Anyone else, taking him over from me, would find it was like an attempt to oust me myself from my own brain. It couldn't be done. To be sure, he doubtless has only a rudimentary set of Anglesey-memories—I do not, for instance, repeat trigonometric theorems while controlling him—but he has enough to be, potentially, a distinct personality.

"As a matter of fact, whenever he wakes up from sleep—there's usually a lag of a few minutes, while I sense the change through my normal psi faculties and get the amplifying helmet adjusted—I have a bit of a struggle. I feel almost a . . . a resistance . . . until I've brought his mental currents completely into phase with mine. Merely dreaming has been enough of a different experience to—"

Anglesey didn't bother to finish the sentence.

"I see," murmured Cornelius. "Yes, it's clear enough. In fact, it's astonishing that you can have such total contact with a being of such alien metabolism."

"I won't for much longer," said the esman sarcastically, "unless you can correct whatever is burning out those K-tubes. I don't have an unlimited supply of spares."

"I have some working hypotheses," said Cornelius, "but there's so little known about psibeam transmission—is the velocity infinite or merely very great, is the beam strength actually independent of distance? How about the possible effects of transmission . . . oh, through the degenerate matter in the Jovian core? Good Lord, a planet where water is a heavy mineral and hydrogen is a metal! What do we know?"

"We're supposed to find out," snapped Anglesey. "That's what this whole project is for. Knowledge. Bull!" Almost, he spat on the floor. "Apparently what little we have learned doesn't even get through to people. Hydrogen is still a gas where Joe lives. He'd have to dig down a few miles to reach the solid phase. And I'm expected to make a scientific analysis of Jovian conditions!"

Cornelius waited it out, letting Anglesey storm on while he himself turned over the problem of K-tube oscillation:

"They don't understand back on Earth. Even here they don't. Sometimes I think they refuse to understand. Joe's down there without much more than his bare hands. He, I, we started with no more knowledge than that he could probably eat the local life. He has to spend nearly all his time hunting for food. It's a miracle he's come as far as he has in these few weeks—made a shelter, grown familiar with the immediate region, begun on metallurgy, hydrurgy, whatever you want to call it. What more do they want me to do, for crying in the beer?"

"Yes, yes—" mumbled Cornelius. "Yes, I—"

Anglesey raised his white bony face. Something filmed over in his eyes.

"What—" began Cornelius.

"Shut up!" Anglesey whipped the chair around, groped for the helmet, slapped it down over his skull. "Joe's waking. Get out of here."

"But if you'll only let me work while he sleeps, how can I—"

Anglesey snarled and threw a wrench at him. It was a feeble toss, even in low-gee. Cornelius backed toward the door. Anglesey was tuning in the esprojector. Suddenly he jerked.

"*Cornelius!*"

"Whatisit?" The psionicist tried to run back, overdid it, and skidded in a heap to end up against the panel.

"K-tube again." Anglesey yanked off the helmet. It must have hurt like blazes, having a mental squeal build up uncontrolled and amplified in your own brain, but he said merely: "Change it for me. Fast. And then get out and leave me alone. Joe didn't wake up of himself. Something crawled into the dugout with me—I'm in trouble down there!"

It had been a hard day's work, and Joe slept heavily. He did not wake until the hands closed on his throat.

For a moment, then, he knew only a crazy smothering wave of panic. He thought he was back on Earth Station, floating in null-gee at the end of a cable while a thousand frosty stars haloed the planet before him. He thought the great I-beam had broken from its moorings and started toward him, slowly, but with all the inertia of its cold tons, spinning and shimmering in the Earthlight, and the only sound himself, screaming and screaming in his helmet, trying to break from the cable. The beam nudged him ever so gently, but it kept on moving. He moved with it. He was crushed against the station wall—nuzzled into it—his mangled suit frothed as it tried to seal its wounded self. There was blood mingled with the foam—his blood! *Joe roared.*

His convulsive reaction tore the hands off his neck and sent a black shape spinning across the dugout. It struck the wall, thunderously, and the lamp fell to the floor and went out.

Joe stood in darkness, breathing hard, aware in a vague fashion that the wind had died from a shriek to a low snarling while he slept.

The thing he had tossed away mumbled in pain and crawled along the wall. Joe felt through lightlessness after his club.

Something else scrabbled. The tunnel! They were coming through the tunnel! Joe groped blind to meet them. His heart drummed thickly and his nose drank an alien stench.

The thing that emerged, as Joe's hands closed on it, was only about half his size, but it had six monstrously taloned feet and a pair of three-fingered hands that reached after his eyes. Joe cursed, lifted it while it writhed, and dashed it to the floor. It screamed, and he heard bones splinter.

"Come on, then!" Joe arched his back and spat at them, like a tiger menaced by giant caterpillars.

They flowed through his tunnel and into the room, a dozen of them entered while he wrestled one that had curled itself around his shoulders and anchored its sinuous body with claws. They pulled at his legs, trying to crawl up on his back. He struck out with claws of his own, with his tail, rolled over and went down beneath a heap of them and stood up with the heap still clinging to him.

They swayed in darkness. The legged seething of them struck the dugout wall. It shivered, a rafter cracked, the roof came down. Anglesey stood in a pit, among broken ice plates, under the wan light of a sinking Ganymede.

He could see, now, that the monsters were black in color and that they had heads big enough to accommodate some brain, less than human but probably more than apes. There were a score of them or so, they struggled from beneath the wreckage and flowed at him with the same shrieking malice.

Why?

Baboon reaction, thought Anglesey somewhere in the back of himself. See the stranger, fear the stranger, hate the stranger, kill the stranger. His chest heaved, pumping air through a raw throat. He yanked a whole rafter to him, snapped it in half, and twirled the iron-hard wood.

The nearest creature got its head bashed in. The next had its back broken. The third was hurled with shattered ribs into a fourth, they went down together. Joe began to laugh. It was getting to be fun.

"Yeee-ow! Ti-i-i-iger!" He ran across the icy ground, toward the pack. They scattered, howling. He hunted them until the last one had vanished into the forest.

Panting, Joe looked at the dead. He himself was bleeding, he ached, he was cold and hungry and his shelter had been wrecked . . . but, he'd whipped them! He had a sudden impulse to beat his chest and howl. For a moment, he hesitated—why not? Anglesey threw back his head and bayed victory at the dim shield of Ganymede.

Thereafter he went to work. First build a fire, in the lee of the spaceship—which was little more by now than a hill of corrosion. The monster pack cried in darkness and the broken ground; they had not given up on him, they would return.

He tore a haunch off one of the slain and took a bite. Pretty good. Better yet if properly cooked. Heh! They'd made a big mistake in calling his attention to their existence! He finished breakfast while Ganymede slipped under the western ice mountains. It would be morning soon. The air was almost still, and a flock of pancake-shaped skyskimmers, as Anglesey called them, went overhead, burnished copper color in the first pale dawn-streaks.

Joe rummaged in the ruins of his hut until he had recovered the water-smelting equipment. It wasn't harmed. That was the first order of business, melt some ice and cast it in the molds of ax, knife, saw, hammer he had painfully prepared. Under Jovian conditions, methane was a liquid that you drank and water was a dense hard mineral. It would make good tools. Later on he would try alloying it with other materials.

Next—yes. To hell with the dugout, he could sleep in the open again for a while. Make a bow, set traps, be ready to massacre the black caterpillars when they attacked him again. There was a chasm not far from here, going down a long ways toward the bitter cold of the metallic-hydrogen strata: a natural icebox, a place to store the several weeks' worth of meat his enemies would supply. This would give him leisure to— Oh, a hell of a lot!

Joe laughed, exultantly, and lay down to watch the sunrise.

It struck him afresh how lovely a place this was. See how the small brilliant spark of the sun swam up out of eastern fog-banks colored dusky purple and veined with rose and gold; see how the light strengthened until the great hollow arch of the sky became one shout of radiance; see how the light spilled warm and living over a broad fair land, the million square miles of rustling low forests and wave-blinking lakes and feather-plumed hydrogen geysers; and see, see, see how the ice mountains of the west flashed like blued steel!

Anglesey drew the wild morning wind deep into his lungs and shouted with a boy's joy.

"I'm not a biologist myself," said Viken carefully. "But maybe for that reason I can better give you the general picture. Then Lopez or Matsumoto can answer any questions of detail."

"Excellent," nodded Cornelius. "Why don't you assume I am totally ignorant of this project? I very nearly am, you know."

"If you wish," laughed Viken.

They stood in an outer office of the xenobiology section. No one else was around, for the station's clocks said 1730 GMT and there was only one shift. No point in having more, until Anglesey's half of the enterprise had actually begun gathering quantitative data.

The physicist bent over and took a paperweight off a desk. "One of the boys made this for fun," he said, "but it's a pretty good model of Joe. He stands about five feet tall at the head."

Cornelius turned the plastic image over in his hands. If you could imagine such a thing as a feline centaur with a thick prehensile tail— The torso was squat, long-armed, immensely muscular; the hairless head was round, wide-nosed, with big deep-set eyes and heavy jaws, but it was really quite a human face. The overall color was bluish gray.

"Male, I see," he remarked.

"Of course. Perhaps you don't understand. Joe is the complete pseudojovian: as far as we can tell, the final model, with all the bugs worked out. He's the answer to a research question that took fifty years to ask." Viken looked sidewise at Cornelius. "So you realize the importance of your job, don't you?"

"I'll do my best," said the psionicist. "But if . . . well, let's say that tube failure or something causes you to lose Joe before I've solved the oscillation problem. You do have other pseudos in reserve, don't you?"

"Oh, yes," said Viken moodily. "But the cost— We're not on an unlimited budget. We do go through a lot of money, because it's expensive to stand up and sneeze this far from Earth. But for that same reason our margin is slim."

He jammed hands in pockets and slouched toward the inner door, the laboratories, head down and talking in a low, hurried voice:

"Perhaps you don't realize what a nightmare planet Jupiter is. Not just the surface gravity—a shade under three gees, what's that? But the gravitational potential, ten times Earth's. The temperature. The pressure . . . above all, the atmosphere, and the storms, and the darkness!

"When a spaceship goes down to the Jovian surface, it's a radio-controlled job; it leaks like a sieve, to equalize pressure, but otherwise it's the sturdiest, most utterly powerful model ever designed; it's loaded with every instrument, every servo-mechanism, every safety device the human mind has yet thought up to protect a million-dollar hunk of precision equipment.

"And what happens? Half the ships never reach the surface at all.

A storm snatches them and throws them away, or they collide with a floating chunk of Ice VII—small version of the Red Spot—or, so help me, what passes for a flock of *birds* rams one and stoves it in!

"As for the fifty per cent which does land, it's a one-way trip. We don't even try to bring them back. If the stresses coming down haven't sprung something, the corrosion has doomed them anyway. Hydrogen at Jovian pressure does funny things to metals.

"It cost a total of—about five million dollars—to set Joe, one pseudo, down there. Each pseudo to follow will cost, if we're lucky, a couple of million more."

Viken kicked open the door and led the way through. Beyond was a big room, low-ceilinged, coldly lit and murmurous with ventilators. It reminded Cornelius of a nucleonics lab; for a moment he wasn't sure why, then recognized the intricacies of remote control, remote observation, walls enclosing forces which could destroy the entire moon.

"These are required by the pressure, of course," said Viken, pointing to a row of shields. "And the cold. And the hydrogen itself, as a minor hazard. We have units here duplicating conditions in the Jovian, uh, stratosphere. This is where the whole project really began."

"I've heard something about that," nodded Cornelius. "Didn't you scoop up air-borne spores?"

"Not I." Viken chuckled. "Totti's crew did, about fifty years ago. Proved there was life on Jupiter. A life using liquid methane as its basic solvent, solid ammonia as a starting point for nitrate synthesis—the plants use solar energy to build unsaturated carbon compounds, releasing hydrogen; the animals eat the plants and reduce those compounds again to the saturated form. There is even an equivalent of combustion. The reactions involve complex enzymes and . . . well, it's out of my line."

"Jovian biochemistry is pretty well understood, then."

"Oh, yes. Even in Totti's day, they had a highly developed biotic technology: Earth bacteria had already been synthesized, and most gene structures pretty well mapped. The only reason it took so long to diagram Jovian life processes was the technical difficulty, high pressure and so on."

"When did you actually get a look at Jupiter's surface?"

"Gray managed that, about thirty years ago. Set a televisor ship down, a ship that lasted long enough to flash him quite a series of pictures. Since then, the technique has improved. We know that

Jupiter is crawling with its own weird kind of life, probably more fertile than Earth. Extrapolating from the air-borne microorganisms, our team made trial syntheses of metazoans and—"

Viken sighed. "Damn it, if only there were intelligent native life! Think what they could tell us, Cornelius, the data, the— Just think back how far we've gone since Lavoisier, with the low-pressure chemistry of Earth. Here's a chance to learn a high-pressure chemistry and physics at least as rich with possibilities!"

After a moment, Cornelius murmured slyly: "Are you certain there *aren't* any Jovians?"

"Oh, sure, there could be several billion of them," shrugged Viken. "Cities, empires, anything you like. Jupiter has the surface area of a hundred Earths, and we've only seen maybe a dozen small regions. But we do know there aren't any Jovians using radio. Considering their atmosphere, it's unlikely they ever would invent it for themselves—imagine how thick a vacuum tube has to be, how strong a pump you need! So it was finally decided we'd better make our own Jovians."

Cornelius followed him through the lab, into another room. This was less cluttered, it had a more finished appearance: the experimenter's haywire rig had yielded to the assured precision of an engineer.

Viken went over to one of the panels which lined the walls and looked at its gauges. "Beyond this lies another pseudo," he said. "Female, in this instance. She's at a pressure of two hundred atmospheres and a temperature of 194 Absolute. There's a . . . an umbilical arrangement, I guess you'd call it, to keep her alive. She was grown to adulthood in this, uh, fetal stage—we patterned our Jovians after the terrestrial mammal. She's never been conscious, she won't ever be till she's 'born.' We have a total of twenty males and sixty females waiting here. We can count on about half reaching the surface. More can be created as required.

"It isn't the pseudos that are so expensive, it's their transportation. So Joe is down there alone till we're sure that his kind *can* survive."

"I take it you experimented with lower forms first," said Cornelius.

"Of course. It took twenty years, even with forced-catalysis techniques, to work from an artificial air-borne spore to Joe. We've used the psibeam to control everything from pseudo-insects on up. Interspecies control is possible, you know, if your puppet's nervous system is deliberately designed for it, and isn't given a chance to grow into a pattern different from the esman's."

"And Joe is the first specimen who's given trouble?"

"Yes."

"Scratch one hypothesis." Cornelius sat down on a workbench, dangling thick legs and running a hand through thin sandy hair. "I thought maybe some physical effect of Jupiter was responsible. Now it looks as if the difficulty is with Joe himself."

"We've all suspected that much," said Viken. He struck a cigarette and sucked in his cheeks around the smoke. His eyes were gloomy. "Hard to see how. The biotics engineers tell me *Pseudocentaurus Sapiens* has been more carefully designed than any product of natural evolution."

"Even the brain?"

"Yes. It's patterned directly on the human, to make psibeam control possible, but there are improvements—greater stability."

"There are still the psychological aspects, though," said Cornelius. "In spite of all our amplifiers and other fancy gadgets, psi is essentially a branch of psychology, even today . . . or maybe it's the other way around. Let's consider traumatic experiences. I take it the . . . the adult Jovian fetus has a rough trip going down?"

"The ship does," said Viken. "Not the pseudo itself, which is wrapped up in fluid just like you were before birth."

"Nevertheless," said Cornelius, "the two hundred atmospheres pressure here is not the same as whatever unthinkable pressure exists down on Jupiter. Could the change be injurious?"

Viken gave him a look of respect. "Not likely," he answered. "I told you the J-ships are designed leaky. External pressure is transmitted to the, uh, uterine mechanism through a series of diaphragms, in a gradual fashion. It takes hours to make the descent, you realize."

"Well, what happens next?" went on Cornelius. "The ship lands, the uterine mechanism opens, the umbilical connection disengages, and Joe is, shall we say, born. But he has an adult brain. He is not protected by the only half-developed infant brain from the shock of sudden awareness."

"We thought of that," said Viken. "Anglesey was on the psibeam, in phase with Joe, when the ship left this moon. So it wasn't really Joe who emerged, who perceived. Joe has never been much more than a biological waldo. He can only suffer mental shock to the extent that Ed does, because it *is* Ed down there!"

"As you will," said Cornelius. "Still, you didn't plan for a race of puppets, did you?"

"Oh, heavens, no," said Viken. "Out of the question. Once we know

Joe is well established, we'll import a few more esmen and get him some assistance in the form of other pseudos. Eventually females will be sent down, and uncontrolled males, to be educated by the puppets. A new generation will be born normally— Well, anyhow, the ultimate aim is a small civilization of Jovians. There will be hunters, miners, artisans, farmers, housewives, the works. They will support a few key members, a kind of priesthood. And that priesthood will be esp-controlled, as Joe is. It will exist solely to make instruments, take readings, perform experiments, and tell us what we want to know!"

Cornelius nodded. In a general way, this was the Jovian project as he had understood it. He could appreciate the importance of his own assignment.

Only, he still had no clue to the cause of that positive feedback in the K-tubes.

And what could he do about it?

His hands were still bruised. *Oh, God,* he thought with a groan, for the hundredth time, *does it affect me that much? While Joe was fighting down there, did I really hammer my fists on metal up here?*

His eyes smoldered across the room, to the bench where Cornelius worked. He didn't like Cornelius, fat cigar-sucking slob, interminably talking and talking. He had about given up trying to be civil to the Earthworm.

The psionicist laid down a screwdriver and flexed cramped fingers. *"Whuff!"* he smiled. "I'm going to take a break."

The half-assembled esprojector made a gaunt backdrop for his wide soft body, where it squatted toad-fashion on the bench. Anglesey detested the whole idea of anyone sharing this room, even for a few hours a day. Of late he had been demanding his meals brought here, left outside the door of his adjoining bedroom-bath. He had not gone beyond for quite some time now.

And why should I?

"Couldn't you hurry it up a little?" snapped Anglesey.

Cornelius flushed. "If you'd had an assembled spare machine, instead of loose parts—" he began. Shrugging, he took out a cigar stub and relit it carefully; his supply had to last a long time. Anglesey wondered if those stinking clouds were blown from his mouth of malicious purpose. *I don't like you, Mr. Earthman Cornelius, and it is doubtless quite mutual.*

"There was no obvious need for one, until the other esmen arrive," said Anglesey in a sullen voice. "And the testing instruments report this one in perfectly good order."

"Nevertheless," said Cornelius, "at irregular intervals it goes into wild oscillations which burn out the K-tube. The problem is why. I'll have you try out this new machine as soon as it is ready, but frankly, I don't believe the trouble lies in electronic failure at all—or even in unsuspected physical effects."

"Where, then?" Anglesey felt more at ease as the discussion grew purely technical.

"Well, look. What exactly is the K-tube? It's the heart of the esprojector. It amplifies your natural psionic pulses, uses them to modulate the carrier wave, and shoots the whole beam down at Joe. It also picks up Joe's resonating impulses and amplifies them for your benefit. Everything else is auxiliary to the K-tube."

"Spare me the lecture," snarled Anglesey.

"I was only rehearsing the obvious," said Cornelius, "because every now and then it is the obvious answer which is hardest to see. Maybe it isn't the K-tube which is misbehaving. Maybe it is you."

"What?" The white face gaped at him. A dawning rage crept red across its thin bones.

"Nothing personal intended," said Cornelius hastily. "But you know what a tricky beast the subconscious is. Suppose, just as a working hypothesis, that way down underneath, you don't *want* to be on Jupiter. I imagine it is a rather terrifying environment. Or there may be some obscure Freudian element involved. Or, quite simply and naturally, your subconscious may fail to understand that Joe's death does not entail your own."

"Um-m-m—" *Mirabile dictu,* Anglesey remained calm. He rubbed his chin with one skeletal hand. "Can you be more explicit?"

"Only in a rough way," replied Cornelius. "Your conscious mind sends a motor impulse along the psibeam to Joe. Simultaneously, your subconscious mind, being scared of the whole business, emits the glandular-vascular-cardiac-visceral impulses associated with fear. These react on Joe, whose tension is transmitted back along the beam. Feeling Joe's somatic fear-symptoms, your subconscious gets still more worried, thereby increasing the symptoms— Get it? It's exactly similar to ordinary neurasthenia, with this exception: that since there is a powerful amplifier, the K-tube, involved, the oscillations can build up uncontrollably within a second or two. You should be thankful the tube does burn out—otherwise your brain might do so!"

For a moment Anglesey was quiet. Then he laughed. It was a hard, barbaric laughter. Cornelius started as it struck his eardrums.

"Nice idea," said the esman. "But I'm afraid it won't fit all the data. You see, I like it down there. I like being Joe."

He paused for a while, then continued in a dry impersonal tone: "Don't judge the environment from my notes. They're just idiotic things like estimates of wind velocity, temperature variations, mineral properties—insignificant. What I can't put in is how Jupiter looks through a Jovian's infrared-seeing eyes."

"Different, I should think," ventured Cornelius.

"Yes and no. It's hard to put into language. Some of it I can't, because man hasn't got the concepts. But . . . oh, I can't describe it. Shakespeare himself couldn't. Just remember that everything about Jupiter which is cold and poisonous and gloomy to us is *right* for Joe."

Anglesey's tone grew remote, as if he spoke to himself:

"Imagine walking under a glowing violet sky, where great flashing clouds sweep the earth with shadow and rain strides beneath them. Imagine walking on the slopes of a mountain like polished metal, with a clean red flame exploding above you and thunder laughing in the ground. Imagine a cool wild stream, and low trees with dark coppery flowers, and a waterfall, methanefall . . . whatever you like . . . leaping off a cliff, and the strong live wind shakes its mane full of rainbows! Imagine a whole forest, dark and breathing, and here and there you glimpse a pale-red wavering will-o'-the-wisp, which is the life radiation of some fleet shy animal, and . . . and—"

Anglesey croaked into silence. He stared down at his clenched fists, then he closed his eyes tight and tears ran out between the lids.

"Imagine being *strong!*"

Suddenly he snatched up the helmet, crammed it on his head and twirled the control knobs. Joe had been sleeping, down in the night, but Joe was about to wake up and—roar under the four great moons till all the forest feared him?

Cornelius slipped quietly out of the room.

In the long brazen sunset light, beneath dusky cloud banks brooding storm, he strode up the hill-slope with a sense of day's work done. Across his back, two woven baskets balanced each other, one laden with the pungent black fruit of the thorntree and one with cable-thick creepers to be used as rope. The ax on his shoulder caught the waning sunlight and tossed it blindingly back.

It had not been hard labor, but weariness dragged at his mind and he did not relish the household chores yet to be performed, cooking and cleaning and all the rest. Why couldn't they hurry up and get him some helpers?

His eyes sought the sky, resentfully. The moon Five was hidden—down here, at the bottom of the air ocean, you saw nothing but the sun and the four Galilean satellites. He wasn't even sure where Five was just now, in relation to himself . . . *wait a minute, it's sunset here, but if I went out to the viewdome I'd see Jupiter in the last quarter, or would I, oh, hell, it only takes us half an Earth-day to swing around the planet anyhow—*

Joe shook his head. After all this time, it was still damnably hard, now and then, to keep his thoughts straight. *I, the essential I, am up in heaven, riding Jupiter V between cold stars. Remember that. Open your eyes, if you will, and see the dead control room superimposed on a living hillside.*

He didn't, though. Instead, he regarded the boulders strewn windblasted gray over the tough mossy vegetation of the slope. They were not much like Earth rocks, nor was the soil beneath his feet like terrestrial humus.

For a moment Anglesey speculated on the origin of the silicates, aluminates, and other stony compounds. Theoretically, all such materials should be inaccessibly locked in the Jovian core, down where the pressure got vast enough for atoms to buckle and collapse. Above the core should lie thousands of miles of allotropic ice, and then the metallic hydrogen layer. There should not be complex minerals this far up, but there were.

Well, possibly Jupiter had formed according to theory, but had thereafter sucked enough cosmic dust, meteors, gases and vapors, down its great throat of gravitation, to form a crust several miles thick. Or more likely the theory was altogether wrong. What did they know, what *could* they know, the soft pale worms of Earth?

Anglesey stuck his—Joe's—fingers in his mouth and whistled. A baying sounded in the brush, and two midnight forms leaped toward him. He grinned and stroked their heads; training was progressing faster than he'd hoped, with these pups of the black caterpillar beasts he had taken. They would make guardians for him, herders, servants.

On the crest of the hill, Joe was building himself a home. He had logged off an acre of ground and erected a stockade. Within the grounds there now stood a lean-to for himself and his stores, a methane well, and the beginnings of a large comfortable cabin.

But there was too much work for one being. Even with the half-intelligent caterpillars to help, and with cold storage for meat, most of his time would still go to hunting. The game wouldn't last forever, either; he had to start agriculture within the next year or so—Jupiter year, twelve Earth years, thought Anglesey. There was the cabin to finish and furnish; he wanted to put a waterwheel, no, methane wheel in the river to turn any of a dozen machines he had in mind, he wanted to experiment with alloyed ice and—

And, quite apart from his need of help, why should he remain alone, the single thinking creature on an entire planet? He was a male in this body, with male instincts—in the long run, his health was bound to suffer if he remained a hermit, and right now the whole project depended on Joe's health.

It wasn't right!

But I am not alone. There are fifty men on the satellite with me. I can talk to any of them, any time I wish. It's only that I seldom wish it, these days. I would rather be Joe.

Nevertheless . . . I, the cripple, feel all the tiredness, anger, hurt, frustration, of that wonderful biological machine called Joe. The others don't understand. When the ammonia gale flays open his skin, it is I who bleed.

Joe lay down on the ground, sighing. Fangs flashed in the mouth of the black beast which humped over to lick his face. His belly growled with hunger, but he was too tired to fix a meal. Once he had the dogs trained—

Another pseudo would be so much more rewarding to educate.

He could almost see it, in the weary darkening of his brain. Down there, in the valley below the hill, fire and thunder as the ship came to rest. And the steel egg would crack open, the steel arms—already crumbling, puny work of worms!—lift out the shape within and lay it on the earth.

She would stir, shrieking in her first lungful of air, looking about with blank mindless eyes. And Joe would come carry her home. And he would feed her, care for her, show her how to walk—it wouldn't take long, an adult body would learn those things very fast. In a few weeks she would even be talking, be an individual, a soul.

Did you ever think, Edward Anglesey, in the days when you also walked, that your wife would be a gray four-legged monster?

Never mind that. The important thing was to get others of his kind down here, female *and* male. The station's niggling little plan would have him wait two more Earth years, and then send him only another dummy like himself, a contemptible human mind looking through eyes which belonged rightfully to a Jovian. It was not to be tolerated!

If he weren't so tired—

Joe sat up. Sleep drained from him as the realization entered. *He* wasn't tired, not to speak of. Anglesey was. Anglesey, the human side of him, who for months had only slept in catnaps, whose rest had lately been interrupted by Cornelius—it was the human body which drooped, gave up, and sent wave after soft wave of sleep down the psibeam to Joe.

Somatic tension traveled skyward; Anglesey jerked awake.

He swore. As he sat there beneath the helmet, the vividness of Jupiter faded with his scattering concentration, as if it grew transparent; the steel prison which was his laboratory strengthened behind it. He was losing contact— Rapidly, with the skill of experience, he brought himself back into phase with the neural currents of the other brain. He willed sleepiness on Joe, exactly as a man wills it on himself.

And, like any other insomniac, he failed. The Joe-body was too hungry. It got up and walked across the compound toward its shack.

The K-tube went wild and blew itself out.

The night before the ships left, Viken and Cornelius sat up late.

It was not truly a night, of course. In twelve hours the tiny moon was hurled clear around Jupiter, from darkness back to darkness, and there might well be a pallid little sun over its crags when the clocks said witches were abroad in Greenwich. But most of the personnel were asleep at this hour.

Viken scowled. "I don't like it," he said. "Too sudden a change of plans. Too big a gamble."

"You are only risking—how many?—three male and a dozen female pseudos," Cornelius replied.

"And fifteen J-ships. All we have. If Anglesey's notion doesn't work, it will be months, a year or more, till we can have others built and resume aerial survey."

"But if it does work," said Cornelius, "you won't need any J-ships, except to carry down more pseudos. You will be too busy evaluating data from the surface to piddle around in the upper atmosphere."

"Of course. But we never expected it so soon. We were going to bring more esmen out here, to operate some more pseudos—"

"But they aren't *needed*," said Cornelius. He struck a cigar to life and took a long pull on it, while his mind sought carefully for words. "Not for a while, anyhow. Joe has reached a point where, given help, he can leap several thousand years of history—he may even have a radio of sorts operating in the fairly near future, which would eliminate the necessity of much of your esping. But without help, he'll just have to mark time. And it's stupid to make a highly trained human esman perform manual labor, which is all that the other pseudos are needed for at this moment. Once the Jovian settlement is well established, certainly, then you can send down more puppets."

"The question is, though," persisted Viken, "can Anglesey himself educate all those pseudos at once? They'll be helpless as infants for days. It will be weeks before they really start thinking and acting for themselves. Can Joe take care of them meanwhile?"

"He has food and fuel stored for months ahead," said Cornelius. "As for what Joe's capabilities are, well, hm-m-m . . . we just have to take Anglesey's judgment. He has the only inside information."

"And once those Jovians do become personalities," worried Viken, "are they necessarily going to string along with Joe? Don't forget, the pseudos are not carbon copies of each other. The uncertainty principle assures each one a unique set of genes. If there is only one human mind on Jupiter, among all those aliens—"

"One *human* mind?" It was barely audible. Viken opened his mouth inquiringly. The other man hurried on.

"Oh, I'm sure Anglesey can continue to dominate them," said Cornelius. "His own personality is rather—tremendous."

Viken looked startled. "You really think so?"

The psionicist nodded. "Yes. I've seen more of him in the past weeks than anyone else. And my profession naturally orients me more toward a man's psychology than his body or his habits. You see a waspish cripple. I see a mind which has reacted to its physical handicaps by developing such a hellish energy, such an inhuman power of concentration, that it almost frightens me. Give that mind a sound body for its use and nothing is impossible to it."

"You may be right, at that," murmured Viken after a pause. "Not that it matters. The decision is taken, the rockets go down tomorrow. I hope it all works out."

He waited for another while. The whirring of ventilators in his little room seemed unnaturally loud, the colors of a girlie picture on the wall shockingly garish. Then he said, slowly:

"You've been rather close-mouthed yourself, Jan. When do you expect to finish your own esprojector and start making the tests?"

Cornelius looked around. The door stood open to an empty hall-way, but he reached out and closed it before he answered with a slight grin: "It's been ready for the past few days. But don't tell any-one."

"How's that?" Viken started. The movement, in low-gee, took him out of his chair and halfway across the table between the men. He shoved himself back and waited.

"I have been making meaningless tinkering motions," said Corne-lius, "but what I waited for was a highly emotional moment, a time when I can be sure Anglesey's entire attention will be focused on Joe. This business tomorrow is exactly what I need."

"*Why?*"

"You see, I have pretty well convinced myself that the trouble in the machine is psychological, not physical. I think that for some rea-son, buried in his subconscious, Anglesey doesn't want to experience Jupiter. A conflict of that type might well set a psionic amplifier circuit oscillating."

"Hm-m-m." Viken rubbed his chin. "Could be. Lately Ed has been changing more and more. When he first came here, he was peppery enough, and he would at least play an occasional game of poker. Now he's pulled so far into his shell you can't even see him. I never thought of it before, but . . . yes, by God, Jupiter must be having some effect on him."

"Hm-m-m," nodded Cornelius. He did not elaborate: did not, for instance, mention that one altogether uncharacteristic episode when Anglesey had tried to describe what it was like to be a Jovian.

"Of course," said Viken thoughtfully, "the previous men were not affected especially. Nor was Ed at first, while he was still controlling lower-type pseudos. It's only since Joe went down to the surface that he's become so different."

"Yes, yes," said Cornelius hastily. "I've learned that much. But enough shop talk—"

"No. Wait a minute." Viken spoke in a low, hurried tone, looking past him. "For the first time, I'm starting to think clearly about this . . . never really stopped to analyze it before, just accepted a bad situation. There *is* something peculiar about Joe. It can't very well involve his physical structure, or the environment, because lower forms didn't give this trouble. Could it be the fact that—Joe is the first puppet in all history with a potentially human intelligence?"

"We speculate in a vacuum," said Cornelius. "Tomorrow, maybe, I can tell you. Now I know nothing."

Viken sat up straight. His pale eyes focused on the other man and stayed there, unblinking. "One minute," he said.

"Yes?" Cornelius shifted, half rising. "Quickly, please. It is past my bedtime."

"You know a good deal more than you've admitted," said Viken. "Don't you?"

"What makes you think that?"

"You aren't the most gifted liar in the universe. And then—you argued very strongly for Anglesey's scheme, this sending down the other pseudos. More strongly than a newcomer should."

"I told you, I want his attention focused elsewhere when—"

"Do you want it that badly?" snapped Viken.

Cornelius was still for a minute. Then he sighed and leaned back.

"All right," he said. "I shall have to trust your discretion. I wasn't sure, you see, how any of you old-time station personnel would react. So I didn't want to blabber out my speculations, which may be wrong. The confirmed facts, yes, I will tell them; but I don't wish to attack a man's religion with a mere theory."

Viken scowled. "What the devil do you mean?"

Cornelius puffed hard on his cigar, its tip waxed and waned like a miniature red demon star. "This Jupiter V is more than a research station," he said gently. "It is a way of life, is it not? No one would come here for even one hitch unless the work was important to him. Those who re-enlist, they must find something in the work, something which Earth with all her riches cannot offer them. No?"

"Yes," answered Viken. It was almost a whisper. "I didn't think you would understand so well. But what of it?"

"Well, I don't want to tell you, unless I can prove it, that maybe this has all gone for nothing. Maybe you have wasted your lives and a lot of money, and will have to pack up and go home."

Viken's long face did not flicker a muscle. It seemed to have congealed. But he said calmly enough: "Why?"

"Consider Joe," said Cornelius. "His brain has as much capacity as any adult human's. It has been recording every sense datum that came to it, from the moment of 'birth'—making a record in itself, in its own cells, not merely in Anglesey's physical memory bank up here. Also, you know, a thought is a sense datum too. And thoughts are not separated into neat little railway tracks; they form a continuous field. Every time Anglesey is in rapport with Joe, and thinks, the thought goes through Joe's synapses as well as his own—and every thought carries its own associations, and every associated memory is recorded. Like if Joe is building a hut, the shape of the logs might remind Anglesey of some geometric figure, which in turn would remind him of the Pythagorean theorem—"

"I get the idea," said Viken in a cautious way. "Given time, Joe's brain will have stored everything that ever was in Ed's."

"Correct. Now a functioning nervous system with an engrammatic pattern of experience—in this case, a *nonhuman* nervous system—isn't that a pretty good definition of a personality?"

"I suppose so—good Lord!" Viken jumped. "You mean Joe is—taking over?"

"In a way. A subtle, automatic, unconscious way." Cornelius drew a deep breath and plunged into it. "The pseudojovian is so nearly perfect a life form: your biologists engineered into it all the experience gained from nature's mistakes in designing *us*. At first, Joe was only a remote-controlled biological machine. Then Anglesey and Joe became two facets of a single personality. Then, oh, very slowly, the stronger, healthier body . . . more amplitude to its thoughts . . . do you see? Joe is becoming the dominant side. Like this business of sending down the other pseudos—Anglesey only thinks he has logical reasons for wanting it done. Actually, his 'reasons' are mere rationalizations for the instinctive desires of the Joe-facet.

"Anglesey's subconscious must comprehend the situation, in a dim reactive way; it must feel his human ego gradually being submerged by the steamroller force of *Joe's* instincts and *Joe's* wishes. It tries to defend its own identity, and is swatted down by the superior force of Joe's own nascent subconscious.

"I put it crudely," he finished in an apologetic tone, "but it will account for that oscillation in the K-tubes."

Viken nodded, slowly, like an old man. "Yes, I see it," he answered. "The alien environment down there . . . the different brain structure . . . good God! Ed's being swallowed up in Joe! The puppet master is becoming the puppet!" He looked ill.

"Only speculation on my part," said Cornelius. All at once, he felt very tired. It was not pleasant to do this to Viken, whom he liked. "But you see the dilemma, no? If I am right, then any esman will gradually become a Jovian—a monster with two bodies, of which the human body is the unimportant auxiliary one. This means no esman will ever agree to control a pseudo—therefore, the end of your project."

He stood up. "I'm sorry, Arne. You made me tell you what I think, and now you will lie awake worrying, and I am maybe quite wrong and you worry for nothing."

"It's all right," mumbled Viken. "Maybe you're not wrong."

"I don't know." Cornelius drifted toward the door. "I am going to try to find some answers tomorrow. Good night."

The moon-shaking thunder of the rockets, crash, crash, crash, leaping from their cradles, was long past. Now the fleet glided on metal wings, with straining secondary ramjets, through the rage of the Jovian sky.

As Cornelius opened the control-room door, he looked at his telltale board. Elsewhere a voice tolled the word to all the stations, *one ship wrecked, two ships wrecked,* but Anglesey would let no sound enter his presence when he wore the helmet. An obliging technician had haywired a panel of fifteen red and fifteen blue lights above Cornelius' esprojector, to keep him informed, too. Ostensibly, of course, they were only there for Anglesey's benefit, though the esman had insisted he wouldn't be looking at them.

Four of the red bulbs were dark and thus four blue ones would not shine for a safe landing. A whirlwind, a thunderbolt, a floating ice meteor, a flock of mantalike birds with flesh as dense and hard as iron—there could be a hundred things which had crumpled four ships and tossed them tattered across the poison forests.

Four ships, hell! Think of four living creatures, with an excellence of brain to rival your own, damned first to years in unconscious night and then, never awakening save for one uncomprehending instant, dashed in bloody splinters against an ice mountain. The wasteful callousness of it was a cold knot in Cornelius' belly. It had to be done, no doubt, if there was to be any thinking life on Jupiter at all; but then let it be done quickly and minimally, he thought, so the next generation could be begotten by love and not by machines!

He closed the door behind him and waited for a breathless moment. Anglesey was a wheelchair and a coppery curve of helmet, facing the opposite wall. No movement, no awareness whatsoever. Good!

It would be awkward, perhaps ruinous, if Anglesey learned of this most intimate peering. But he needn't, ever. He was blindfolded and ear-plugged by his own concentration.

Nevertheless, the psionicist moved his bulky form with care, across the room to the new esprojector. He did not much like his snooper's role, he would not have assumed it at all if he had seen any other hope. But neither did it make him feel especially guilty. If what he suspected was true, then Anglesey was all unawares being twisted into something not human; to spy on him might be to save him.

Gently, Cornelius activated the meters and started his tubes warming up. The oscilloscope built into Anglesey's machine gave him the other man's exact alpha rhythm, his basic biological clock. First you adjusted to that, then you discovered the subtler elements by feel, and when your set was fully in phase you could probe undetected and—

Find out what was wrong. Read Anglesey's tortured subconscious and see what there was on Jupiter that both drew and terrified him. *Five ships wrecked.*

But it must be very nearly time for them to land. Maybe only five would be lost in all. Maybe ten would get through. Ten comrades for—Joe?

Cornelius sighed. He looked at the cripple, seated blind and deaf to the human world which had crippled him, and felt a pity and an anger. It wasn't fair, none of it was.

Not even to Joe. Joe wasn't any kind of soul-eating devil. He did not even realize, as yet, that he *was* Joe, that Anglesey was becoming a mere appendage. He hadn't asked to be created, and to withdraw his human counterpart from him would very likely be to destroy him.

Somehow, there were always penalties for everybody, when men exceeded the decent limits.

Cornelius swore at himself, voicelessly. Work to do. He sat down and fitted the helmet on his own head. The carrier wave made a faint pulse, inaudible, the trembling of neurones low in his awareness. You couldn't describe it.

Reaching up, he tuned to Anglesey's alpha. His own had a somewhat lower frequency, it was necessary to carry the signals through a heterodyning process. Still no reception . . . well, of course he had to find the exact wave form, timbre was as basic to thought as to music. He adjusted the dials, slowly, with enormous care.

Something flashed through his consciousness, a vision of clouds roiled in a violet-red sky, a wind that galloped across horizonless immensity—he lost it. His fingers shook as he tuned back.

The psibeam between Joe and Anglesey broadened. It took Cornelius into the circuit. He looked through Joe's eyes, he stood on a hill and stared into the sky above the ice mountains, straining for sign of the first rocket; and simultaneously, he was still Jan Cornelius, blurrily seeing the meters, probing about for emotions, symbols, any key to the locked terror in Angelsey's soul.

The terror rose up and struck him in the face.

Psionic detection is not a matter of passive listening in. Much as a radio receiver is necessarily also a weak transmitter, the nervous system in resonance with a source of psionic-spectrum energy is itself emitting. Normally, of course, this effect is unimportant; but when you pass the impulses, either way, through a set of heterodyning and amplifying units, with a high negative feedback—

In the early days, psionic psychotherapy vitiated itself because the amplified thoughts of one man, entering the brain of another, would combine with the latter's own neural cycles according to the ordinary vector laws. The result was that both men felt the new beat frequencies as a nightmarish fluttering of their very thoughts. An analyst, trained into self-control, could ignore it; his patient could not, and reacted violently.

But eventually the basic human wave-timbres were measured, and psionic therapy resumed. The modern esprojector analyzed an incoming signal and shifted its characteristics over to the "listener's" pattern. The *really* different pulses of the transmitting brain, those which could not possibly be mapped onto the pattern of the receiving neurones—as an exponential signal cannot very practicably be mapped onto a sinusoid—those were filtered out.

Thus compensated, the other thought could be apprehended as comfortably as one's own. If the patient were on a psibeam circuit, a skilled operator could tune in without the patient being necessarily aware of it. The operator could either probe the other man's thoughts or implant thoughts of his own.

Cornelius' plan, an obvious one to any psionicist, had depended on this. He would receive from an unwitting Anglesey-Joe. If his theory were right, and the esman's personality was being distorted into that of a monster—his thinking would be too alien to come through the filters. Cornelius would receive spottily or not at all. If his theory was wrong, and Angelsey was still Anglesey, he would receive only a normal human stream-of-consciousness, and could probe for other trouble-making factors.

His brain roared!

What's happening to me?

For a moment, the interference which turned his thoughts to sawtoothed gibberish struck him down with panic. He gulped for breath, there in the Jovian wind, and his dreadful dogs sensed the alienness in him and whined.

Then, recognition, remembrance, and a blaze of anger so great that it left no room for fear. Joe filled his lungs and shouted it aloud, the hillside boomed with echoes:

"Get out of my mind!"

He felt Cornelius spiral down toward unconsciousness. The overwhelming force of his own mental blow had been too much. He laughed, it was more like a snarl, and eased the pressure.

Above him, between thunderous clouds, winked the first thin descending rocket flare.

Cornelius' mind groped back toward the light. It broke a watery surface, the man's mouth snapped after air and his hands reached for the dials, to turn his machine off and escape.

"Not so fast, you." Grimly, Joe drove home a command that locked Cornelius' muscles rigid. "I want to know the meaning of this. Hold still and let me look!" He smashed home an impulse which could be rendered, perhaps, as an incandescent question mark. Remembrance exploded in shards through the psionicist's forebrain.

"So. That's all there is? You thought I was afraid to come down here and be Joe, and wanted to know why? But I *told* you I wasn't!"

I should have believed—whispered Cornelius.

"Well, get out of the circuit, then." Joe continued growling it vocally. "And don't ever come back in the control room, understand? K-tubes or no, I don't want to see you again. And I may be a cripple, but I can still take you apart cell by cell. Now—sign off— leave me alone. The first ship will be landing in minutes."

You a cripple . . . you, Joe Anglesey?

"What?" The great gray being on the hill lifted his barbaric head as if to sudden trumpets. "What do you mean?"

Don't you understand? said the weak, dragging thought. *You know how the esprojector works. You know I could have probed Anglesey's mind in Anglesey's brain without making enough interference to be noticed. And I could not have probed a wholly nonhuman mind at all, nor could it have been aware of me. The filters would not have passed such a signal. Yet you felt me in the first fractional second. It can only mean a human mind in a nonhuman brain.*

You are not the half-corpse on Jupiter V any longer. You're Joe— Joe Anglesey.

"Well, I'll be damned," said Joe. "You're right."

He turned Anglesey off, kicked Cornelius out of his mind with a single brutal impulse, and ran down the hill to meet the spaceship.

Cornelius woke up minutes afterward. His skull felt ready to split apart. He groped for the main switch before him, clashed it down, ripped the helmet off his head and threw it clanging on the floor. But it took a little while to gather the strength to do the same for Anglesey. The other man was not able to do anything for himself.

They sat outside sickbay and waited. It was a harshly lit barrenness of metal and plastic, smelling of antiseptics: down near the heart of the satellite, with miles of rock to hide the terrible face of Jupiter.

Only Viken and Cornelius were in that cramped little room. The rest of the station went about its business mechanically, filling in the time till it could learn what had happened. Beyond the door, three biotechnicians, who were also the station's medical staff, fought with death's angel for the thing which had been Edward Anglesey.

"Nine ships got down," said Viken dully. "Two males, seven females. It's enough to start a colony."

"It would be genetically desirable to have more," pointed out Cornelius. He kept his own voice low, in spite of its underlying cheerfulness. There was a certain awesome quality to all this.

"I still don't understand," said Viken.

"Oh, it's clear enough—now. I should have guessed it before, maybe. We had all the facts, it was only that we couldn't make the simple, obvious interpretation of them. No, we had to conjure up Frankenstein's monster."

"Well," Viken's words grated, "we have played Frankenstein, haven't we? Ed is dying in there."

"It depends on how you define death." Cornelius drew hard on his cigar, needing anything that might steady him. His tone grew purposely dry of emotion:

"Look here. Consider the data. Joe, now: a creature with a brain of human capacity, but without a mind—a perfect Lockean *tabula rasa*, for Anglesey's psibeam to write on. We deduced, correctly enough—if very belatedly—that when enough had been written, there would be a personality. But the question was: whose? Because, I suppose, of normal human fear of the unknown, we assumed that any personality in so alien a body had to be monstrous. Therefore it must be hostile to Anglesey, must be swamping him—"

The door opened. Both men jerked to their feet.

The chief surgeon shook his head. "No use. Typical deep-shock traumata, close to terminus now. If we had better facilities, maybe—"

"No," said Cornelius. "You cannot save a man who has decided not to live any more."

"I know." The doctor removed his mask. "I need a cigarette. Who's got one?" His hands shook a little as he accepted it from Viken.

"But how could he—decide—anything?" choked the physicist. "He's been unconscious ever since Jan pulled him away from that . . . that thing."

"It was decided before then," said Cornelius. "As a matter of fact, that hulk in there on the operating table no longer has a mind. I know. I was there." He shuddered a little. A stiff shot of tranquilizer was all that held nightmare away from him. Later he would have to have that memory exorcised.

The doctor took a long drag of smoke, held it in his lungs a moment, and exhaled gustily. "I guess this winds up the project," he said. "We'll never get another esman."

"I'll say we won't." Viken's tone sounded rusty. "I'm going to smash that devil's engine myself."

"Hold on a minute!" exclaimed Cornelius. "Don't you understand? This isn't the end. It's the beginning!"

"I'd better get back," said the doctor. He stubbed out his cigarette and went through the door. It closed behind him with a deathlike quietness.

"What do you mean?" Viken said it as if erecting a barrier.

"*Won't* you understand?" roared Cornelius. "Joe has all Anglesey's habits, thoughts, memories, prejudices, interests . . . oh, yes, the different body and the different environment, they do cause some changes—but no more than any man might undergo on Earth. If you were suddenly cured of a wasting disease, wouldn't you maybe get a little boisterous and rough? There is nothing abnormal in it. Nor is it abnormal to want to stay healthy—no? Do you see?"

Viken sat down. He spent a while without speaking.

Then, enormously slow and careful: "Do you mean Joe is Ed?"

"Or Ed is Joe. Whatever you like. He calls himself Joe now, I think—as a symbol of freedom—but he is still himself. What *is* the ego but continuity of existence?

"He himself did not fully understand this. He only knew—he told me, and I should have believed him—that on Jupiter he was strong and happy. Why did the K-tube oscillate? A hysterical symptom! Anglesey's subconscious was not afraid to stay on Jupiter—it was afraid to come back!

"And then, today, I listened in. By now, his whole self was focused on Joe. That is, the primary source of libido was Joe's virile body, not Anglesey's sick one. This meant a different pattern of impulses—not too alien to pass the filters, but alien enough to set up interference. So he felt my presence. And he saw the truth, just as I did—

"Do you know the last emotion I felt, as Joe threw me out of his mind? Not anger any more. He plays rough, him, but all he had room to feel was joy.

"I *knew* how strong a personality Anglesey had! Whatever made me think an overgrown child-brain like Joe's could override it? In there, the doctors—bah! They're trying to salvage a hulk which has been shed because it is useless!"

Cornelius stopped. His throat was quite raw from talking. He paced the floor, rolled cigar smoke around his mouth but did not draw it any farther in.

When a few minutes had passed, Viken said cautiously: "All right. You should know—as you said, you were there. But what do we do now? How do we get in touch with Ed? Will he even be interested in contacting us?"

"Oh, yes, of course," said Cornelius. "He is still himself, remember. Now that he has none of the cripple's frustrations, he should be more amiable. When the novelty of his new friends wears off, he will want someone who can talk to him as an equal."

"And precisely who will operate another pseudo?" asked Viken sarcastically. "I'm quite happy with this skinny frame of mine, thank you!"

"Was Anglesey the only hopeless cripple on Earth?" asked Cornelius quietly.

Viken gaped at him.

"And there are aging men, too," went on the psionicist, half to himself. "Someday, my friend, when you and I feel the years close in, and so much we would like to learn—maybe we, too, would enjoy an extra lifetime in a Jovian body." He nodded at his cigar. "A hard, lusty, stormy kind of life, granted—dangerous, brawling, violent—but life as no human, perhaps, has lived it since the days of Elizabeth the First. Oh, yes, there will be small trouble finding Jovians."

He turned his head as the surgeon came out again.

"Well?" croaked Viken.

The doctor sat down. "It's finished," he said.

They waited for a moment, awkwardly.

"Odd," said the doctor. He groped after a cigarette he didn't have. Silently, Viken offered him one. "Odd. I've seen these cases before. People who simply resign from life. This is the first one I ever saw that went out smiling—smiling all the time."

Didn't

He

Ramble

by CHAD OLIVER

The old man sat in a soundproof room. He was elegantly dressed in evening clothes, although he had discarded his formal cape at the moment, and his well-manicured fingers were busily tapping out time against the frosted side of his cocktail glass.

The old man's name was Theodore Pearsall, a fact of some importance since he was one of the richest men in the world. Money did not interest him, however; it was only a means to an end.

He reached out a soft pink hand and made a slight adjustment, turning one of the twenty-two knobs on his chair-arm a fraction to the left.

"Play that thing!" Theodore Pearsall shouted, surprisingly. "Do it, Dippermouth!"

Dippermouth obliged.

A gleaming tape, preserving music almost two hundred years old, slid into position behind the transparent plastic safety shield. It fed itself into the shining player, and music surged from the ultrahigh-fidelity speaker that spanned one entire wall.

Louis Armstrong, of course. One of the good old good ones, as Satchmo himself used to say: "Potato Head Blues," cut by the Hot

Seven away back in 1927, with Louis still sticking to the vibrant cornet.

Pearsall closed his eyes, and smiled. His whole face relaxed. His polished shoe thumped on the thick carpet. There was Johnny Dodds's driving clarinet, and those wonderful tailgate smears from Kid Ory's trombone. . . .

"Those were the days," Pearsall whispered happily.

He was quite lost now.

The speaker tirelessly recreated the past, and the legendary men played again: Sidney Bechet's inventive soprano sax, King Oliver swapping breaks with Little Louis, and Bix, impossible Bix, blowing those springwater-pure notes so cleanly it broke your heart—

Jelly Roll Morton then, singing out his genius and his despair:

> *I could sit right here and think a thousand miles away,*
> *I could sit right here and think a thousand miles away. . . .*

The thick door opened and slammed with a jarring crash.

Pearsall turned, expecting a robot, but it wasn't a robot—at least not quite.

It was Laura, his wife.

She was wearing her crucified expression.

"In case you've forgotten, Theodore, we're Having A Party upstairs tonight." (She said it in capital letters, as always.) "The least you could do would be to come up and *mingle* with our guests."

Pearsall considered the matter, silently.

"Can't you turn that thing off while I'm talking to you? Are you drunk, Theodore?"

"Not yet," he assured her, and turned Jelly Roll back into the long silence of the centuries.

He looked at his wife, without pleasure. Laura was beautifully dressed, of course, all silks and ruffles, and she had kept her figure well. He wondered if he had ever loved her.

"Are you coming?"

"Looks that way, chicken."

She beamed at him. "We're playing charades," she said triumphantly, and hurried out the door.

Theodore Pearsall shuddered, drained his drink, and stood up.

"One more night," he told himself, savoring the words.

He looked around the friendly room and smiled a little.

Then he marched upstairs, much as a man might stroll out to greet a firing squad in the cold gray light of dawn.

He hooked his thumbs in his evening suspenders, more to annoy Laura than anything else, and surveyed the scene.

There's no place like home, he thought sourly.

It was plush, he had to give it that. The furnishings of the huge living room were flamboyantly non-functional, as modern trends demanded: heavy wine drapes flopping over the leaded windows, glittering chandeliers blazing down on thick flowered carpeting, a profusion of tastefully worm-eaten antique chairs, a couple of iron-hard couches covered in stiff brocade, a scattering of spindly tables, gewgaws, and assorted gingerbread.

He snapped his fingers.

"Sir?" said the gleaming robot that flashed to his side.

"A glass of gin, if you will be so kind."

Robots are not equipped with a look of disapproval, but this one made a creditable try.

"Sir?"

"Put an olive in it so it'll look like a martini. And hurry."

The robot glided toward the bar with a distinct air of aloofness.

There was a lot of well-mannered laughter, and some of it quite possibly was genuine. The room was full of antiseptically clean people. All the men had red faces and distinguished gray hair. All the women were delicately pale, in stunning slither-gowns, as lovely as butterflies and with brains to match.

One portly gentleman, with a kind of desperate gravity, was imitating a rocket in outer space.

The robot arrived with a sweating glass on a tray.

Pearsall took the glass, popped the olive into his mouth, and fortified himself with a slug of clear gin. He affixed a transparently false smile to his face and moved forward.

It was, he reflected, precisely the sort of party that the scandal tapes were always screaming about. IS THEODORE PEARSALL A HEDONIST? WHAT'S WITH THE DOLL IN PEARSALL'S HALL? IS TEDDY A BEAR?

The item the tapes forgot to mention was that the whole business was a crashing bore.

A perfumed hand touched him.

"Here you are, you nice man!" It was Jenny, wife of one of the vice-presidents of one of his companies. She had been a looker once upon a time, and still dressed like a siren. Unhappily, she was incurably vivacious. "We're going to be partners!"

"Goody," said Pearsall, allowing himself to be led toward the crowd.

An old, old song was spinning through his head:

> *Lord, I'd rather drink muddy water,*
> *Sleep in a hollow log . . .*

Big Gate, there. Jack Teagarden. Born down in Texas, raised in Tennessee—

One more night.

He patted Jenny absently on the head, and did his duty in an interminable game of charades.

Much later, after the guests had departed and Laura had gone to her bedroom, Pearsall hurried down into his soundproof vault and locked the door behind him.

His mind was quite clear, despite the gin, and he was as excited as a boy about to snag his first brook trout.

He pulled out a concealed phone line. It was a direct hook-up; no need to touch the dial.

"Williams?"

"Ah, Mr. Pearsall! We thought you might have forgotten us."

"Hardly." He sneaked a look around the room to reassure himself. "Is everything ready?"

"It's waiting for you, sir. And a fine job it is, if I do say so myself."

"Well, make it snappy, Williams. My affairs here are all in order, and there's a trust fund to take care of Laura. I'm ready to go."

"Now?"

"Now. Tonight. As soon as possible."

"As you wish, sir. Ah, there's one small item—"

"Yes?"

"The girls, as you specified, will be real ones, working in relays. Excellent—ummm—local color. Now, the Patrol has made discreet inquiries of this office, Mr. Pearsall. They seem to feel that as long as the girls are there—so close to home, as it were—they were wondering whether it would be permissible for off-duty Patrolmen to . . . how shall I say it—make use of the unusual facilities available—"

Pearsall snapped his fingers. "Excellent!" he beamed. "A gasser!"

"I beg your pardon?"

"I mean, it's wonderful. The money, of course, will go to help defray the expense of the project?"

"A businessman to the end, Mr. Pearsall! Precisely what we had in mind."

"And Laura will never know where I am?"

"You may rely on our absolute discretion, sir. In fifty years of service, our firm has never had a complaint."

"Tonight, then, Williams. Step on it. Use the rear entrance."

"As you wish, sir. Our representative will carry the contract with him; please read it carefully on the trip out. If I may be of any further service, it will be my pleasure."

"Thank you, Williams."

He broke the connection. He had never felt so alive, so eager. He paced the floor, his face beaming.

He cut in the music.

"Muskrat Ramble!"

"Save It Pretty Mama!"

"Way Down Yonder In New Orleans!"

They came for him at four in the morning, long before Laura was awake.

As far as the world he had known was concerned, he vanished without a trace.

The ship climbed into the sunrise on a ladder of flame. She lanced through mountains of clouds, and then the familiar blue of the sky faded and darkened, and she was in space.

Pearsall had been in space before, and it did not enchant him. True, the cold lights of the stars were lovely against their backdrop of velvet, and the sun was a yellow blaze of glory. But it was life that called to Pearsall, all the life that he had missed, all the smells and sounds and joys and heartaches he had heard about and read about, but never experienced.

And space was an infinite sea of death.

It was not for him.

Not yet.

His old blue eyes skipped over the contract.

". . . and on the basis of the Purchaser's life expectancy as determined by the Company's physicians, and verified by the Purchaser's personal physicians, the Company agrees to provide, supply, and maintain said Project according to the Purchaser's specifications, until such a time as said Project can no longer be of any use to the Purchaser, whereupon said Project and Property revert to the Company, for whatever use . . ."

He read the rest of it, and signed it.

He knew, of course, that it was now possible for doctors to calculate a patient's very hour of death with certainty. Accidents could kill a man before his time, but there had been no case since the year 2100 of a man living *past* his expected death date—and techniques of diagnosis and prognosis had improved some since then. Naturally, this was one item of information that doctors were forbidden by law to give to their patients.

It was better not to know.

He sat back in his seat, his eyes closed. The power was off now, as the ship coasted silently toward Mars, and beyond. He couldn't sleep, didn't want to sleep. He felt no regret for what he was leaving behind him. He had no children, and his marriage to Laura had been one of convenience, nothing more. His money had been inherited for the most part, and had brought him no happiness. Earth itself was a fossil; exciting things were happening on other worlds, but he had not been qualified to go.

No, he was well rid of it—all of it.

It was what was ahead that counted.

A world of his own, his kind of world, with his kind of people. His heart hammered in his chest, his eyes grew bright.

This won't do, he thought. *Mustn't overexcite myself.*

He took two sleeping pills, and dozed off.

The ship had nosed into the Company's section of the Asteroid Belt between Mars and Jupiter and was braking her acceleration before he woke up. He brushed the white hair out of his eyes and stared out through the viewscreen. Thousands of tiny worlds hung there in space, moving through tightly-calculated orbits.

Each world was a man's dream come true, and each one was different. He had heard rumors of some of the early ones: a world where there was a major sporting event every four hours, a world that was a hunter's paradise of swift streams and fearless animals, a world that was an erotic dream come to life . . .

The ship matched velocities exactly with a dimly glimpsed shape. There was a *chunk* as the two coupled together, airlock to airlock.

"We're here, sir," a voice said.

Theodore Pearsall stood up, his fists clenched tightly, his breath coming very fast.

"We're here," he repeated.

He moved toward the door.

Then he was inside and the ship was gone.

He smelled it first: a wet, heavy river-smell. He drew it into his lungs, tasting it, savoring it. It hung over the city like a sweet, invisible fog.

The River.

Ole Miss.

Then he heard it. His eyes misted. Music: clear as a bell, liquid as the river itself, lifting into the air like a buoyant, living thing. It sent a shiver down his spine and he began to run, just a little.

He hardly saw the old frame buildings with their towers and chimneys, didn't feel any of the smiling people he bumped into, ignored the whispered invitation that drifted down from behind a second-story shutter.

He started to turn in through two white swinging doors at a place called Tom Anderson's. He was close enough to the music to reach out and touch it, but he stopped. He listened.

More music.

Coming down the street.

There it was, rounding the corner. A wagon, pulled by a team of horses. A sign on the wagon, advertising a dance. And a band, letting fly with "Milneburg Joys." No piano, of course, but drums, guitar, and string bass. A youngster on cornet, sitting on a box. An older man playing clarinet, sitting beside him. And sitting on the back edge of the wagon, his feet dangling down, his golden trombone slide flashing in the sun—

Kid Ory.

He was younger than in most of the pictures you saw, even though the Kid had never really aged. He looked perhaps twenty-five, a handsome Creole man, and the power in his horn shored up the band like a rock-solid two-by-four. As Pearsall watched, Ory took his lips away from the mouthpiece and shouted something to him in French.

Pearsall flushed; he couldn't catch the words. But he grinned and waved back at him. The Kid nodded, counted with his horn, swung into the intricate slides of "Ory's Creole Trombone."

The wagon passed by, the music still lingering in the warm, humid air, like a crisp painting slowly fading in the sun.

Pearsall walked into Tom Anderson's and stepped up to the bar.

"Mistah Theodore Pearsall!" the bartender said, beaming from ear to ear.

"Call me Ted," Pearsall said. It was the first time in his life he had ever said it. It felt good.

"Yassuh. What'll it be?"

"Scotch and water, please."

The man poured it out, handed it to him. Pearsall reached for his money.

"Don't cost you nothin', Mistah Ted. On the house."

Pearsall turned away, feeling better than he had felt in years. He had to hand it to the Company: they were doing the job up brown.

The leader of the band, a Negro Pearsall didn't recognize at first, nodded gravely to him, tapped his foot, and blew into his horn—blew down into it, digging for the low ones. "Tishomingo Blues"—Lord, it was Bunk, Bunk Johnson and the boys. It was flowing, under-stated New Orleans jazz, and it was the whole group that played it, not a crew of soloists.

Pearsall watched and listened and sipped his drink. He thought: *They're all out there, right now, waiting for me. Louis and Sidney and Buddy and Jelly Roll. And Bix, Bix had to be there, even if he hadn't been there in real life. For when dreams come true, they're better than real life ever was, that's why they're dreams. . . .*

He stayed for two hours, just being happy, and then he walked over to his apartment, still in the French Quarter. It was plain but comfortable, with a big brass bed and open windows over the street. The curtains fluttered in the breeze off the river, and he heard a clarinet wailing from far away.

Dodds? Fazola, maybe?

No matter.

There was a newspaper on the stand by the bed, a *real* newspaper, not a tape. He glanced at the date.

June 17, 1917.

If he caught the significance of that date, he gave no sign.

But he never again read a newspaper, and he deliberately lost track of time.

A cornet, stabbing out the melody.

A trombone, sliding and stomping, backing it up.

A clarinet, a lyric clarinet, weaving around them, singing.

Three rhythm, propelling it, giving it a base to walk on: drums, string bass, guitar. (Sure, they had used a banjo in those days—but dreams are better.)

Living music, music from the heart, music to blow your blues away. Living music, by men who once had lived. Living music that could not die, but could never come again.

Heaven, Utopia, Paradise. It had many names. It was different for every man. To Theodore Pearsall, raised in an easy world of certainties and automation, this was It: everything he yearned for, all the people he wanted, all the happiness and the laughter and the sorrow. He had heard the music once in a museum, and it had called him.

He had answered.

It took money, time, engineering genius. A tiny planetoid between Mars and Jupiter, with a bubble to hold in the air. Artificial gravity, so a man could walk. And a rebuilt Storyville: not all of it, but enough.

The music was real, you couldn't fake it. It had been played by real men, long ago, and caught on records. Then it had been remastered, built into tapes. You couldn't even see the tapes in the horns.

And Louis and Kid and Jelly Roll, all the great ones?

Robots, of course—or androids, to give them their proper names. Brilliant ones. You couldn't tell the difference unless you looked too close. And who would look too close, with all the music, all the booze, all the laughter?

Only some of the girls were real.

No robot was *that* good.

Men build different monuments. There were some, Pearsall knew, who would have been shocked by what he had done with his money. Most would not understand. But here he had found what he wanted: peace and love and music and good times to remember all the days of his life.

He was an old man.

He knew what was important, and what wasn't. A man always knew, looking back.

Others could go conquer the stars, and doubtless it was all worth the effort.

He strolled out of his room, a graceful gal on each arm, a black cigar in his mouth. He moved towards the lights and the music.

Somewhere out on the river, a steamboat whistled.

Pearsall quickened his steps.

It was the Fourth of July, and that was a very important day.

Everybody knew what had happened on the Fourth of July. Back in the year 1900, it was.

Yes, sir.

Louis Armstrong's birthday.

Ted Pearsall sought him out. He was still a kid, still in his teens, but he could already stand up, with that handkerchief in his hand, and the power in his horn was something to hear.

Pearsall dined on a Poor Boy sandwich: half a loaf of French bread sliced down the middle, stuffed with barbecued ham. He tried to take Satch to Antoine's for a real meal, but the kid stuck to red beans and rice.

The evening got rolling.

> *I wish I could shimmy like my sister Kate. . . .*
> *I thought I heard Buddy Bolden say . . .*

Oh, it was all there.

Basin Street. Canal Street. Burgundy Street.

And all the great old places: Lulu White's Mahogany Hall, Countess Willie's, Josie Arlington's Five Dollar House. You could look them all up in Tom Anderson's Blue Book, which sold for two bits and listed all the more reputable houses of ill repute—all two hundred of them.

> *If you get a good man and don't want him taken from you,*
> *Don't ever tell your gal friend what your man can do. . . .*

And it was all on the house—or, rather, houses.

He loved it all, the balconies on the houses, the hot evenings as the sun went down, the palm tree in the vacant lot.

He even got a kick out of the smartly uniformed Patrolmen when they came to town. They always dropped in when they were in the vicinity. Sure, they were square as a block of cement, and boneheaded to boot. But it was nice to know that even a Space Cadet had glands.

They all thought he was crazy.

Pearsall sort of had them figured the same way.

August, September, October.

> *I gotta momma, she live right back o' the jail.*
> *I gotta sweet momma . . .*

Mister Jelly Lord, playing his solo piano like an orchestra, beating out "King Porter" in a bar. Brass bands in the streets, swinging by "In Gloryland."

Pearsall stayed up as late as he could, slept when he could, drunk on music.

And then it was November.

November, 1917.

He was sitting in Tom Anderson's when it happened.

He had felt the change all day, without knowing what it was. There was a tension in the air, a waiting. Girls leaning out of windows, looking for something. A dog howling down by the river. A horn sobbing out the blues, somewhere, far away.

He sat at his table. He felt the sweat in the palms of his hands. *Don't let this be the day. Please don't let this be the day.*

But it was.

A Patrol officer walked into Tom's, looked around. He was big brass. He nailed something on the wall, something white.

A notice.

Pearsall didn't have to read it. He knew what it said.

It was in November, 1917, that Storyville had been shut down, killed off by the Navy. That had been the end, the time when the houses had to auction off their furniture and Countess Willie got only a buck and a quarter for her famous white piano, the time when the musicians had to pack up and leave, go to Chicago, go to Los Angeles, go up the river, go anywhere.

Do you know what it means to miss New Orleans . . .

And it was happening again. The Patrol was the Navy now, and they were putting the old padlock on the Land of Dreams.

Pearsall wasn't afraid, but he knew what was coming.

". . . the Company agrees to provide, supply, and maintain said Project . . . until such a time as said Project can no longer be of any use to the Purchaser. . . ."

They had known that he was dying. The doctors knew everything. Well, hell.

It was nice and artistic, the way they were doing it.

He had no regrets.

The road to the cemetery was lined with people.

There was a lot of crying and wailing, but the people were listening, too. That was as it should be, for there had never been a band like this before.

Louis was there, and Bix, and Bunk. Ory's trombone, and Teagarden's. Bechet and Dodds and Fazola on clarinets. Minor Hall, his drum muffled with a handkerchief.

They played the plaintive "Flee As A Bird" all the way to the graveyard, where the bearers lowered the body into the ground. The preacher said the words.

Minor Hall took the handkerchief out of his snare.

He hit the march beat, the happy beat, and the band fell into line.

That was the way it was in New Orleans: sadness that a man had died, then joy that he was marching with the saints.

What did they play?

They blew "Didn't He Ramble."

First Louis had the lead, then Bix, then Bunk.

> *Oh, didn't he ramble!*
> *He rambled round the town*
> *Till the Butcher cut him down.* . . .

They played it with all their hearts, played it for the last time, marching back to Storyville, back to the already-emptying land of dreams.

And as they marched, as the clarinets soared, the Company might, or might not, have been surprised to hear Louis turn to Bix and say, "Old Pops went out in style."

Bix nodded. "It was good to play again," he said, and lifted his cornet toward the river.

The

Queen's

Messenger

by JOHN J. MCGUIRE

"Which one will he be?"

Dr. Gilbert Blanding, head of the Research Bureau, World Government Department of Agriculture, had been expecting that question.

His friend and occasional companion in research, Dr. Karl Gorski, had been a successful revolutionary against the Soviets. He was an expert at reaching for one thing and grasping another. But even Karl's skill in planning had not prevented the deaths of three other men who had tried to carry their message to Mars.

"I took nineteen cards, added the joker, riffled and shuffled them," Gil said. "Cavendish came out as number nine."

"Sufficiently random," the old Pole approved. "A good method, yes."

"But the man, no," Gilbert finished.

"No."

The flat finality in Gorski's tone angered Blanding. To Gil, knowing as well as could be known how many men Gorski had killed while a young patriot, the statement seemed utterly unreasonable.

"We will discuss Cavendish in a moment," Gorski continued. "Let us first complete the details on this one we just spoke with—"

"Clancy," said Blanding. "James Terence. Weight, 120. In for armed robbery. Caught, if I understand this record correctly, only because a cashier had more courage than good sense. Hobby, amateur magician. Has worked as a knife-thrower—"

"You miss the essentials." Gorski's interruption was that of a chief surgeon instructing an interne. "First, he is a physical type that we are supposed to need. Second, he comes from the kitchen in this prison."

"For the same reason that you are taking that chef who tried to poison the political convention." Gil felt himself beginning to understand Karl's reasoning.

"Yes. You want one particular man, so we hide him by taking a dozen similar cases."

Gil responded to the stress Gorski had given the word *you*. "Karl, who else can do the job?"

"That is the unanswerable argument. But I would still prefer to let him stay in prison."

"Why? Because he was a murderer and killed his wife and her lover? And yet you are willing to take the chef who tried to poison an entire political convention. And yourself, how many have you killed? Ever think about them?"

"Almost every night, Gilbert. I can only hope that those I have saved since I began to practice my profession begins to cancel that number.

"And there is exactly, explicitly, why I do not like Dr. Cavendish. He took an oath to save human lives, yet he deliberately used his enormous medical skill to try to hide his crime."

"He convicted himself," Blanding argued.

"He did?" The old Pole was openly derisive. "How? The old man who was peeping in the window, the fact that the police 'copter was in the immediate neighborhood, the young policeman who had the hunch about putting the plug back into the drain—this is self-incrimination?"

"His book," Gilbert mumbled.

Gorski became abruptly more judicial in tone. "Yes, in that sense you are right. His own work on trace elements allowed the District Attorney to present proof positive that the liquid in the tub had been human beings. But enough of this. I cannot dispute your essential point."

"You mean—?" Gilbert could not follow the sudden change in Karl's attitude.

"We need him. Maybe this time the end will justify the means. And one other little point—"

"Yes?"

"I think he is the proper man to match against that other murderer, Kushalik."

Frank Cavendish forced himself to sit calmly, await his turn without *open* impatience. Inwardly, he seethed. Although the routine of a prisoner's life was always at the disposal of the authorities, he had work to do, work which they knew was important. He should be over at the kitchen now, especially when half his crew had been called in for these interviews.

Well, there was nothing he could do about his kitchen or his sewage plant problems until this interview was over. So . . . he forced himself to think about the reason this group was assembled.

Something about dietary experiments on concentrates for Mars, the prison grapevine had said. And the grapevine in Jackson Prison —The Hermitage, some literate prisoner had dubbed it, because the men who came here were here to stay—was uncannily accurate.

Strange that they were still experimenting with concentrates though. The journals he received as a reward for good conduct, although barren of definite information, had implied to his trained mind the fact that the problem of feeding both Earth and Mars had been whipped several years ago.

"Number nine."

Frank stood up and walked to his place between Garth and Jones.

Interesting though the work might be, his answer was no. He himself had killed the only reason why life outside this maximum-security jail had ever been attractive.

The shadows from the barred window behind them fell across the desk they shared. The decision made, there was not much need to talk to each other. The silence was broken only by the snap of Gorski's lighter or the steamy breathing of Gil's pipe.

Too much silence in this place, thought Gil. Too much silence and too much grayness. There was not even a tiny click to the latch of the door when it opened to admit the two guards and the next prisoner. The steps of the trio were soundless on the bare floor.

The guards guided the prisoner to the chair in front of the desk, then moved to stand on either side of him. Gorski shook his head and Gil spoke for both: "We have permission to see all of them in private."

The older guard hesitated, said, "This one—"

Blanding motioned to the privilege-slip on the desk.

The guard shrugged his shoulders, motioned to his companion. They left as silently as they had come.

When the door had closed, Blanding stared openly at the man across the desk. The prisoner's attitude was puzzling. Not arrogant, not submissive, but—Gil groped for the word, found it—neutral, a sort of chameleon response to the gray walls and the silence.

Only once during those first few moments did the man in the salt and pepper uniform show a flicker of emotion. That came when the prisoner's glance touched upon a card, the summary of his life complete with number, picture and crime. With a raised eyebrow he looked at Gil. Hint of laughter, question clear but unspoken: *You need this?*

Karl stirred restlessly, his fingers drummed on the plexi-protected top of the desk. Blanding took a deep breath, began, "Dr. Gorski, may I present Dr. Frank Cavendish?"

"It is an honor to meet you in person. My most highly-prized and constantly-used book is still your 'Tables of Trace Element Variants in Common Dietary Changes.' The work was . . . how you could—" Gorski subsided, red-faced, regarding a corner of the room with embarrassed intentness.

The prisoner's attitude did not change nor did any gesture mar his attitude of patient waiting.

A minute dragged by before Gil realized that he must be the one to break the silence. "We need you, doctor. We need you desperately."

There was no response, not even that of curiosity, in the face or body of the man opposite him, but Gil plugged on. "Not just we two who came here, not just this world, but the planets and worlds to come. They need something only you—"

Gil stopped, found his own glance following the prisoner's roving gaze. The yellow card, striped by the shadows of the barred window; the gray walls; deliberately, a long look back to the door behind which the guards waited. Suddenly, Blanding saw these things through the prisoner's eyes. In a swift surge of sympathy, he realized how empty his words had echoed in the hollowness of a prisoner's life. He turned to Gorski for help.

The help came from Cavendish. "Go ahead, doctors, but without the heroics, please. I know I owe you at least the courtesy of listening."

Gorski took over. "We have completed your work, Dr. Cavendish.

We now have the total picture of the place of trace elements in the diet."

"Congratulations. I was fairly sure that you had done so. I am glad to learn my guess was correct."

Gorski heaved a gusty sigh. "We have also, I think, immortalized you. The series of equations are in your name.

"But that is as it should be. It was your expansion of the lock and key analogy, your experiments with the vitamin antagonists, which showed us the questions to ask. Knowing what we had to find out, the rest was almost automatic."

Cavendish, who had been leaning forward, now settled back to as much comfort as his straight chair allowed. "Thank you for the pleasant information, but I am sure that you did not come here just to cheer me up. Nor," and he looked at Gil, "do you have me here simply to ask me to be a guinea pig. What do you want?"

"I told you," said Gil. "We need your help."

"How? What help can I be? If your problem is theory, I can offer little. The journals have been too barren of information for me to keep up to date.

"And if it's a problem of application, you know as well as I that the answers are best found by research teams working on Mars itself. Not, I'm sure, in anything I can do or suggest."

"You are utterly wrong," contradicted Gorski flatly. "There is something very vital you can try to do, something three men have died attempting."

Cavendish suddenly leaned forward again, caught as Gil had seen a lazing trout fling itself at the right bait. The prisoner focused his attention on Gorski, then followed the direction of Karl's glance and fixed his eyes on Gil.

Gil began with a bitter pill. "You were among those who insisted on a long-term contract for those who wanted to settle on Mars."

"Yes, certainly, including the testing program to screen out the psychos—"

"That long-term program was a mistake."

The prisoner's face set in the stubborn lines that Gil knew so well. "How? You can't colonize with fly-by-nights. History has proven that a score of times. Real building is done with what we planned, people with families who really need the land. They stay, they have the reasons to stick out the first few bitter years."

Gorski shook his huge head. "But fly-by-nights also have a place in the scheme of things."

"Where?"

Gorski showed no impatience at the caustic tone. "We should have had a check on the colonists through people who came and went in days or months. Then the First Family would not have been such an agonizing error."

"Agonizing error." Cavendish rolled the words around his tongue like a man discovering a new flavor in an old and familiar drink.

"Our hydroponic diet was not complete or perfect," Gil began.

"Of course not. But it should have been . . . it was . . . close enough for people to survive until we had perfection." Cavendish dismissed the objection.

"But adults adapted to it by gradual replacement. And children were born into it."

Abruptly the prisoner's glance dulled, became the vacant, introspective look that Gil knew so well. "Even the technical journals called it food poisoning."

"Yes, the First Family," agreed Gorski. "Picked by lottery to return. Given the full treatment, including a banquet of the best and richest foods on Earth as compensation for what they had endured."

Cavendish reached the logical conclusion. "Literally, they did die from food poisoning. And their deaths must have been unpleasant."

Gorski's bass-viol voice was muted. "I attended them. The youngest died in seven hours, the father lived three days."

Gil had been watching Frank's hands and he was ready with what their movements showed the prisoner needed.

Cavendish carefully lit the slim cigar and then said, "I was wrong. But, tell me, do they still—"

"Oh, yes, they still go to Mars, though not in such numbers. Nor, with . . . well, we called those who went during the first years, the joyous ones.

"But they still go, and for the same reasons. Land virtually for the asking, the right to have children freely, these things would make Mankind colonize Hell without waiting to die.

"But they don't return. Or if they do, they die in a hurry and very badly."

Gil knew the light tone Gorski had used had been a deliberate taunting. But Frank asked his questions in the way he leaned toward them.

The answers came from Gorski, definitely the superior in political matters.

"Directly, Dr. Cavendish, it was the Atomic Energy Law. In-

directly, it is the fact that sending food to Mars in the form of concentrates is now a gigantic business and our Bureau is still under
the World Government's Department of Agriculture."

"The Global Grange—do you still call them that—prevents publication because you used radioactive tracer isotopes?" asked Cavendish. "Yes, I see how under the law they could. You appealed, of
course."

"The Council on Grievances, which hears all complaints against
the World Government, will get to our case . . . in about five years,"
explained Gil.

Cavendish leaned back, his face again expressionless.

Once more Gil yielded to Gorski.

"They go to Mars for freedom," said the man who had given his
youth to that ideal, "and find themselves in a jail. For all practical
purposes, our slaves. Yes, I said slaves, because what they earn is
barely enough to buy what they need to live.

They will not be content to remain so."

The surprise on the prisoner's face was also a question.

"You know these whom we are sending out. Or rather, you know
the tests which weed them out so that only our finest can go. Follow
the implications of that to the logical conclusion history has taught:
How long do pioneers remain slaves?"

Gorski lit another cigarette, inhaled slowly, continued: "However,
that is not the major, the ultimate problem. In the long run, while
we keep them and the others to come tied by an umbilicus cord to
Earth, Man can never hope to reach the stars."

Silence for an eternity of two heartbeats, and Frank accepted:
"What can I do?"

Blanding picked up a paper, laid it with a pen in front of Cavendish. "Taste-testing concentrates bound for Mars is at present the
major part of our work. We want you as one of twenty volunteers for
the next series of tests."

"And then?"

"Well," Gil began—

"One moment, please!" Gorski's voice was crisp, his manner that
of a man speaking from deep experience. "If by any chance something would go wrong, the less you know, the less you can tell. You
know they have ways to persuade anyone to tell everything."

"I've heard of those ways," Frank agreed. Then in a quick burst of
the rage that Gil recalled so vividly, "Why can't you plow the lid
off the whole stinking mess with a little publicity?"

Gorski leaned forward, put his elbows on the table, looked directly into the prisoner's eyes. "Dr. Cavendish, you always were a political fool. Few men, however, have ever shown that fact as clearly as you have by your presence here. So I am going to speak to you as the child you are.

"Neither we, nor those that we are fighting, dare to bring this matter out into the open. Neither of us can be sure who would win.

"You would say along with my idealistic colleague here that the great moral sense of humanity would spring instantly to our support. You may be right. But we cannot risk that until the message is delivered. Then, the moral sense will find itself supporting an accepted fact. It is much easier to hail a conquest than to fight the battle leading to it."

Gorski drew back from the table and his voice deepened. "And we cannot be sure that they will support us even then. To understand me, look at the world about you.

"We are still not recovered from the shattering effects of the Great War. To almost every man the first necessity is the grim one of earning a livelihood.

"And we in one blow propose to destroy the economic foundations of millions of people. Farmers, manufacturers, transport workers of the trade routes on Earth and off of it, whose livelihood comes from feeding Mars.

"Add to them those who sincerely believe, or could be led to believe, that the safety of our planet will lie in keeping the colonies dependent, not free. Think how quickly suppressing us could become a sacred war.

"Now ask yourself, in justice to our cause, dare we take the risk of open battle?"

Cavendish reached for the pen.

Gorski sighed deeply. "But in all fairness to you I must tell you that this will mean your apparent and perhaps your actual death."

The pen did not waver.

But before he pushed the button to summon the guards, Gil had to ask the question that had haunted him for years: "Frank, why did you do it?"

The prisoner turned and spoke with all pretense in his manner gone. Sadly, nakedly, he called for understanding. "You, Gil, you too ask that? You who knew how much she was in my life, how much I blindly trusted her because I blindly needed her?

"I gave her everything that she asked and found it was less than nothing to her. She was by instinct not made for open love. She preferred the sneaky, stolen pleasure.

"I have but one regret. That the police arrived before I drained the tank."

Cavendish turned to the door now opening slowly behind him, opening on gray blank walls and silence. But, Gil thought, not half as gray, not half as silent, as some parts of that man's life and mind.

Guards from the prison herded the convicts to the plane. But once inside the plane, only the presence of two officers seated facing the group and the consciousness of two more at the rear, reminded Frank that he was still a prisoner. The convicts were allowed to seat and group themselves as they pleased.

Cavendish found himself with Clancy, his meat-cutter, beside him and Jesper, his head cook, ahead of him.

"Keesters, Doc, we got practically no guard at all," Clancy observed. "Four of them and twenty of us. We could take over this plane."

Frank closed his eyes briefly, then opened them and shook his head. "Not a chance, Clancy. First of all, you know if we started trouble, our brother cons would jump us faster than those Security Cops. This volunteer business means too much to them. Second, you can't get into the pilot's compartment from this side of the plane. Third, there's this—" He pointed to the tiny, almost invisible vent in the window frame.

"Don't tell me, I know," Clancy moaned. "They can douse us but good with hypno-gas. I wish I could catch the guy who invented that stuff. The face-full that bank clerk gave me is what caught me. Say, how did you know that vent was there, Doc? Ah, why ask. You probably read it or heard it somewhere and I know by now how that memory of yours is."

The little crook bent over Frank for a glance out of the window. The plane had taken off and the barren pattern of Jackson Prison was clearly visible.

Clancy leaned back into his chair, a thoughtful look on his face. "You know, Doc, they say no one ever got out of there, but I bet you and I could have done it. I could have made sure that any guard who could have seen us wasn't watching," and he made that inimitable, graceful gesture of hand and wrist which only a true knife-thrower acquires, "and even those electron-locks couldn't have held you. Don't kid me, Doc, I know. I've seen you work. One look, or one touch, and you've got whatever you saw or heard or touched in your head like it was part of you. I'm right, ain't I?"

It was not the first time Frank had faced that question, but many sleepless nights had given him his answer. "Yes, Clancy, I think we could have. But I never wanted to."

Frank caught the sidewise glance his little friend gave him, but Clancy went on with his biggest interest.

"How about where we're goin', Doc? What's the chances to skip out of there? You've worked on this stuff, how tightly will we be watched?"

"I think we're going to Wiscinois, Clancy, where the big hobby is hunting. And you know as well as I what happens if a prisoner takes off from a government project. They just run it on the telecasts, 'Five Thousand Alive, Ten Thousand Dead, No Questions Asked!' Even if you got through the woods to New Chicago, how long would you last in the big town with that over you?"

And I hope Gorski has thought of that, Frank added for himself.

"Yeah, I forgot about that for a minute," and Clancy subsided.

But Jesper, the chef who had expressed his opinion about the government by trying to poison an entire political convention, was ready with more questions.

"Doctor, I volunteered for this because it offers a chance for a pardon and a pension. What exactly did I let myself in for?"

Only Jesper's long, lean face was visible over the back of his chair. But Frank knew that his chief cook's body was an extension of the face. A tall, lank frame barely covered with skin, with nowhere an ounce of fat. The man looked like anything except what he had been, the top chef for a string of hotels.

And Frank couldn't restrain a laugh.

"Jes, you're here for one reason, to eat everything put in front of you and tell what you think of it. And to make sure you do eat, you also are going to exercise. Every muscle in your body is going to get a workout."

Jesper's eyes widened with horror, but Clancy had the pertinent question. "Doc, how can eating be dangerous?"

Frank stopped laughing. "We'll be trying new things, Clancy, looking for the perfect combination. Storable, transportable, containing everything that is needed to keep a man alive. But they don't know what those things are and so they put everything into the concentrates. Now, maybe one of the things they put in won't hurt you, but in combination with something else in the mixture—well, you make out a will before we start."

"I get it, Doc. I like strawberries and I like cream. But boy, what the two of them together do to me. Keesters, just once and never again—"

Although this was the sixteenth day that Frank had ground out the required ten miles on the stationary bikes, his legs felt as they had on the first day. They seemed as limp as wet macaroni as he weaved, not walked, across the gym floor.

Never thought that I would consider a gym mat equal to a feather bed, he reflected.

A thud on the mat beside him. Clancy, wet and dripping with sweat.

"Doc," the little pirate moaned, "you sure weren't kidding when you told us that we would exercise. You'd think they were training us for a fight and an honest one at that."

Cavendish sat up, wiped his face with his towel. "It's that last mile which gets me, when they change the gears."

"Me, too. I can take the other nine, it's that tenth one which never ends. And look at Jes. All these years he's been cooking and never gained a bit of weight. The fanciest stuff in the world, he sampled all of it and still looked like a walking skeleton. Then on this sawdust they're feeding us, he picks up four pounds in two weeks."

Frank glanced over at the tall man grimly pedaling away. "It's the combination of food and something he never did before, Jimmy. Regular exercise."

He lay back on the mat again, covered his face with his forearm. The glance at Jesper had also given him a look at the clock and confirmed what he had begun to feel. Any minute now those twinges would be a solid pain.

"Say, Doc, I know you think I'm full of questions," Clancy began— And there it was, an agony that doubled him.

"Doc!"

Cavendish caught the note of fear in Clancy's voice, found a moment to think, *the little guy liked me.* Then the tearing hand was at his stomach again. A roaring in his ears, blackness shot with lightning before his eyes—had Gorski miscalculated, made this too realistic?

At a great distance he could hear Clancy shouting for help with a garnish of obscenities. A sound of running feet. Then, simply, nothing.

He was weak, which probably helped to make the morgue seem colder than any other he remembered. But the coffee Blanding had brought was helping to both strengthen and warm him.

A key scratched in the lock and Gorski lumbered in. After checking the lock, he waddled over to the dissecting table and leaned against it, puffing heavily.

"Well?" Blanding was sharply impatient.

"One moment, please. It was not difficult, but they infected me with their frantic excitement." Gorski lit a cigarette, drained half a cup of coffee in a gulp. "I finally got to Pritchard. He's the only under-secretary with any brains or backbone."

"And he agreed?" Gil asked.

Frank found himself tensing, even though there had been nothing he could do in this part of the plan.

"He agreed with all we want. Keep it as secret as possible, of course. He emphasized that more than I did. Naturally. The Grange has no desire to let anyone know that its wares might kill you. He will also help with this end. The agricultural agent for this area is a power in local politics. Our certificate of death will be accepted without any question. And there, he hinted, that the cause of death had better be officially unrelated to our work.

"I think, Dr. Cavendish, I shall have to discover an unsuspected weakness in your heart, a condition aggravated by exercise, not your diet.

"Also, he will cover us on our hasty autopsy. It will be done on orders from above."

"Good." Gil's very posture showed his relief.

"I have more, even better because he will think it was his idea. Dr. Cavendish, we will perform the autopsy on you tonight, to determine the exact cause of death. But immediately after we have determined the cause, we are to cremate you. Our findings are to be sent directly to Pritchard, marked TOPSEC.

"Your ashes are to receive a quiet burial tomorrow."

The old Pole shifted his cigarette to his left hand, waved the smoke away from his face with his right. His manner was abruptly sober.

"Dr. Cavendish, you are now officially dead. Not only to the world outside of this room, but in a few minutes, and only for the most vital contacts, you are also dead to us.

"My part, aside from dirtying the laboratory and sealing some ashes in a bottle, is done. This is my good-by and though I do not believe that you know what I mean, I wish you Godspeed."

The hand-clasp, though not especially friendly, was firm and strong.

Cavendish slipped from the table, tottered for a moment as his full weight came down on his legs and found them still wobbly.

"Dr. Gorski," he said, "I will always remember you as a man who missed his real vocation of directing realistic dramas. You had even me convinced that I was dying."

The Pole's rumbling chuckle followed them to the door. There, while Gil reconnoitered the route ahead, Frank turned for one last look at Gorski.

Under the Atomic Energy Law, both Karl and Gil faced prison, and more, if anything went wrong.

But the old man was seated in a chair large enough to bear his weight, clearly set to enjoy himself with the last of the coffee before starting to work. He seemed completely relaxed, blowing out smoke rings aimed at encircling a cup on the table before him.

Wish I felt that confident, Frank thought.

Kushalik—

Maybe a man, maybe just a name, maybe an organization, any one, any two, or all of these. We do not know with certainty. Only of this can we be sure: his is the striking arm for that coalition of transport companies, farmer unions, and bureaucrats which we call the Global Grange. He kills for them—

Frank Fitzgerald looked at the figures in his sales book. They represented a week's work for the Mellon Drug Company and if the other salesmen were doing comparably, the company would have to declare an extra dividend.

He leaned back to light a cigarette while he estimated his commission. Let's see, that total put him in the two per cent overwrite bracket—

With a grunt he bent forward and stubbed out his cigarette. He put his guess-timate—a guess because he was still uncertain about the arbitrary deductions—in his personal record and leaned back again.

Suddenly, he looked at his ashtray and laughed.

This time there had been no need to fight against the impulse to pinch off the glowing tip and stow the butt away for future use. Freedom and its luxuries were no longer new. The habits of prison, where tobacco had been the stable medium of exchange, had been replaced by the careless gestures of an unrationed man.

Frank Cavendish had come a long way in two months.

And, looking at his hand-luggage in the corner of his hotel room, Frank reminded himself that he had a longer way to go.

He lifted the bottle on his desk up to the light. Dammit, the chambermaid had been after it again. But there was enough left for three good drinks. Carefully spaced, they would carry him through the last of his preparations for the trip to Mars.

Let's see, what was left to do?

He rose from his chair and walked over to the bed where his few personal possessions were spread. You couldn't take much with you, even today, when the IO drive had made interplanetary transportation a business, not an adventure.

The sample case went with him. He would feel lost without it.

"You must live this role, not act it. Otherwise, you have no chance to get by Kushalik."

He opened the case and looked at the rows of tiny bottles. Each gleaming cylinder was filled to its top with one type of pill, tablet or capsule. The collection rivaled the spectrum in colors and a cross-section of humanity in sizes. The important part of the display, however, was not the tubes, but the cryptic symbols beneath each one.

Those symbols were married to his notebook, which would have to remain behind for his successor.

He leafed the pages of the notebook, remembering how it had almost made a schizophrenic of him.

The first page was a time-schedule, listing the days on which he should visit each part of the city. The rest of the notebook was divided according to that schedule and named alphabetically the doctors on his routes. Each doctor had a page and a careful analysis. Estimated number of patients and income according to that basis, a method borrowed from the Internal Revenue Bureau. Previous sales. When to suggest re-orders. Habits and prejudices. Best time to go to each office—

Yes, he reflected, putting the book down, this almost made a schizo of me. Until I learned that the coded prices under each tube were just as important as the contents. He flipped open a page and glanced at the income of a General Practitioner. A rare bird in these days of specialists working together in clinics, a GP earned every penny of his income.

And what an income!

He turned back to his desk and poured a second drink, chuckling to himself as he did so. That last thought, consideration of a doctor's income, showed how much the personality of Dr. Frank Cavendish, research specialist, had been submerged in the character of Frank Fitzgerald, drug salesman.

"Keep your first name, it's a common one. And you won't be surprised when people use it."

Then again his thoughts jumped back to the money that GP made each year and suddenly his wife's face was in front of him. Not as she had been alive, but with the facial muscles loosely flaccid, as she had looked when he had severed that classic head from that beautiful body.

Had he been wrong, dedicating himself to research? Would there have been any difference if he had made a lot of money for them, given his wife the income that the wife of that GP had?

The visiphone buzzed gently and he lit his screen. "Mr. Fitzgerald, Mellon Drug representative, speaking."

And I am Frank Fitzgerald again, a part of him discovered.

"Cut your screen, Frank, someone may look over my shoulder. There was a traitor in the Bureau. He didn't have a chance to report much, Gorski saw to that. But he did get the word out that another messenger is on the way.

"If there's any more we dare to do for you, we'll try. But I don't know what it could be. Nothing, probably.

"So it's all up to you. Good luck and good-by."

The click and buzz of an ended call.

Frank snapped off the 'phone and stared at the bottle. Well, Gil, I don't know what I can do, either. Keep my eyes wider open, sure. Thank you for the warning, of course. But anything else—

Wish I had lived in other times, he thought. Then a man with a message carried a silver greyhound on his watch chain. Merely by showing that symbol, the messenger got the best in transportation and services, including police protection.

He disdained the glass, finished the bottle by picking it up and draining the last shot.

There was so much he didn't know, would probably never know —where was the real Frank Fitzgerald, whose place he had taken? What had happened when he had been supposed to report to the home office for psychiatric clearance before the flight to Mars?

He himself had simply gone to Philly for two days and returned to find papers in his room stating that he was a certified Planet Pioneer.

Most important, who and where was Kushalik?

The flavor of the whiskey was still in his throat as he got into bed, appreciating for the last time the convenience of a hotel apartment.

And two names drifted together as he slipped into sleep. Kushalik and the real Frank Fitzgerald.

One part of our race laboring to tie us down and the other working just as hard to cut the ropes.

Frank took a long, deep breath before he entered the room. So far, he had passed each of the final examinations which InterPlanetary Transport insisted on before they risked the delicate movement of a human body to the spaceship already building up overhead.

All his baggage had been taken from him, and, he was sure, scrutinized with care. His physical person had been examined minutely. No one carrying any type of container anywhere in his body could have gotten past those precise searches, personal and assisted by every mechanical aid.

The psychiatric was the last.

He opened the door and gave the room a quick, skimming glance as he walked to the chair facing the psychiatrist.

And he found that the days he had spent being a drug salesman, meeting all types of doctors, were all of a sudden a source of strength. I had been ready to tell Gorski that whoever picked that job for me had been joking, he remembered.

"Frank Fitzgerald?" The doctor checked the form, glancing up occasionally as he sped through the routine. Abruptly he stopped speaking, but kept on reading.

He's come to it, Frank decided.

"I see that you are a drug salesman, Mr. Fitzgerald."

"Yes, sir. A very interesting occupation. Doctors are nice people to meet and know, even in a business way."

"Mellon Company—" thoughtfully.

"Yes, sir, the biggest and the best." A reminder of how much IPT profited by carrying Mellon Company cargoes both ways.

"I see that you've already had psychiatric preparation for the trip."

This was the gamble. "No, sir, I haven't."

"What's that!"

"Just what I said, sir. All I did was go into a room and sit down to talk to the Company doctor the way I'm talking to you. It seemed to me that we only talked about five minutes, but I checked my watch later and it must have been longer. Anyhow, we just talked, then he stood up and said I was ready to go."

Frank shook his head as though puzzled. "From what I'd heard, I thought there was going to be more. But I didn't get any more, so I finally figured that they thought I didn't need it."

All through his speech Frank had carefully watched the doctor for signs that his character as a man who had been gassed and conditioned without knowing it was being accepted.

They came. That tightness which had jumped around the doctor's mouth when Frank had first said no preparation had been made, the little crease between the eyebrows—both disappeared. A short nod, probably approval of a job well done—

The next question came smoothly. "You seem to me to be very well adjusted, Mr. Fitzgerald. However, I cannot possibly know you as well as your Company physician and I would like to test the totality of the adjustment. Would you consent to a whiff of hypno-gas? It takes—"

"No, sir."

Frank made the statement firmly, like a man sure of his rights.

"You know, of course, that I can insist, to the extent of refusing you passage."

"The answer is still no. The Company warned me about this, told me if you . . . listen, all salesmen know things which the Company doesn't want made general knowledge—"

"I won't insist," the psychiatrist cut in, "you are obviously ready to go. Congratulations, Mr. Fitzgerald. You have the spirit that this age needs more of. Just wait in your room for further instructions."

Back in that cubicle, and only then, Frank allowed himself to relax completely.

The cheapest way to go to Mars was in "deep sleep." But Frank preferred to travel awake and Mellon Drugs, delighted to have a volunteer for the work on Mars, paid the enormous difference without objection.

The first "day" was rough, even with Frank's background of experience on the artificial satellites while doing research on the proper foods in a weightless environment. But the tumble-bug gyros at last established Up and Down and Frank began to meet the other Planet Pioneers also making the trip awake.

There were a number of very attractive, single women making the journey. They were bright lights against the drab walls and almost every man on board became a moth.

Frank remained aloof until one of the women said to him, "You're a funny sort of traveling salesman, never looking more than once at any girl."

The remark alerted him. He understood why these lovelies were making the trip. And making themselves available.

"I'll have to be careful with you," the girl giggled. "You're a drug salesman and you may put something in my drink that wouldn't be good for me."

"Wouldn't be good for you?" Frank asked.

"You know, might make me do things that a nice girl doesn't do on her first date with a man."

"Honey, you're safe with me," he assured her and proceeded to make himself a liar.

You must live this part, not act it.

Both pleasure and self-protection kept him with Clarissa for the ten days that the IO drive needed to get them to Mars.

It was easy to laugh with her.

Both of them especially enjoyed the busybody professor who spent endless hours running in and out of a special compartment. In a day, everyone knew the rabbity little man's business. He was shepherding a supply of whole blood in vacuseal to protect some high IPT officials from anemia.

A fact for Gorski, Frank reflected, confirming what he thinks. This coalition is not as solid as it looks. Show IPT how they can make or save money by having the planets independent—

Then Mars Satellite Number One was outside the ship and routine became inescapable. Frank could break the chain only long enough to say a passionate good-by to Clarissa and make plans to meet her on Mars.

But he knew he would never see her again.

Kushalik would surely have other plans for her and those with her.

Frank waited for two days before he went to the Science Clinic. During those two days he went through the process of setting himself up as Mellon Drugs' new representative: A room at the hotel; baggage checked and stored; identifying himself to the sad-faced, weak-lunged secretary; establishing credit at the bank; freight to the Mellon warehouse; putting the office in order.

Then he took a sample of Mellon's new version of a multi-vitamin and went to the Clinic.

"Dr. Richards, please," he told the young man at the reception desk.

"Whom shall I say is calling and for what purpose, sir?"

"Frank Fitzgerald, for Mellon Drugs, about arranging an oxidation test for some new compounds. He'll understand. The speed here will be different."

The young man fiddled with the jack for a moment before he made the call. "Mellon Drugs," the boy said. "You must be the new one."

"I am. Just landed a couple of days ago. Why?"

"You'll either have to confirm the old contract or sign a new one. Will you remind Dr. Richards, sir? And he's down that hall to the very end, go left, then watch on your right for L-14. Go right through the office. He's in the lab beyond it."

Long, eager strides and a few moments later, Frank introduced himself to a harassed man in a white smock. The doctor was so obviously trying to conceal his irritation at being interrupted that Frank decided to play his role to the very last minute.

"I regret disturbing you," he apologized, "but I believe my business is sufficiently important to warrant it. If you have the materials available, I would like to dictate a new contract between the Mellon Company, your clinic and yourself. On perma-tape, please."

For a moment Richards was impressed, as Frank meant him to be. The request for perma-tape indicated a long-term contract and probably more money for the doctor and the clinic.

Then again Richards looked harassed. He hesitated, said, "I wonder if you would mind dictating here. I had this set up," and he indicated the recorder on the lab table, "so that I could make a running account of this dissection. I could save a lot of time by just switching the tapes back and forth."

"Glad to," Frank agreed. He seated himself where the doctor had been, studied the specimen until Richards returned.

"Looks like a sort of 'possum," Frank commented.

"What? Oh, yes, it does. In fact, we call it a Marsupial." Richards blew across the mike, his eyes on a dial. "Go ahead, it's ready."

Frank closed his eyes for a moment, opened them. In an even, unemphasized tone he started dictating what he had memorized while he had been Dr. Blanding's guinea pig. When he started, he saw three scalpels lying on the table in front of him. An edge of his mind remembered what Clancy had taught him, and as he spoke, he played with the razor-edged knives.

And that part of his brain which made him the perfect messenger, a true eidetic memory, continued to produce smoothly the message which was in effect a declaration of independence for Mars and for every other place where the human race would try to find a future.

The Message. Twenty-four closely-typed and printed pages of analysis, beginning with the original formulation and broken down to the variations that naturally exist among men. The differences between a pygmy in the rain-leached jungles of Malaya, an Eskimo's winter diet and a suburbanite roving the restaurants of New York.

The Message. Mankind was now free to reach for all the planets, even the stars. They would no longer be bound to living on Earth-grown concentrates. No other water would ever be like Earth water. But now they knew exactly what to add, down to the most minute trace element, to make a hydroponic diet both beneficial and easily available anywhere.

The Message. Finally past the men of IPT. Men able to censor mail because it had to be microfilmed; allowed to examine baggage; permitted to screen would-be passengers with hypno-gas and psychiatric examination—all this in the name of the twin gods called Weight Limits and Safety Precautions.

Gods who had been only masks for an ancient one called Greed.

To Frank, Dr. Richards was only a figure on the edge of his consciousness. But he became vaguely aware that the doctor was becoming more and more restless.

Abruptly Richards' hand jumped forward and snapped off the recorder. "Impossible!"

Frank felt as he always did when something interfered with his memory's function of reporting without error. A great light within himself snapped off and the lesser light around him gradually came back into focus.

"What did you say?"

"These so-called formulae you are dictating. You're too late, you impostor! We got this yesterday as liquids."

"Then I was not the only messenger," Frank said, strangely disappointed.

"The only one? You're not even the real one. There's only ever been one man that I know of who could do what you're pretending to do, and he died months ago!"

"In . . . one . . . of . . . Dr. Blanding's . . . diet . . . tests—"

The last words had come more and more slowly. Dr. Richards reseated himself, gaze fixed on Frank's face.

"I never met the man," Richards said in a whisper, "but of course

I've heard of him. What he wrote is required reading. And I saw his picture just last week, in an old Journal I was checking.

"Go ahead, Mr. . . . Fitzgerald."

"Please sit still."

Closing the door from the office as quietly as he had opened it, stood a man distinguishable from thousands seen on any street only because he had a gun in his hand.

"Congratulations, my dear sir." The man spoke with sober precision. "You deceived my entire organization. You almost deceived me, except that I could not believe Blanding and Gorski would try anything so desperately obvious as that blood bank. However, those fools who work for me would have had it so. There is only one messenger, they insisted.

"One messenger! Fools!"

"You must be Kushalik himself," Frank said.

"But he delivered the blood bank!" Richards could not hide his feelings, spoke like a man in shock.

"He's not the man who brought it from Earth. And I hate to think what would have happened if you would have used it as a guide," Frank stated grimly.

"When they do use it," Kushalik corrected the statement, "because—"

He did not finish the statement directly, did not have to. Instead, "And I think I shall have to end Gorski and Blanding also. This last has been too much."

He regarded them as a man will look at a chess problem. "Too bad you shut off that recorder, Dr. Richards. I could have used part of that tape to make this more realistically a double murder. But—"

Frank weighed the chances and considered both results. In a deep breath, he reached his decision and he spoke to distract the gunman.

"Kushalik, do you know why prison foods are prepared so that they can be cut with a fork?"

The nondescript man paid no attention. "Dr. Richards, will you please move to this side of the table." He indicated a place opposite to Frank with a gesture of his gun hand.

The first scalpel Frank threw went into that gun hand just above the wrist. Kushalik's head went back at the shock of the sudden pain and when the second knife struck, it hit below the aiming point. It buried itself to the hilt where the chin became the neck. The third missed the left eyeball completely and made only a long gash along the scalp.

But the third one hadn't been needed, Frank noted. The second had done the job.

"Thank you, Clancy," Frank said aloud.

"What did you say?" Richards' voice was hoarse.

"Nothing important, just a comment on how ignorance can kill a man."

He walked around the table and looked down on the enemy. Kushalik's eyes were flickering.

"Not dead, just paralyzed," Frank said. "Must have gone through and caught the spine, which is why he didn't shoot."

He reached down, pulled the knife out of Kushalik's throat and drove it into the gunman's heart. "You've got good scalpels, doctor."

Absently, his mind busy with the larger problem, he picked up a handful of paper towels from the table and laid them over Kushalik's throat.

"Don't want too much blood around here," he went on, thinking and planning aloud. "Let's see, we could claim self-defense, get away with it, too. That gun in his hand . . . yes. But then his organization would know that there *had* been another messenger. And that wouldn't be good. I don't think they'll break up just because this one is dead.

"Now, how did he know that I was here? Got it, sure, that boy at the reception desk. But I'll bet the kid doesn't know anything except to call a particular number when a certain type of stranger shows up. I think we can count him out."

"Richards!" He spoke sharply and the doctor began to come out of his daze. "Kushalik will have to disappear. They'll hunt for him, but because of the way he seems to work, they won't start hunting for a couple of days. With luck, they'll never be sure of what happened to him.

"In any event, we'll have the time we need, time to get out enough copies of the formulae so that it can never be suppressed. Yes, and we'll get the fact that it exists in the newscasts, too."

Coldly, Frank measured Dr. Richards and he liked what he saw. The man had made a fast recovery.

Cavendish glanced around the lab. "We'll use that large sink. By the way, it does drain directly into the main sewer, doesn't it? Good.

"Now, we'll need some stuff from the chem lab. And outside of that, there won't be much for you to do. I'll take care of the rest.

"You may remember," he said easily, taking a long look into his past, "that I have had experience with this business."

The
Other
People

by LEIGH BRACKETT

I ran down Buckhorn Mountain in the cloud and rain, carrying the boy in my arms. The green lightning flashed among the trees. Buckhorn is no stranger to lightning, but this was different. It did not come from the clouds, and there was no thunder with it. It ran low, searching the thickets, the brush-choked gullies, the wet hollows full of brambles and poison ivy. Thick green hungry snakes looking for something. Looking for me.

Looking for the boy who had started it all.

He peered up at me, clinging like a lemur to my coat as I went headlong down the slope. His eyes were copper-colored. They had seen a lot for all the two-and-a-half years they had been open on this world. They were frightened now, not just vaguely as you might expect from a child his age, but intelligently. And in his curiously sweet shrill voice he asked:

"Why mus' they kill us?"

"Never mind," I said, and ran and ran, and the green lightning hunted us down the mountainside.

It was Doc Callendar, the County Health Officer, who got me in on the whole thing. I am Hank Temple, owner, editor, feature writer, legman, and general roustabout of the *Newhale News*, serving New-hale and the rural and mountain areas around it. Doc Callendar, Sheriff Ed Betts and I are old friends, and we work together, helping out where we can. So one hot morning in July my phone rang and it was Doc, sounding kind of dazed.

"Hank?" he said. "I'm at the hospital. Would you want to take a run up here for a minute?"

"Who's hurt?"

"Nobody. Just thought something might interest you."

Doc was being cagey because anything you say over the phone in Newhale is public property. But even so the tone of his voice put prickles between my shoulder-blades. It didn't sound like Doc at all.

"Sure," I said. "Right away."

Newhale is the county seat, a small town, and a high town. It lies in an upland hollow of the Appalachians, a little clutter of old red brick buildings with porches on thin wooden pillars, and frame houses ranging from new white to weathered silver-gray, centered around the dumpy courthouse. A very noisy stream bisects the town. The tannery and the feed-mill are its chief industries, with some mining nearby. The high-line comes down a neat cut on Tunkhan-nock Ridge to the east and goes away up a neat cut on Goat Hill to the west. Over all towers the rough impressive hump of Buckhorn Mountain, green on the ridges, shadowed blue in the folds, wrapped more often than not in a mist of cloud.

There is not much money nor any great fame to be made in New-hale, but there are other reasons for living here. The girl I wanted to marry couldn't quite see them, and it's hard to explain to a woman why you would rather have six pages of small-town newspaper that belong to you than the whole of the *New York Times* if you only work for it. I gave up trying, and she went off to marry a gray flannel suit, and every time I unlimber my fishing-rod or my deer rifle I'm happy for her.

The hospital is larger than you might expect, since it serves a big part of the county. Sitting on a spur of Goat Hill well away from the tannery, it's an old building with a couple of new wings tacked on. I found Doc Callendar in his office, with Bossert. Bossert is the resi-dent doctor, a young guy who knows more, in the old phrase, than a jackass could haul downhill. This morning he looked as though he wasn't sure of his own name.

"Yesterday," Doc said, "one of the Tate girls brought her kid in, a little boy. I wasn't here, I was out testing those wells up by Pinecrest. But I've seen him before. He's a stand-out, a real handsome youngster."

"Precocious," said Jim Bossert nervously. "Very precocious for his age. Physically, too. Coordination and musculature well developed. And his coloring—"

"What about it?" I asked.

"Odd. I don't know. I noticed it, and then forgot it. The kid looked as though he'd been through a meat-grinder. His mother said the other kids had ganged up and beaten him, and he hadn't been right for several days, so she reckoned she'd better bring him in. She's not much more than nineteen herself. I took some X-rays—"

Bossert picked up a couple of pictures from the desk and shoved them at me. His hands shook, making the stiff films rattle together.

"I didn't want to trust myself on these. I waited until Callendar could check them, too."

I held the pictures up and looked at them. They showed a small, frail bony structure and the usual shadowy outline of internal organs. It wasn't until I had looked at them for several minutes that I began to realize there was something peculiar about them. There seemed to be too few ribs, the articulation of the joints looked queer even to my layman's eyes, and the organs themselves were a hopeless jumble.

"Some of the innards," said Doc, "we can't figure out at all. There are organs we've never seen nor heard of before."

"Yet the child seems normal and perfectly healthy," said Bossert. "Remarkably so. From the beating he'd taken he should have had serious injuries. He was just sore. His body must be as flexible and tough as spring steel."

I put the X-rays back on the desk. "Isn't there quite a large literature on medical anomalies?"

"Oh, yes," said Doc. "Double hearts, upside-down stomachs, extra arms, legs, heads—almost any distortion or variation you can think of. But not like this." He leaned over and tapped his finger emphatically on the films. "This isn't a distortion of anything. This is *different*. And that's not all."

He pushed a microscope slide toward me.

"That's the capper, Hank. Blood sample. Jim tried to type it. I tried to type it. We couldn't. There isn't any such type."

I stared at them. Their faces were flushed, their eyes were bright, they quivered with excitement, and suddenly it got to me too.

"Wait a minute," I said. "Are you trying to tell me—"

"We've got something here," said Doc Callendar. "Something—" He shook his head. I could see the dreams in it. I could see Callendar standing ten feet tall on a pedestal of medical journals. I could see him on podiums addressing audiences of breathless men, and the same dreams were in Bossert's eyes.

I had my own. The *Newhale News* suddenly a famous name on the wire-services, and one Henry Temple bowing with modest dignity as he accepted the Pulitzer Prize for journalism.

"Big," said Bossert softly. "The boy is more than a freak. He's something new. A mutation. Almost a new species. The blood-type alone—"

Something occurred to me and I cut him short. "Listen," I said. "Listen, are you sure you didn't make a mistake or something? How could the boy's blood be so different from his mother's?" I hunted for the word. "Incompatibility. He'd never have been born."

"Nevertheless," said Doc Callendar mildly, "he was born. And nevertheless, there is no such blood-type. We've run tests backward and forward, together and independently. Kindly allow us to know what we're talking about, Hank. The boy's blood obviously must have been compatible with his mother's. Possibly it's a more advanced Type O, universally compatible. This is only one of the many things we have to study and evaluate."

He picked up the X-ray films again and looked at them, with an expression of holy ecstasy in his eyes.

I lighted another cigarette. My hands were shaking now, like theirs. I leaned forward.

"Okay," I said. "What's the first thing we do?"

Doc's station wagon, with COUNTY HEALTH SERVICE painted on its side, slewed and snorted around the turns of the steep dirt road. Jim Bossert had had to stay at the hospital, but I was sitting beside Doc, hunched forward in a sweat of impatience. The road ran up around the shoulder of Tunkhannock Ridge. We had thick dark woods on our right going up, and thick dark woods on our left going down. Buckhorn hung in the north like a curtain across the sky.

"We'll have to be careful," Doc was saying. "I know these people pretty well. If they get the idea we're trying to pull something, we'll never get another look at the kid."

"You handle it," I said. "And by the way, nobody's mentioned the boy's father. Doesn't he have one?"

"Do you know the Tate girls?"

"No. I've been through Possum Creek all right, but through it is all."

"You must have gone fast," said Doc, grinning. "The answer is physiologically yes, legally are you kidding?" He shifted into second, taking it easy over a place where the road was washed and gullied. "They're not a bad bunch of girls at that, though," he added reflectively. "I kind of like them. Couple of them are downright married."

We bucketed on through the hot green shadows, the great centers of civilization like Newhale forgotten in the distance behind us, and finally in a remote pocket just under Tunkhannock's crest we came upon a few lean spry cattle, and then the settlement of Possum Creek.

There were four ancient houses straggled out along the side of the stream. One of them said GENERAL STORE and had a gas pump in front of it. Two old men sat on the step.

Doc kept on going. "The Tates," he said, straight-faced, "live out a little from the center of town."

Two more turns of the road, which was now only a double-rutted track, brought us to a rural mailbox which said TATE. The house behind it was pretty well run down, but there was glass in most of the windows and only half the bricks were gone from the chimney. The clapboards were sort of a rusty brown, patched up with odds and ends of tarpaper. A woman was washing clothes in an old galvanized tub set on a stand in the side yard. There was a television aerial tied on cockeyed to the gable of the house. There was a sow with a litter in a pen right handy to the door, and a little way at the back was a barn with the ridge-pole swayed like an old horse. A tarpaper shack and a battered house-trailer were visible among the trees—probably the homes of the married daughters. An ancient man sat in an ancient rocking-chair on the porch and peered at us, and an ancient dog beside him rose up heavily and barked.

I've known quite a lot of families like the Tates. They scratch out enough corn for their pigs and their still-houses, and enough garden for themselves. The young men make most of their money as guides during hunting season, and the old men make theirs selling moonshine. They have electricity now, and they can afford radios and even television sets. City folks call them lazy and shiftless. Actually, they find the simple life so pleasant that they hate to let hard work spoil their enjoyment of it.

Doc drove his station wagon into the yard and stopped. Instantly there was an explosion of dogs and children and people.

"There he is," Doc said to me, under cover of the whooping and woofing and the banging of screen doors. "The skinny little chap with the red hair. There, just coming down the steps."

I looked over and saw the boy.

He was an odd one, all right. The rest of the Tate tribe all had straight hair ranging from light brown to honey-blond. His was close and curly to his head and I saw what Jim Bossert had meant about his coloring. The red had undertones of something else in it. One would almost, in that glare of sunlight, have said silver. The Tates had blue eyes. His were copper-colored. The Tates were fair and sunburned, and so was he, but there was a different quality of fairness to his skin, a different shading to the tan.

He was a little boy. The Tate children were rangy and big boned. He moved among them lightly, a gazelle among young goats, with a totally unchildlike grace and sureness. His head was narrow, with a very high arch to the skull. His eyes were grave, precociously wise. Only in the mouth was there genuine childishness, soft and shy.

We got out of the car. The kids—a dozen of them, give or take a couple—all stopped as though on a signal and began to study their bare feet. The woman came from the washtub, wiping her hands on her skirt. Several others came out of the house.

The little boy remained at the foot of the steps. His hand was now in the hand of a buxom girl. Judging by Bossert's description, this would be his mother. Not much over nineteen, handsome, big-breasted, full-hipped. She was dressed in tight jeans and a boy's shirt, her bare feet stuck into sandals, and a hank of yellow hair hung down her back.

Doc spoke to them all, introducing me as a friend from town. They were courteous, but reserved. "I want to talk to Sally," he said, and we moved closer to the steps. I tried not to look at the boy lest the glitter in my eye give me away. Doc was being so casual and hearty it hurt. I could feel a curious little prickle run over my skin as I got close to the child. It was partly excitement, partly the feeling that here was a being different from myself, another species. There was a dark bruise on the child's forehead, and I remembered that the others had beaten him. Was this *otherness* at the bottom of their resentment? Did they sense it without the need for blood samples and X-rays?

Mutant. A strange word. A stranger thing to come upon here in these friendly familiar hills. The child stared at me, and the July sun turned cold on my back.

Doc spoke to Sally, and she smiled. She had an honest, friendly smile. Her mouth was wide and full, frankly sensuous but without coquetry. She had big blue eyes, and her sunburned cheeks were flushed with health, and she looked as uncomplicated and warmly attractive as a summer meadow. I wondered what strange freak of genetics had made her the fountainhead of a totally new race.

Doc said, "Is this the little boy you brought in to the hospital?"

"Yes," she said. "But he's better now."

Doc bent over and spoke to the boy. "Well," he said. "And what's your name, young man?"

"Name's Billy," he answered, in a grave sweet treble that had a sound in it of bells being rung far off. "Billy Tate."

The woman who had come from the washtub said with unconcealed dislike, "He ain't no Tate, whatever he might be."

She had been introduced as Mrs. Tate, and was obviously the mother and grandmother of this numerous brood. She had lost most of her teeth and her gray-blonde hair stood out around her head in an untidy brush. Doc ignored her.

"How do you do, Billy Tate," he said. "And where did you get that pretty red hair?"

"From his daddy," said Mrs. Tate sharply. "Same place he got his sneaky-footed ways and them yellow eyes like a bad hound. I tell you, Doctor, if you see a man looks just like that child, you tell him to come back and get what belongs to him!"

A corny but perfectly fitting counterpoint to her words, thunder crashed on Buckhorn's cloudy crest, like the ominous laughter of a god.

Sally reached down suddenly and caught up the boy into her arms. . . .

The thunder quivered and died on the hot air. I stared at Doc and he stared at me, and Sally Tate screamed at her mother.

"You keep your dirty mouth off my baby!"

"That ain't no way to talk to Maw," said one of the older girls. "And anyway, she's right."

"Oh," said Sally. "You think so, do you?" She turned to Doc, her cheeks all white now and her eyes blazing. "They set their young ones on my baby, Doctor, and you know why? They're jealous. They're just sick to their stomachs with it, because they all got big hunkety kids that can't do nothin' but eat, and big hunkety men that treat them like they was no better'n brood sows."

She had reached her peak of fury so quickly that it was obvious this row had been going on for a long while, probably ever since the child was born.

Possibly even before, judging by what she said then.

"Jealous," she said to her sisters, showing her teeth. "Every last one of you was dancing up and down to catch his eye, but it was me he took to the hayloft. *Me.* And if he ever comes back he can have me again, for as often and as long as he wants me. And I won't hear no ill of him nor the baby!"

I heard all this. I understood it. But not with all, or even most of my mind. That was busy with another thing, a thing it didn't want to grapple with at all and kept shying away from, only to be driven back shivering.

Doc put it into words.

"You mean," he said, to no one in particular, "the boy looks just like his father?"

"Spit an' image," said Sally fondly, kissing the red curls that had that queer glint of silver in them. "Sure would like to see that man again, I don't care what they say. Doctor, I tell you, he was beautiful."

"Handsome is as handsome does," said Mrs. Tate. "He was no good, and I knew it the minute I saw—"

"Why, Maw," said Mr. Tate, "he had you eating out of his hand, with them nicey ways of his." He turned to Doc Callendar, laughing. "She'd a' gone off to the hayloft with him herself if he'd asked her, and that's a fact. Ain't it, Harry?"

Harry said it was, and they all laughed.

Mrs. Tate said furiously, "It'd become you men better to do something about getting some support for that brat from its father, instead of making fool jokes in front of strangers."

"Seems like, when you bring it up," said Mr. Tate, "it would become us all not to wash our dirty linen for people who aren't rightly concerned." He said courteously to Doc, "Reckon you had a reason for coming here. Is there something I can do?"

"Well—," said Doc uncertainly, and looked at the boy. "Just like his father, you say."

And if that is so, I thought, *how can he be a mutant? A mutant is something new, something different, alien from the parent stem. If he is the spit an' image outside, then build and coloring bred true. And if build and coloring bred true, probably blood-type and internal organs—*

Thunder boomed again on Buckhorn Mountain. And I thought, *Well, and so his father is a mutant, too.*

But Doc said, "Who was this man, Sally? I know just about everybody in these hills, but I never saw anyone to answer that description."

"His name was Bill," she said, "just like the boy's. His other name was Jones. Or he said it was."

"He lied," said Mrs. Tate. "Wasn't Jones no more than mine is. We found that out."

"How did he happen to come here?" asked Doc. "Where did he say he was from?"

"He come here," Mrs. Tate said, "driving a truck for some appliance store, Grover's I think it was, in Newhale. Said the place was just new and was making a survey of teevees around here, and offering free service on them up to five dollars, just for goodwill. So I let him look at ours, and he fussed with it for almost an hour, and didn't charge me a cent. Worked real good afterward, too. That would 'a been the end of it, I guess, only Sally was under his feet all the time and he took a shine to her. Kept coming back, and coming back, and you see what happened."

I said, "There isn't any Grover's store in Newhale. There never has been."

"We found that out," said Mrs. Tate. "When we knew the baby was coming we tried to find Mr. Jones, but it seems he'd told us a big pack of lies."

"He told me," Sally said dreamily, "where he come from."

Doc said eagerly, "Where?"

Twisting her mouth to shape the unfamiliar sounds, Sally said, "Hrylliannu."

Doc's eyes opened wide. "Where the hell is that?"

"Ain't no place," said Mrs. Tate. "Even the schoolteacher couldn't find it in the atlas. It's only another of his lies."

But Sally murmured again, "Hrylliannu. Way he said it, it sounded like the most beautiful place in the world."

The stormcloud over Buckhorn was spreading out. Its edges dimmed the sun. Lightning flicked and flared and the thunder rolled. I said, "Could I take a look at your television?"

"Why," said Mrs. Tate, "I guess so. But don't you disturb it, now. Whatever else he done, he fixed that teevee good."

"I won't disturb it," I said. I went up the sagging steps past the old man and the fat old dog. I went into the cluttered living room, where the springs were coming out of the sofa and there was no rug on the floor, and six kids apparently slept in the old brass bed in the corner. The television set was maybe four years old, but it was the best and biggest made that year. It formed a sort of shrine at one end of the room, with a piece of red cloth laid over its top.

I took the back off and looked in. I don't know what I expected to see. It just seemed odd to me that a man would go to all the trouble of faking up a truck and tinkering with television sets for nothing. And apparently he hadn't. What I did see I didn't understand, but even to my inexpert eye it was obvious that Mr. Jones had done something quite peculiar to the wiring inside.

A totally unfamiliar component roosted on the side of the case, a little gadget not much bigger than my two thumbnails.

I replaced the back and turned the set on. As Mrs. Tate said, it worked real good. Better than it had any business to. I got a peculiar hunch that Mr. Jones had planned it that way, so that no other serviceman would have to be called. I got the hunch that that component was important somehow to Mr. Jones.

I wondered how many other such components he had put in television sets in this area, and what they were for.

I turned off the set and went outside. Doc was still talking to Sally.

". . . some further tests he wants to make," I heard him say. "I can take you and Billy back right now . . ."

Sally looked doubtful and was about to speak. But the decision was made for her. The boy cried out wildly, "No! No!" With the frantic strength of a young animal he twisted out of his mother's arms, dropped to the ground, and sped away into the brush so swiftly that nobody had a chance even to grab for him.

Sally smiled. "All them shiny machines and the funny smells frightened him," she said. "He don't want to go back. Isn't anything wrong with him, is there? The other doctor said he was all right."

"No," said Doc reluctantly. "Just something about the X-rays he wanted to check on. It could be important for the future. Tell you what, Sally. You talk to the boy, and I'll come back in a day or two."

"Well," she said. "All right."

Doc hesitated, and then said, "Would you want me to speak to the sheriff about finding this man? If that's his child he should pay something for its support."

A wistful look came into her eyes. "I always thought maybe if he knew about the baby—"

Mrs. Tate didn't give her time to finish. "Yes, indeed," she said.

"You speak to the sheriff. Time somebody did something about this, 'fore that brat's a man grown himself."

"Well," said Doc, "we can try."

He gave a last baffled glance at the woods where the boy had disappeared, and then we said goodbye and got into the station wagon and drove away. The sky was dark overhead now, and the air was heavy with the smell of rain.

"What do you think?" I said finally.

Doc shook his head. "I'm damned if I know. Apparently the external characteristics bred true. If the others did—"

"Then the father must be a mutant too. We just push it back one generation."

"That's the simplest explanation," Doc said.

"Is there any other?"

Doc didn't answer that. We passed through Possum Creek, and it began to rain.

"What about the television set?" he asked.

I told him. "But you'd have to have Jud or one of the boys from Newhale Appliance look at it, to say what it was."

"It smells," said Doc. "It stinks, right out loud."

The bolt of lightning came so quickly and hit so close that I wasn't conscious of anything but a great flare of livid green. Doc yelled. The station wagon slewed on the road that now had a thin film of mud over it, and I saw trees rushing at us, their tops bent by a sudden wind so that they seemed to be literally leaping forward. There was no thunder. I remembered that, I don't know why. The station wagon tipped over and hit the trees. There was a crash. The door flew open and I fell out through a wet whipping tangle of branches and on down to the steep-tilted ground below. I kept on falling, right down the slope, until a gully pocket caught and held me. I lay there dazed, staring up at the station wagon that now hung over my head. I saw Doc's legs come out of it, out the open door. He was all right. He was letting himself down to the ground. And then the lightning came again.

It swallowed the station wagon and the trees and Doc in a ball of green fire, and when it went away the trees were scorched and the paint was blistered on the wrecked car, and Doc was rolling over and over down the slope, very slowly, as if he was tired and did not want to hurry. He came to rest not three feet away from me. His hair and his clothes were smoldering, but he wasn't worrying about it. He wasn't worrying about anything, any more. And for the second time there had not been any thunder, close at hand where the lightning was.

The rain came down on Doc in heavy sheets, and put the smoldering fire out.

Jim Bossert had just come from posting Doc Callendar's body. For the first time I found myself almost liking him, he looked so sick and beat-out. I pushed the bottle toward him, and he drank out of it and then lighted a cigarette and just sat there shaking.

"It was lightning," he said. "No doubt at all."

Ed Betts, the sheriff, said, "Hank still insists there was something screwy about it."

Bossert shook his head at me. "Lightning."

"Or a heavy electric charge," I said. "That comes to the same thing, doesn't it?"

"But you saw it hit, Hank."

"Twice," I said. "Twice."

We were in Bossert's office at the hospital. It was late in the afternoon, getting on for supper time. I reached for the bottle again, and Ed said quietly,

"Lightning does do that, you know. In spite of the old saying."

"The first time, it missed," I said. "Just. Second time it didn't. If I hadn't been thrown clear I'd be dead too. And there wasn't any thunder."

"You were dazed," Bossert said. "The first shock stunned you."

"It was green," I said.

"Fireballs often are."

"But not lightning."

"Atmospheric freak." Ed turned to Jim Bossert. "Give him something and send him home."

Bossert nodded and got up, but I said, "No. I've got to write up a piece on Doc for tomorrow's paper. See you."

I didn't want to talk any more. I went out and got my car and drove back to town. I felt funny. Hollow, cold, with a veil over my brain so I couldn't see anything clearly or think about anything clearly. I stopped at the store and bought another bottle to see me through the night, and a feeling of cold evil was in me, and I thought of green, silent lightning, and little gimcracks that didn't belong in a television set, and the grave wise face of a child who was not quite human. The face wavered and became the face of a man. A man from Hrylliannu.

I drove home, to the old house where nobody lives now but me. I wrote my story about Doc, and when I was through it was dark and the bottle was nearly empty. I went to bed.

I dreamed Doc Callendar called me on the phone and said, "I've found him but you'll have to hurry." And I said, "But you're dead. Don't call me, Doc, please don't." But the phone kept ringing and ringing, and after a while I woke part way up and it really was ringing. It was two-forty-nine A.M.

It was Ed Betts. "Fire up at the hospital, Hank. I thought you'd want to know. The south wing. Gotta go now."

He hung up and I began to put clothes on the leaden dummy that was me. The south wing, I thought, and sirens went whooping up Goat Hill. The south wing. That's where X-ray is. That's where the pictures of the boy's insides are on file.

What a curious coincidence, I thought.

I drove after the sirens up Goat Hill, through the clear cool night with half a moon shining silver on the ridges, and Buckhorn standing calm and serene against the stars, thinking the lofty thoughts that seem to be reserved for mountains.

The south wing of the hospital burned brightly, a very pretty orange color against the night.

I pulled off the road and parked well below the center of activity and started to walk the rest of the way. Patients were being evacuated from the main building. People ran with things in their hands. Firemen yelled and wrestled with hoses and streams of water arced over the flames. I didn't think they were going to save the south wing. I thought they would be doing well to save the hospital.

Another unit of the fire department came hooting and clanging up the road behind me. I stepped off the shoulder and as I did so I looked down to be sure of my footing. A flicker of movement on the slope about ten feet below caught my eye. Dimly, in the reflected glow of the fire, I saw the girl.

She was slim and light as a gazelle, treading her furtive way among the trees. Her hair was short and curled close to her head. In that light it was merely dark, but I knew it would be red in the sunshine, with glints of silver in it. She saw me or heard me, and she stopped for a second or two, startled, looking up. Her eyes shone like two coppery sparks, as the eyes of an animal shine, weird in the pale oval of her face. Then she turned and ran.

I went after her. She ran fast, and I was in lousy shape. But I was thinking about Doc.

I caught her.

It was dark all around us under the trees, but the firelight and the moonlight shone together into the clearing where we were. She didn't struggle or fight me. She turned around kind of light and stiff to face me, holding herself away from me as much as she could with my hands gripping her arms.

"What do you want with me?" she said, in a breathless little voice. It was accented, and sweet as a bird's. "Let me go."

I said, "What relation are you to the boy?"

That startled her. I saw her eyes widen, and then she turned her head and looked toward the darkness under the trees. "Please let me go," she said, and I thought that some new fear had come to her.

I shook her, feeling her small arms under my hands, wanting to break them, wanting to torture her because of Doc. "How was Doc killed?" I asked her. "Tell me. Who did it, and how?"

She stared at me. "Doc?" she repeated. "I do not understand." Now she began to struggle. "Let me go! You hurt me."

"The green lightning," I said. "A man was killed by it this morning. My friend. I want to know about it."

"Killed?" she whispered. "Oh, no. No one has been killed."

"And you set that fire in the hospital, didn't you? Why? Why were those films such a threat to you? Who are you? Where—"

"Hush," she said. "Listen."

I listened. There were sounds, soft and stealthy, moving up the slope toward us.

"They're looking for me," she whispered. "Please let me go. I don't know about your friend, and the fire was—necessary. I don't want anyone hurt, and if they find you like this—"

I dragged her back into the shadows underneath the trees. There was a huge old maple there with a gnarly trunk. We stood behind it, and now I had my arm around her waist and her head pressed back against my shoulder, and my right hand over her mouth.

"Where do you come from?" I asked her, with my mouth close to her ear. "Where is Hrylliannu?"

Her body stiffened. It was a nice body, very much like the boy's in some ways, delicately made but strong, and with superb coordination. In other ways it was not like the boy's at all. I was thinking of her as an enemy, but it was impossible not to think of her as a woman, too.

She said, her voice muffled under my hand, "Where did you hear that name?"

"Never mind," I said. "Just answer me."

She wouldn't.

"Where do you live now? Somewhere near here?"

She only strained to get away.

"All right," I said. "We'll go now. Back up to the hospital. The sheriff wants to see you."

I started to drag her away up the hill, and then two men came into the light of the clearing.

One was slender and curly-headed in that particular way I was beginning to know. He looked pleasantly excited, pleasantly stimulated, as though by a game in which he found enjoyment. His eyes picked up the fitful glow of the fire and shone eerily, as the girl's had.

The other man was a perfectly ordinary type. He was dark and heavy-set and tall, and his khaki pants sagged under his belly. His face was neither excited nor pleasant. It was obvious that to him this was no game. He carried a heavy automatic, and I thought he was perfectly prepared to use it.

I was afraid of him.

". . . to send a dame, anyway," he was saying.

"That's your prejudice speaking," said the curly-haired man. "She was the only one to send." He gestured toward the flames. "How can you doubt it?"

"She's been caught."

"Not Vadi." He began to call softly. "Vadi? Vadi!"

The girl's lips moved under my hand. I bent to hear, and she said in the faint ghost of a whisper:

"If you want to live, let me go to them."

The big dark man said grimly, "She's been caught. We'd better do something about it, and do it quick."

He started across the clearing.

The girl's lips shaped one word. "Please!"

The dark man came with his big gun, and the curly-headed one came a little behind him, walking as a stalking cat walks, soft and springy on its toes. If I dragged the girl away they would hear me. If I stayed where I was, they would walk right onto me. Either way, I thought, I would pretty surely go to join Doc on the cold marble.

I let the girl go.

She ran out toward them. I stood stark and frozen behind the maple tree, waiting for her to turn and say the word that would betray me.

She didn't turn, and she didn't say the word. The curly-headed man put his arms around her and they talked rapidly for perhaps half a minute, and I heard her tell the dark man that she had only waited to be sure they would not be able to put the fire out too soon. Then all three turned and went quickly away among the dark trees.

I stayed where I was for a minute, breathing hard, trying to think. Then I went hunting for the sheriff.

By the time I found Ed Betts, of course, it was already too late. But he sent a car out anyway. They didn't find a trace of anyone on the road who answered the descriptions I gave.

Ed looked at me closely in the light of the dying fire, which they had finally succeeded in bringing under control. "Don't get sore at me now, Hank," he said. "But are you real sure you saw these people?"

"I'm sure," I said. I could still, if I shut my eyes and thought about it, *feel* the girl's body in my arms. "Her name was Vadi. Now I want to talk to Croft."

Croft was the Fire Marshal. I watched the boys pouring water on what was left of the south wing, which was nothing more than a pile of hot embers with some pieces of wall standing near it. Jim Bossert joined us, looking exhausted and grimy. He was too tired even to curse. He just wailed a little about the loss of all his fine X-ray equipment, and all his records.

"I met the girl who did it," I said. "Ed doesn't believe me."

"Girl?" said Bossert, staring.

"Girl. Apparently an expert at this sort of thing." I wondered what the curly-haired man was to her. "Was anybody hurt?"

"By the grace of God," said Bossert, "no."

"How did it start?"

"I don't know. All of a sudden I woke up and every window in the south wing was spouting flame like a volcano."

I glanced at Ed, who shrugged. "Could have been a short in that high-voltage equipment."

Bossert said, "What kind of a girl? A lunatic?"

"Another one like the boy. There was a man with her, maybe the boy's father, I don't know. The third one was just a man. Mean looking bastard with a gun. She said the fire was necessary."

"All this, just to get rid of some films?"

"It must be important to them," I said. "They had already killed Doc. They tried to kill me. What's a fire?"

Ed Betts swore, his face twisted between unbelief and worry. Then Croft came up. Ed asked him, "What started the fire?"

Croft shook his head. "Too early to tell yet. Have to wait till things cool down. But I'll lay you any odds you like, it was started by chemicals."

"Deliberately?"

"Could be," said Croft, and went away again.

I looked at the sky. It was almost dawn, that beautiful bleak time when the sky is neither dark nor light and the mountains are cut from black cardboard, without perspective. I said, "I'm going up to the Tates'. I'm worried about the boy."

"All right," said Ed quickly, "I'll go with you. In my car. We'll stop in town and pick up Jud. I want him to see that teevee."

"The hell with Jud," I said. "I'm in a hurry." And suddenly I was. Suddenly I was terribly afraid for that grave-faced child who was obviously the unwitting key to some secret that was important enough to justify arson and murder to those who wanted to keep it.

Ed hung right behind me. He practically shoved me into his car. It had COUNTY SHERIFF painted on its door, and I thought of Doc's station wagon with its COUNTY HEALTH SERVICE, and it seemed like a poor omen but there was nothing I could do about it.

There was nothing I could do about stopping for Jud Spofford, either. Ed went in and routed him out of bed, taking the car keys with him. I sat smoking and looking up at Tunkhannock Ridge, watching it brighten to gold at the crest as the sun came up. Finally Jud came out grumbling and climbed in the back seat, a tall lanky young fellow in a blue coverall with *Newhale Electric Appliance Co.* embroidered in red on the pocket. His little wife watched from the doorway, holding her pink wrapper together.

We went away up Tunkhannock Ridge. There was still a black smudge of smoke above the hospital on Goat Hill. The sky over Buckhorn Mountain was clear and bright.

Sally Tate and her boy were already gone.

Mrs. Tate told us about it, while we sat on the lumpy sofa in the living room and the fat old dog watched us through the screen door, growling. Sally's sisters, or some of them at least, were in the kitchen listening.

"Never was so surprised at anything in my life," said Mrs. Tate. "Pa had just gone out to the barn with Harry and J. P.—them's the two oldest girls' husbands, you know. I and the girls was washing up after breakfast, and I heard this car drive in. Sure enough it was him. I went out on the stoop—"

"What kind of a car?" asked Ed.

"Same panel truck he was driving before, only the name was painted out. Kind of a dirty blue all over. 'Well,' I says, 'I never expected to see *your* face around here again!', I says, and he says—"

Boiled down to reasonable length, the man had said that he had always intended to come back for Sally, and that if he had known about the boy he would have come much sooner. He had been away, he said, on business, and had only just got back and heard about Sally bringing the child in to the hospital, and knew that it must be his. He had gone up to the house, and Sally had come running out into his arms, her face all shining. Then they went in together to see the boy, and Bill Jones had fondled him and called him Son, and the boy had watched him sleepily and without affection.

"They talked together for a while, private," said Mrs. Tate, "and then Sally come and said he was going to take her away and marry her and make the boy legal, and would I help her pack. And I did, and they went away together, the three of 'em. Sally didn't know when she'd be back."

She shook her head, smoothing her hair with knotted fingers. "I just don't know," she said. "I just don't know."

"What?" I asked her. "Was there something wrong?" I knew there was, but I wanted to hear what she had to say.

"Nothing you could lay your hand to," she said. "And Sally was so happy. She was just fit to burst. And he *was* real pleasant, real polite to me and Pa. We asked him about all them lies he told, and he said they wasn't lies at all. He said the man he was working for did plan to open a store in Newhale, but then he got sick and the plan fell through. He said his name was Bill Jones, and showed us some cards and things to prove it. And he said Sally just misunderstood the name of the place he come from because he give it the old Spanish pronunciation."

"What did he say it was really?" Ed asked, and she looked surprised.

"Now I think of it, I guess he didn't say."

"Well, where's he going to live, with Sally?"

"He isn't settled yet. He's got two or three prospects, different places. She was so happy," said Mrs. Tate, "and I ought to be too, 'cause Lord knows I've wished often enough he would come back and get that peaky brat of his, and Sally too if she was minded. But I ain't. I ain't happy at all, and I don't know why."

"Natural reaction," said Ed Betts heartily. "You miss your daughter, and probably the boy too, more than you know."

"I've had daughters married before. It was something about this man. Something—" Mrs. Tate hesitated a long time, searching for a word. "Queer," she said at last. "Wrong. I couldn't tell you what. Like the boy, only more so. The boy has Sally in him. This one—" She made a gesture with her hands. "Oh, well, I expect I'm just looking for trouble."

"I expect so, Mrs. Tate," said Ed, "but you be sure and get in touch with me if you don't hear from Sally in a reasonable time. And now I'd like this young man to look at your teevee."

Jud, who had been sitting stiff and uncomfortable during the talking, jumped up and practically ran to the set. Mrs. Tate started to protest, but Ed said firmly, "This may be important, Mrs. Tate. Jud's a good serviceman, he won't upset anything."

"I hope not," she said. "It does run real good."

Jud turned it on and watched it for a minute. "It sure does," he said. "And in this location, too."

He took the back off and looked inside. After a minute he let go a long low whistle.

"What is it?" said Ed, going closer.

"Damnedest thing," said Jud. "Look at that wiring. He's loused up the circuits, all right—and there's a couple tubes in there like I never saw before." He was getting excited. "I'd have to tear the whole thing down to see what he's really done, but somehow he's boosted the power and the sensitivity way up. The guy must be a wizard."

Mrs. Tate said loudly, "You ain't tearing anything down, young man. You just leave it like it is."

I said, "What about that dingus on the side?"

"Frankly," said Jud, "that stops me. It's got a wire to it, but it don't seem to hitch up anywhere in the set." He turned the set off and began to poke gently around. "See here, this little hairline wire that comes down and bypasses the whole chassis? It cuts in here on the live line, so it draws power whether the set's on or not. But I don't see how it can have anything to do with the set operating."

"Well, take it out," said Ed. "We'll take it down to the shop and see whether we can make anything of it."

"Okay," said Jud, ignoring Mrs. Tate's cry of protest. He reached in and for the first time actually touched the enigmatic little unit, feeling for what held it to the side of the case.

There was a sharp pop and a small bright flare, and Jud leaped back with a howl. He put his scorched fingers in his mouth and his eyes watered. Mrs. Tate cried, "Now, you've done it, you've ruined my teevee!" There was a smell of burning on the air. The girls came running out of the kitchen and the old dog barked and clawed the screen.

One of the girls said, "What happened?"

"I don't know," Jud said. "The goddamned thing just popped like a bomb when I touched it."

There was a drift of something gray—ash or dust—and that was all. Even the hairline wire was consumed.

"It looks," I said, "as though Mr. Jones didn't want anybody else to look over his technological achievements."

Ed grunted. He looked puzzled and irresolute. "Hurt the set any?" he asked.

"Dunno," said Jud, and turned it on.

It ran as perfectly as before.

"Well," said Mrs. Tate, "thank goodness."

"Yeah," said Ed. "I guess that's all, then. What do you say, Hank? We might as well go."

I said we might as well. We climbed back into Ed's car and started—the second time for me—back down Tunkhannock Ridge.

Jud was still sucking his fingers. He wondered out loud if the funny-looking tubes in the set would explode the same way if you touched them, and I said probably. Ed didn't say anything. He was frowning deeply. I asked him what he thought about it.

"I'm trying to figure the angle," he said. "This Bill Jones. What does he get out of it? What does he *make*? On the television gag, I mean. People usually want to get paid for work like that."

Jud offered the opinion that the man was a nut. "One of these crazy guys like in the movies, always inventing things that make trouble. But I sure would like to know what he done to that set."

"Well," said Ed, "I can't see what more we can do. He did come back for the girl, and apart from that he hasn't broken any laws."

"Hasn't he?" I said, looking out the window. We were coming to the place where Doc had died. There was no sign of a storm today. Everything was bright, serene, peaceful. But I could feel the cold feeling of being watched. Someone, somewhere, knew me. He watched where I went and what I did, and decided whether or not to send the green lightning to slay me. It was a revelation, like the moments you have as a young child when you become acutely conscious of God. I began to shake. I wanted to crawl down in the back seat and hide. Instead I sat where I was and tried to keep the naked terror from showing too much. And I watched the sky. And nothing happened.

Ed Betts didn't mention it, but he began to drive faster and faster until I thought we weren't going to need any green lightning. He didn't slow down until we hit the valley. I think he would have been glad to get rid of me, but he had to haul me all the way back up Goat Hill to get my car. When he did let me off, he said gruffly,

"I'm not going to listen to you again till you've had a good twelve hours' sleep. And I need some myself. So long."

I went home, but I didn't sleep. Not right away. I told my assistant and right-hand man, Joe Streckfoos, that the paper was all his today, and then I got on the phone. I drove the local exchange crazy, but by about five o'clock that afternoon I had the information I wanted.

I had started with a map of the area on my desk. Not just Newhale, but the whole area, with Buckhorn Mountain roughly at the center and showing the hills and valleys around its northern periphery. By five o'clock the map showed a series of red pencil dots. If you connected them together with a line they formed a sprawling, irregular, but unbroken circle drawn around Buckhorn, never exceeding a certain number of miles in distance from the peak.

Every pencil dot represented a television set that had within the last three years been serviced by a red-haired man—for free.

I looked at the map for a long time, and then I went out in the yard and looked up at Buckhorn. It seemed to me to stand very high, higher than I remembered. From flank to crest the green unbroken forest covered it. In the winter time men hunted there for bear and deer, and I knew there were a few hunting lodges, hardly more than shacks, on its lower slopes. These were not used in summer, and apart from the hunters no one ever bothered to climb those almost perpendicular sides, hanging onto the trees as onto a ladder, up to the fog and storm that plagued the summit.

There were clouds there now. It almost seemed that Buckhorn pulled them down over his head like a cowl, until the gray trailing edges hid him almost to his feet. I shivered and went inside and shut the door. I cleaned my automatic and put in a full clip. I made a sandwich and drank the last couple of drinks in last night's bottle.

I laid out my boots and my rough-country pants and a khaki shirt. I set the alarm. It was still broad daylight. I went to bed.

The alarm woke me at eleven-thirty. I did not turn on any lamps. I don't know why, except that I still had that naked feeling of being watched. Light enough came to me anyhow from the intermittent sulfurous flares in the sky. There was a low mutter of thunder in the west. I put the automatic in a shoulder holster under my shirt, not to hide it but because it was out of the way there. When I was dressed I went downstairs and out the back door, heading for the garage.

It was quiet, the way a little town can be quiet at night. I could hear the stream going over the stones, and the million little songs of the crickets, the peepers, and the frogs were almost stridently loud.

Then they began to stop. The frogs first, in the marshy places besides the creek. Then the crickets and the peepers. I stopped too, in the black dark beside a clump of rhododendrons my mother used to be almost tiresomely proud of. My skin turned cold and the hair bristled on the back of my neck and I heard soft padding footsteps and softer breathing on the heavy air.

Two people had waded the creek and come up into my yard.

There was a flare and a grumble in the sky and I saw them close by, standing on the grass, looking up at the unlighted house.

One of them was the girl Vadi, and she carried something in her hands. The other was the heavy-set dark man with the gun.

"It's okay," he told her. "He's sleeping. Get busy."

I slid the automatic into my palm and opened my mouth to speak, and then I heard her say:

"You won't give him a chance to get out?"

Her tone said she knew the answer to that one before she asked it. But he said with furious sarcasm:

"Why certainly, and then you can call the sheriff and explain why you burned the house down. And the hospital. Christ. I told Arnek you weren't to be trusted." He gave her a rough shove. "Get with it."

Vadi walked five careful paces away from him. Then very swiftly she threw away, in two different directions, whatever it was she carried. I heard the two things fall, rustling among grass and branches where it might take hours to find them even by daylight. She spun around. "Now," she said in a harsh defiant voice, "what are you going to do?"

There was a moment of absolute silence, so full of murder that the far-off lightning seemed feeble by comparison. Then he said:

"All right, let's get out of here."

She moved to join him, and he waited until she was quite close to him. Then he hit her. She made a small bleating sound and fell down. He started to kick her, and then I jumped out and hit him over the ear with the flat of the automatic. It was his turn to fall down.

Vadi got up on her hands and knees. She stared at me, sobbing a little with rage and pain. Blood was running from the corner of her mouth. I took the man's gun and threw it far off and it splashed in the creek. Then I got down beside the girl.

"Here," I said. "Have my handkerchief."

She took it and held it to her mouth. "You were outside here all the time," she said. She sounded almost angry.

"It just happened that way. I still owe you thanks for my life. And my house. Though you weren't so tender about the hospital."

"There was no one to be killed there. I made sure. A building one can always rebuild, but a life is different."

She looked at the unconscious man. Her eyes burned with that catlike brilliance in the lightning flares.

"I could kill him," she said, "with pleasure."

"Who is he?"

"My brother's partner." She glanced toward Buckhorn and the light went out of her eyes. Her head became bowed.

"Your brother sent you to kill me?"

"He didn't say—"

"But you knew."

"When Marlin came with me I knew."

She had begun to tremble.

"Do you make a career of arson?"

"Arson? Oh. The setting of fires. No. I am a chemist. And I wish I—"

She caught herself fiercely and would not finish.

I said, "Those things are listening devices, then."

She had to ask me what I meant. Her mind was busy with some thorny darkness of its own.

"The little gadgets your brother put in the television sets," I said. "I figured that's what they were when I saw how they were placed. A string of sentry posts all around the center of operations, little ears to catch every word of gossip, because if any of the local people get suspicious they're bound to talk about it and so give warning. He heard my calls this afternoon, didn't he? That's why he sent you. And he heard Doc and me at the Tates'. That's why—"

Moving with that uncanny swiftness of hers, she rose and ran away from me. It was like before. She ran fast, and I ran after her. She went splashing through the shallow stream and the water flew back against me, wetting my face, spattering my clothes. On the far bank I caught her, as I had before. But this time she fought me.

"Let me go," she said, and beat her hands against me. "Do you know what I've done for you? I've asked for the knife for myself. Let me go, you clumsy fool—"

I held her tighter. Her soft curls pressed against my cheek. Her body strove against me, and it was not soft but excitingly strong.

"—before I regret it," she said, and I kissed her.

It was strange, what happened then.

I've kissed girls who didn't want to be kissed, and I've kissed girls who didn't like me particularly. I've kissed a couple of the touch-me-not kind who shrink from any sort of physical contact. I've had my face slapped. But I never had a girl *withdraw* from me the way she did. It was like something closing, folding up, shutting every avenue of contact, and yet she never moved. In fact she had stopped moving entirely. She just stood with my arms around her and my lips on hers, and kind of a coldness came out of her, a rejection so total I couldn't even get mad. I was shocked, and very much puzzled, but you can't get mad at a thing that isn't personal. This was too deep for that. And suddenly I thought of the boy.

"A different breed," I said. "Worlds apart. Is that it?"

"Yes," she said quietly. "Worlds apart."

And the coldness spread through me. I stood on the bank of the stream in the warm night, the bank where I had stood ten thousand times before, boy and man, and saw the strange shining of her eyes, and I was more than cold, I was afraid. I stepped back away from her, still holding her but in a different way.

"It wasn't like this," I said, "between your brother and Sally Tate."

The girl-thing said, "My brother Arnek is a corrupt man."

"Vadi," I said. "Where is Hrylliannu?"

The girl-thing looked past my shoulder and said, "Marlin is running away."

I looked too, and it was so. The big man's head was harder than I had thought. He had got up, and I saw him blundering rapidly away along the side of my house, heading for the street.

"Well," I said, "he's gone now. You must have come in a car, didn't you?"

She nodded.

"Good," I said. "It won't be challenged as soon as mine. We'll take it."

"Where are you going?" she asked, catching her breath sharply.

"Where I was going when you stopped me. Up Buckhorn."

"Oh no," she said. "No, you can't, you mustn't." She was human again, and afraid. "I saved your life, isn't that enough for you? You'll never live to climb Buckhorn and neither will I if—"

"Did Sally and the boy live to climb it?" I asked her, and she hung her head and nodded. "Then you'll see to it that we do."

"But tonight!" she said in a panic. "Not tonight!"

"What's so special about tonight?" She didn't answer, and I shook her. "What's going on up there?"

She didn't answer that, either. She said with sudden fierceness, "All right, then, come on. Climb Buckhorn and see. And when you're dying, remember that I tried to stop you."

She didn't speak again. She led me without protest to the car parked on the dirt road. It was a panel truck. By day it would have been a dirty blue.

"He's going to kill them, isn't he?" I said. "He killed Doc. You admit he wants to kill me. What's going to save Sally and the child?"

"You torture me," she said. "This is a world of torture. Go on. Go on, and get it done."

I started the panel truck. Like the television set, it worked better than it had any business to. It fled with uncanny strength and swiftness over the dirt roads toward Buckhorn, soft-sprung as a cloud, silent as a dream.

"It's a pity," I said. "Your brother has considerable genius."

She laughed. A bitter laugh. "He couldn't pass his second year of technical training. That's why he's here."

She looked at Buckhorn as though she hated the mountain, and Buckhorn, invisible behind a curtain of storm, answered her look with a sullen curse, spoken in thunder.

I stopped at the last gas station on the road and honked the owner out of bed and told him to call Sheriff Betts and tell him where I'd gone. I didn't dare do it myself for fear Vadi would get away from me. The man was very resentful about being waked up. I hoped he would not take out his resentment by forgetting to call.

"You're pretty close to Buckhorn," I told him. "The neck you save may be your own."

I left him to ponder that, racing on toward the dark mountain in that damned queer car that made me feel like a character in one of my own bad dreams, with the girl beside me—the damned queer girl who was not quite human.

The road dropped behind us. We began to climb the knees of the mountain. Vadi told me where to turn, and the road became a track, and the track ended in the thick woods beside a rickety little lodge the size of a piano-box, with a garage behind it. The garage only looked rickety. The headlights showed up new and sturdy timbers on the inside.

I cut the motor and the lights and reached for the handbrake. Vadi must have been set on a hair-trigger waiting for that moment. I heard her move and there was a snap as though she had pulled something from a clip underneath the dashboard. The door on her side banged open.

I shouted to her to stop and sprang out of the truck to catch her. But she was already out of the garage, and she was waiting for me. Just as I came through the door there was a bolt of lightning, bright green, small and close at hand. I saw it coming. I saw her dimly in the backflash and knew that in some way she had made the lightning with a thing she held in her hand. Then it hit me and that was all.

When I came to I was all alone and the rain was falling on me just the way it had on Doc. . . .

But I wasn't dead.

I crawled around and finally managed to get up, feeling heavy and disjointed. My legs and arms flopped around as though the coordinating controls had been burned out. I stood inside the garage out of the rain, rubbing my numb joints and thinking.

All the steam had gone out of me. I didn't want to climb Buckhorn Mountain any more. It looked awfully black up there, and awfully lonesome, and God alone knew what was going on under the veil of cloud and storm that hid it. The lightning flashes—real sky-made lightning—showed me the dripping trees going right up into nothing, with the wind thrashing them, and then the following thunder cracked my eardrums. The rain hissed, and I thought, it's crazy for one man to go up there alone.

. Then I thought about Sally Tate and the little red-headed kid, and

I thought how Ed Betts might already be up there somewhere, plowing his way through the woods looking for me. I didn't know how long I'd been out.

I made sure I still had my gun, and I did have. I wished I had a drink, but that was hopeless. So I started out. I didn't go straight up the mountain. I figured the girl would have had time to find her brother and give him warning, and that he might be looking for me to come that way. I angled off to the east, where I remembered a ravine that might give me some cover. I'd been up Buckhorn before, but only by daylight, with snow on the ground and a couple of friends with me, and not looking for anything more sinister than a bear.

I climbed the steep flank of the mountain, leaning almost into it, worming and floundering and pulling my way between the trees. The rain fell and soaked me. The thunder was a monstrous presence, and the lightning was a great torch that somebody kept tossing back and forth so that sometimes you could see every vein of every leaf on the tree you were fighting with, and sometimes it was so dark that you knew the sun and stars hadn't been invented yet. I lost the ravine. I only knew I was still going up. There wasn't any doubt about that. After a while the rain slacked off and almost stopped.

In an interval between crashes of thunder I heard voices.

They were thin and far away. I tried to place them, and when I thought I had them pegged I started toward them. The steep pitch of the ground fell away into a dizzying downslope and I was almost running into a sort of long shallow trough, thickly wooded, its bottom hidden from any view at all except one directly overhead. And there were lights in it, or at least a light.

I slowed down and went more carefully, hoping the storm would cover any noise I made.

The voices went on, and now I could hear another sound, the scrinch and screek of metal rubbing on metal.

I was on the clearing before I knew it. And it wasn't a clearing at all really, just one of those natural open places where the soil is too thin to support trees and runs to brush instead. It wasn't much more than ten feet across. Almost beside me were a couple of tents so cleverly hidden among the trees that you practically had to fall on them, as I did, to find them at all.

From one of them came the sleepy sobbing of a child.

In the small clearing Vadi and Arnek were watching a jointed metal mast build itself up out of a pit in the ground. The top of it was already out of sight in the cloud but it was obviously taller than the trees. The lamp was on the ground beside the pit.

The faces of Vadi and her brother were both angry, both set and obstinate. Perhaps it was their mutual fury that made them seem less human, or more unhuman, than ever, the odd bone-structure of cheek and jaw accentuated, the whole head elongated, the silver-red hair fairly bristling, the copper-colored eyes glinting with that unpleasantly catlike brilliance in the light. They had been quarreling, and they still were, but not in English. Arnek had a look like a rattlesnake.

Vadi, I thought, was frightened. She kept glancing at the tents, and in a minute the big man, Marlin, came out of one of them. He was pressing a small bandage on the side of his head, over his ear. He looked tired and wet and foul-tempered, as though he had not had an easy time getting back to base.

He started right in on Vadi, cursing her because of what she had done.

Arnek said in English, "I didn't ask her to come here, and I'm sending her home tonight."

"That's great," Marlin said. "That's a big help. We'll have to move our base anyway now."

"Maybe not," said Arnek defiantly. He watched the slim mast stretching up and up with a soft screeking of its joints.

"You're a fool," said Marlin, in a tone of cold and bitter contempt. "You started this mess, Arnek. You had to play around with that girl and make a kid to give the show away. Then you pull that half-cocked trick with those guys in the station wagon and you can't even do that right. You kill the one but not the other. And then *she* louses up the only chance we got left. You know how much money we're going to lose? You know how long it'll take us to find a location half as good as this? You know what I ought to do?"

Arnek's voice was sharp, but a shade uncertain. "Oh, stop bitching and get onto those scanners. All we need is another hour and then they can whistle. And there are plenty of mountains."

"Are there," said Marlin, and looked again at Vadi. "And how long do you think she'll keep her mouth shut at *your* end?"

He turned and walked back into the tent. Arnek looked uncertainly at Vadi and then fixed his attention on the mast again. Vadi's face was the color of chalk. She started once toward the tent and Arnek caught her roughly and spoke to her in whatever language they used, and she stopped.

I slid around the back of the tents to the one Marlin was in. There was a humming and whining inside. I got down on my hands and knees and crawled carefully over the wet grass between the tents, toward the front. The mast apparently made its last joint because it stopped and Arnek said something to Vadi and they bent over what seemed to be a sunken control box in the ground. I took my chance and whipped in through the tent flap.

I didn't have long to look around. The space inside was crammed with what seemed to be electronic equipment. Marlin was sitting hunched up on a stool in front of a big panel with a dozen or so little screens on it like miniature television monitors. The screens, I just had time to see, showed an assortment of views of Buckhorn and the surrounding areas, and Marlin was apparently, by remote control, rotating one by one the distant receivers that sent the images to the screens. They must have been remarkably tight-beamed, because they were not much disturbed by static. I knew now how the eye of God had watched Doc and me on Tunkhannock Ridge.

I didn't know yet how the lightning-bolts were hurled, but I was pretty sure Ed Betts would get one if his car showed up on a scanner screen, and who would be the wiser? Poor Ed hit by lightning just like old Doc, and weren't the storms something fierce this summer?

Marlin turned around and saw it wasn't Arnek. He moved faster than I would have thought possible. He scooped up the light stool he was sitting on and threw it at me, leaping sideways himself in a continuation of the same movement. In the second in which I was getting my head out of the way of the stool he pulled a gun. He had had a spare, just as he must have had a car stashed somewhere in or near the town.

He did not quite have time to fire. I shot him twice through the body. He dropped but I didn't know if he was dead. I kicked the gun out of his hand and jumped to stand flat against the canvas wall beside the front flap, not pressing against it. The canvas was light-proof, and the small lamps over the control panels did not throw shadows.

Arnek did not come in.

After a second or two I got nervous. I could hear him shouting "Marlin! Marlin!" I ran into the narrow space behind the banks of equipment, being extremely careful how I touched anything. I did not see any power leads. It dawned on me that all this stuff had come up out of a pit in the ground like the mast and that the generator must be down there below. The floor wasn't canvas at all, but some dark gray material to which the equipment was bolted.

I got my knife out and started to slit the canvas at the back. And suddenly the inside of the tent was full of green fire. It sparked off every metal thing and jarred the gun out of my hand. It nearly knocked me out again. But I was shielded by the equipment from the full force of the shock. It flicked off again almost at once. I got the canvas cut and squirmed through it and then I put three or four shots at random into the back of the equipment just for luck.

Then I raced around the front and caught Arnek just as he was deciding not to enter the tent after all.

He had a weapon in his hand like the one Vadi had used on me. I said, "Drop it," and he hesitated, looking evil and upset. "Drop it!" I told him again, and he dropped it. "Now stand away," I said. "Walk out toward your sister, real slow, one step at a time."

He walked, and I picked up the weapon.

"Good," I said. "Now we can all relax." And I called Sally Tate, telling her it was safe to come out now.

All this time since I was where I could see her Vadi had stood with one hand over her mouth, looking up into the mist.

Sally Tate came out of the other tent. She was carrying the boy, and both their faces were pale and puffy-eyed and streaked with tears.

"It's all right now," I said. "You can go—" I was going to say "home," and then there was a sound in the sky that was not wind or thunder, that was hardly a sound at all, but more of a great sigh. The air pressed down on me and the grass was flattened as by a down-driven wind and all the branches of the trees bowed. The mist rolled, boiled, was rent, torn apart, scattered.

Something had come to rest against the top of the mast.

Arnek turned and ran to Vadi and I did not stop him. I moved closer to Sally Tate, standing with her mouth open and her eyes big and staring.

The mast began to contract downward, bringing the thing with it.

I suppose I knew then what the thing was. I just didn't want to admit it. It was cylindrical and slender, about fifty feet long, with neither wings nor jets. I watched it come slowly and gracefully down, attached by its needle-sharp nose to the magnetic grapple on top of the mast. The mast acted as automatic guide and stabilizer, dropping the ship into a slot between the trees as neatly as you would drop a slice of bread into the slot of a toaster.

And all the time the bitter breath of fear was blowing on me and little things were falling into place in my mind and I realized that I had known the answer for some time and had simply refused to see it.

A port opened in the side of the ship. And as though that was the final symbolic trigger I needed, I got the full impact of what I was seeing. Suddenly the friendly protecting sky seemed to have been torn open above me as the veiling cloud was torn, and through the rent the whole Outside poured in upon me, the black freezing spaces of the galaxy, the blaze and strangeness of a billion billion suns. I shrank beneath that vastness. I was nothing, nobody, an infinitesimal fleck in a cosmos too huge to be borne. The stars had come too close. I wanted to get down and howl and grovel like a dog.

No wonder Arnek and Vadi and the boy were queer. They were not mutants—they were not even that Earthly. They came from another world.

A little ladder had extended itself downward from the port. A man came briskly to the ground and spoke to Arnek. He resembled Arnek except that he was dressed in a single close-fitting garment of some dark stuff. Arnek pointed to me, speaking rapidly. The man turned and looked at me, his body expressing alarm. I felt childish and silly standing there with my little gun. Lone man of Earth at an incredible Thermopylae, saying, "You shall not land."

All the time Arnek and the stranger had been talking there had been other activities around the ship. A hatch in the stern had opened and now from both hatches people began to come out helter-skelter as though haste was the chief necessity. There were men and women both. They all looked human. Slightly odd, a little queer perhaps, but human. They were different types, different colors, sizes, and builds, but they all fitted in somewhere pretty close to Earthly types. They all looked a little excited, a little scared, considerably bewildered by the place in which they found themselves. Some of the women were crying. There were maybe twenty people in all.

I understood then exactly what Arnek and Marlin had been up to and it seemed so grotesquely familiar and prosaic that I began to laugh.

"Wetbacks," I said aloud. "That's what you're doing, smuggling aliens."

Aliens. Yes indeed.

It did not seem so funny when I thought about it.

The stranger turned around and shouted an order. The men and women stopped, some of them still on the ladders. More voices shouted. Then those on the ladders were shoved aside and eight men in uniform jumped out, with weapons in their hands.

Sally Tate let go one wild wavering shriek. The child fell out of her arms. He sat on the wet ground with the wind knocked out of him so he couldn't cry, blinking in shocked dismay. Sally tottered. Her big strong healthy body was sunken and collapsed, every muscle slack. She turned and made a staggering lunge for the tent and fell partly in through the doorway, crawled the rest of the way like a hurt dog going under a porch, and lay there with the flap pulled over her head.

I didn't blame her. I don't even know what obscure force kept me from joining her.

Of the eight men, five were not human. Two of them not even remotely.

I can't describe them. I can't remember what they looked like, not clearly.

Let's be honest. I don't *want* to remember.

I suppose if you were used to things like that all your life it would be different. You wouldn't think anything about it.

I was not used to things like that. I knew that I never would be, not if we ourselves achieved space-flight tomorrow. I'm too old, too set in the familiar pattern of existence that has never been broken for man since the beginning. Perhaps others are more resilient. They're welcome to it.

I picked up the boy and ran.

It came on again to rain. I ran down Buckhorn Mountain, carrying the boy in my arms. And the green lightning came after us, hunting us along the precipitous slope.

The boy had got his breath back. He asked me why we had to die. I said never mind, and kept on running.

I fell with him and rolled to the bottom of a deep gully. We were shaken. We lay in the dripping brush looking up at the lightning lancing across the night above us. After a while it stopped. I picked him up again and crept silently along the gully and onto the slope below.

And nearly got shot by Ed Betts and a scratch posse, picking their cautious way up the mountainside.

One of the men took the child out of my arms. I hung onto Ed and said inanely, "They're landing a load of wetbacks."

"Up there?"

"They've got a ship," I told him. "They're aliens, Ed. Real aliens."

I began to laugh again. I didn't want to. It just seemed such a hellishly clever play on words that I couldn't help it.

Fire bloomed suddenly in the night above us. A second later the noise of the explosion reached us.

I stopped laughing. "They must be destroying their installations. Pulling out. Marlin said they'd have to. Christ. And Sally is still up there."

I ran back up the mountain, clambering bearlike through the trees. The others followed.

There was one more explosion. Then I came back to the edge of the clearing. Ed was close behind me. I don't think any of the others were really close enough to see. There was a lot of smoke. The tents were gone. Smoking trees were slowly toppling in around the edges of a big raw crater in the ground. There was no trace of the instruments that had been in the tents.

The ship was still there. The crew, human and unhuman, were shoving the last of the passengers back into the ship. There was an altercation going on beside the forward port.

Vadi had her arm around Sally Tate. She was obviously trying to get her aboard. I thought I understood then why Sally and the boy were still alive. Probably Vadi had been insisting that her brother send them along where they wouldn't be any danger to him, and he hadn't quite had the nerve to cross her. He was looking uncertain now, and it was the officer who was making the refusal. Sally herself seemed to be in a stupor.

Vadi thrust past the officer and led Sally toward the ladder. And Sally went, willingly. I like to remember that, now, when she's gone.

I think—I hope—that Sally's all right out there. She was younger and simpler than I, she could adapt. I think she loved Bill Jones—Arnek—enough to leave her child, leave her family, leave her world, and still be happy near him.

Ed and I started to run across the clearing. Ed had not said a word. But his face was something to look at.

They saw us coming but they didn't bother to shoot at us. They seemed in a tremendous hurry. Vadi screamed something, and I was sure it was in English and a warning to me, but I couldn't understand it. Then she was gone inside the ship and so were Arnek and Sally and the officer and crewmen, and the ladders went up and the ports shut.

The mooring mast began to rise and so did the ship, and the trees were bent with the force of its rising.

I knew then what the warning was.

I grabbed Ed bodily and hauled him back. The ship didn't have to be very high. Only above the trees. I hauled him as far as blind instinct told me I could go and then I yelled, "Get down! Get down!" to everybody within earshot and made frantic motions. It all took possibly thirty seconds. Ed understood and we flopped and hugged the ground.

The mast blew.

Dirt, rocks, pieces of tree rained down around us. The shock wave pounded our ears. A few moments later, derisive and powerful, a long thin whistling scream tore upward across the sky, and faded, and was gone.

We got up after a while and collected the muddy and startled posse and went to look at what was left of the clearing. There was nothing. Sally Tate was gone as though she had never existed. There was no shred of anything left to prove that what Ed and I had seen was real.

We made up a story, about a big helicopter and an alien racket. It wasn't too good a story, but it was better than the truth. Afterward, when we were calmer, Ed and I tried to figure it out for ourselves. How it was done, I mean, and why.

The "how" was easy enough, given the necessary technology. Pick a remote but not too inconveniently isolated spot, like the top of Buckhorn Mountain. Set up your secret installation—a simple one, so compact and carefully hidden that hunters could walk right over it and never guess it was there when it was not in use. On nights when conditions are right—that is to say, when the possibility of being observed is nearest to zero—run your cargo in and land it. We figured that the ship we saw wasn't big enough to transport that many people very far. We figured it was a landing-craft, ferrying the passengers down from a much bigger mother-ship way beyond the sky.

A star-ship. It sounded ridiculous when you said it. But we had seen the members of the crew. It is generally acknowledged by nearly everybody now that there is no intelligent life of any terrestrial sort on the other planets of our own system. So they had to come from farther out.

Why? That was a tougher one to solve. We could only guess at it.

"There must be a hell of a big civilization out there," said Ed, "to build the ships and travel in them. They obviously know we're here."

Uneasy thought.

"Why haven't they spoken to us?" he wondered. "Let us in on it too."

"I suppose," I said, "they're waiting for us to develop space-flight on our own. Maybe it's a kind of test you have to pass to get in on their civilization. Or maybe they figure we're so backward they don't want to have anything to do with us, all our wars and all. Or both. Pick your own reason."

"Okay," said Ed. "But why dump their people on us like that? And how come Marlin, one of our own people, was in on it?"

"There *are* Earthmen who'll do anything for money," I said. "Like Marlin. It'd not be too hard to contact men like him, use them as local agents."

"As for why they dump their people on us," I went on, "it probably isn't legal, where they came from. Remember what Marlin said about Vadi? *How long will she keep her mouth shut at* your *end?* My guess is her brother was a failure at home and got into a dirty racket, and she was trying to get him out of it. There must be other worlds like Earth, too, or the racket wouldn't be financially sound. Not enough volume."

"But the wetbacks," Ed said. "Were they failures, too? People who couldn't compete in the kind of a society they must have? And how the hell many do you suppose they've run in on us already?"

I've wondered about that myself. How many aliens has Marlin, and probably others like him, taken off the star-boats and dressed and instructed and furnished with false papers, in return doubtless for all the valuables the poor devils had? How many of the people you see around you every day, the anonymous people that just look a little odd somehow, the people about whom you think briefly that they don't even look human—the queer ones you notice and then forget—how many of them *aren't* human at all in the sense that we understand that word?

Like the boy.

Sally Tate's family obviously didn't want him back. So I had myself appointed his legal guardian, and we get on fine together. He's a bright kid. His father may have been a failure in his own world, but on ours the half-bred child has an I.Q. that would frighten you. He's also a good youngster. I think he takes after his aunt.

I've thought of getting married since then, just to make a better home for the boy, and to fill up a void in my own life I'm beginning to feel. But I haven't quite done it yet. I keep thinking maybe Vadi will come back some day, walking with swift grace down the side of Buckhorn Mountain. I do not think it is likely, but I can't quite put it out of my mind. I remember the cold revulsion that there was between us, and then I wonder if that feeling would go on, or whether you couldn't get used to that idea of differentness in time.

The trouble is, I guess, that Vadi kind of spoiled me for the general run of women.

I wonder what her life is like in Hrylliannu, and where it is. Sometimes on the bitter frosty nights when the sky is diamond-clear and the Milky Way glitters like the mouth of hell across it, I look up at the stars and wonder which one is hers. And old Buckhorn sits black and silent in the north, and the deep wounds on his shoulder are healing into grassy scars. He says nothing. Even the thunder now has a hollow sound. It is merely thunder.

But, as Arnek said, there are plenty of mountains.

Into

Your Tent

I'll Creep

by ERIC FRANK RUSSELL

Morfad sat in the midship cabin and gloomed at the wall. He was worried and couldn't conceal the fact. The present situation had the frustrating qualities of a gigantic rat trap. One could escape it only with the combined help of all the other rats.

But the others weren't likely to lift a finger either on his or their own behalf. He felt sure of that. How can you persuade people to try to escape a jam when you can't convince them that they're in it, right up to the neck?

A rat runs around a trap only because he is grimly aware of its existence. So long as he remains blissfully ignorant of it, he does nothing. On this very world a horde of intelligent aliens had done nothing about it through the whole of their history. Fifty skeptical Altairans weren't likely to step in where three thousand million Terrans had failed.

He was still sitting there when Haraka came in and informed, "We leave at sunset."

Morfad said nothing.

"I'll be sorry to go," added Haraka. He was the ship's captain, a big, burly sample of Altairan life. Rubbing flexible fingers together, he went on, "We've been lucky to discover this planet, exceedingly lucky. We've become blood brothers of a life-form fully up to our own standard of intelligence, space-traversing like ourselves, friendly and cooperative."

Morfad said nothing.

"Their reception of us has been most cordial," Haraka continued enthusiastically. "Our people will be greatly heartened when they hear our report. A great future lies before us, no doubt of that. A Terran-Altairan combine will be invincible. Between us we can explore and exploit the entire galaxy."

Morfad said nothing.

Cooling down, Haraka frowned at him. "What's the matter with you, Misery?"

"I am not overjoyed."

"I can see that much. Your face resembles a very sour *shamsid* on an aged and withered bush. And at a time of triumph, too! Are you ill?"

"No." Turning slowly, Morfad looked him straight in the eyes. "Do you believe in psionic faculties?"

Haraka reacted as if caught on one foot. "Well, I don't know. I am a captain, a trained engineer-navigator, and as such I cannot pretend to be an expert upon extraordinary abilities. You ask me something I am not qualified to answer. How about you? Do you believe in them?"

"I do—*now*."

"Now? Why now?"

"The belief has been thrust upon me." Morfad hesitated, went on with a touch of desperation. "I have discovered that I am telepathic."

Surveying him with slight incredulity, Haraka said, "You've discovered it? You mean it has come upon you recently?"

"Yes."

"Since when?"

"Since we arrived on Terra."

"I don't understand this at all," confessed Haraka, baffled. "Do you assert that some peculiarity in Terra's conditions has suddenly enabled you to read my thoughts?"

"No, I cannot read your thoughts."

"But you've just said that you have become telepathic."

"So I have. I can hear thoughts as clearly as if the words were being shouted aloud. But not your thoughts nor those of any member of our crew."

Haraka leaned forward, his features intent. "Ah, you have been hearing *Terran* thoughts, eh? And what you've heard has got you bothered? Morfad, I am your captain, your commander. It is your bounden duty to tell me of anything suspicious about these Terrans." He waited a bit, urged impatiently, "Come on, speak up!"

"I know no more about these humanoids than you do," said Morfad. "I have every reason to believe them genuinely friendly but I don't know what they think."

"But by the stars, man, you—"

"We are talking at cross-purposes," Morfad interrupted. "Whether I do or do not overhear Terran thoughts depends upon what one means by Terrans."

"Look," said Haraka, "whose thoughts *do* you hear?"

Steeling himself, Morfad said flatly, "Those of Terran dogs."

"Dogs?" Haraka lay back and stared at him. "*Dogs?* Are you serious?"

"I have never been more so. I can hear dogs and no others. Don't ask me why because I don't know. It is a freak of circumstance."

"And you have listened to their minds ever since we jumped to Earth?"

"Yes."

"What sort of things have you heard?"

"I have had pearls of alien wisdom cast before me," declared Morfad, "and the longer I look at them the more they scare the hell out of me."

"Get busy frightening me with a few examples," invited Haraka, suppressing a smile.

"Quote: the supreme test of intelligence is the ability to live as one pleases without working," recited Morfad. "Quote: the art of retribution is that of concealing it beyond all suspicion. Quote: the sharpest, most subtle, most effective weapon in the cosmos is flattery."

"Huh?"

"Quote: if a thing can think, it likes to think that it is God—treat it as God and it becomes your willing slave."

"Oh, no!" denied Haraka.

"Oh, *yes!*" insisted Morfad. He waved a hand toward the nearest port. "Out there are three thousand million petty gods. They are eagerly panted after, fawned upon, gazed upon with worshiping eyes. Gods are very gracious toward those who love them." He made a spitting sound that lent emphasis to what followed. "The lovers know it—and love comes cheap."

Haraka said, uneasily, "I think you're crazy."

"Quote: to rule successfully the ruled must be unconscious of it." Again the spitting sound. "Is that crazy? I don't think so. It makes sense. It works. It's working out there right now."

"But—"

"Take a look at this." He tossed a small object into Haraka's lap. "Recognize it?"

"Yes, it's what they call a cracker."

"Correct. To make it, some Terrans plowed fields in all kinds of weather, rain, wind and sunshine, sowed wheat, reaped it with the aid of machinery other Terrans had sweated to build. They transported the wheat, stored it, milled it, enriched the flour by various processes, baked it, packaged it, shipped it all over the world. When humanoid Terrans want crackers they've got to put in man-hours to get them."

"So—?"

"When a dog wants one he sits up, waves his forepaws and admires his god. That's all. Just that."

"But, darn it, man, dogs are relatively stupid."

"So it seems," said Morfad, dryly.

"They can't really *do* anything effective."

"That depends upon what one regards as effective."

"They haven't got hands."

"And don't need them—having brains."

"Now see here," declaimed Haraka, openly irritated, "we Altairans invented and constructed ships capable of roaming the spaces between the stars. The Terrans have done the same. Terran dogs have not done it and won't do it in the next million years. When one dog has the brains and ability to get to another planet I'll eat my cap."

"You can do that right now," Morfad suggested. "We have two dogs on board."

Haraka let go a grunt of disdain. "The Terrans have given us those as a memento."

"Sure they gave them to us—at whose behest?"

"It was wholly a spontaneous gesture."

"Was it?"

"Are you suggesting that dogs put the idea into their heads?" Haraka demanded.

"I know they did," retorted Morfad, looking grim. "And we've not been given two males or two females. Oh no, sir, not on your life. One male and one female. The givers said we could breed them.

Thus in due course our own worlds can become illuminated with the undying love of man's best friend."

"Nuts!" said Haraka.

Morfad gave back, "You're obsessed with the old, out-of-date idea that conquest must be preceded by aggression. Can't you understand that a wholly alien species just naturally uses wholly alien methods? Dogs employ their own tactics, not ours. It isn't within their nature or abilities to take us over with the aid of ships, guns and a great hullabaloo. It *is* within their nature and abilities to creep in upon us, their eyes shining with hero-worship. If we don't watch out, we'll be mastered by a horde of loving creepers."

"I can invent a word for your mental condition," said Haraka. "You're suffering from caniphobia."

"With good reasons."

"Imaginary ones."

"Yesterday I looked into a dogs' beauty shop. Who was doing the bathing, scenting, powdering, primping? Other dogs? Hah! Humanoid females were busy dolling 'em up. Was *that* imaginary?"

"You can call it a Terran eccentricity. It means nothing whatever. Besides, we've quite a few funny habits of our own."

"You're dead right there," Morfad agreed. "And I know one of yours. So does the entire crew."

Haraka narrowed his eyes. "You might as well name it. I am not afraid to see myself as others see me."

"All right. You've asked for it. You think a lot of Kashim. He always has your ear. You will listen to him when you'll listen to nobody else. Everything he says makes sound sense—to you."

"So you're jealous of Kashim, eh?"

"Not in the least," assured Morfad, making a disparaging gesture. "I merely despise him for the same reason that everyone else holds him in contempt. He is a professional toady. He spends most of his time fawning upon you, flattering you, pandering to your ego. He is a natural-born creeper who gives you the Terradog treatment. You like it. You bask in it. It affects you like an irresistible drug. It works —and don't tell me that it doesn't because all of us know that it *does*."

"I am not a fool. I have Kashim sized up. He does not influence me to the extent you believe."

"Three thousand million Terrans have four hundred million dogs sized up and are equally convinced that no dog has a say in anything worth a hoot."

"I don't believe it."

"Of course you don't. I had little hope that you would. Morfad is telling you these things and Morfad is either crazy or a liar. But if Kashim were to tell you while prostrate at the foot of your throne you would swallow his story hook, line and sinker. Kashim has a Terradog mind and uses Terradog logic, see?"

"My disbelief has better basis than that."

"For instance?" Morfad invited.

"Some Terrans are telepathic. Therefore if this myth of subtle mastery by dogs were a fact, they'd know of it. Not a dog would be left alive on this world." Haraka paused, finished pointedly, "They don't know of it."

"Terran telepaths hear the minds of their own kind but not those of dogs. I hear the minds of dogs but not those of any other kind. As said before, I don't know why this should be. I know only that it *is*."

"It seems nonsensical to me."

"It would. I suppose you can't be blamed for taking that viewpoint. My position is difficult; I'm like the only one with ears in a world that is stone-deaf."

Haraka thought it over, said after a while, "Suppose I were to accept everything you've said at face value—what do you think I should do about it?"

"Refuse to take the dogs," responded Morfad, promptly.

"That's more easily said than done. Good relations with the Terrans are vitally important. How can I reject a warm-hearted gift without offending the givers?"

"All right, don't reject it. Modify it instead. Ask for two male or two female dogs. Make it plausible by quoting an Altairan law against the importation of alien animals that are capable of natural increase."

"I can't do that. It's far too late. We've already accepted the animals and expressed our gratitude for them. Besides, their ability to breed is an essential part of the gift, the basic intention of the givers. They've presented us with a new species, an entire race of dogs."

"You said it!" confirmed Morfad.

"For the same reason we can't very well prevent them from breeding when we get back home," Haraka pointed out. "From now on we and the Terrans are going to do a lot of visiting. Immediately they discover that our dogs have failed to multiply they'll become generous and sentimental and dump another dozen on us. Or maybe a hundred. We'll then be worse off than we were before."

"All right, all right." Morfad shrugged with weary resignation. "If you're going to concoct a major objection to every possible solution we may as well surrender without a fight. Let's abandon ourselves to becoming yet another dog-dominated species. Requote: to rule successfully the ruled must be unconscious of it." He gave Haraka the sour eye. "If I had my way, I'd wait until we were far out in free space and then give those two dogs the hearty heave-ho out the hatch."

Haraka grinned in the manner of one about to nail down a cock-eyed tale once and for all. "And if you did that it would be proof positive beyond all argument that you're afflicted with a delusion."

Emitting a deep sigh, Morfad asked, "Why would it?"

"You'd be slinging out two prime members of the master race. Some domination, eh?" Haraka grinned again. "Listen, Morfad, according to your own story you know something never before known or suspected and you're the only one who does know it. That should make you a mighty menace to the entire species of dogs. They wouldn't let you live long enough to thwart them or even to go round advertising the truth. You'd soon be deader than a low-strata fossil." He walked to the door, held it open while he made his parting shot. "You look healthy enough to me."

Morfad shouted at the closing door, "Doesn't follow that because I can hear their thoughts they must necessarily hear mine. I doubt that they can because it's just a freakish—"

The door clicked shut. He scowled at it, walked twenty times up and down the cabin, finally resumed his chair and sat in silence while he beat his brains around in search of a satisfactory solution.

"The sharpest, most subtle, most effective weapon in the cosmos is flattery."

Yes, he was seeking a means of coping with four-footed warriors incredibly skilled in the use of Creation's sharpest weapon. Professional fawners, creepers, worshipers, man-lovers, ego-boosters, trained to near-perfection through countless generations in an art against which there seemed no decisive defense.

How to beat off the coming attack, contain it, counter it?

"Yes, God!"

"Certainly, God!"

"Anything you say, God!"

How to protect oneself against this insidious technique, how to quarantine it or—

By the stars! that was it—*quarantine* them! On Pladamine, the useless world, the planet nobody wanted. They could breed there to their limits and meanwhile dominate the herbs and bugs. And a soothing reply would be ready for any nosey Terran tourist.

"The dogs? Oh, sure, we've still got them, lots of them. They're doing fine. Got a nice world of their very own. Place called Pladamine. If you wish to go see them, it can be arranged."

A wonderful idea. It would solve the problem while creating no hard feelings among the Terrans. It would prove useful in the future and to the end of time. Once planted on Pladamine no dog could ever escape by its own efforts. Any tourists from Terra who brought dogs along could be persuaded to leave them in the canine heaven specially created by Altair. There the dogs would find themselves unable to boss anything higher than other dogs, and, if they didn't like it, they could lump it.

No use putting the scheme to Haraka who was obviously prejudiced. He'd save it for the authorities back home. Even if they found it hard to credit his story, they'd still take the necessary action on the principle that it is better to be sure than sorry. Yes, they'd play safe and give Pladamine to the dogs.

Standing on a cabin seat, he gazed out and down through the port. A great mob of Terrans, far below, waited to witness the coming take-off and cheer them on their way. He noticed beyond the back of the crowd a small, absurdly groomed dog dragging a Terran female at the end of a thin, light chain. Poor girl, he thought. The dog leads, she follows yet believes *she* is taking *it* some place.

Finding his color-camera, he checked its controls, walked along the corridor and into the open air lock. It would be nice to have a picture of the big send-off audience. Reaching the rim of the lock he tripped headlong over something four-legged and stubby-tailed, that suddenly intruded itself between his feet. He dived outward, the camera still in his grip, and went down fast through the whistling wind while shrill feminine screams came from among the watching crowd.

Haraka said, "The funeral has delayed us two days. We'll have to make up the time as best we can." He brooded a moment, added, "I am very sorry about Morfad. He had a brilliant mind but it was breaking up toward the end. Oh well, it's a comfort that the expedition has suffered only one fatality."

"It could have been worse, sir," responded Kashim. "It could have been you. Praise the heavens that it was not."

"Yes, it could have been me." Haraka regarded him curiously. "And would it have grieved you, Kashim?"

"Very much indeed, sir. I don't think anyone aboard would feel the loss more deeply. My respect and admiration are such that—"

He ceased as something padded softly into the cabin, laid its head in Haraka's lap, gazed soulfully up at the captain. Kashim frowned with annoyance.

"Good boy!" approved Haraka, scratching the newcomer's ears.

"My respect and admiration," repeated Kashim in louder tones, "are such that—"

"Good boy!" said Haraka again. He gently pulled one ear, then the other, observed with pleasure the vibrating tail.

"As I was saying, sir, my respect—"

"Good boy!" Deaf to all else, Haraka slid a hand down from the ears and massaged under the jaw.

Kashim favored Good Boy with a glare of unutterable hatred. The dog rolled a brown eye sidewise and looked at him without expression. From that moment Kashim's fate was sealed.

Nor

Dust

Corrupt

by JAMES MCCONNELL

The room seemed more a mausoleum than an office, but that was as
had been intended. Perhaps thirty feet high, fifty feet wide, it
stretched a good hundred feet in length. It was paneled entirely in
jet black onyx, which gave a sense of infinity to it. The floor was a
thick lawn of heavy black pile carpeting. Only two areas of the
room offered mitigation to this oppressive gloom. Just past the middle, bathed in a haze of light, was placed a large black desk, and
behind it sat a man. At the far end of the room, slightly elevated,
was an alabaster statue, an abstraction of incredible beauty and
poignancy. The statue too was wrapped in a soft nimbus. Few visitors
to this room ever had to be told the title of this work of art, for its
meaning was apparent in its every line—*Bereavement*.

The man behind the big black desk belonged to the room as much
as did the onyx walls, the thick carpet or the alabaster statue. Without the presence of this man the chamber seemed strangely empty,
strangely morbid, and few of the man's associates cared to remain
in the room when he was not there. Somehow the warm air of
benevolence to be found in his fair, pinkish face softened the harsh
somberness of the appointments, while the gentle strength in his
dark and mournful eyes gave amelioration to the atmosphere of

despair. His job was to be a Janus, looking from the cheery rubric of today towards the unknown but dimmer colors of tomorrow—to be a bridge between present pleasures and future fears. There was no better man for the task in all the Galaxy than Consolator Steen.

At the moment Consolator Steen sat waiting, thinking, planning. Soon through the huge doors facing him would come a man, one Joseph Krieg by name, who sought Steen's assistance. The fact that Krieg was one of the richest men in all the known universe made the impending interview a most important one, for Consolator Steen's assistance depended entirely upon the price that could be paid.

Steen's fingers flicked over the set of hidden controls on his desk. Everything was in readiness. "And another innocent fish gets hooked," he muttered to himself. He sighed once, shortly, then touched an invisible button. "I will see Joseph Krieg now." In the outer office Steen's aide-de-camp, Assistant Consolator Braun, sprang to an attitude of proper deference as the huge bronze doors swung open. Braun bowed slightly as Joseph Krieg strode past him and into the onyx chamber.

Steen's eyes narrowed in admiration as he examined the man walking towards him. Joseph Krieg was a huge person, just past middle age but still retaining the hardened appearance of late youth. His face had a chiseled squareness to it, and his manner indicated not so much wealth as it did an obvious determination to succeed. This would be an interesting fish to play with indeed, Steen thought.

About half-way to the desk Krieg stumbled slightly, but recovered his pace with the cumbersome grace of some massive animal. A smile flickered briefly over Steen's face. The thickness of the carpet had more purposes than one. When Krieg was almost upon him, Steen stood up.

Krieg stopped in front of the desk, facing Steen, as if waiting for some signal. Steen, who knew the value of silence, remained absolutely still. After a few seconds, obviously perplexed, Krieg smiled nervously. "Consolator Steen?"

"Welcome to Earth, Joseph Krieg. Welcome to the Heart of the Galaxy." Steen's voice was rich, mellifluous, and the words fell from his mouth like benedictions. He extended a hand. "Won't you please be seated?"

The chair received Krieg's body as if it were the most precious burden it had ever held. Its soft contours almost demanded that he relax, yield the tenseness of his muscles to its smooth and welcoming shape. Its surface closed around him as if it were a second skin, then began to tingle in gentle caress. Joseph Krieg had never felt so comforted in his life.

Consolator Steen seated himself behind his desk, then waited until his assistant, Braun, had taken a chair some feet away. He smiled paternally. "May I ask you one favor? Would it seem presumptuous if I called you Joseph? Perhaps you would feel it an impertinence on my part, but . . ." Consolator Steen gestured slightly with both his hands, as if to implore forgiveness.

Joseph Krieg smiled, nodded his head. "Of course I won't mind if you use my first name. It would be an honor, Sir." The smile continued on his face, but his eyes narrowed as if he were attempting to puzzle out the figure behind the desk.

"You will excuse me too if I say that you've come too soon, Joseph," the Consolator said.

"Too soon?" Krieg replied quizzically. "I don't think I . . ."

Steen smiled warmly. "I only mean that you look still so young, so strong and vibrant with life. And yet, perhaps you are the wiser to come now, still in the vigor of living. It shows an honesty with yourself, an ability to face the facts, which is much to be admired."

"Thank you, Sir," Krieg replied. He continued to stare at the Consolator.

Steen knew full well the turmoil that was stirring within the man. The entire interview had been psychologically planned to evoke dark and dormant emotions which, when released, would destroy Krieg's normal ability to judge situations impassively. Proof that things were going as intended came from Krieg's continual use of the word "Sir." Krieg's commercial empires spanned the Universe; from perfume to starships, from food to fertilizers, he was king. And yet he would never understand that it was Steen's quiet paternal power, the fact that he wore wise sorrow wrapped around him the way some men wear a cloak, that called forth this unfamiliar reverence. The psychological survey done on Krieg had cost the Consolator a small fortune, and he didn't intend to waste it.

"You must realize, Joseph, that the things which you have come to discuss are matters of the deepest concern for all of us here on Earth." Steen gesticulated towards Braun as if Braun represented somehow all the other billions on Earth. "The problem is one that touches deep within all of us, and we are anxious to be of whatever service possible. But more than anything else, we want you to know that we *understand*."

"Thank you, Sir," Krieg repeated. He frowned for a moment, then seemed to smile. "But if you don't mind, maybe we could begin our discussion of terms."

Steen raised one eyebrow slightly. The man showed a remarkable lack of sentimentality. Corrections would have to be made in the approach . . .

"Of course. I am delighted to get on with things. And I must say, I find your attitude extraordinarily sane. The problem is, really, a simple one best met head on. You are here because you know that as it comes to all men, death must come to you too. And you feel the necessity to make certain that when your time comes, you will be brought to Earth to your final rest. You are a son of Earth. This is your great ancestral home."

Krieg started slightly, then relaxed almost in reverie. Steen smiled inwardly at the power of words, repeated, to invoke long forgotten memories. For Steen knew that when Krieg had been no more than a toddling child, learning to read, learning to respond to affection, his simple-syllabled books had spoken in reverent tones of "The Great Ancestral Home." In later years, all of Krieg's studies had had hidden at their core an emotional dependence upon Earth. No place was finer, more beautiful, more important. No, not all the rest of the stars put together. He had been told it a million times until it had become an inseparable part of his very personality, just so the words would have the desired effect at this moment. *The Great Ancestral Home.*

"You are so fortunate, my son," the Consolator continued. "So very few of Earth's teeming children will ever have the opportunity that lies within your grasp. You must make the most of it."

As Steen watched, Krieg seemed to shake some of the feeling of awe from him. "I intend to make the most of it, Sir," he said, offering Steen his most charming smile. "It just depends on how hard a bargain you want to drive."

Consolator Steen gave Krieg a look of mild reproach. "There is no 'bargaining' to be done, Joseph. The monetary considerations are set by law, and we have no choice in the matter. All that we can do is to explain the services which we are prepared to extend to you, and then help you as best we can to arrive at the most suitable decision. Our position is simply that of catering to your individual wants as best we can."

"My wants are simple," Krieg replied, and it seemed to Steen that far too much of the man's usual forcefulness was returning to his voice. "I wish to be buried on Earth when I die, and I want you to arrange this for me."

"Of course, of course, my son," Steen said, letting just a glint of steel appear in his eyes. "But what do we mean by burial? We have such different problems here on Earth than you do elsewhere in the Galaxy. You must understand that. We are forced to such strange solutions to these problems. But perhaps if I merely show you the various types of burial which we undertake, then you will understand." Steen laughed to himself. The fish appeared fat and hungry, and now it was time to drop in the bait.

The Consolator touched a hidden switch atop his desk and one of the black onyx walls rippled and seemed to dissolve in mist. A replica of Earth swam through the haze and into view. "Earth. Such an incredibly small planet, Joseph. But the heart of the Galaxy none the less." The replica seemed to swell in size and geographical details became apparent. "Earth. Once a world of gentle, rolling plains, winding rivers, thick forests, wide oceans and soaring mountains. Just like any other habitable planet. And now look at it. One solid mass of buildings and machines, Joseph. We've drained the oceans and filled in their beds with metal. We've destroyed the forests and the rolling plains and planted the land for miles above and below with throbbing inorganic monsters. We've hollowed out the very mountains to make more space. Space for nine hundred billion people, Joseph. And still we are cramped almost beyond belief. We need to expand a hundredfold. But we cannot. There simply is no room left.

"No room for the living, Joseph, and this means no more room for the dead, either. Here, let me show you." The scene changed, showing first a huge building, and then, the bottom floor of the edifice. "This is one of our larger buildings, Joseph. It is more than fifty miles long and one hundred miles wide. The bottom floor alone is more than one quarter mile high. This huge space is completely filled with cubes two inches square. Each cube holds the ashes of one human being who wished to find his final resting place on Earth."

Consolator Steen made a motion of resignation. "Notice that I said 'on Earth,' Joseph, and not 'in Earth.' This is our 'pauper's field,' the burial ground of those devoted souls who could not afford to be buried *in* the Earth itself."

Joseph Krieg frowned. "But surely underneath the building . . ."

"Underneath the bottom floor of that building are the bodies of many millions more, Joseph, just as there are bodies under all of our buildings. Bodies of those wealthy few who could afford to escape cremation and find surcease of life in the loamy substance of the Earth itself. I shudder to tell you how tightly packed they are, of the skin-tight coffins which we had to devise, of the geometrical tricks involved in jamming as many bodies as possible in the least amount of space. And yet, it *is* burial, and it is *in* the Earth itself. No granite monuments, of course, no vases of flowers, no green grass. Just a perpetual flame burning in the main lobby of the building, and a micro-film file available somewhere listing the vital statistics of all those souls whose remains lie in the basement—or below."

Krieg's face was furrowed with a heavy frown. Steen's words had been as shocking to the man as Steen had hoped they would be. "But the Parks . . ."

"Ah, yes, Joseph. The Parks . . ." Consolator Steen leaned forward slightly. The fish was sniffing at the bait quite properly now. "Our Parks, which are the one remaining link with the past. Those green and grassy meadows in the midst of our metallic forests. The last places on Earth where you can be buried out in the open, with flowers over your head and birds singing above. You want to be buried in one of the Parks, don't you Joseph?" When the man nodded briefly, Steen continued. "Which Park, Joseph?"

"Manhattan . . ."

Steen drew himself up with a sudden, silent movement. The fish had taken a good look at the bait. Now to remove it from sight for a while. Steen closed his eyes briefly, then raised a hand as if to brush away a sudden tear. "I'm sorry, Joe. Very sorry indeed. I was afraid that was what you wanted, and yet, there was always . . ." He blinked his eyes. "Manhattan Park is impossible, Joe. Confucius Park in Hong Kong, perhaps. I think there are still some plots available in Frogner Park in Oslo. I'm certain that we could get you into Amundsen Park at the South Pole. But Manhattan . . . No, Joe. That's one dream I'm afraid you'll just have to give up."

"Why?" Joseph Krieg asked quietly but determinedly.

"Have you ever seen it, Joe? I thought not. It's perhaps the most beautiful part of this most beautiful planet in the Galaxy. Would you like to see Manhattan?"

Manhattan. Steen was quite aware that to Joseph Krieg this was a word of a hundred thousand associations, each of them connected with love, security, devotion and repose. It was like asking a starving man if he would care for something to eat.

Steen did not even wait for a reply. "I think it could be managed,

as a special favor. Permission to enter Manhattan Park is difficult
to get, you know, but I think this once . . ." Steen turned to Braun.
"Put a call through to the President's office . . ."

Atop grassy knolls, supple willows trailed languid branches to
the ground. Silver-throated birds sang secret melodies while bees
hummed a scarcely audible background. Narrow graveled paths
wound through this gentle landscape, now hugging the edge of a
tinkling stream, now plunging through carpets of gorgeous flowers.
The three men sat silent on a rough stone bench observing the pas-
toral scene.

Finally Consolator Steen spoke softly. "I understand how you feel,
Joe. The first time any of us see it, we are afflicted with silence. Its
beauty is almost painful, the memories it invokes almost beyond
bearing. Lincoln is buried there, just beyond that hillock; Landow-
ski not far from him. Shakespeare's grave is there to the right, and
close by is the body of Sharon, the poet of the Galaxy. Einstein's
final resting place is a mile or so away, and near to it you'll find Chi
Wan, who gave us Stardrive. Humanity's Valhalla, Joe."

Joseph Krieg had not cried openly since childhood, and yet now
there were tears in his eyes. "This has always been my dream . . ."

Consolator Steen placed a friendly arm around the man's shoulders. "Yes, now you have seen it. Your dream has come true." He
paused for just a moment, then said, "And now, Joe, perhaps we had
better go."

Joseph Krieg turned towards the man with an abrupt motion. "Go?
Why should we go? We've been here scarcely ten minutes."

"Because the longer you stay, the harder it will be for you to leave,
Joe. And the less attractive the other parks will seem to you. So,
I'd like for us to leave at once." His voice became businesslike.
"First, I'd like to show you Hong Kong, and then . . ."

"I don't want to see Hong Kong, or any place else. This is where I
want to be buried, Steen. Whatever the price is, I'll pay."

Consolator Steen sighed deeply. "I don't think you understand,
Joe. It isn't a matter of price. Manhattan is simply not available to
you, for the reason that it is not for sale. I know that you have heard
otherwise; I am sure that rumors have reached your ears that burial
in Manhattan could be effected for a mere trillion credits. But these
fantastic tales are incorrect—for two reasons.

"The first reason, Joe, is a financial one. To the average man, a
mere million credits is such a gigantic, unobtainable sum that he is

sure anything in the Galaxy could be obtained for a trillion. This is not so, as you and I both know. Why, a million credits will scarcely get you a burial in a two-inch-square cube in the bottom floor of one of our huge buildings. Remember? I called those huge bargain basements 'pauper's fields.' And that they are—available to those poor people throughout the Universe who have only a few millions to their names. Incredible, isn't it?

"A trillion credits? Why, it takes a hundred billion to make you eligible for burial *under* one of the buildings, where you're packed in like a sardine with millions of other bodies. And how many people in the Galaxy can lay their hands on a hundred billion credits? The answer, Joe, is too many people indeed. Some of them have so much more money than that, they can actually afford to be buried in one of the Parks.

"A trillion credits? Yes, that will get you buried in Hong Kong Park, or in Frogner, or Amundsen. But not for long. You can rent a temporary grave in Hong Kong, for example, for a mere billion credits a day. At that rate, for a trillion credits, you'd stay buried on Earth for less than three years, and then your body would have to be moved elsewhere. Very few people can afford to purchase a permanent plot in one of these parks. But they are available—at a cost of something like one quadrillion credits. And just how many men in the Galaxy *have* a quadrillion credits or so?"

Consolator Steen knew the answer to this question exactly—he also knew that Joseph Krieg was one of these men. Krieg could have afforded a quadrillion credits, but it would have exhausted his fortune. Steen waited until he was sure that the other man was deep in mental turmoil and then he continued, his voice now softer, less commercial sounding. "And having given you 'the prices,' so to speak, of the lesser treasures, I will now surprise you by saying that the entry ticket to Manhattan Park is free."

Joseph Krieg looked at the man intently, a curious fire of hope in his eyes. "Free?"

Steen nodded. "And because it is free, it is unobtainable. It is not generally known, Joe, but the only way one can be buried in Manhattan Park is by permission of the Galactic Congress. Only certified heroes are so honored, and they are few and far between. Remember the great bacteriologist Manuel de Artega? It took the Galactic Congress more than fifty years of debate after he died to decide to let him in—but after all, the only claim to fame he had was that he saved a few trillion lives from the Green Plague. He was buried here some thirteen years ago. There has been no one since, and no one in sight."

Steen patted the man on the shoulder. "Now, come along, Joe. I want you to take a look at Amundsen Park before you make up your mind. It's not at all cold at the Pole these days—lovely flowers, trees . . ."

"No!" Joseph Krieg cried, standing up. Steen and Braun both rose too. "There must be a way!"

The Consolator smiled inwardly. *The fish was responding magnificently. Now to push the bait just a little closer* . . .

"Now, now, Joe. You mustn't get upset about this. The other Parks are just as fine, I assure you," Steen murmured in consolation.

Krieg shook his head. "You can't tell me that sometime or other someone didn't buy his way into Manhattan. It stands to reason . . ."

"Now, Joe. You're taking this much too hard . . ."

"I tell you, I know people. And that's all the Galactic Congress is made up of—people. Tell me the truth, Steen. Has anyone ever bribed his way into this Park?"

Steen frowned and turned his head slightly away from the man. *Just a flick or two more of the line* . . .

"I wish you wouldn't ask me questions like that, Joe. When I say that it's impossible, I mean just that. You'll just excite yourself needlessly by listening to foolish rumors . . ."

Krieg pounced on the word jubilantly. "What do you mean, rumors? Then there *has* been someone who bought his way in! Who was it, Steen? I swear, if you don't tell me, I'll move heaven and earth to find out."

Consolator Steen seemed to consider for a moment, then sighed. *Hooked.* "All right, Joe. But believe me, you'll wish you hadn't asked. For what happened to . . . to this other person is unattainable to you."

"Who was it?" Krieg asked excitedly.

"Who was the richest man who ever lived, Joe?"

"You mean . . ."

"Who was it that founded the University you went to, the hospital in which you were born? Who gave a magnificent library to every city in the known universe, who was it . . ."

Krieg interrupted. "Old C. T. himself . . ."

Steen nodded. "Yes, old C. T. Anderman himself. Years ago, Joe, he faced the same problem you face now, and he reacted the same way you have. So he set out on a campaign to get into Manhattan the only way he knew how—with money. There was one difference, Joe. Where you are fabulously wealthy, C. T. Anderman was wealthy beyond all dreams. Do you know that he gave away more than one quintillion credits—*gave it away!* Just to make his name universally known. 'The Philanthropist of the Galaxy,' they called him. One quintillion credits! No wonder they voted him a hero's grave. But what the press and the public never knew is that it cost him more than twice that much—for he had to spend another one quintillion credits for bribes and influence. It took him fifty years, Joe, to pack the Galactic Congress with enough of his men to swing the trick. But he finally did it."

There was a short silence, then Steen continued. "Now you see why I didn't want to tell you, Joe—to raise false hopes. Only one man in the Galaxy was ever wealthy enough to buy his way into Manhattan. And he had to give up his entire fortune to do it. I'm afraid that you'll never make the grade, Joe."

Krieg stood stunned. Steen was aware that two quintillion credits was beyond Krieg's wildest dreams, for Steen knew that Joseph Krieg had come to Earth determined to purchase his burial lot and then retire from the business world.

Steen pulled lightly at Krieg's arm. "Now, come along, Joe. Let's go take a look at Hong Kong." The three men started off down the path, but before they had gone ten feet, a robot scurried out of the bushes and dashed over to the bench they had been sitting on. It clucked softly to itself, put forth several arms, and in a matter of seconds had completely washed and disinfected the bench.

Joseph Krieg, an empty and numb look on his face, stopped to watch the process. He stared for a few seconds, then asked hoarsely, "What's that?"

Consolator Steen smiled. "One of the Guardians, Joe. Superb—and completely incorruptible. Within minutes after we leave, every vestige of our visit will be gone—each piece of gravel we tread on will be scrubbed clean or replaced, each piece of grass we touch uprooted and destroyed, even the very air we breathe will be sterilized to remove our traces. We have our problem of vandals too, you know," Steen said, a wisp of a smile playing about the corners of his mouth. "But these are vandals who want to get in and leave something, not like those of ancient times on Earth who broke into burial grounds to loot and destroy. Yes, Joe, we found long ago that the only safe method was to employ mechanical devices to guard against clandestine burials. So even the gardeners who keep this Park in blossom are mechanical. See, there's another one over there, hard at work."

Joseph Krieg turned and saw to one side, by a large bed of red flowers, another robot with dozens of visible appendages. It purred an almost silent tune as it clipped and pruned, dug and spaded, trimmed and cleaned the beds, occasionally sprinkling a rich fertilizer dust here and there.

"The Guardians of Valhalla, Joe. They were set into motion centuries ago, and not even the President knows how to change their orders. They can't be bribed, even if their human masters can be."

Joseph Krieg stooped down beside the bed of flowers. He reached out and picked up a handful of the fine dirt and let it slip pensively through his fingers. "Dust unto dust," he said slowly. "Man was created from the soil of Earth, and to dust he returneth." There was a long silence as Steen let the emotion run its course. Then he touched Krieg lightly on the arm and the man stood up again. They started off down the path, ignoring the machine that skittered along behind them, cleansing each bit of gravel they stepped upon.

To Steen, this was always the most important part of the interview. While the fish was masticating the bait, he had to prattle on to keep the hook from becoming too visible. "Some day I must tell you of all the ways people have tried to get themselves buried on Earth without paying for the privilege, Joe. It makes a fascinating story. We're in a difficult position here, you know, for we have to import every single bit of food we eat, every machine we use, each piece of clothing that we wear. But every single item that we import is carefully scanned to make sure that no one has concealed so much as a single human hair in the process." Steen watched Krieg's face closely as they walked. The man should be going through hell just now, but not too much of it showed on his face. Steen continued his prattle, a little puzzled.

"Oh, it's incredible the ways that people have tried to cheat. Some of the methods used are too ugly to relate, some of them humorous beyond belief. But this is why we've resorted to mechanical guards all the way round—to maintain our incorruptibility. Even Anderman with all of his quintillions could not have bribed his way past our machines." Steen's voice betrayed none of the anxiety that he felt. For Joseph Krieg was almost smiling now, was apparently feeling none of the great confusion that Steen had counted upon.

They reached the gates. "Well, Joe. I think we'll head straight for

Hong Kong, if you don't mind. It will be early morning there by now, and that's the best time . . ."

Joseph Krieg turned to face the man. "Thank you very much, Consolator, but I don't think that will be necessary. You see, I've changed my mind."

Steen repressed a frown. "Changed your mind?" he asked blandly.

"Yes. After giving it due consideration, I think that it would be foolish to squander all of my fortune on a burial on Earth. My family would be cheated out of its inheritance if I did, and after all, if my sons carry on in their father's tradition, that's enough for me." Krieg extended his hand. "I wish to thank you, Steen, for your kindness. I regret that I have troubled you for nothing."

Steen shook the man's hand warmly, using his free hand to grasp Krieg's arm in friendly fashion. "It was no trouble at all, I assure you. But please understand, Joseph, if I can ever be of service to you in *any* way, if I can ever be of assistance in any manner whatsoever, please do not hesitate to call upon me. After all, even Anderman had certain problems which . . ." Steen smiled knowingly.

Krieg returned the smile. "I think I understand. And I appreciate your offer, although I must tell you that there is little likelihood that I will be forced to take it up. Again my thanks. And now, good-bye." Krieg turned and strode through the gates.

Consolator Steen and his assistant, Braun, stood watching the man as he disappeared into the distance. Then Steen turned and walked over to one of the benches in the Park near to the gates. He sat down wearily.

"Braun," he said, "I don't like it. Not at all. He should have been beside himself with worry, he should have pumped me for more information, he should have done a thousand other things. But he didn't. He just turned and left. I tell you, I don't like it at all."

Braun frowned. "He seemed to take the bait, Sir."

"And then, after sniffing it over carefully, he turned and spat it right back in our faces. We can't afford mistakes like this, Braun. Earth needs the money too badly. It's our only means of support, and we can't let a fish like Krieg get off the hook."

"There are other fish around, Sir."

Steen's face took on an angry look. "Of course there are. But none with the potentialities that Krieg showed. Don't you realize that ever since that sad day when Earth realized that she was a has-been, she's had to take advantage of every single opportunity offered her, just to keep alive? Oh, they were clever, those ancient ones who realized that if a civilization is to be kept together, it must have a myth. And so they gave our civilization its myth—that of Earth, the Great Ancestral Home. Just accidentally, it also offered Earth a means of retaining at least a part of her power."

Steen waved his hands in the air. "From an economic viewpoint it was nice too. Only the very wealthy could afford an Earth burial, and so it became a means of hidden, graduated taxation—Earth soaked the rich and ignored the poor, and cut her overt taxes while doing so. Burial became so costly that it helped break up the huge estates, it helped leaven out the wealth. Our propaganda was sharpened to the point where we could take a man like Anderman and drive him all of his life towards an almost unattainable goal, force him to expend his tremendous energies in the accumulation of great wealth, extending the frontiers of the Galaxy as he did so, building up our civilization's strength in the process, and then, in the end, make him turn all of his wealth over to Earth in one form or another. Oh, I tell you, Braun, those ancient ones were clever."

The tirade halted. The air hung silent for a moment, and the twittering of a near-by bird could be heard.

"They were very, very clever. They gave us all the tools, and somehow we've failed to use them correctly. What was it, Braun? What did we do, or fail to do, that let Krieg get away from us?"

Braun frowned. "I don't know, Sir. Perhaps he just changed his mind about Earth."

Steen snorted. "Impossible! He's had too many years' exposure to our propaganda for that. He can no more give up his dream of burial in Manhattan than he can give up his very personality. No, Braun, I think we just underestimated the man. Somewhere along the line he had an idea, he saw something that we failed to see.

Braun shrugged his shoulders. "But what are we going to do about it?"

Consolator Steen pursed his lips. "I tell you what I'm going to do about it. I'm going straight back to the office and sit and think, and think, and then think some more. Krieg's got a good fifty years ahead of him yet, and that means I've got exactly that long to guess what's on his mind. I'll get that quintillion credits if it's the last thing I do."

They had no more than reached the gate when one of the mechanical Guardians appeared from behind a bush, chortled to itself and scurried over to the bench. It cleansed the rough-hewn stone, then washed the path the two men had taken. Then, its exceptional chores accomplished, it went back to its normal pursuits.

It approached a bed of begonias nearby. One appendage extended itself and began digging up the dirt around the plants. Meanwhile, inside the machine, other appendages ripped open a small bag and spilled the fine dust inside the bag into a small trough. The empty bag was rolled up and stuck in a disposal bin along with several other bags, all with identical markings:

JOSEPH KRIEG AND SONS,
BY APPOINTMENT,
PURVEYORS OF FINE FERTILIZERS
TO THE GALACTIC GOVERNMENT ON EARTH

The machine clucked quietly to itself as it sprinkled the dust evenly over the black, yielding earth. It patted the fertilizer gently into the rich soil, making sure that each plant got its fair share. Then it scurried off silently to tend to a bed of calla lilies nearby.

Nightsound

by ALGIS J. BUDRYS

The heavy oak-veneer desk in the attic had been the family catch-all for years. The pigeonholes under the jammed rolltop were crammed with unimportant letters, receipted bills, circulars from the Department of Agriculture and all the other papers that might, someday, have become important but never had.

Now Sam Dundy's father was dead, collapsed over his last straight furrow, the tired heart finally pushed too far, and Sam was home from State College. There were arrangements to be made, the estate to be put in order, and his mother was unable to bring herself to it. Sunk within himself, his emotions numb, Sam had been doing the best he could.

He had gone through the main records, down in the dining room desk, but there still might be something up here in the attic that he ought to know about—some record of a loan, or an insurance policy, that would mean another debt left behind by his father, or—Sam knew how little hope there was in this—some money due the estate.

He pulled open the bottom drawer, and lifted off a bundle of brittle yellow newspapers. Under these was a worn book, with a cheap red binding that had become faded and splotched. The imitation gold stamping was flaked and half-gone. Sam picked up the book and squinted at the title page in the dim light coming through the attic window. The attic wasn't wired.

With dusk falling, he should have brought a flashlight. But he had been doing things like that for the past two days—moving in shock, forgetting things, making mistakes, falling into long periods of mental drifting while he stopped wherever he was and simply daydreamed.

The book was something called *Every Farmer's Home Cyclopedia of Simple Veterinary Science.* He'd never heard of it, but he wasn't surprised. It was the kind of book salesmen were continually selling on farms, for one dollar down and thirty-five cents a week for twenty weeks. He couldn't imagine his father spending the money, but, as he leafed through the pretentiously printed, cheap paper pages, he saw the heavy underlinings and notations in the margins, done in his father's hand with a pencil stub.

Sam looked at it, weighing it in his hand, slowly shaking his head. It was like handling a piece of the past—like knowing suddenly, without any doubt, exactly what was going on inside a man's head.

Here it was—the long-forgotten first sign of his father's resolve to have him go to veterinary school, perhaps the source of it. Sam looked at the sections that had drawn most of his father's attention.

A chapter on Animal Surgery had its pages smudged from what must have been incessant reading. Sitting in the near-dark, Sam had no trouble picturing his father, in the worn armchair under the standing lamp in the parlor, with the book in his lap and his blunt forefinger moving slowly under each line, his face set in a frown of concentration.

Lying on the table next to him would be the grammar school dictionary, most of its pages loose in the binding. At intervals, his father would hold his place with one finger while he leafed through the dictionary, either muttering the definition over and over until he had memorized it or else scowling in momentary anger when the dictionary failed to include the word that had puzzled him.

The annotations almost covered the type on some of the pages. In several places, there was a curt *Won't work.* Once or twice, he saw *Try it,* following an underscored paragraph, and he wondered what his father had been doing.

At the end of the chapter, his father had blocked in a characteristic comment—*Can't pay the price for the tools, anyway. Don't know enough to make some. Haven't got the brains to handle them right, if I did. Have to give this up and try something else.*

In the same way his father had talked to the plow and the water pump, his father had talked to the book.

Sam smiled in the dark. Every bit of work his father did was accompanied by a steady drive of short, declarative sentences. "Gotta lift you *over* that rock . . ." "Push this part *in* here . . ." "Gonna fence you *this* Fall . . ."

So here was the record of something else planned, possibly attempted and angrily abandoned, because there were too many things against its achievement.

At this thought, Sam's smile faded. His father's life had been over-full of such defeats. The old, hard-jawed man had fought his losing battle every step of the way, trying with strength and hard work and stubbornness to do what money would have accomplished.

Sam remembered his father's harsh snort. "If farmers had money, youngster, most of 'em wouldn't be farmers."

So here was another time his father hadn't been able to carry something through. It must have been a long time ago, because he couldn't remember it at all.

He closed the book and put it down on top of the newspapers. It would look strange, sitting on his bookshelf at college alongside the legitimate texts. But it would sit there, if he ever went back.

Sam looked down into the drawer. There was still something else in there, something that looked like a flat box in this light. He took it out, surprised to find that it was hard—not as cold as metal, but not as slickly smooth as plastic. He held it up to the fading light, but there was nothing to see except a faint seam, that marked off a lid, and a catch.

Frowning, he pushed at the little metal square, seeking to unfasten it as a pressure latch first, then trying to slide it open. It didn't work in either way. Finally, he found the hairline that divided it in two, and pushed in opposite ways. The latch opened, but, when he tried to lift the lid, it stayed locked. The catch had slipped back as soon as he let it go.

Annoyed at the designer, who seemed to have thought that people had three hands, he fumbled the lid up with his little fingers, while holding the catch open, and saw that the box was a portable radio.

He frowned at the three knobs, the dial, and the two-inch grill that were set into the surface of the box under the lid. The dial was glowing luminously, and he wondered what kind of paint had managed to store up light for so long. But he wondered more about the radio's being there at all.

There was an old Sears-Roebuck set downstairs, sitting in the parlor, with its veneer splitting from old age. But it played well enough to get the weather bulletins and the Farm and Home Hour. Why had his father spent the money on a late-model transistor set and hidden it away up here, in the attic?

He couldn't figure out what make it was, either. The dial was hard to read—it looked like some trick system, all symbols instead of numbers, which didn't make any sense at all. It might be a cheap Japanese set—something like that—from the looks of the symbols, but the Japs used regular American numbers on the ones they sold over here.

He tried to turn one of the knobs, and found that to do so required more strength than he had expected. It didn't seem to do anything, either. The next one moved the pointer on the dial. So the third one had to be the switch. He twisted it and felt the box begin to vibrate softly in his hands.

But nothing happened after he had waited a long minute, and he wondered if the first knob was a volume control that he had turned all the way down. He twisted it back toward its first position.

It had turned completely dark in the attic. There was still some light outside, but, toward the east, the stars were out, shining pure white in the purple-black sky.

There was a click as he reset the first knob.

Faraway, and thin, he heard: *"N'fera, n'feri, n'fero . . . n'fera, n'feri, n'fero .... d'anclaf, n'fera."*

There was a pause. And then, still far, still thin, but nearer, he heard the reply, in another voice as dry and rustling as the first had been soft and lilting. *"N'fera, socsim. Socsim. D'anclaf, n'feri."*

Something frightened him. He reached out and closed the radio's lid, and sat looking up at the distant stars, wondering what language he had heard . . .

He rapped softly on his mother's door, his face troubled. He didn't want to bother her, but he had to get the radio business settled. He frowned as he tried to think of how he was going to ask her. If she didn't know anything about it, he didn't want to upset her any more.

"Who is it?"

His mother's voice was nervous and apprehensive.

"It's Sammy, Mom," he said patiently, though there was no one else it could have been. "May I talk to you for a minute?"

"Oh—Sammy. I wasn't asleep yet—just dozing. Were you upstairs?"

"Up in the attic, Mom," he reminded her.

"Looking through the old desk? Did you find anything?" she asked.

"I don't know, for sure. May I come in and talk to you?" He knew that, if he didn't remind her, she'd forget what he wanted.

"Yes, of course, Sammy." He heard her bedclothes rustle, and opened the door. There was no light on, and he blinked as he made his way to her bed and sat down on the chair beside it. He took her hand.

"How are you, Mom?" he asked gently. He could see the paleness of her face in the dim light, and as his eyes slowly became accustomed to it, he saw that she was keeping her eyes closed. Her hand was limp in his, and her breathing was shallow.

"Pretty well," she replied wanly. The fingers of her left hand twisted at the edge of the comforter. "I think I'll be able to get to sleep all right tonight. Is everything all right on the farm?"

He nodded. "Everything's fine, Mom," he answered uncomfortably, remembering. "We've got to take good care of Annie," his father had often said, shaking his head angrily, with that frequent anger which came over him, and was coming over his son, now, at things he couldn't do anything about.

"I guess there's some women shouldn't ever have to farm," he had said slowly. "But what else can we do, boy? If a man's got a farm, he's got to work it. If a man's been a farmer all his life, he's got to stick with that. But you take care of her, if I can't. You're my hope, boy. You're the best hope I've got in this world."

"Did you find anything in the attic, Sammy?" his mother asked, forgetting again.

She hadn't been made for a life of never having enough, Sam thought to himself. She wasn't intended to live as she had had to for thirty years, out here in country where winter froze you for half the year, and the summer baked the blood out of your body. Just one child to help her, and that one not a daughter but a son to work with his father—working at the very thing that ground her life down flat, too, and not able to work enough to make it pay, no matter how little you slept, or how your arms and back ached. It couldn't be done. Two men couldn't make it pay—they could only drag enough out of the land so they could hang on, year after year, slipping downhill by inches.

But you had the land, and you were born to it, and what else could you do? You hung on, hoping for you didn't know what. Going to school, grudging every hour of time, but knowing there wasn't any way out at all, without the schooling. Going on to the State College, because, if you didn't, then it would be one more generation of Dundys that bled their life into the ground, hoping for something better for the next.

Six years at veterinary school, then, and two more to go, taking two semesters for every single semester's credits, because you had to work part-time for clothes and lodging and a little extra to send home.

Two years to go—Sam's lips tightened into a straight white line.

There wasn't any money to pay a hired man to work the farm. Even if there had been, no hired man—no two men—would sweat and stretch themselves as his father had.

"I don't know, Mom," he replied finally. He still didn't know how to go about asking her. He didn't even know what the radio's being in the desk could mean. But his father must have had some good reason for having it.

"Do you know if anybody ever left anything with Dad for safe-keeping?" he asked at last. "Tools, or equipment of some kind? Or maybe somebody paid off a loan by giving Dad something like a radio? Do you know if he ever did anything like that?"

"Did you find some papers?" His mother's hand tightened in his, and her voice grew with hope. "Does somebody owe Tom? Do you think it'll be enough so you can keep going to school?" Then her hand grew limp again.

"No," she whispered, "that couldn't be. There's no sense trying to wish something into being true."

She had been with Tom Dundy for thirty years, working beside him as much as she had it in her to, and more. She had drawn on faith in her man for strength, through all that time, and the habit was still there.

Sam didn't have any way of doing anything for her. But he found himself wishing that she didn't have enough hope in her to be weaker every time that it died.

"You don't remember Dad's having anything like that around the house, Mom?" he kept at her, sorry he had started and wanting to get it finished.

"No, Sammy, not ever."

"All right, Mom. I thought there might be something, but I guess I was wrong. I'll keep looking."

He slipped his hand free of hers, leaned forward and kissed her. "Good night, Mom. I'm pretty sure I can work something out."

"Good night, Sammy. Don't stay up too late."

He left her room quietly, closing the door softly behind him. You kept hoping, somehow—Tom Dundy had taught both of them that. It wasn't a blind thing. It was knowing, deep inside yourself, that a man's strength and a man's mind ought to be enough in this world, that, if you held out long enough, things had to turn your way. But it was hard, losing the man.

He and his mother had both lived with his father, following him, taking the way he picked. Now he was gone, and they were both lost for a while. But there'd be a way out. The world hadn't changed merely because one man was gone.

Sam came into his own room and looked at the radio on the dresser . . .

The crops grew, and the rain came down. There was always food growing, always a roof to live under. They were strong factors—permanent things that were rooted in more than one man's life. It was just that these factors didn't seem useful any longer.

Why had his father had that radio? Sam went to it and opened it without knowing exactly why, except that he was trying to find something to do.

Far away—farther than the first voices he'd heard—there was a burst of crystalline chiming, and a fainter answer. He twisted the stiff dial, moving down the band, and whisps of voices grew to clarity, faded, and were gone again. *reinni ser*—. . . . *grut tagat vol*

"*Ssthethannn . . . flahmit somahal . . . dundi, wat*—"

His fingers froze.

"Dundy! *Dundy!*" The voice was harsh and deep, like no voice he had ever heard speaking English before. "Dundy, answer me, please! What's happened to you?"

Somewhere, among those people who spoke along these bandwidths, someone else was lost and uncertain because Tom Dundy was dead . . .

It was late at night, but Sam didn't look at his watch to check the time. For several hours, now, he had been sitting on the edge of his bed, listening to the radio calling his father's name at intervals, in a voice that sounded like the note of some heavy machine crushing out a tunnel in the rock far underground.

Of all the people in the world, if you knew anybody, you knew your parents. You knew the sound and mood of every kind of footstep they could take, the meaning of every cough that cleared their throats before they spoke to you. You knew the touch of their hands and the rustle of their clothes.

He tried to picture his father, sitting and listening to that voice—answering it somehow—but he couldn't. Nothing he knew or remembered was any help to him.

His father was a man who had kept much to himself. If he had wanted to talk to somebody over that radio, without letting anybody know about it, there was always time during the day when he could have used it in privacy. But Sam couldn't think of any reason for his doing it.

He remembered something his father had told him once—"Youngster, it's no good talking about something you're doing. If it works out, then you got something better to talk about. If it don't, nobody knows you've been a damn fool but you."

That would explain his father's not telling him. But it didn't explain what the radio was all about.

It might have been going on for years. His father had seen too many seasons come and go and come back again, to act for tomorrow, or next month.

"Son, how about you going off to vet school up at State College? Seems to me we could swing it."

He remembered that with absolute clarity. His father, twelve years ago, had turned to him at supper one night and said it, with the idea thought over in his head for nobody knew how long beforehand.

"State pays for your schooling—no trouble there. Be a little tight, with clothes and food to pay for, and us missing your help here, but it's worth it."

It was. It was worth the extra work his father had to go back to doing, an older man than the one he had been before Sam could do a man's work. A veterinary didn't have to kill himself over a plow for his food and his roof. A veterinary's mother could live in a house in town, with no more chores to do, and a veterinary's wife wouldn't dry up and grow into a thin, pale woman with creases in her forehead and the skin chapping on her hands until it cracked open.

So now Sam was three-quarters of the way to being a graduate veterinary. And Tom Dundy had killed himself to get him there. That had been twelve years in the planning.

Sam raised his head. The voice on the radio was saying something else.

"I know someone is listening. I repeat—I know someone is listening to me. It is imperative that anyone connected with Thomas Dundy of Minnesota reply to this message." The voice was still heavy, still deep, but now it was desperate.

Sam didn't move. He wasn't sure that he should—he knew he didn't want to.

"Please—anyone with information regarding the present whereabouts of Thomas Dundy—it is urgent that I hear from him immediately. If he is unavailable, please locate someone truly able to speak for him."

Sam got to his feet and stood over the radio, his fists clenched.

"To operate the transmitting apparatus, move the first button to the—the left. Repeat—to transmit, switch the first button to the left. Speak toward the grill. I will now wait two minutes for a reply."

Sam reached out toward the knob, wondering who it was that wasn't quite sure of left and right.

Then he snapped the knob over, because he didn't dare not do it. "This is Sam Dundy," he said shakily. "Who are you?"

He waited, but there wasn't any answer until he realized he ought to switch the knob back.

"—dy's son? Are you Tom Dundy's son? The student?"

"Yes. Look, who are you?"

"I can't tell you that if your father is available. Is he all right?"

"He's dead, mister. I found the radio by accident. I don't know anything about this. If you want anything, you'd better explain."

"Dundy died? How long ago?"

"Three days."

There was an odd, unidentifiable noise before the voice answered. Then it said, "You are almost finished with your studies, aren't you?"

"It'll be two years yet, mister."

"Two *years!* I don't know whether I can . . ." A pause, then, "I'm sorry for you about your father. Will you help me?"

Sam clamped his jaws together. "Not unless I know who I'm helping and what this is all about."

"I'm sorry—I'm being hasty. But I have a very good reason. If I do not have help soon, I shall be dead, too. When I lost contact with your father, I . . . You understand? I lost my composure. I don't— that is, I'm not in a position to extend my trust to very many people.

"Your father found me a number of years ago, but he could not help me. I gave him the communicator so we could keep in contact, and he could advise me when circumstances had changed. I have slowed my metabolism to nearly the critical level, but if you cannot help me soon, it will be too late. I apologize for my . . . brusqueness, but I am also prey to emotions. I ask you again—will you help me?"

Sam looked down at the radio—the communicator. He knew his face was pale. He wiped his hand across his face, and his fingers were damp when they came away.

Outside, he knew, the stars were shining cold and clear on this moonless night, and he knew, too, that there were voices whispering across the night between the stars.

He took a deep breath. "I don't know," he answered slowly. "I'd have to see you. How far away are you?"

The voice made the odd sound again. It might have been a sigh. "Somewhere on your father's holding. I don't know where, in relation to your domicile. I came down at night, and too quickly . . . I will broadcast a beam of sound. Walk along it, and I will guide you. You are a student—you are aware that not all organisms must resemble one of your race—that intelligence and emotion may nevertheless be present?"

"I'll be coming."

"I thank you."

Quietly, Sam walked downstairs and got the flashlight. Holding the communicator, he stepped out into the yard, listening as the voice said, "I will start the beam now." A series of sharp clicks began to come from the speaker.

Walking slowly in the darkness, picking his way with the flashlight's help, Sam left the yard, sometimes having to go off the beam and find it again, when confronted by a building or a fence.

He figured out where he was headed almost immediately. There was a section of woods that he and his father had never cleared, or had ever intended to, what with so many other things to take care of.

He came down at night, Sam thought, and quickly. I wonder where he's from? I wonder which of the languages I heard is the one his people speak?

The earth under his feet felt different, somehow, than it had ever felt before—not as solid, yet better. He walked into the woods, threading his way between the trees.

"I hear your footsteps." The beam was cut off, and the voice spoke to him again. "Walk slowly. Look down."

Some of the trees were half-toppled, leaning against others, as though a windstorm had pushed them over. He must have walked through here a hundred times.

"Stop."

He looked down, and the dead leaves stirred, a few feet in front of him. He saw movement under them, something that looked like a sluggish rock, not too big. He saw a stir of thick arms that were like petrified tree roots, bending under enormous pressure.

"I have internal injuries," the voice said, booming and grating out from the ground, instead of from the communicator. Sam switched it off and shut the lid automatically. "I cannot dig out my ship and repair it, as I am. I have no access to my medical supplies or the interstellar transmitter. I have only my personal kits." The rock twisted itself sideward, and he saw an oval patch on its side, with a dark stain in its center.

"I was thrown clear. We are a tough people, and the ship is made of the same substance as the communicator case, but I cannot reach it. I'm at your mercy. If you help me, my bargain with your father will hold. I will tell you how to construct some of the circuits which make the communicator and the ship's propulsion fields possible. I understand such knowledge is negotiable here."

Sam nodded. "Yes, it is. There's a patent office, and companies that build electronic instruments. But I think I'd help you anyway." He thought about the old *Veterinary Cyclopedia,* with his father's stubborn notes. "I think I can do it. If not right now, *very* soon."

"Thank you. You are much like your father."

"I hope so, mister," Sam answered, "I hope so!"

The Tunesmith

by LLOYD BIGGLE, JR.

Everyone calls it the Center. It has another name, a long one, that gets listed in government appropriations and can be looked up in the encyclopedia, but no one uses it. From Bombay to Lima, it is— the Center. You can stagger out of the rolling mists of Venus, elbow your way up to a bar, and begin, "When I was at the Center . . ." And every stranger within hearing will listen attentively. You can mention the Center in the depths of London, or on a Martian desert, or at the solitary outpost on Pluto, and know you are understood.

No one ever explains the Center. It isn't possible, and it isn't necessary. From the babe in arms to the centenarian looking forward to retirement, everyone has been there, and plans to go again next year, and the year after that. It is the vacation land of the Solar System. It is square miles of undulating American middle-west farm land, transfigured by ingenious planning and relentless labor and incredible expense. It is a monumental summary of man's cultural achievements, and like a phoenix, it has emerged suddenly, inexplicably, at the end of the twenty-fourth century, from the corroded ashes of a shocking cultural decay.

The Center is colossal, spectacular and magnificent. It is inspiring, edifying and amazing. It is awesome, it is overpowering, it is—everything.

And though few of its visitors know about this, or care, it is also haunted.

You are standing in the observation gallery of the towering Bach

Monument. Off to the left, on the slope of a hill, you see the tense spectators who crowd the Grecian Theatre for Aristophanes. Sunlight plays on their brightly-colored clothing. They watch eagerly, delighted to see in person what millions are watching on visiscope.

Beyond the theatre, the tree-lined Frank Lloyd Wright Boulevard curves off into the distance, past the Dante Monument and the Michelangelo Institute. The twin towers of a facsimile of the Rheims Cathedral rise above the horizon. Directly below, you see the curious landscaping of an eighteenth century French *jardin,* and nearby, the Molière Theatre.

A hand clutches your sleeve, and you turn suddenly, irritably, and find yourself face to face with an old man.

The leathery face is scarred and wrinkled, the thin strands of hair glistening white. The hand on your arm is a gnarled claw. You stare, take in the slumping contortion of one crippled shoulder and the hideous scar of a missing ear, and back away in alarm.

The sunken eyes follow you. The hand extends in a sweeping gesture that takes in the far horizon, and you notice that the fingers are maimed or missing. The voice is a harsh cackle. "Like it?" he says, and eyes you expectantly.

Startled, you say, "Why, yes. Of course."

He takes a step forward, and his eyes are eager, pleading. "I say, do you like it?"

In your perplexity, you can do no more than nod as you turn to hurry away. But your nod brings a strange response. A strident laugh, an innocent, childish smile of pleasure, a triumphant shout. "I did it! I did it all!"

Or you stand in resplendent Plato Avenue, between the Wagnerian Theatre, where the complete *Der Ring des Nibelungen* is performed daily without interruptions, and the reconstruction of the sixteenth century Globe Theatre, where Shakespearean Drama is present morning, afternoon and evening.

A hand paws at you. "Like it?"

If you respond with a torrent of ecstatic praise, the old man eyes you impatiently, and only waits until you have finished to ask again, "I say, do you like it?"

But a smile and a nod is met with beaming pride, a gesture, a shout. "I did it!"

In the lobby of one of the thousand spacious hotels, in the waiting room of the remarkable library where a copy of any book you request is reproduced for you free of charge, in the eleventh balcony of

Beethoven Hall, a ghost shuffles haltingly, clutches an arm, asks a question.

And shouts proudly, "I did it!"

Erlin Baque sensed her presence behind him, but he did not turn. He leaned forward, his left hand tearing a rumbling bass figure from the multichord while his right hand fingered a solemn melody. With a lightning flip of his hand he touched a button, and the thin treble tones were suddenly fuller, more resonant, almost clarinet-like. ("But God, how unlike a clarinet!" he thought.)

"Must we go through all that again, Val?" he said.

"The landlord was here this morning."

He hesitated, touched a button, touched several buttons, and wove weird harmonies out of the booming tones of a brass choir. (But what a feeble, distorted brass choir!)

"How long does he give us this time?"

"Two days. And the food synthesizer's broken down again."

"Good. Run down and buy some fresh meat."

"With what?"

He slammed his fists down on the keyboard, and shouted above the shattering dissonance. "I will not rent a harmonizer. I will not turn my arranging over to hacks. If a Com goes out with my name on it, it's going to be *composed*. It may be idiotic, and it may be sickening, but it's going to be done right. It isn't much, God knows, but it's all I have left."

He turned slowly and glared at her, this pale, drooping, worn-out woman who had been his wife for twenty-five years. Then he looked away, telling himself stubbornly that he was no more to be blamed than she. When sponsors paid the same rates for good Coms that they paid for hackwork . . .

"Is Hulsey coming today?" she asked.

"He told me he was coming."

"If we could get some money for the landlord . . ."

"And the food synthesizer. And a new visiscope. And new clothes. There's a limit to what can be done with one Com."

He heard her move away, heard the door open, and waited. It did not close. "Walter-Walter called," she said. "You're the featured tunesmith on today's Show Case."

"So? There's no money in that."

"I thought you wouldn't want to watch, so I told Mrs. Rennik I'd watch with her."

"Sure. Go ahead. Have fun."

The door closed.

Baque got to his feet, and stood looking down at his chaos-strewn worktable. Music paper, Com-lyric releases, pencils, sketches, half-finished manuscripts were cluttered together in untidy heaps and overflowed onto the floor. Baque cleared a corner for himself and sat down wearily, stretching his long legs out under the table.

"Damn Hulsey," he muttered. "Damn sponsors. Damn visiscope. Damn Coms."

Compose something. You're not a hack, like the other tunesmiths. You don't punch your melodies out on a harmonizer's keyboard and let a machine harmonize them for you. You're a musician, not a melody monger. Write some music. Write a—a sonata, for multichord. Take the time now, and compose something.

His eyes fell on the first lines of a Com-lyric release. "If your flyer jerks and clowns, if it has its ups and downs . . ."

"Damn landlord," he muttered, reaching for a pencil.

The tiny wall clock tinkled the hour, and Baque leaned over to turn on the visiscope. A cherub-faced master of ceremonies smiled out at him ingratiatingly. "Walter-Walter again, ladies and gentlemen. It's Com time on today's Show Case. Thirty minutes of Commercials by one of today's most talented tunesmiths. Our Com spotlight is on—"

A noisy brass fanfare rang out, the tainted brass tones of a multichord.

"Erlin Baque!"

The multichord swung into an odd, dipsey melody Baque had done five years before, for Tamper Cheese, and a scattering of applause sounded in the background. A nasal soprano voice mouthed the words, and Baque groaned unhappily. "We age our cheese, and age it, age it, age it, the old-fashioned way . . ."

Walter-Walter cavorted about the stage, moving in time with the melody, darting down into the audience to kiss some sedate house-wife-on-a-holiday, and beaming at the howls of laughter.

The multichord sounded another fanfare, and Walter-Walter leaped back onto the stage, both arms extended over his head. "Now listen to this, all you beautiful people. Here's your Walter-Walter exclusive on Erlin Baque." He glanced secretively over his shoulder, tiptoed a few steps closer to the audience, placed his finger on his lips, and then called out loudly, "Once upon a time there was another composer named Baque, spelled B-A-C-H, but pronounced Baque.

He was a real atomic propelled tunesmith, the boy with the go, according to them that know. He lived some four or five or six hundred years ago, so we can't exactly say that that Baque and our Baque were Baque to Baque. But we don't have to go Baque to hear Baque. We like the Baque we've got. Are you with me?"

Cheers. Applause. Baque turned away, hands trembling, a choking disgust nauseating him.

"We start off our Coms by Baque with that little masterpiece Baque did for Foam Soap. Art work by Bruce Combs. Stop, look— and *listen!*"

Baque managed to turn off the visiscope just as the first bar of soap jet propelled itself across the screen. He picked up the Com lyric again, and his mind began to shape the thread of a melody.

"If your flyer jerks and clowns, if it has its ups and downs, ups and downs, ups and downs, you need a WARING!"

He hummed softly to himself, sketching a musical line that swooped and jerked like an erratic flyer. Word painting, it was called, back when words and tones meant something. Back when the B-A-C-H Baque was underscoring such grandiose concepts as heaven and hell.

Baque worked slowly, now and then checking a harmonic progression at the multichord and rejecting it, straining his mind for some fluttering accompaniment pattern that would simulate the sound of a flyer. But then—no. The Waring people wouldn't like that. They advertised that their flyers were noiseless.

He was suddenly aware of urgently-sounding door chimes. He walked over to flip on the scanner, and Hulsey's pudgy face grinned out at him.

"Come on up," Baque told him. Hulsey nodded, and disappeared.

Five minutes later he waddled through the door, sank into a chair that sagged dangerously under his bulky figure, plunked his briefcase on the floor, and mopped his face. "Whew! Wish you'd get yourself on a lower level. Or into a building with some modern conveniences. Those elevators scare me to death!"

"I'm thinking of moving," Baque said.

"Good. It's about time."

"But it'll probably be somewhere higher up. The landlord has given me two days' notice."

Hulsey winced, and shook his head sadly. "I see. Well, I won't keep you in suspense, then. Here's the check for the Sana-Soap Com."

Baque took the check, glanced at it, and scowled.

"You were behind in your guild dues," Hulsey said. "Have to deduct them, you know."

"Yes. I'd forgotten."

"I like to do business with Sana-Soap. Cash right on the line. Too many companies wait until the end of the month. Sana-Soap wants a couple of changes, but they paid anyway." He snapped open the briefcase, and pulled out a folder. "You've got some sly bits in this, Erlin my boy. They like it. Particularly this 'sudsey, sudsey, sudsey' thing in the bass. They kicked on the number of singers, at first, but not after they heard it. Now right here they want a break for a straight announcement."

Baque glanced, and nodded. "How about keeping the 'sudsey, sudsey' ostinato going as a background to the announcement?"

"Sounds good. That's a sly bit, that—what'd you call it?"

"Ostinato."

"Ah—yes. Wonder why the other tunesmiths don't work in bits like that."

"A harmonizer doesn't produce effects," Baque said dryly. "It just —harmonizes."

"You give them about thirty seconds of that 'sudsey' for background. They can cut it if they don't like it."

Baque nodded, and scribbled a note on the manuscript.

"And the arrangement," Hulsey went on. "Sorry, Erlin, but we can't get a French horn player. You'll have to do something else with that part."

"No horn player? What's wrong with Rankin?"

"Blacklisted. The Performers' Guild has him blacklisted. He went out to the west coast to play. Played for nothing, and even paid his own expenses, so they blacklisted him."

"I remember," Baque said softly. "The Monuments of Art Society. He played a Mozart Horn Concerto for them. Their last concert, too. Wish I could have heard it, even if it was with multichord."

"He can play it all he wants to, now, but he'll never get paid for playing again. You can work that horn part into the multichord line, or I might be able to get you a trumpet player. He could use a converter."

"It'll ruin the effect."

Hulsey chuckled. "Sounds the same to everyone but you, my boy. *I* can't tell the difference. We got your violins, and a cello player. What more do you want?"

"Doesn't the London Guild have a horn player?"

"You want me to bring him over for one three-minute Com? Be reasonable, Erlin! Can I pick this up tomorrow?"

"Yes. I'll have it ready in the morning."

Hulsey reached for his briefcase, dropped it again, and leaned forward. "Erlin, I'm worried about you. I have twenty-seven tunesmiths in my agency. You make the least money of any of them. Your net last year was twenty-two hundred. The next-highest netted eleven thousand."

"That isn't news to me," Baque said.

"This may be. You have as many accounts as any of the others. Did you know that?"

"No," Baque said. "No, I didn't know that."

"That's right. You have as many accounts, but you don't make any money. Want to know why? Two reasons. You spend too much time on a Com, and you write it too well. Sponsors can use one of your Coms for months—or sometimes even years, like that Tamper Cheese thing. People like to hear them. Now if you just didn't write so damned well, you could work faster, and the sponsors would have to use more of your Coms, and you could turn out more."

"I've thought about that. Even if I didn't, Val would keep reminding me. But it's no use. That's the way I have to work. If there was some way to get the sponsors to pay more for a *good* Com . . ."

"There isn't. The guild wouldn't stand for it, because good Coms mean less work, and most tunesmiths couldn't write a really good Com. Now don't think I'm concerned about my agency. Of course I make more money when you make more, but I'm doing well enough with my other tunesmiths. I just hate to see my best man making so little money. You're a throwback, Erlin. You waste time and money collecting those antique—what do you call them?"

"Phonograph records."

"Yes. And those moldy old books about music. I don't doubt that you know more about music than any living man, and what does it get you? Not money, certainly. You're the best there is, and you keep trying to be better, and the better you get the less money you make. Your income drops lower every year. Couldn't you manage to be mediocre now and then?"

"No," Baque said. "I couldn't manage it."

"Think it over."

"These accounts I have. Some of the sponsors really like my work.

They'd pay more, if the guild would let them. Supposing I left the guild?"

"You can't, my boy. I couldn't handle your stuff—not and stay in business long. The Tunesmiths' Guild would put on the pressure, and the Performers' and Lyric Writers' Guilds would blacklist you. Jimmy Denton plays along with the guilds, and he'd bar your stuff from visiscope. You'd lose all your accounts—fast. No sponsor is big enough to fight all that trouble, and none of them would want to bother. So just try to be mediocre now and then. Think about it."

Baque sat staring at the floor. "I'll think about it."

Hulsey struggled to his feet, clasped Baque's hand briefly, and waddled out. Baque got up slowly, and opened the drawer where he kept his meager collection of old phonograph records. Strange and wonderful music.

Three times in his career, Baque had written Coms that were a full half-hour in length. On rare occasions he got an order for fifteen minutes. Usually he was limited to five, or less. But composers like the B-A-C-H Baque wrote things that lasted an hour or more—even wrote them without lyrics.

And they wrote for real instruments, even some amazing-sounding instruments that no one played any more, like bassoons, piccolos and pianos.

"Damn Denton. Damn visiscope. Damn the guilds."

Baque rummaged tenderly among the discs until he found one bearing Bach's name. *Magnificat*. Then, because he felt too despondent to listen, he pushed it away.

Six months before the Performers' Guild had blacklisted its last oboe player. Now its last horn player, and there just weren't any young people learning to play instruments. Why should they, when there were so many marvelous contraptions that ground out the Coms without any effort on the part of the performer? Even multichord players were becoming scarce, and the multichord could, if one desired, practically play itself.

Baque stood looking uncertainly about the room, from multichord to worktable to the battered plastic bookcase that held his old books on music. The door jerked open, and Val hurried in.

"Did Hulsey . . ."

Baque handed her the check. She took it eagerly, glanced at it, and looked up in dismay.

"My guild dues," he said. "I was behind."

"Oh. Well, it's a help, anyway."

Her voice was flat, emotionless, as if one more disappointment really didn't matter. They stood facing each other awkwardly.

"I watched part of *Morning with Marigold*," Val said. "She talked about your Coms."

"I should hear soon on that Slo-Smoke Com," Baque said. "Maybe we can hold the landlord off for another week. Right now—I'm going to walk around a little."

"You should get out more . . ."

He closed the door behind him, slicing her sentence off neatly. He knew what followed. Get a job somewhere. Be good for your health to get out of the apartment a few hours a day. Write Coms in your spare time—they don't bring in more than a part-time income, anyway. At least do it until we get caught up. All right. If you won't, I will.

But she never did. A prospective employer never wanted more than one look at her slight body and her worn, sullen face. And Baque doubted that he would receive any better treatment.

He could get work as a multichord player, and make a good income. But then he'd have to join the Performers' Guild, which meant he'd have to resign from the Tunesmiths' Guild. So if he did that he could no longer write Coms.

"Damn Coms!"

When he reached the street, he stood for a moment watching the crowds shooting by on the swiftly-moving conveyer. A few people glanced at him, and saw a tall, gawky, balding man in a frayed, badly-fitting suit. Baque hunched up his shoulders, and walked awkwardly along the stationary sidewalk. They would consider him just another derelict from a shabby neighborhood, he knew, and they would quickly look the other way while they hummed a snatch from one of his Coms.

He turned in at a crowded restaurant, found a table at one side, and ordered a beer. On the rear wall was an enormous visiscope screen, where the Coms followed each other without interruption. Baque listened to the Coms for a time, first curious to see what the other tunesmiths were doing, and then disgusted. Around him, the customers watched and listened while they ate. Some of them nodded their heads jerkily in time with the music. A few young couples were dancing on the small dance floor, skillfully changing steps as the music shifted from one Com to another.

Baque watched them sadly, and thought about the way things had changed. At one time, he knew, there had been special music for dancing, and special groups of instruments to play it. And people had gone to concerts by the thousands, sitting in seats with nothing to look at but the performers.

All of it was gone. Not only the music, but art, and literature, and poetry. The plays he had read in his grandfather's school books were forgotten.

James Denton's *Visiscope International* decreed that people must look and listen at the same time. James Denton's *Visiscope International* decreed that the public attention span wouldn't tolerate long programs. So there were Coms.

Damn Coms!

When Val returned to the apartment an hour later, Baque was sitting in the corner staring at the crumbly volumes he had collected from the days when books were still printed on paper—a scattering of biographies, books on music history and technical books on music theory and composition. Val looked twice around the room before she noticed him, and then she confronted him anxiously, stark tragedy written on her face.

"The man's coming to fix the food synthesizer."

"Good," Baque said.

"But the landlord won't wait. If we don't pay him day after tomorrow—pay him everything—we're out."

"So we're out."

"Where will we go? We can't get in anywhere without paying something in advance."

"So we won't get in anywhere."

She fled sobbing into the bedroom.

The next morning Baque resigned from the Tunesmiths' Guild and joined the Performers' Guild. Hulsey's round face drooped mournfully when he heard the news. He loaned Baque enough money to pay his guild registration fee and quiet the landlord, and expressed his sorrow in eloquent terms as he hurried Baque out of his office. He would, Baque knew, waste no time in assigning Baque's clients to his other tunesmiths—to men who worked faster and not so well.

Baque went to the guild hall, where he sat for five hours waiting for a multichord assignment. He was finally escorted into the secretary's office, and brusquely motioned into a chair. The secretary eyed him suspiciously.

"You belonged to the Performers' Guild twenty years ago, and you left it to become a tunesmith. Right?"

"Right," Baque said.

"You lost your seniority after three years. You knew that, didn't you?"

"I didn't, but I didn't think it mattered. There aren't many good multichord players around."

"There aren't many good jobs around, either. You'll have to start at the bottom." He scribbled on a slip of paper, and thrust it at Baque. "This one pays well, but we have a hard time keeping a man there. Lankey isn't easy to work for. If you don't irritate him too much—well, then we'll see."

Baque found himself outside the door, staring hard at the slip of paper.

He rode the conveyer out to the New Jersey Space Port, floundered about through a rattle-trap slum area getting his directions hopelessly confused, and finally found the place almost within radiation distance of the port. The sprawling building had burned at some time in the remote past. Stubby remnants of walls rose out of the weed-choked rubble. A walk curved back from the street towards a dimly lit cavity at one corner of the building. Steps led uncertainly downwards. Overhead, an enormous sign pointed its flowing colors in the direction of the port. The *Lankey-Pank Out*.

Baque stepped through the door, and faltered at the onslaught of extraterrestrial odors. Lavender-tinted Venusian tobacco smoke hung like a limp blanket midway between floor and ceiling. The revolting, cutting fumes of Martian whiskey staggered him. He had a glimpse of a scattered gathering of tough spacers and tougher prostitutes before the doorman planted his bulky figure and scarred caricature of a face in front of him.

"You looking for someone?"

"Mr. Lankey."

The doorman jerked a thumb towards the bar, and noisily stumbled back into the shadows. Baque walked towards the bar.

He had no trouble picking out Lankey. The proprietor sat on a tall stool behind the bar, and thrust his bald head forward to watch him coldly as he approached. In the dim, smoke-streaked light his taut pale face had a spectral grimness. He planted one elbow on the bar, fingered his flattened stump of a nose with the two remaining fingers on one hairy hand, and stared at Baque with burning, bloodshot eyes.

"I'm Erlin Baque," Baque said.

"Yeh. The multichord player. Can you play that multichord, fellow?"

"Why, yes, I can play . . ."

"That's what they all say. And I've had maybe two in the last five years that could really play. Most of them come out here figuring they'll set the thing on automatic, and fuss around with one finger. I want that multichord *played*, fellow, and I'll tell you right now—if you can't play you might as well jet for home base, because there isn't any automatic on my multichord. I had it disconnected."

"I can play," Baque told him.

"All right. I'll find out soon enough. The guild rates this place as Class Four, but I pay Class One rates if you can play. If you can really play, I'll slip you some bonuses the guild won't know about. Hours are from six P.M. to six A.M., but you get plenty of breaks, and if you get hungry or thirsty just ask for what you want. Only go easy on the hot stuff. I won't do with a drunk multichord player, no matter how good he is. Rose!"

He bellowed a second time, and a woman stepped out of a door at the side of the room. She wore a faded dressing gown, and her tangled hair hung untidily about her shoulders. She turned a small, pretty face towards Baque, and studied him boldly.

"Multichord," Lankey said. "Show him."

Rose beckoned, and Baque followed her towards the rear of the room. Suddenly he stopped in amazement.

"What's the matter?" Rose said.

"No visiscope!"

"No. Lankey says the spacers want better things to look at than soap suds and air cars." She giggled. "Something like me, for example."

"I never heard of a restaurant without visiscope."

"Neither did I, until I came here. But Lankey's got three of us to sing the Coms, and you're to do the multichord with us. I hope you make the grade. We haven't had a multichord player for a week, and it's hard singing without one."

"I'll make out all right," Baque said.

A narrow platform stretched across the end of the room, where any other restaurant Baque had seen had its visiscope screen. There had been one here at one time, he noticed. He could see the unpatched scars in the wall where it had been torn out.

"Lankey ran a joint on Venus back when they didn't have visiscope there," Rose said. "He has his own ideas about how to entertain customers. Want to see your room?"

Baque did not answer. He was examining the multichord. It was a battered old instrument, and it bore the marks of more than one brawl. He fingered the filter buttons, and swore softly to himself. Most of them were broken. Only the flute and violin filters clicked into place properly. So he would have to spend twelve hours a day with the twanging tones of an unfiltered multichord.

"Want to see your room?" Rose said again. "It's only five. Might as well relax before we have to go to work."

Rose showed him a cramped enclosure behind the bar. He stretched out on a hard cot and tired to relax, and then it was six o'clock, and Lankey stood in the door beckoning at him.

He took his place at the multichord, and sat fingering the keys. He felt no nervousness. There wasn't anything he didn't know about Coms, and he knew he wouldn't have trouble with the music. But the atmosphere disturbed him. The haze of smoke was thicker, and he blinked his smarting eyes and felt the whiskey fumes tear at his nostrils when he took a deep breath.

There was still only a scattering of customers—mechanics in grimy work suits, swaggering pilots, a few civilians who liked their liquor strong and didn't mind the surroundings. And women. Two women, he guessed, for every man in the room.

There was a sudden stirring, a yelp of approval, and an unrestrained stomping of feet. Lankey was crossing the platform with Rose, and the other singers. Baque's first horrified impression was that the girls were nude, but as they came closer he made out their brief plastic costumes. Lankey was right, he thought. The spacers would much prefer looking at that than at animated Coms on a visiscope screen.

"You met Rose," Lankey said. "This is Zanna and Mae. Let's get going."

He walked away, and the girls gathered around the multichord. "What Coms do you know?" Rose said.

"I know them all."

She looked at him doubtfully. "We sing together, and then we take turns. You're—sure you know them all?"

Baque flipped on the power, and sounded a chord. "You sing, and I'll handle this."

"We'll start out with a Tasty-Malt Com. It goes like this." She hummed softly. "Know that one?"

"I wrote it," Baque said.

They sang better than he had expected. He followed them easily, and was able to keep his eyes on the customers. Heads were jerking in time with the music, and he quickly caught the mood and began to experiment. His fingers shaped a rolling rhythm in the bass, fumbled with it tentatively, and then expanded it. He abandoned the melodic line, leaving the girls to carry on by themselves while he searched the entire keyboard to ornament the driving rhythm.

Feet began to stomp. The girl's bodies were swaying wildly, and Baque felt himself rocking back and forth as the music swept on recklessly. The girls finished their lyrics, and when he did not stop they started in again. Spacers were on their feet, now, clapping and swaying. Some seized their women and began dancing in the narrow spaces between the tables. Finally Baque forced a cadence and slumped forward, panting and mopping his forehead. One of the girls collapsed on the stage, and the others hauled her upright. They fled to a frenzy of applause.

Baque felt a hand on his shoulder. Lankey. His ugly, expressionless face eyed Baque, turned to study the wildly enthusiastic customers, turned back to Baque. He nodded, and walked away.

Rose came back alone, still breathing heavily. "How about a Sally Ann Perfume Com?"

"Tell me the words," Baque said.

She recited them tonelessly. A tragic little story about the shattered romance of a girl who did not use Sally Ann. "Shall we make them cry?" Baque said. "Just concentrate on that. It's a sad story, and we're going to make them cry."

She stood by the multichord, and sang plaintively. Baque fashioned a muted, tremulous accompaniment, and when the second verse started he improvised a drooping countermelody. The spacers sat in hushed suspense. The men did not cry, but some of the women sniffed audibly, and when Rose finished there was a taut silence.

"Quick," Baque hissed. "We'll brighten things up. Sing something —anything!"

She launched into another Com, and Baque brought the spacers to their feet with the driving rhythm of his accompaniment.

The other girls took their turns, and Baque watched the customers detachedly, bewildered at the power that surged in his fingers. He carried them from one emotional extreme to the other, and back again, improvising, experimenting. And his mind fumbled haltingly with an idea.

"Time for a break," Rose said finally. "Better get something to eat."

Seven-thirty. An hour and a half of continuous playing. Baque felt drained of strength and emotion, and he accepted his dinner tray indifferently and took it to the enclosure they called his room. He did not feel hungry. He sniffed doubtfully at the food, tasted it—and ate ravenously. Real food, after months of synthetics!

He sat for a while on the cot, wondering how much time the girls took between appearances. Then he went looking for Lankey.

"I don't like sitting around," he said. "Any objection to my playing?"

"Without the girls?"

"Yes."

Lankey planted both elbows on the bar, cupped his chin in one fist, and sat looking absently at the far wall. "You going to sing yourself?" he said finally.

"No. Just play."

"Without any singing? Without words?"

"Yes."

"What will you play?"

"Coms. Or I might improvise something."

A long silence. Then—"Think you could keep things moving while the girls are out?"

"Of course I could."

Lankey continued to concentrate on the far wall. His eyebrows contracted, relaxed and contracted again. "All right," he said. "I was just wondering why I never thought of it."

Unnoticed, Baque took his place at the multichord. He began softly, making the music an unobtrusive background to the rollicking conversation that filled the room. As he increased the volume, faces turned in his direction.

He wondered what those people were thinking, hearing for the first time music that was not a Com, music without words. He watched intently, and satisfied himself that he was holding their attention. Now—could he bring them out of their seats with nothing more than the sterile tones of a multichord? He gave the melody a rhythmic snap, and the stomping began.

As he increased the volume again, Rose came stumbling out of a doorway and hurried across the stage, perplexity written on her pert face.

"It's all right," Baque told her. "I'm just playing to amuse myself. Don't come back until you're ready."

She nodded, and walked away. A red-faced spacer near the platform looked up at the revealed outline of her young body, and leered. Fascinated, Baque studied the coarse, demanding lust in his face, and searched the keyboard to express it. This? Or—this? Or—

He had it. His body rocked as he felt himself caught up in the relentless rhythm. His foot tightened on the volume control, and he turned to watch the customers.

Every pair of eyes stared hypnotically at his corner of the room. A bartender stood at a half crouch, mouth agape. There was uneasiness, a strained shuffling of feet, a restless scraping of chairs. Baque's foot dug harder at the volume control.

Terrified, he sat watching the scene that erupted below him. Lasciviousness twisted every face. Men were on their feet, reaching for the women, clutching, pawing. A chair crashed to the floor, and a table, and no one seemed to notice. A woman's dress fluttered crazily downwards, and the pursued were pursuers while Baque's fingers raced onward, out of control.

With a violent effort he wrenched his hands from the keys, and the moment of silence crashed into the room like thunder. Fingers trembling, he began to play softly, indifferently. Order was restored when he looked again, the chair and table were upright, and the customers were seated in apparent relaxation—except for one woman, struggling back into her dress in obvious embarrassment.

Baque continued to play quietly until the girls returned.

Six A.M. Body aching with weariness, hands aching, legs cramped, Baque climbed down from the multichord. Lankey stood waiting for him.

"Class One rates," he said. "You've got a job with me as long as you want it. But take it a little easy with that stuff, will you?"

Baque thought about Val, cramped in the dreary apartment, eating synthetic food. "Would I be out of order to ask for an advance?"

"No," Lankey said. "Not out of order. I told the cashier to give you a hundred on your way out. Call it a bonus."

Weary from his long conveyer ride, Baque walked quietly into his dim apartment and looked about. No sign of Val—she would still be sleeping. He sat down at his own multichord and touched the keys.

Unbelievable. Music without Coms, without words, could make people laugh and cry, and dance, and cavort madly.

And it could turn them into lewd animals.

Wonderingly he played the music that had incited such uncon-cealed lust, played it louder, and louder . . .

And felt a hand on his shoulder, and turned to look into Val's passion-twisted face.

He asked Hulsey to come and hear him that night, and later Hulsey sat slumped on the cot in his room, and shuddered. "It isn't right. No man should have that power over people. How do you do it?"

"I don't know," Baque said. "I saw that young couple sitting there, and they were happy, and I felt their happiness. And as I played everyone in the room was happy. And then another couple came in, quarreling, and the next thing I knew I had everyone mad."

"Almost started a fight at the next table," Hulsey said. "And what you did after that . . ."

"Yes. But not as much as I did last night. You should have seen it last night."

Hulsey shuddered again.

"I have a book about Greek music," Baque said. "Ancient Greece—way back. They had something they called *ethos*. They thought that the different musical scales affected people in different ways. Music could make men sad, or happy, or enthused—or drive them crazy. They even claimed that a musician named Orpheus could move trees and soften rocks with his music. Now listen. I've had a chance to experiment, and I've noticed that my playing is most effective when I don't use the filters. There are only two filters that work on that multichord, anyway—flute and violin—but when I use either of them the people don't react so strongly. I'm wondering if it wasn't the Greek instruments, rather than the scales, that produced those ef-fects. I'm wondering if the tone of an unfiltered multichord doesn't have something in common with the tone of the ancient Greek *kithara* or *aulos*."

Hulsey grunted. "I don't think it's instruments, or scales, either. I think it's Baque, and I don't like it. You should have stayed a tune-smith."

"I want you to help me," Baque said. "I want to find a place where we can put a lot of people—a thousand, at least—not to eat, or watch Coms, but just to listen to one man play on a multichord."

Hulsey got up abruptly. "Baque, you're a dangerous man. I'm damned if I'll trust any man who can make me feel the way you made me feel tonight. I don't know what you're trying to do, but I won't have any part of it."

He stomped away in the manner of a man about to slam a door.

But a male multichordist in the *Lankey-Pank Out* did not rate the luxury of a door on his room. Hulsey paused uncertainly in the doorway, and disappeared. Baque followed, and stood watching him weave his way impatiently past the tables towards the exit.

From his place behind the bar, Lankey looked at Baque, and glanced after the disappearing Hulsey. "Troubles?" he said.

Baque turned away wearily. "I've known that man for twenty years. I never thought he was my friend. But then—I never thought he was my enemy, either."

"It works out that way, sometimes," Lankey said.

Baque shook his head. "I'd like to try some Martian whiskey. I've never tasted the stuff."

Two weeks made Baque an institution at the *Lankey-Pank Out,* and the place was jammed to capacity from the time he went to work until he left the next morning. When he performed alone, he forgot about the Coms, and played what he wanted. He'd even played some pieces by Bach for the customers, and received generous applause—though nothing like the tumultuous enthusiasm that followed his improvisations.

Sitting behind the bar, eating his evening meal and watching the customers, Baque felt vaguely happy. For the first time in years he had plenty of money. He enjoyed the work he was doing.

And he had begun to wonder how he could go about eliminating the Coms altogether.

As Baque pushed aside his tray, he saw Biff the doorman step forward to greet another pair of customers, halt suddenly, and back away in stupefied amazement. And no wonder—evening clothes at the *Lankey-Pank Out!*

The couple strolled into the room, blinking in the dim, smoke-tinted light, and looking about curiously. The man was bronze and handsome, but no one noticed him. The woman's striking beauty flashed like a meteor against the drab surroundings. She moved in an aura of shining loveliness. Her fragrance routed the foul tobacco and whiskey odors. Her hair gleamed golden, her shimmering, flowing gown clung seductively to her voluptuous figure.

Baque stared, and suddenly recognized her. Marigold, of *Morning with Marigold.* Worshiped around the Solar System by the millions of devotees to her visiscope program. Mistress, it was said, to James Denton, the czar of visiscope. Marigold Manning.

She raised her hand to her mouth in mock horror, and the bright tones of her laughter dropped tantalizingly among the spellbound spacers.

"What an odd place," she said. "Where did you ever hear about a place like this?"

"I need some Martian whiskey, damn it," the man muttered.

"So stupid of the Port Bar to run out. With all those ships from Mars coming in, too. Are you sure we can get back in time? Jimmy'll raise hell if we aren't there when his ship lands."

Lankey touched Baque's arm. "After six," he said, without taking his eyes from Marigold Manning. "They'll be getting impatient."

Baque nodded, and started for the multichord. And as soon as the customers saw him, the tumult began. He paused before taking his seat, and saw Marigold Manning and her escort staring open-mouthed. The sudden uproar had brought them up short, and they turned from the stomping, howling customers to examine this nondescript man who inspired such undignified enthusiasm.

Miss Manning's exclamation rang out sharply above the noise. "What the hell!"

Baque shrugged, and started to play. When Miss Manning finally left, after a brief conference with Lankey, her escort still hadn't gotten his Martian whiskey.

The next evening Lankey greeted Baque with both fists full of telenotes. "What a hell of a mess this is! You see this Marigold dame's program this morning?"

"Don't think I've watched visiscope since I came to work here."

"In case it interests you, you were—what does she call it?—a 'Marigold Exclusive' on visiscope this morning. Erlin Baque, the famous tunesmith, is now playing the multichord in a queer little restaurant called the *Lankey-Pank Out*. If you want to hear some amazing music, wander out by the New Jersey Space Port, and hear Baque. Don't miss it. The experience of a lifetime." Lankey swore, and waved the telenotes. "Queer, she calls us. Now I've got ten thousand requests for reservations, some from as far away as Budapest and Shanghai. And our capacity is five hundred, counting standing room. Damn that woman! We already had all the business we could handle."

"You need a bigger place," Baque said.

"Yes. Well, confidentially, I've got my eye on a big warehouse. It'll seat a thousand, at least. We'll clean up. I'll give you a contract to take charge of the music."

Baque shook his head. "How about opening a big place up town? Attract people that have more money to spend. You run it, and I'll bring in the customers."

Lankey caressed his flattened nose solemnly. "How do we split?"

"Fifty-fifty," Baque said.

"No," Lankey said thoughtfully. "I play fair, Baque, but fifty-fifty wouldn't be right on a deal like that. I'd have to put up all the money myself. I'll give you one-third, and you're to handle the music."

They had a lawyer draw up a contract. Baque's lawyer. Lankey insisted on that.

In the bleak grey of early morning Baque sleepily rode the crowded conveyer towards his apartment. It was the rush hour, when commuters jammed against each other and snarled grumpily when a neighbor shifted his feet. Was the crowd heavier than usual? Baque shrugged off the jostling and elbowing, and lost himself in thought.

It was time he found a better place to live. He hadn't minded the dumpy apartment as long as he couldn't afford a better place, but Val had been complaining for years. And now when they could move, when they could have a luxury apartment or even a small home over in Pennsylvania, Val refused to go. Didn't want to leave her friends, she said.

Baque mulled over this problem of feminine contrariness, and realized suddenly that he was approaching his own stop. He started to push his way towards a deceleration strip—he shoved firmly, he attempted to step between his fellow riders, he applied his elbows, gently, at first, and then viciously. The crowd about him did not yield.

"I beg your pardon," Baque said, making another attempt. "I get off here."

This time a pair of brawny arms barred his way. "Not this morning, Baque. You got an appointment up town."

Baque flung a glance at the circle of faces about him. Hard faces, grim, grinning faces. With a sudden effort Baque hurled himself sideways, fighting with all his strength—and was hauled back roughly.

"Up town, Baque. If you want to go dead, that's your affair."

"Up town," Baque agreed.

At a public air strip they left the conveyer. A flyer was waiting for them, a plush, private job that displayed a high-priority X registration number. They flew swiftly towards down-town Manhattan, cutting recklessly across the air lanes, and veered in for a landing on the towering *Visiscope International* Building. Baque was bundled down an anti-gravity shaft, led through a labyrinth of corridors, and prodded none too gently into an office.

A huge office. It was sparsely furnished, with a desk, some chairs, a bar in the far corner, an enormous visiscope screen—and a multi-chord. It was crowded. Baque's gaze swept the blur of faces and found one that was familiar. Hulsey.

The plump agent took two steps forward, and stood glaring at Baque. "Day of reckoning, Erlin," he said coldly.

A hand rapped sharply on the desk. "I take care of any reckoning that's done around here, Hulsey. Please sit down, Mr. Baque."

Baque arranged himself uncomfortably on the chair that was thrust foward from somewhere. He waited, his eyes on the man behind the desk.

"My name is James Denton. Does my fame extend to such out-of-the-way places as the *Lankey-Pank Out?*"

"No," Baque said. "But I've heard of you."

James Denton. Czar of *Visiscope International.* Ruthless arbitrator of public taste. He was no more than forty, with a swarthy, handsome face, flashing eyes, and a ready smile.

He nodded slowly, tapped a cigar on the edge of his desk, and carefully placed it in his mouth. Men on either side of him extended lighters. He chose one without glancing up, nodded again, and puffed deeply.

"I won't bore you with introductions to this gathering, Baque. Some of these men are here for professional reasons. Some are here because they're curious. I heard about you for the first time yesterday, and what I heard made me think you might be a problem. Mind you, I said 'might be'—that's what I aim to find out.

"When I have a problem, Baque, I do one of two things. I solve it, or I eliminate it, and I waste no time either way." He chuckled. "As you can see from the fact that I had you brought in at the earliest moment you were—shall we say—available?"

"The man's dangerous, Denton!" Hulsey blurted out.

Denton flashed his smile. "I like dangerous men, Hulsey. They're useful to have around. If I can use whatever it is Mr. Baque has, I'll make him an attractive offer. I'm sure he'll accept it gratefully. If I can't use it, I aim to make damned certain that he won't be inconveniencing me. Do I make myself clear, Baque?"

Baque stared at the floor, and said nothing.

Denton leaned forward. His smile did not waver, but his eyes narrowed, and his voice was suddenly icy. "Do I make myself clear, Baque?"

"Yes," Baque muttered weakly.

Denton jerked a thumb towards the door, and half of those present, including Hulsey, solemnly filed out. The others waited, talking in whispers, while Denton puffed steadily on his cigar. Suddenly Denton's intercom rasped out a single word. "Ready!"

Denton pointed at the multichord. "We crave a demonstration of your skill, Mr. Baque. And take care that it's a good demonstration. Hulsey is listening, and he can tell us if you try to stall."

Baque nodded, and took his place at the multichord. He sat with fingers poised, and grinned at the circle of staring faces. Overlords of business, they were, and never in their lives had they heard real music. As for Hulsey—yes, Hulsey would be listening, but over Denton's intercom, over a communication system designed to carry voices!

And Hulsey had a terrible ear for music.

Still grinning, Baque touched the violin filter, touched it again, and faltered.

Denton chuckled dryly. "I neglected to inform you, Mr. Baque. On Hulsey's advice, we've had the filters disconnected. Now—"

Anger surged within Baque. He jammed his foot down hard on the volume control, insolently tapped out a visiscope fanfare, and started to play his Tamper Cheese Com. Face flushed, Denton leaned forward and snarled something. The men beside him stirred uneasily. Baque shifted to another Com, improvised some variations, and began to watch the faces around him. Overlords of the business world. It would be amusing, he thought, to make them dance and stomp their feet. His fingers shaped a compelling rhythm, and they began to sway restlessly.

Suddenly he forgot his caution. Laughing silently to himself, he released an overpowering torrent of sound that set the men dancing. He froze them in ridiculous postures with an outburst of surging emotion. He made them stomp recklessly, he brought tears to their eyes, and he finished off with the pounding force that Lankey called the "Sex Music."

Then he slumped over the keyboard, terrified at what he had done.

Denton was on his feet, face pale, hands clenching and unclenching. "My God!" he muttered.

He snarled a word at his intercom. "Reaction?"

"Negative," came the prompt answer.

"Let's wind it up."

Denton sat down, passed his hand across his face, and turned to Baque with a bland smile. "An impressive performance, Mr. Baque. We'll know in a few minutes—ah, here they are."

Those who had left earlier filed back into the room, and several men huddled together in a whispered conference. Denton got up from his desk, and paced the floor. The other men in the room, including Hulsey, remained standing and waited awkwardly.

Baque kept his place at the multichord, glancing uneasily about the room. In shifting his position he accidently touched a key, and the single tone shattered the poise of the conferees, spun Denton around wildly, and startled Hulsey into two steps towards the door.

"Mr. Baque is getting impatient," Denton called. "Can't we finish this?"

"One moment, sir."

They returned, finally, and arranged themselves in two lines in front of Denton's desk. The spokesman, a white-haired, scholarly looking man with a delicate pink complexion, cleared his throat self-consciously, and waited for Denton's nod.

"It is established," he said, "that those in this room were powerfully affected by the music. Those listening on the intercom experienced no reaction except a mild boredom."

"Any fool could figure that out," Denton snapped. "How does he do it?"

"We can only offer a working hypothesis . . ."

"So you're guessing. Let's have it."

"Erlin Baque has the ability to telepathically project his emotional experience. When the projection is subtly reinforced by the tones of the multichord, the experience of those in his immediate presence is intense. It has no effect upon those listening to his music at a distance."

"And—visiscope?"

"Baque's playing would have no effect upon visiscope listeners."

"I see," Denton said. He scowled thoughtfully. "What about his long-term success?"

"It is difficult to predict . . ."

"Predict, damn it!"

"The novelty of his playing would attract attention, at first. In time he might develop a group of followers who would use the emotional experience of his playing as a kind of narcotic."

"Thank you, gentlemen," Denton said. "That will be all."

The room emptied quickly. Hulsey paused in the doorway, glared hatefully at Baque, and then walked out meekly.

"So I can't use you, Baque," Denton said. "But it seems you are no problem. I know what you and Lankey are up to. If I say the word, you would never, in this lifetime, find a place for your new restaurant. I could have the *Lankey-Pank Out* closed down by evening. But it would hardly be worth the trouble. I won't even insist on a visiscope screen in your new restaurant. If you can develop a cult for yourself, why—perhaps it will keep the members out of worse mischief. You see I feel generous this morning, Baque. Now you'd better leave before I change my mind."

Baque nodded, and got to his feet. At that moment Marigold Manning swept into the room, radiantly lovely, exotically perfumed, her glistening blonde hair swept up into the latest Martian hair style.

"Jimmy, darling—oh!"

She stared at Baque, stared at the multichord, and stammered, "Why, you're—you're—Erlin Baque! Jimmy, why didn't you tell me?"

"Mr. Baque has been favoring me with a private performance," Denton said brusquely. "I think we understand each other, Baque. Good morning!"

"You're going to use him on visiscope!" Miss Manning exclaimed. "Jimmy, that's wonderful. May I have him first? I can work him in this morning."

Denton shook his head slowly. "Sorry, darling. We've decided that Mr. Baque's talent is—not quite suitable for visiscope."

"At least I can have him for a guest. You'll be my guest, won't you, Mr. Baque? There's nothing wrong with giving him a guest spot, is there Jimmy?"

Denton chuckled. "No. After all the fuss you stirred up, it might be a good idea for you to guest him. It'll serve you right when he flops."

"He won't flop. He'll be wonderful on visiscope. Will you come in this morning, Mr. Baque?"

"Well . . ." Baque began. Denton nodded emphatically. "We'll be opening a new restaurant soon," Baque went on. "I wouldn't mind being your guest on opening day."

"A new restaurant? That's wonderful! Does anyone know? I'll give it out this morning as an exclusive!"

"It isn't exactly settled, yet," Baque said apologetically. "We haven't found a place . . ."

"Lankey found a place yesterday," Denton said. "He'll be signing a lease this morning. Just let Miss Manning know your opening date, Baque, and she'll arrange a spot for you. Now if you don't mind . . ."

It took Baque half an hour to find his way out of the building, but he plodded aimlessly along the corridors and disdained asking directions. He hummed happily to himself, and now and then he broke into a laugh.

The overlords of the business world—and their scientists—knew nothing about overtones.

"So that's the way it is," Lankey said. "I think we were lucky, Baque. Denton should have made his move when he had a chance—when I wasn't expecting it. When he wises up, I'll see that it's too late."

"What can we do if he really decides to put us out of business?"

"I have some connections myself, Baque. They don't run in high society, like Denton, but they're every bit as dishonest. And Denton has a lot of enemies who'll be glad to back us up. Said he could close me down by evening, eh? It's a funny deal. There's not much we can do that would hurt Denton, but there's plenty we can do to keep him from hurting us."

"I think we're going to hurt Denton," Baque said.

Lankey moved over to the bar, and came back with a tall glass of pink, foaming liquid. "Drink it," he said. "You've had a long day, and you're getting delirious. How could we hurt Denton?"

"Coms. Visiscope depends on Coms. We'll show the people they can have entertainment without them. We'll make our motto NO COMS AT LANKEY'S!"

"Great," Lankey drawled. "I just invest a thousand in fancy new costumes for the girls—they can't wear those plastic things in our new place, you know—and you decide not to let them sing."

"Certainly they're going to sing."

Lankey leaned forward, caressing his nose. "And no Coms. Then what are they going to sing?"

"I took some lyrics out of an old school book my grandfather had. They're called poems, and I'm writing music for them. I was going to try them out here, but Denton might hear about it, and there's no use starting trouble before it's necessary."

"No. Save them for the new place. And you'll be on Morning with Marigold the day we open. Are you certain about this overtones stuff,

Baque? You really could be projecting emotions, you know. Not that it will make any difference in the restaurant, but on visiscope . . ."

"I'm certain. How soon can we open?"

"I've got three shifts remodeling the place. We'll seat twelve hundred, and have room for a nice dance floor. Should be ready in two weeks. But I'm not sure this visiscope deal is wise, Baque."

"I want to do it."

Lankey went back to the bar, and got a drink for himself. "All right. You do it. If your stuff comes over, all hell is going to break loose, and I might as well start getting ready for it." He grinned. "Damned if it won't be good for business!"

Marigold Manning had changed her hair styling to the latest creation of Zann of Hong Kong, and she dallied for ten minutes in deciding which profile she would present to the cameras. Baque waited patiently, a bit uncomfortable in the most expensive dress suit he had ever owned. He was wondering if perhaps he really did project emotions.

"I'll have it this way," Miss Manning said finally, waving a pilot screen in front of her face for a last, searching look. "And you, Mr. Baque? What will we do with you?"

"Just put me at the multichord," Baque said.

"But you can't just play. You'll have to say something. I've been announcing this every day for a week, and we'll have the biggest audience in years, and you'll just *have* to say something."

"Gladly," Baque said. "If I can talk about *Lankey's*."

"But of course, you silly man. That's why you're here. You talk about *Lankey's*, and I'll talk about Erlin Baque."

"Five minutes," a voice announced crisply.

"Oh, dear," she said. "I'm always so nervous just before."

"Be happy you're not nervous during," Baque said.

"That's so right. Jimmy just makes fun of me, but it takes an artist to understand another artist. Do you get nervous?"

"When I'm playing, I'm much too busy."

"That's just the way it is with me. Once my program starts, I'm much too busy . . ."

"Four minutes . . ."

"Oh, bother!" She seized the pilot screen again. "Maybe I would have been better the other way."

Baque seated himself at the multichord. "You're perfect the way you are."

"Do you really think so? It's a nice thing to say, anyway. I wonder if Jimmy will take the time to watch."

"I'm sure he will."

"Three minutes . . ."

Baque threw on the power, and sounded a chord. Now he *was* nervous. He had no idea what he was going to play. He'd intentionally refrained from preparing something, because it was his improvisations that affected people so strangely. Only one thing was certain —there would be no Sex Music. Lankey had warned him about that.

He lost himself in thought, failed to hear the final warning, and looked up startled at Miss Manning's cheerful, "Good morning, everyone. It's *Morning with Marigold!*"

Her bright voice wandered on and on. Erlin Baque. His career as a tunesmith. Her amazing discovery of him playing in the *Lankey-Pank Out*. She ran the Tamper Cheese Com. Finally she finished her remarks, and risked the distortion of her lovely profile to glance in his direction. "Ladies and gentlemen, with admiration, with pride, with pleasure, I give you a Marigold Exclusive, Erlin Baque!"

Baque grinned nervously, and coyly tapped out a scale with one finger. "This is my first speech," he said. "Probably it'll be my last. The new restaurant opens tonight. *Lankey's,* on Broadway. Unfortunately I can't invite you to join us, because thanks to Miss Manning's generous comments this past week all space is reserved for the next two months. After that we'll be setting aside a limited number of reservations for visitors from distant places. Jet over and see us!

"You'll find something different at *Lankey's.* There is no visiscope screen. Maybe you've heard about that. We have attractive young ladies to sing for you. I play the multichord. We know you'll enjoy our music. We know you'll enjoy it because you'll hear no Coms at *Lankey's.* Remember that—*No Coms at Lankey's.* No soap with your soup. No air cars with your steaks. No shirts with your desserts. No Coms! Just good music played for your enjoyment—like this."

He brought his hands down on the keyboard.

It was a strange experience, playing with no audience, or practically no audience. There was only Miss Manning, and the visiscope engineers, and Baque was suddenly apprehensive that his audiences were responsible for his success. He'd always had a throng of faces to watch, and he had paced his playing according to their reactions. People were listening all over the Western Hemisphere. And later it would be all over Earth, and all over the Solar System. Would they be clapping and stomping? Would they be thinking awesomely, "So that's how music sounds without words, without Coms?" Or would they be listening in mild boredom?

Baque caught a glimpse of Miss Manning's pale face, of the engineers watching with mouths agape, and thought maybe everything was all right. He lost himself in the music, and played fervently.

He continued to play after he knew that something had gone wrong. Miss Manning leaped to her feet and hurried towards him, the engineers were moving about confusedly, and the distant pilot screen was blank. Baque slowed down, and brought his playing to a halt.

"We were cut off," Miss Manning said tearfully. "Who would do such a thing to me? Never, never, in all the time I've been on visiscope—George, who cut us off?"

"Orders."

"Whose orders?"

"My orders!" James Denton strode towards them, and he was not smiling. His lips were tight, his face pale, his eyes gleaming violence and sudden death. "Pretty bright boy, aren't you?" he said to Baque. "I don't know how you worked that trick, but no man fools James Denton more than once. Now you've made yourself a problem, and I'm not going to bother solving it. Consider yourself eliminated."

"Jimmy!" Miss Manning wailed. "My program—cut off. How could you?"

"Shut up, damn it! I'll give you any odds you want, Baque, that Lankey's doesn't open tonight. Not that it's going to make any difference to you."

Baque smiled gently. "I think you've lost, Denton. I think enough music got over to beat you. I'll give you any odds *you* want that you'll have several thousand complaints by tomorrow. So will the government. And then you'll find out who really runs *Visiscope International.*"

"*I* run *Visiscope International.*"

"No, Denton. It belongs to the people. They've let things slide for a long time, and taken anything you'd give them. But if they know what they want, they'll get it. I know I gave them at least three minutes of what they want. That was more than I'd hoped for."

"How did you work that trick in my office?"

"You tricked yourself, Denton—because you didn't know about overtones. Your intercom wasn't built to carry music. It doesn't carry the upper frequencies at all, so the multichord sounded dead to the men in the other room. But visiscope has the frequency range of live sound."

Denton nodded. "Clever. I'll have the heads of some scientists, for that. And I'll have your head, Baque."

He stalked away, and as the automatic door closed behind him, Marigold Manning clutched Baque's arm. "Quick! Follow me!" As Baque hesitated, she hissed, "Don't stand there like an idiot! He'll have you killed."

She led him through a control room, and out into a small corridor. They raced down it, darted through a reception room past a startled secretary, and out a rear door into another corridor. She jerked him after her into an anti-grav lift, and they shot upwards. At the top of the building she hurried him to the air car landing strip, and left him standing in a doorway.

"When I give you a signal, you walk out," she said. "Don't run, just walk."

She walked out calmly, and Baque heard an attendant's surprised greeting. "Through early this morning, Miss Manning?"

"We're running a lot of Coms," she said. "I want the big Waring."

"Coming right up."

Peering around the corner, Baque saw her step into the flyer. As soon as the attendant's back was turned, she waved frantically. Baque walked carefully towards her, keeping the Waring between the attendant and himself. A moment later they were shooting upwards, and below them a siren sounded faintly.

"We did it!" she gasped. "If you hadn't gotten out before that alarm sounded, you wouldn't have gotten out at all."

Baque took a deep breath, and looked back at the *Visiscope International* Building. "Well, thanks," he said. "But surely that wasn't necessary. This is a civilized planet."

"*Visiscope International* is not civilized!" she snapped.

He looked at her wonderingly. Her face was flushed, her eyes wide with fear, and for the first time Baque saw her as a human being, a woman, a lovely woman. As he looked, she turned away and burst into tears.

"Now Jimmy'll have me killed, too. And where will we go?"

"*Lankey's,*" Baque said. "Look—you can see it from here."

She pointed the air car at the freshly painted letters on the strip above the new restaurant, and Baque, looking backwards, saw a crowd forming in the street by *Visiscope International.*

Lankey floated his desk over to the wall, and leaned back comfortably. He wore a trim dress suit, and he had carefully groomed himself for the role of a jovial host, but in his office he was the same ungainly Lankey that Baque had first seen leaning over a bar.

"I told you all hell would break loose," he said flatly. "There are five thousand people over by *Visiscope International*, screaming for Erlin Baque. And the crowd is growing."

"I didn't play for more than three minutes," Baque said. "I thought a lot of people might write in to complain about their cutting me off, but I didn't expect anything like that."

"You didn't, eh? Five thousand people. Probably ten thousand, by now, and nobody knows where it will stop. And Miss Manning, here, risks her neck to get you out of the place—ask her why, Baque."

"Yes," Baque said. "Why go to all that trouble for me?"

She shuddered. "Your music does things to me."

"It sure does," Lankey said. "Baque, you fool, you gave a quarter of Earth's population three minutes of Sex Music!"

Lankey's opened on schedule that evening, with crowds filling the street outside, and struggling in as long as there was standing room. The shrewd Lankey had instituted an admission charge. The standees bought no food, and Lankey couldn't see the point in furnishing free music, even if people were willing to stand to hear it.

There was one last-minute change. Lankey decided that the customers would prefer a glamorous hostess to a flat-nosed old host, and he hired Marigold Manning. She moved about gracefully, the deep blue of her flowing gown offsetting her golden hair.

When Baque took his place at the multichord, the frenzied ovation lasted for twenty minutes.

Midway through the evening, Baque sought out Lankey. "Has Denton tried anything?"

"Not a thing. Everything is running smoothly."

"It seems odd. He swore we wouldn't open tonight."

Lankey chuckled. "He's had troubles of his own to worry about. The authorities are on his neck about that rioting this afternoon. I was afraid they would blame you, but they didn't. Denton put you on, and then he cut you off, and they figure he's responsible. And according to my last report, *Visiscope International* has had more than ten million complaints. Don't worry, Baque. We'll hear from Denton soon enough—and the guilds, too."

"The guilds? Why the guilds?"

"The Tunesmiths' Guild will be damned furious about your cutting out the Coms. The Lyric Writers' Guild will go along with them, on account of the Coms, and on account of your using music without words. The Performers' Guild won't like you because not many of its members can play worth a damn. By tomorrow morning, Baque, you'll be the most popular man in the Solar System, and the sponsors, and the visiscope people, and the guilds are going to hate your guts. I'm giving you a twenty-four hour bodyguard, and Miss Manning, too. I want you to come out of this alive."

"Do you really think Denton would . . ."

"Denton would."

The next morning the Performers' Guild blacklisted *Lankey's*, and ordered all the musicians, including Baque, to sever relations. The musicians respectfully declined, and found themselves blacklisted before noon. Lankey called in a lawyer, the most sinister, furtive, disreputable-looking individual Baque had ever seen.

"They're supposed to give us a week's notice," Lankey said, "and another week if we decide to appeal. I'll sue them for five million."

The Commissioner of Public Safety called, and a little later, the Liquor Commissioner. Both conferred briefly with Lankey, and departed grim-faced.

"Denton's moving too late," Lankey said gleefully. "I got to both of them a week ago, and recorded our conversations. They don't dare take any action."

A riot broke out in front of *Lankey's* that night. Lankey had his own riot squad ready for action, and the customers never noticed the disturbance. Lankey's informants estimated that more than fifty million complaints had been received by *Visiscope International*. An anti-Com demonstration erupted spontaneously, and five hundred visiscope screens were smashed in Manhattan restaurants.

Lankey's finished its first week unmolested, entertaining capacity crowds daily. Reservations were pouring in from as far away as Venus and Mars. Baque sent to Berlin for a multichordist to understudy him, and Lankey hoped by the end of the month to have the restaurant open twenty-four hours a day.

At the beginning of the second week, Lankey told Baque, "We've got Denton licked. I've countered every move he's made, and now we're going to make a few moves. You're going on visiscope again. I'm making application today. We're legitimate business, and we've got as much right to buy time as anyone else. If he won't give it to us, I'll sue. He won't dare refuse."

"Where do you get the money for all this?" Baque said.

Lankey grinned. "I saved it up. And I've had a little help from people who don't like Denton."

Denton didn't refuse. Baque did an Earth-wide program direct from *Lankey's,* with Marigold Manning introducing him. He omitted only the Sex Music.

Quitting time at *Lankey's.* Baque was in his dressing room, wearily changing. Lankey had already left for an early-morning conference with his lawyer. They were speculating on Denton's next move.

Baque was uneasy. He was, he told himself, only a dumb musician. He didn't understand legal problems, or the tangled web of connections and influence that Lankey negotiated so easily. He knew James Denton was the incarnation of evil. He also knew that Denton had enough money to buy Lankey a thousand times over. Or pay for the murder of anyone who got in his way. What was he waiting for? With enough time, Baque might deliver a death-blow to the whole institution of Coms. Denton would know that.

So what was he waiting for?

The door burst open, and Marigold Manning stumbled in half undressed, her pale face the bleached whiteness of her plastic breast cups. She slammed the door and leaned against it, sobs shaking her body.

"Jimmy," she gasped. "I got a note from Carol—that's his secretary. She was a good friend of mine. She says Jimmy's bribed our guards, and they're going to kill us on the way home this morning. Or let Jimmy's men kill us."

"I'll call Lankey," Baque said. "There's nothing to worry about."

"No! If they suspect anything they won't wait. We won't have a chance."

"Then we'll just wait until Lankey gets back."

"Do you think it's safe to wait? They know we're getting ready to leave."

Baque sat down heavily. It was the sort of move he expected Denton to make. Lankey picked his men carefully, he knew, but then—Denton had enough money to buy any man. And yet . . .

"Maybe it's a trap," he said. "Maybe that note's a fake."

"No. I saw that fat little man Hulsey talking with one of your guards last night, and I knew Jimmy was up to something."

So that was it. Hulsey. "What do you want to do?" Baque said.

"Could we get out the back way?"

"I don't know. We'd have to get past at least one guard."

"Couldn't we try?"

Baque hesitated. She was frightened. She was sick with fright. But she knew far more about this sort of thing than he did. And she knew James Denton. He'd never have gotten out of *Visiscope International* without her help.

"If you think that's the thing to do, we'll try it."

"I'll have to finish changing."

"Go ahead, then. Let me know when you're ready."

She looked cautiously out the door, and turned back, fear overcoming modesty. "No. You come with me."

Baque and Miss Manning walked leisurely along the corridor at the back of the building, nodded to the two guards that sat there alertly, and with a sudden movement were through the door. Running. A shout of surprise came from behind them, nothing more. They dashed frantically down an alley, turned off, reached another intersection, and hesitated.

"The conveyer is that way," she gasped. "If we can reach the conveyer . . ."

"Let's go!"

They ran on, hand in hand. Far ahead of them the alley opened onto a street. Baque glanced anxiously upwards for air cars, and saw none. Exactly where they were he did not know.

"Are we—being followed?"

"I don't think so. There aren't any air cars, and I didn't see anyone behind us when we stopped."

"Then we got away!"

Thirty feet ahead of them, a man stepped abruptly out of the dawn shadows. As they halted, stricken dumb with panic, he walked towards them. A hat was pulled low over his face, but there was no mistaking the smile. James Denton.

"Good morning, beautiful," he said. "*Visiscope International* hasn't been the same without your lovely presence. And a good morning to you, Mr. Baque."

They stood silently, Miss Manning's hand clutching Baque's arm, her nails cutting through his shirt and into his flesh. He did not move.

"I thought you'd fall for that little gag, beautiful. I thought you'd be just frightened enough, by now, to fall for it. I have every exit blocked, but I'm grateful to you for picking this one. Very grateful. I like to settle in person for a double cross."

Suddenly he whirled on Baque, his voice an angry snarl. "Get going, Baque. It isn't your turn, yet. I have other plans for you."

Baque stood rooted to the damp pavement.

"Move, Baque, before I change my mind."

Miss Manning released his arm. Her voice was a choking whisper. "Go!" she said.

"Baque!"

"Go, quickly," she whispered again.

Baque took two hesitant steps.

"Run!" Denton shouted.

Baque ran. Behind him there was the evil crack of a gun, a scream, and silence. Baque faltered, saw Denton looking after him, and ran on.

"So I'm a coward," Baque said.

"No, Baque." Lankey shook his head slowly. "You're a brave man, or you wouldn't have gotten into this. It wouldn't have been bravery, to try something there. It would have been foolishness. It's my fault, for thinking he'd move first against the restaurant. I owe Denton something for this, Baque, and I'm a man who pays his debts."

A troubled frown creased Lankey's ugly face. He looked oddly at Baque, and scratched his bald head. "She was a brave and beautiful woman, Baque. But I wonder why Denton let you go."

The air of tragedy that hung heavily over *Lankey's* that night did not affect the customers. They gave Baque a thunderous ovation as he moved towards the multichord. As he paused for a half-hearted bow, three policemen closed in on him.

"Erlin Baque?"

"That's right."

"You're under arrest."

Baque grinned. Denton wasn't long in making his next move. "What's the charge?" he said.

"Murder."

The murder of Marigold Manning.

Lankey pressed his mournful face against the bars, and talked unhurriedly. "They have some witnesses," he said, "honest witnesses, who saw you run out of that alley. They have several dishonest witnesses, who saw you fire the shot. One of them is your friend Hulsey, who just happened to be taking an early-morning stroll along that alley—or so he'll testify. Denton would probably spend a million to convict you, but he won't have to. He won't even have to bribe the jury. The case against you is that good."

"What about the gun," Baque said.

"They found it. No fingerprints, of course. But someone will claim you were wearing gloves, or someone will have seen you wipe it off."

Baque nodded. Things were out of his hands, now. He'd worked for a cause that no one understood—perhaps he didn't understand himself what he was trying to do. And he'd lost.

"What happens next?"

Lankey shook his head. "I'm not one to hold back bad news. It means life. They're going to send you to the Ganymede rock pits for life."

"I see," Baque said. He added anxiously, "You're going to carry on?"

"Just what were you trying to do, Baque? You weren't only working for *Lankey's*. I couldn't figure it out, but I went along with you because I like you. And I like your music. What was it?"

"I don't know." A concert? A thousand people gathered together to hear music? Was that what he wanted? "Music, I suppose," he said. "Get rid of the Coms—or some of them."

"Yes. Yes, I think I understand. *Lankey's* will carry on, Baque, as long as I have any breath left. That new multichord player isn't bad. He's nothing like you were, but then—there'll never be another one like you were. We're still turning people away. Several other restaurants are doing away with visiscope and trying to imitate us, but we have a big head start. We'll carry on the way you had things set up, and your one-third still stands. I'll have it put in trust for you. You'll be a wealthy man when you get back."

"When I get back!"

"Well—a life sentence doesn't necessarily mean life. See that you behave yourself."

"Val?"

"She'll be taken care of. I'll give her a job of some kind, to keep her occupied."

"Maybe I can send you music for the restaurant," Baque said. "I should have plenty of time."

"I'm afraid not. It's music they want to keep you away from. So—no writing of music. And they won't let you near a multichord. They think you could hypnotize the guards, and turn all the prisoners loose."

"Would they—let me have my record collection?"

"I'm afraid not."

"I see. Well, if that's the way it is . . ."

"It is. Now I owe Denton two debts."

The unemotional Lankey had tears in his eyes as he turned away.

The jury deliberated for eight minutes, and brought in a verdict of guilty. Baque was sentenced to life imprisonment. There was some editorial grumbling on visiscope, because life in the Ganymede rock pits was frequently a very short life.

And there was a swelling undertone of whispering among the little people that the verdict was bought and paid for by the sponsors, by visiscope. Erlin Baque was framed, it was said, because he gave the people music.

And on the day Baque left for Ganymede, announcement was made of a public exhibition, by H. Vail, multichordist, and B. Johnson, violinist. Admission one dollar.

Lankey collected evidence with painstaking care, rebribed one of the bribed witnesses, and petitioned for a new trial. The petition was denied, and the long years limped past.

The New York Symphony Orchestra was organized, with twenty members. One of James Denton's plush air cars crashed, and he was instantly killed. An unfortunate accident. A millionaire who once heard Erlin Baque play on visiscope endowed a dozen conservatories of music. They were to be called the Baque Conservatories, but a musical historian who had never heard of Baque got the name changed to Bach.

Lankey died, and a son-in-law carried on his efforts as a family trust. A subscription was launched to build a new hall for the New York Symphony, which now numbered forty members. Interest spread like an avalanche, and a site was finally picked in Ohio, to be within easier commuting distance of all parts of the North American continent. Beethoven Hall was erected, to seat forty thousand people. The first series of concerts was fully subscribed forty-eight hours after tickets went on sale.

Opera was given on visiscope for the first time in two hundred years. An opera house was built on the Ohio site, and then an art institute. The Center grew, first by private subscription, and then under government sponsorship. Lankey's son-in-law died, and a nephew took over the management of *Lankey's*—and the campaign to free Erlin Baque. Thirty years passed, and then forty.

And forty-nine years, seven months and nineteen days after Baque received his life sentence, he was paroled. He still owned a third interest in Manhattan's most prosperous restaurant, and the profits that had piled up over the years made him a wealthy man. He was ninety-six years old.

Another capacity crowd at Beethoven Hall. Vacationists from all parts of the Solar System, music lovers who commuted for the concerts, old people who had retired to the Center, forty-thousand of them, stirred restlessly and searched the wings for the conductor. Applause thundered down from the twelve balconies as he strode forward.

Erlin Baque sat in his permanent seat at the rear of the main floor. He adjusted his binoculars and peered at the orchestra, wondering again what a contrabassoon sounded like. His bitterness he had left behind on Ganymede. His life at the Center was an unending revelation of miracles.

Of course no one remembered Erlin Baque, tunesmith and murderer. Whole generations of people could not even remember the Coms. And yet Baque felt that he had accomplished all this, just as surely as if he had built this building—built the Center—with his own hands. He spread his hands before him, hands deformed by the years in the rock pits, fingers and tips of fingers crushed off, his body maimed by cascading rocks. He had no regrets. He had done his work well.

Two ushers stood in the aisle behind him. One jerked a thumb in his direction, and whispered, "Now there's a character for you. Comes to every concert. Never misses one. And he just sits there in the back row watching people. They say he was one of the old tunesmiths, years and years ago."

"Maybe he likes music," the other said.

"Naw. Those old tunesmiths never knew anything about music. Besides—he's deaf."

Hunting Machine

by CAROL EMSHWILLER

It sensed Ruthie McAlister's rapid heartbeat, just as it sensed any other animal's. The palms of her hands were damp, and it felt that, too—it also felt the breathing, in and out. And it heard her nervous giggle.

She was watching her husband, Joe, as he leaned over the control unit of the thing that sensed heartbeats—the grey-green thing they called the hound, or Rover, or sometimes the bitch.

"Hey," she said. "I guess it's OK, huh?"

Joe turned a screw with his thumb nail and pulled out the wire attached to it. "Gimme a bobby pin."

Ruthie reached to the back of her head. "I mean it's not dangerous is it?"

"Naw."

"I don't just mean about *it*." She nodded at the grey-green thing. "I mean, I know you're good at fixing things like this, like the time you got beer for nothing out of the beer vendor and, golly, I guess we haven't paid for a TV show for years. I mean, I *know* you can fix things right, only won't they know when we bring it back to be checked out?"

"Look, these wardens are country boys, and besides, I can put this thing back so *nobody* knows."

The grey-green thing squatted on its six legs where Joe could lean over it; it sensed that Ruthie's heartbeat had slowed almost to normal, and it heard her sigh.

"I guess you're pretty good at this, huh, Joe?" She wiped her damp hands on her green tunic. "That's the weight dial, isn't it?" she asked, watching him turn the top one.

He nodded. "Fifteen hundred pounds," he said slowly.

"Oo, was he really and truly that big?"

"Bigger." And now the thing felt Joe's heart and breathing surge.

They had been landed day before yesterday, with them geodesic tent, pneumatic form beds, automatic camping stove, and pocket air conditioner. Plus portable disposal automatic blow-up chairs and tables, pocket TV set, four disposable hunting costumes apiece (one for each day), and two folding guns with power settings.

In addition, there was the bug-scat, go-snake, sun-stop, and the grey-green hunter, sealed by the warden and set for three birds, two deer and one black bear. They had only the bear to go; now, Joe McAlister had unsealed the controls, released the governor and changed the setting to brown bear, 1500 pounds.

"I don't care," he said, "I want that bear."

"Do you think he'll still be there tomorrow?"

Joe patted one of the long jointed legs of the thing. "If he's not, ol' bitch here will find him for us."

Next day, was clear and cool, and Joe breathed big, expanding breaths and patted his beginning paunch. "Yes sir," he said, "this is the day for something big—something really big, that'll put up a real fight."

He watched the red of the sunrise fade out of the sky while Ruthie turned on the stove and then got out her make-up kit. She put sun-stop on her face, then powdered it with a tan powder. She blackened her eyelids and purpled her lips; after that, she opened the stove and took out two disposable plates with eggs and bacon.

They sat in the automatic blow-up chairs, at the automatic blow-up table. Joe said that there was nothing like North air to give you an appetite, and Ruthie said she bet they were sweltering back in the city. Then she giggled.

Joe leaned back in his chair and sipped his coffee. "Shooting deer is just like shooting a cow," he said. "No fight to 'em at all. Even when ol' hound here goads 'em, they just want to run off. But this bear's going to be different. Of course bears are shy too, but ol' hound knows what to do about that."

"They say it's getting to be so there aren't many of the big kind left."

"Yes, but one more won't hurt. Think of a skin and head that size in our living room. I guess anybody that came in there would sure sit up and take notice."

"It won't match the curtains," his wife said.

"I think what I'll do is pack the skin up tight and leave it some-where up here, till the warden checks us through. Then, maybe a couple of days later, I'll come back and get it."

"Good idea." Ruthie had finished her coffee and was perfuming herself with bug-scat.

"Well, I guess we'd better get started." They hung their folded-up guns on their belts. They put their dehydrated, self-heating lunch in their pockets. They slung on their cold-unit canteens. They each took a packet containing chair, table and sun shade; then Joe fas-tened on the little mike that controlled the hunter. It fit on his shoul-der where he could turn his head to the side and talk into it.

"All right, houn' dog," he said, shoulder hunched and head tilted, "get a move on, boy. Back to that spot where we saw him yesterday. You can pick up the scent from there."

The hunting machine ran on ahead of them. It went faster than anything it might have to hunt. Two miles, three miles—Joe and Ruthie were left behind. They followed the beam it sent back to them, walking and talking and helping each other over the rough spots.

About eleven o'clock, Joe stopped, took off his red hunting hat and mopped his balding forehead with the new bandana he'd bought at Hunter's Outfitters in New York. It was then he got the signal. *Sighted, sighted, sighted . . .*

Joe leaned over his mike. "Stick on him boy. How far are you? Well, try to move him down this way if you can." He turned to his wife. "Let's see, about three miles . . . we'll take half hour out for lunch. Maybe we'll get there a couple of hours from now. How's it going, kid?"

"Swell," Ruthie said.

The big bear sat on the rocks by the stream. His front paws were wet almost to the elbows. There were three torn fishheads lying be-side him. He ate only the best parts because he was a good fisher; and he looked, now, into the clean cold water for another dark blue back that would pause on its way upstream.

It wasn't a smell that made him turn. He had a keen nose, but the hunting machine was made to have no smell. It was the grey dead lichen's crackle that made him look up. He stood still, looking in the direction of the sound and squinting his small eyes, but it wasn't until it moved that he saw it.

Three quarters of a ton, he was; but like a bird, or a rabbit, or a snake, the bear avoided things that were large and strange. He turned back the way he always took, the path to his rubbing tree and to his home. He moved quietly and rapidly, but the thing followed.

He doubled back to the stream again, then, and waded down it on the opposite side from the thing—but still it followed, needing no scent. Once the hunting machine sighted, it never lost its prey.

Heart beat normal, respiration normal, it sensed. Size almost 1600 pounds.

The bear got out on the bank and turned back, calling out in low growls. He stood up on his hind legs and stretched his full height. Almost two men tall, he stood and gave warning.

The hunting machine waited twenty yards away. The bear looked at it a full minute; then he fell back on all fours and turned south again. He was shy and he wanted no trouble.

Joe and Ruthie kept on walking north at their leisurely pace until just noon. Then they stopped for lunch by the side of the same stream the bear had waded, only lower down. And they used its cold water on their dehydrated meal—beef and onions, mashed potatoes, a lettuce salad that unfolded in the water like Japanese paper flowers. There were coffee tablets that contained a heating unit too, and fizzled in the water like firecracker fuses until the water was hot, creamy coffee.

The bear didn't stop to eat. Noon meant nothing to him. Now he moved with more purpose, looking back and squinting his small eyes.

The hunter felt the heart beat faster, the breathing heavy, pace increasing. Direction generally south.

Joe and Ruthie followed the signal until it suddenly changed. It came faster; that meant they were near.

They stopped and unfolded their guns. "Let's have a cup of coffee first," Ruthie said.

"OK, Hon." Joe released the chairs which blew themselves up to size. "Good to take a break so we can really enjoy the fight."

Ruthie handed Joe a fizzing cup of coffee. "Don't forget you want ol' Rover to goad some."

"Uh huh. Bear's not much better than a deer without it. Good you reminded me." He turned and spoke softly into the little mike.

The hunting machine shortened the distance slowly. Fifteen feet, ten, five. The bear heard and turned. Again he rose up, almost two men tall, and roared his warning sound to tell the thing to keep back.

Joe and Ruthie shivered and didn't look at each other. They heard it less with their ears, and more with their spines—with an instinct they had forgotten.

Joe shook his shoulder to shake away the feeling of the sound. "I guess the ol' bitch is at him."

"Good dog," Ruthie said. "Get 'im, boy."

The hunter's arm tips drew blood, but only in the safe spots—shoulder scratches at the heavy lump behind his head, thigh punctures. It never touched the veins, or arteries.

The bear swung at the thing with his great paw. His claws screeched down the body section but didn't so much as make a mark on the metal. The blow sent the thing thirty feet away, but it got up and came back so fast the bear couldn't see it until it was there, thrusting at him again. He threw it again and again, but it came back every time. The muscles, claws and teeth were nothing to it. It was made to withstand easily more than what one bear could do, and it knew with its built-in knowledge, how to make a bear blind-angry.

Saliva came to the bear's mouth and flew out over his chin as he moved his heavy head sideways and back. It splashed, gummy on his cheeks and made dark, damp streaks across his chest. Only his rage was real to him now, and he screamed a deep rasp of frustration again and again.

Two hundred yards away, Joe said, "Some roar!"

"Uh huh. If noise means anything, it sounds like he's about ready for a real fight."

They both got up and folded up the chairs and cups. They sighted along their gun barrels to see that they were straight. "Set 'em at medium," Joe said. "We want to start off slow."

They came to where the bear was, and took up a good position on a high place. Joe called in his mike to the hunter thing. "Stand by, houn' dog, and slip over here to back us up." Then he called to the bear. "Hey, boy. This way, boy. This way."

The grey-green thing moved back and the bear saw the new enemy, two of them. He didn't hesitate; he was ready to charge anything that moved. He was only five feet away when their small guns popped. The force knocked him down, and he rolled out of the way, dazed; he turned again for another charge, and came at them, all claws and teeth.

Joe's gun popped again. This time the bear staggered, but still came on. Joe backed up, pushing at his gun dial to raise the power.

He bumped into Ruthie behind him and they both fell. Joe's voice was a crazy scream. "Get him."

The hunting machine moved fast. Its sharp forearm came like an upper cut, under the jaw, and into the brain.

He lay, looking smaller, somehow, but still big, his ragged fur matted with blood. Fleas were alive on it, and flies already coming. Joe and Ruthie looked down at him and took big breaths.

"You shouldna got behind me," Joe said as soon as he caught his breath. "I coulda kept it going longer if you'da just stayed out of the way."

"You told me to," Ruthie said. "You told me to stay right behind you."

"Well, I didn't mean *that* close."

Ruthie sniffed. "Anyway," she said, "how are you going to get the fur off it?"

"Hmmmph."

"I don't think that moth-eaten thing will make much of a rug. It's pretty dirty, too, and probably full of germs."

Joe walked around the bear and turned its head sideways with his toe. "Be a big messy job, all right, skinning it. Up to the elbows in blood and gut, I guess."

"I didn't expect it to be like *this* at all," Ruthie said. "Why don't you just forget it. You had your fun."

Joe stood, looking at the bear's head. He watched a fly land on its eye and then walk down to a damp nostril.

"Well come *on.*" Ruthie took her small pack. "I want to get back in time to take a bath before supper."

"OK" Joe leaned over his mike. "Come on ol' Rover, ol' hound dog. You did fine."

The Science-Fiction Book Index

Compiled by EARL KEMP

The Index that follows covers in detail the fiction titles published in the field of imaginative literature, in the English language. There are three lists, Number One: Books published between January 1, 1956 and December 31, 1956; Number Two: Books published between January 1, 1957 and December 31, 1957; Number Three: Related, Associational and Non-fiction Works. There has been no attempt in List Three to separate the books published in 1956 from those published in 1957. Acknowledgment is made to Edward Wood and James O'Meara for their assistance and to Kenneth Slater of England whose invaluable British indexing serves to complete this list.

The imprint *Avalon* is used exclusively by the firm of Thomas Bouregy and Company.

An asterisk, preceding the title of the book, denotes the original first edition publication of the title insofar as it is possible to establish.

The following key is applicable:

(B)	- British	J	- Juvenile
(C)	- Canadian	pa	- Paper back
BCE	- Book Club Edition†	°	- Original edition

† *Sidgwick and Jackson* is the British Science Fiction Book Club, corresponding to *Doubleday* here in the States.

LIST ONE

January 1, 1956 through December 31, 1956

Abbott, George & Wallop, Douglas
  °DAMN YANKEES /The Year the Yankees Lost the Pennant/ $2.95 *Random House*
Abrashkin, Raymond & Williams, Jay
  °DANNY DUNN AND THE ANTI-GRAVITY PAINT J $2.50 *Whittlesey*
Adler, Allen A. See Stuart, W. J.
Anderson, Poul
  °PLANET OF NO RETURN 35¢ *Ace Double* pa
  °STAR WAYS $2.50 *Avalon*
  STAR WAYS $2.75 *Ryerson* (C)

Appleton, Victor, II (Group pseudonym)
   °TOM SWIFT AND HIS OUTPOST IN SPACE J 95¢ *Grosset & Dunlap*
Ash, Alan
     CONDITIONED FOR SPACE 6s *Ward, Lock* (B) New Edition
     CONDITIONED FOR SPACE 2s *Ward, Lock* (B) pa
Asimov, Isaac (See also Paul French, pseudonym)
     THE CAVES OF STEEL 5s6d *Sidgwick and Jackson* BCE (B)
     THE END OF ETERNITY $1.15 *Doubleday* BCE
     I, ROBOT 35¢ *Signet* pa
Asquith, Cynthia ed
     THE SECOND GHOST BOOK 2s *Pan* (B) pa
Atkins, John (Alfred)
     TOMORROW REVEALED $3.50 *Burns & MacEachern* (C)
     TOMORROW REVEALED $4.00 *Roy*
Auden, W(ystan) H(ugh) & Kallman, Chester
   °THE MAGIC FLUTE $3.50 *Random House*
Baker, Frank
   °TALK OF THE DEVIL 12s6d *Angus & Robertson* (Australia)
Barnes, Arthur K.
   °INTERPLANETARY HUNTER $3.00 *Gnome* Illustrated by Emsh (Edward
     Alexander Emshwiller)
Benson, Msgr. Robert Hugh
     LORD OF THE WORLD $3.00 *Dodd, Mead* New Edition
Bester, Alfred
   °TIGER! TIGER! 12s6d *Sidgwick and Jackson* (B)
Biemiller, Carl L(udwig)
   °STARBOY J $2.50 *Holt*
Black, Irving See Stuart, W. J.
Bleiler, Everett F(ranklin) & Dikty, T. E. eds
     THE BEST SCIENCE FICTION STORIES *Fifth Series* 10s6d *Grayson &
     Grayson* (B)
Blish, James
     EARTHMAN, COME HOME $1.15 *Doubleday* BCE
     EARTHMAN, COME HOME 12s6d *Faber & Faber* (B)
     EARTHMAN, COME HOME $3.75 *T. Allen* (C)
   °THEY SHALL HAVE STARS 12s6d *Faber & Faber* (B)
Bliss, Sidney
   °CRY HUNGER $2.75 *Vantage*
Boland, John
   °NO REFUGE 12s6d *Michael Joseph* (B)
Boston, L. M.
   °THE CHILDREN OF GREEN KNOWE J $2.75 *Harcourt, Brace*
Boucher, Anthony ed
   °THE BEST FROM FANTASY AND SCIENCE FICTION *Fifth Series* $3.50
     Doubleday
     THE BEST FROM FANTASY AND SCIENCE FICTION *Fifth Series* $4.25
     Doubleday (C)
     THE BEST FROM FANTASY AND SCIENCE FICTION *Fifth Series* $1.15
     Doubleday BCE
Bounds, Sydney J.
   °THE WORLD WRECKER 8s6d *Foulsham* (B)

Bowles, Paul
    THE DELICATE PREY 25¢ *Signet* pa New Edition

Brackett, Leigh (Mrs. Edmond Hamilton)
    THE LONG TOMORROW $1.15 *Doubleday* BCE
    THE SWORD OF RHIANNON 9s6d *Boardman* (B)

Bradbury, Ray
    THE GOLDEN APPLES OF THE SUN 2s *Corgi* (B) pa
    THE OCTOBER COUNTRY 50¢ *Ballantine* pa
    THE OCTOBER COUNTRY 15s *Rupert Hart-Davis* (B)
    THE SILVER LOCUSTS /The Martian Chronicles/ 2s *Corgi* (B) pa
———& ed
    °THE CIRCUS OF DR. LAO AND OTHER IMPROBABLE STORIES (Title novel
      by Charles G. Finney) 35¢ *Bantam* pa

Bradley, Willis T. Translator
    °JOURNEY TO THE CENTER OF THE EARTH, by Jules Verne 35¢ *Ace
      Double* pa
    JOURNEY TO THE CENTER OF THE EARTH, by Jules Verne $2.95 *Wyn*

Bromfield, Louis
    THE STRANGE CASE OF MISS ANNIE SPRAGG 25¢ *Berkley* pa

Brown, Fredric
    MARTIANS, GO HOME 35¢ *Bantam* pa
    STAR SHINE /Angels and Spaceships/ 25¢ *Bantam* pa

Brown, Slater
    SPACEWARD BOUND J $2.82 *Prentice Hall* (Magic Windows Edition)
      Schools only

Burke, Jonathan
    °PURSUIT THROUGH TIME 10s6d *Ward, Lock* (B)
    PURSUIT THROUGH TIME $2.25 *British Book Service* (Import)

Burman, Lucien Ben
    °SEVEN STARS FOR CATFISH BEND $2.75 *Funk & Wagnalls*

Cameron, E.
    °STOWAWAY TO THE MUSHROOM PLANET J $2.75 *Little, Brown*

Campbell, John W., Jr.
    THE MOON IS HELL! $1.00 *Fantasy Press* pa
———& ed
    THE ASTOUNDING SCIENCE FICTION ANTHOLOGY (excerpts from) 35¢
      Berkley pa

Capon, Paul
    °INTO THE TENTH MILLENNIUM J 13s6d *Heinemann* (B)
    LOST: A MOON J $2.75 *Bobbs-Merrill*

Carr, John Dickson (See Carter Dickson, pseudonym)

Charters, David Wilton
    °GROTTO $3.50 *Pageant*
    GROTTO $4.00 *Smithers* (C)

Chilton, Charles
    °THE RED PLANET 19s6d *Herbert Jenkins* (B)

Christopher, John (Pseudonym of Christopher S. Youd)
    °THE DEATH OF GRASS 10s6d *Michael Joseph* (B)
    THE DEATH OF GRASS $2.75 *Collins* (C)

Clarke, Arthur C(harles)
    CHILDHOOD'S END 2s *Pan* (B) pa

°THE CITY AND THE STARS　/Against the Fall of Night/　$3.75　*Harcourt, Brace*

THE CITY AND THE STARS　/Against the Fall of Night/　$4.25　*Longmans, Green*　(C)

THE CITY AND THE STARS　/Against the Fall of Night/　$1.15　*Doubleday*　BCE

THE CITY AND THE STARS　/Against the Fall of Night/　13s6d　*Frederick Muller*　(B)

°REACH FOR TOMORROW　35¢　*Ballantine*　pa

REACH FOR TOMORROW　$2.00　*Ballantine*

Clement, Hal　(Pseudonym of Harry Clement Stubbs)

°RANGER BOYS IN SPACE　J　$2.75　*Page*

RANGER BOYS IN SPACE　J　19s6d　*Harrap*　(B)

Coles, Manning

°THE FAR TRAVELLER　$3.00　*Doubleday*

Collins, Hunt　(Pseudonym of Evan Hunter)

TOMORROW AND TOMORROW　35¢　*Pyramid*　pa　/same as Tomorrow's World/

°TOMORROW'S WORLD　$2.50　*Avalon*　/Malice in Wonderland/

TOMORROW'S WORLD　$2.75　*Ryerson*　(C)

Conklin, (Edward) Groff　ed

A WAY HOME, by Theodore Sturgeon (excerpts from)　35¢　*Pyramid*　pa

°SCIENCE-FICTION ADVENTURES IN MUTATION　$3.75　*Vanguard*

SCIENCE-FICTION ADVENTURES IN MUTATION　$4.25　*Copp*　(C)

SCIENCE FICTION OMNIBUS　(excerpts from)　35¢　*Berkley*　pa

Correy, Lee　(Pseudonym of G. Harry Stine)

°CONTRABAND ROCKET　35¢　*Ace Double*　pa

°ROCKET MAN　J　$2.75　*Holt*

Crispin, Edmund (Pseudonym of R. B. Montgomery)　ed

°BEST SF TWO　15s　*Faber & Faber*　(B)

BEST SF TWO　$3.25　*British Book Service*　(Import)

Cummings, Ray

THE MAN WHO MASTERED TIME　35¢　*Ace Double*　pa

Dallas, Paul V.

°THE LOST PLANET　J　$2.00　*Winston*

Dawson, Basil

°DAN DARE ON MARS　J　7s6d　*Hulton*　(B)

de Camp, L(yon) Sprague & Howard, Robert E.

°TALES OF CONAN　$3.00　*Gnome*

del Rey, Lester (See also Erik van Lhin, pseudonym)

°MISSION TO THE MOON　J　$2.00　*Winston*

°NERVES　35¢　*Ballantine*　pa

NERVES　$2.00　*Ballantine*

STEP TO THE STARS　J　10s6d　*Hutchinson*　(B)

Derleth, August　ed

THE OTHER SIDE OF THE MOON　10s6d　*Grayson & Grayson*　(B)

THE OTHER SIDE OF THE MOON　$5.00　*McLeod*　(C)

PORTALS OF TOMORROW　12s6d　*Cassell*　(B)

Dern, Dorothy Louise

°THE DOCTOR'S SECRET　$2.50　*Pageant*

Dick, Philip K(endrick)
°THE MAN WHO JAPED 35¢ *Ace Double* pa
°THE WORLD JONES MADE 35¢ *Ace Double* pa
WORLD OF CHANCE /Solar Lottery/ 9s6d *Rich & Cowan* (B)

Dickson, Carter (Pseudonym of John Dickson Carr)
°FEAR IS THE SAME $3.50 *Morrow*

Dickson, Gordon R.
°ALIEN FROM ARCTURUS 35¢ *Ace Double* pa
°MANKIND ON THE RUN 35¢ *Ace Double* pa

Dikty, T. E. ed
°THE BEST SCIENCE FICTION STORIES AND NOVELS 1956 $3.50 *Fell*
THE BEST SCIENCE FICTION STORIES AND NOVELS 1956 $4.75 *Mc-Leod* (C)
THE BEST SCIENCE FICTION STORIES AND NOVELS 1956 $1.15 *Double-day* BCE
————& Bleiler, E. F. eds
THE BEST SCIENCE FICTION STORIES *Fifth Series* 10s6d *Grayson & Grayson* (B)

Drake, Leah Bodine
°THIS TILTING DUST /Verse/ $2.00 *Golden Quill*

Duncan, David
ANOTHER TREE IN EDEN /Beyond Eden/ 12s6d *Heinemann* (B)

Eager, Edward
°KNIGHT'S CASTLE J $2.75 *Harcourt, Brace*

Elam, Richard M.
YOUNG VISITOR TO MARS J $1.00 *Grosset & Dunlap*

Elridge, Paul Viereck, George Sylvester
MY FIRST TWO THOUSAND YEARS 35¢ *Crest (Fawcett)* pa

Eliott, E. C.
°KEMLO AND THE GRAVITY RAYS J 6s *Nelson* (B)

Elton, John
THE GREEN PLANTATIONS 6s *Ward, Lock* (B) New Edition
THE GREEN PLANTATIONS 6s *Ward, Lock* (B) pa

Emshwiller, Edward Alexander See Barnes, Arthur K.

Endore, Guy
NIGHTMARE /Methinks the Lady/ 25¢ *Dell* pa

Evans, I. O. ed
°JULES VERNE, MASTER OF SCIENCE FICTION 12s6d *Sidgwick and Jackson* (B)
THE SHORT STORIES OF JULES VERNE 12s6d *Sidgwick and Jackson* (B)

Ewing, Frederick R. (Pseudonym of Edward Hamilton Waldo, better known as Theodore Sturgeon. See item in *List Three*.)

Fagan, Henry A.
°NINYA 13s6d *Jonathan Cape* (B)
NINYA $2.75 *Clarke, Irwin* (C)

Finney, Charles G.
THE CIRCUS OF DR. LAO (and Other Improbable Stories, ed by Ray Bradbury) 35¢ *Bantam* pa

Fortune, Dion
MOON MAGIC 16s *Aquarian* (B)

Frank, Pat
  °FORBIDDEN AREA $3.50 *Lippincott*
  FORBIDDEN AREA $1.65 *Doubleday* (Best-in-Books)
  FORBIDDEN AREA $1.15 *Doubleday* (Literary Guild)

French, Paul (Pseudonym of Isaac Asimov)
  °LUCKY STARR AND THE BIG SUN OF MERCURY J $2.50 *Doubleday*

Golding, William, Wyndham, John & Peake, Mervyn
  °SOMETIME, NEVER 12s6d *Eyre & Spottiswoode* (B)

Gordon, Rex (Pseudonym of S. B. Hough)
  °NO MAN FRIDAY 13s6d *Heinemann* (B)
  NO MAN FRIDAY $3.00 *British Book Service* (Import)

Gowland, John Stafford
  °BEYOND MARS 9s6d *Gryphon Books* (B)

Gunn, James E. & Williamson, Jack
  STAR BRIDGE 35¢ *Ace Single* pa

Haggard, H. Rider
  ALLAN QUATERMAIN 6s *Nelson* (B) (Winchester Classics Edition)
  AYESHA 10s6d *Macdonald* (B)

Harris, John Beynon (See John Wyndham, pseudonym)

Heinlein, Robert A(nson)
  °DOUBLE STAR $2.95 *Doubleday*
  DOUBLE STAR $3.50 *Doubleday* (C)
  DOUBLE STAR $1.15 *Doubleday* BCE
  THE GREEN HILLS OF EARTH 2s *Pan* (B) pa
  °TIME FOR THE STARS J $2.75 *Scribner's*
  TIME FOR THE STARS J $3.25 *Saunders* (C)

Herbert, Frank
  °THE DRAGON IN THE SEA $2.95 *Doubleday*
  THE DRAGON IN THE SEA $3.50 *Doubleday* (C)
  THE DRAGON IN THE SEA $1.15 *Doubleday* BCE

Hingley, R.
  °UP, JENKINS 12s6d *Longmans* (B)

Holden, Richard (Cort)
  SNOW FURY 25¢ *Pocket Perma* pa

Hough, S. B. (See Rex Gordon, pseudonym)

Howard, D.
  DIANE: SHE CAME FROM VENUS 12s6d *Regency Press* (B)

Howard, Robert E. & de Camp, L. Sprague
  °TALES OF CONAN $3.00 *Gnome*

Hoyland, R.
  ETHELBERT GOES TO THE MOON J $1.50 *Collins* (C)

Hume, Cyril See Stuart, W. J.

Hunger, Anna & Miller, R. De Witt
  °THE MAN WHO LIVED FOREVER 35¢ *Ace Double* pa

Hunter, Evan (See Hunt Collins, pseudonym)

James, Henry
  THE TURN OF THE SCREW AND DAISY MILLER 35¢ *Dell* pa New
    Edition
  THE TURN OF THE SCREW AND OTHER STORIES 7s6d *Collins* (B)

Jameson, Malcolm
  °TARNISHED UTOPIA 35¢ *Galaxy Novels* pa

Jenkins, Will F.   (See Murray Leinster, pseudonym)

Johns, W. E.
  °Now to the Stars   J   7s6d   *Hodder & Stoughton*   (B)

Jones, Raymond F.
  °The Secret People $2.50   *Avalon*
  The Secret People $2.75   *Ryerson*   (C)

Jones, Tupper
  °The Building of the Alpha One $3.00   *Exposition*

Kallman, Chester & Auden, W. H.
  °The Magic Flute $3.50   *Random House*

Kelleam, Joseph E.
  °Overlords From Space   35¢   *Ace Double*   pa

Klass, Philip   (See William Tenn, pseudonym)

Kornbluth, C(yril) M.
  Christmas Eve   /Not This August/   10s6d   *Michael Joseph*   (B)
  Not This August $1.15   *Doubleday*   BCE
  Not This August   35¢   *Bantam*   pa
——& Pohl, Frederik
  °Presidential Year   35¢   *Ballantine*   pa

Kuttner, Henry   (See also Lewis Padgett, pseudonym)
  Fury   5s6d   *Sidgwick and Jackson*   BCE   (B)

Large, E. C.
  °Dawn in Andromeda   15s   *Jonathan Cape*   (B)
  Dawn in Andromeda $3.00   *Clarke, Irwin*   (C)

Lee, Vernon
  °Pope Jacynth and More Supernatural Tales   15s   *Rowen*   (B)

Leinster, Murray   (Pseudonym of Will F. Jenkins)
  The Forgotten Planet   35¢   *Ace Double*   pa
  Operation: Outer Space $1.00   *Fantasy Press*   pa

Lernet-Holenia, Alexander
  °Count Luna $4.00   *Criterion*

Lewin, Albert   See Switzer, Robert

Lewis, C. S.
  Out of the Silent Planet   35¢   *Avon*   pa   New Edition

Lewis, Wyndham
  The Human Age, Book I: Childermass   25s   *Methuen*   (B)

Lott, S. Makepeace
  °Escape to Venus   10s6d   *Rich & Cowan*   (B)

Lovecraft, H(oward) P(hillips)
  The Dream Quest of Unknown Kadath $1.25   *Shroud*   pa

Low, Prof. A. M.
  °Adrift in the Stratosphere   3s6d   *Tower: Blackie*   (B)
  °Satellite in Space   J   10s6d   *Herbert Jenkins*   (B)

McClary, Thomas Calvert
  3 Thousand Years   35¢   *Ace Double*   pa

MacGregor, James Murdoch   (See J. T. McIntosh, pseudonym)

McIlwain, David   (See Charles Eric Maine, pseudonym)

McIntosh, J. T.   (Pseudonym of James Murdoch MacGregor)
  Born Leader   25¢   *Pocket Perma*   pa

ONE IN THREE HUNDRED   10s6d   *Museum Press*   (B)
RULE OF THE PAGBEASTS   /The Fittest/   25¢   *Crest (Fawcett)*   pa

MacKenzie, Nigel
   DAY OF JUDGMENT   9s6d   *Wright & Brown*   (B)

McVicar, Angus
   °THE ATOM CHASERS   J   7s6d   *Burke*   (B)
   °SECRET OF THE LOST PLANET   J   7s6d   *Burke*   (B)

Maine, Charles Eric (Pseudonym of David McIlwain)
   °ESCAPEMENT   12s6d   *Hodder and Stoughton*   (B)
   TIMELINER   35¢   *Bantam*   pa

Mantley, John
   °THE 27th DAY   12s6d   *Michael Joseph*   (B)

Mason, Gregory
   °THE GOLDEN ARCHER $3.50   *Twayne*

Matheson, Richard
   BORN OF MAN AND WOMAN   10s6d   *Max Reinhardt*   (B)
   I AM LEGEND   2s   *Corgi*   (B)   pa
   °THE SHRINKING MAN   35¢   *Gold Medal (Fawcett)*   pa

Mead, Harold
   THE BRIGHT PHOENIX   35¢   *Ballantine*   pa
   THE BRIGHT PHOENIX $2.00   *Ballantine*

Mead, Shepherd
   THE BIG BALL OF WAX   35¢   *Ballantine*   pa

Merril, Judith   ed
   °SF THE YEAR'S GREATEST SCIENCE-FICTION AND FANTASY   35¢   *Dell*
      1st Editions   pa
   SF THE YEAR'S GREATEST SCIENCE-FICTION AND FANTASY $3.95   *Gnome*

Merritt, A(braham)
   THE MOON POOL   35¢   *Avon*   pa   New Edition

Miller, R. De Witt & Hunger, Anna
   °THE MAN WHO LIVED FOREVER   35¢   *Ace Double*   pa

Mines, Samuel   ed
   MOMENT WITHOUT TIME   5s6d   *Sidgwick and Jackson*   BCE   (B)

Mingston, R. G.
   °TEN DAYS TO THE MOON   J   15s   *Maclellan*   (B)

Mogridge, S.
   °PETER AND THE MOON BOMB   J   8s6d   *Hutchinson*   (B)

Montgomery, R. B. (See Edmund Crispin, pseudonym)

Moore, C. L. (Mrs. Henry Kuttner. See Lewis Padget, pseudonym in collabora-
      tion with Henry Kuttner.)

Moore, Patrick A.
   °THE DOMES OF MARS   J   7s6d   *Burke*   (B)
   °WHEEL IN SPACE   J   6s6d   *Lutterworth*   (B)
   °WORLD OF MISTS   J   7s6d   *Frederick Muller*   (B)

Moore, Ward
   CLOUD BY DAY   15s   *Heinemann*   (B)

Morley, Felix
   °GUMPTION ISLAND $5.00   *Caxton*

Munro, H. H.   (See Saki, pseudonym)

Nielsen, H.
 °Deep in the Sky $3.00 *Exposition*
North, Andrew (Pseudonym of Alice Mary Norton)
 °Plague Ship J $2.75 *Gnome*
North, J.
 °Emperor of the Moon J 8s6d *G. Bles* (B)
Norton, Alice Mary (See Andrew North and Andre Norton, pseudonyms)
Norton, Andre (Pseudonym of Alice Mary Norton)
 °The Crossroads of Time 35¢ *Ace Double* pa
  Star Guard 35¢ *Ace Double* pa
 ————& ed
 °Space Police $2.75 *World*
Nourse, A(lan) E(dward)
  Trouble on Titan J 10s6d *Hutchinson* (B)
O'Brien, C. E.
 °Earth Waits for Dawn $3.75 *Vantage*
Orwell, George
  Animal Farm 25¢ *Signet* pa
Padgett, Lewis (Pseudonym of Henry Kuttner and C. L. Moore in collaboration.)
  Chessboard Planet /The Fairy Chessmen/ 35¢ *Galaxy Novels* pa
Patchett, M(ary) E(lwyn)
  Flight to the Misty Planet J $2.75 *Bobbs-Merrill*
 °Send for Johnny Danger J 6s6d *Lutterworth* (B)
Peake, Mervyn, Wyndham, John & Golding, William
 °Sometime, Never 12s6d *Eyre & Spottiswoode* (B)
Pohl, Frederik
 °Alternating Currents 35¢ *Ballantine* pa
  Alternating Currents $2.00 *Ballantine*
 ————& Kornbluth, C. M.
 °Presidential Year 35¢ *Ballantine* pa
 ————& Williamson, Jack
 °Undersea Fleet J $2.75 *Gnome*
Powys, John Cooper
 °The Brazen Head 18s *Macdonald* (B)
Richards, Guy
  Two Rubles to Times Square $3.50 *Duel, Sloan & Pearce-Little, Brown*
Richardson, Robert S(hirley)
  Second Satellite J $2.75 *Whittlesey*
Robinson, Frank M.
 °The Power $3.00 *Lippincott*
  The Power $3.50 *Longmans, Green* (C)
  The Power $1.15 *Doubleday* BCE
Rockwell, Carey (Group pseudonym)
 °The Robot Rocket J $1.00 *Grosset & Dunlap*
Rohmer, Sax (Pseudonym of Arthur Sarsfield Ward)
  The Si-Fan Mysteries 7s6d *Methuen* (B)
 °Sinister Madonna 25¢ *Gold Medal (Fawcett)* pa
  Sinister Madonna 10s6d *Jenkins* (B)
  The Drums of Fu-Manchu 7s6d *Cassell* (B)

THE ISLAND OF FU-MANCHU 7s6d *Cassell* (B)
THE MOON IS RED 5s *Jenkins* (B)

Russell, Eric Frank
DEEP SPACE 12s6d *Eyre & Spottiswoode* (B)
°MEN, MARTIANS AND MACHINES 9s6d *Dobson* (B)
MEN, MARTIANS AND MACHINES $3.00 *Roy*
°THREE TO CONQUER $2.50 *Avalon*
THREE TO CONQUER $2.75 *Ryerson* (C)

St. Clair, Margaret
°AGENT OF THE UNKNOWN 35¢ *Ace Double* pa
°THE GREEN QUEEN 35¢ *Ace Double* pa

SAKI (Pseudonym of H. H. Munro)
76 SHORT STORIES OF 7s6d *Collins* (B)

Schealer, John M.
°ZIP ZIP AND HIS FLYING SAUCER J $2.50 *Dutton*
ZIP ZIP AND HIS FLYING SAUCER J $2.85 *Smithers* (C)

Schneider, John G.
°THE GOLDEN KAZOO $3.50 *Rinehart*
THE GOLDEN KAZOO 35¢ *Dell* pa

Sellings, Arthur
°TIME TRANSFER 12s6d *Michael Joseph* (B)

Sharp, Margery
THE STONE OF CHASTITY 2s6d *Fontana:Collins* (B) pa

Simak, Clifford D.
°STRANGERS IN THE UNIVERSE $3.50 *Simon & Schuster*
TIME AND AGAIN 12s6d *Heinemann* (B)

Sloane, William
THE UNQUIET CORPSE /The Edge of Running Water/ 25¢ *Dell* pa
————& ed
STORIES FOR TOMORROW 18s *Eyre & Spottiswoode* (B)

Smith, Edward E(lmer)
GALACTIC PATROL $1.00 *Fantasy Press* pa

Smith, George O.
°HIGHWAYS IN HIDING $3.00 *Gnome*

Smith, H. Allen
THE AGE OF THE TAIL $1.49 *Grosset & Dunlap*
THE AGE OF THE TAIL 35¢ *Bantam* pa

Sohl, Jerry
°THE MARS MONOPOLY 35¢ *Ace Double* pa

Sorenson, V.
°STRANGE STORIES 12s6d *Secker* (B)

Stark, Raymond
°CROSSROADS TO NOWHERE 10s6d *Ward, Lock* (B)
CROSSROADS TO NOWHERE $2.25 *British Book Service* (Import)

Steen, Marguerite
°THE UNQUIET SPIRIT $3.75 *Doubleday*

Stewart, George R.
EARTH ABIDES 3s6d *Corgi Giant* (B) pa

Stine, G. Harry (See Lee Correy, pseudonym)

Stoker, Bram
DRACULA 7s6d *Rider* (B) New Edition

Stuart, W. J.
°FORBIDDEN PLANET (from the screenplay by Cyril Hume, from the story
by Irving Black and Allen A. Adler) $3.00 *Farrar, Straus & Cudahy*
FORBIDDEN PLANET (ibid) 35¢ *Bantam* pa
FORBIDDEN PLANET (ibid) 2s *Corgi* (B) pa

Stubbs, Harry Clement (See Hal Clement, pseudonym)

Sturgeon, Theodore (Pseudonym of Edward Hamilton Waldo. See also Fred-
erick R. Ewing, pseudonym in *List Three.*)
A WAY HOME, ed by Groff Conklin (excerpts from) 35¢ *Pyra-
mid* pa
E PLURIBUS UNICORN 35¢ *Ballantine* pa
MORE THAN HUMAN 5s6d *Sidgwick and Jackson* BCE (B)

Summers, Montague ed
THE SUPERNATURAL OMNIBUS 12s6d *Gollancz* (B)

Swann, Thomas Burnett
°WOMBATS AND MOONDUST /Verse/ $2.50 *Wings*

Switzer, Robert
°THE LIVING IDOL (from the screenplay by Albert Lewin) 25¢ *Signet* pa

Temple, William F.
°MARTIN MAGNUS ON MARS J 9s6d *Frederick Muller* (B)

Tenn, William (Pseudonym of Philip Klass)
°THE HUMAN ANGLE 35¢ *Ballantine* pa
THE HUMAN ANGLE $2.00 *Ballantine*
OF ALL POSSIBLE WORLDS 12s6d *Michael Joseph* (B)

Thurber, James
°FURTHER FABLES FOR OUR TIMES $3.50 *Simon & Schuster*

Timperley, Rosemary
°CHILD IN THE DARK $3.50 *Crowell*

Todd, Ruthven
SPACE CAT VISITS VENUS J 7s6d *Chatto & Windus* (B)

Tolkien, J. R. R.
THE RETURN OF THE KING $5.00 *Houghton Mifflin*

Trevor, M.
°THE OTHER SIDE OF THE MOON J 9s6d *Collins* (B)
THE OTHER SIDE OF THE MOON J $2.00 *Collins* (C)

Tubb, E. C.
ALIEN DUST 5s6d *Sidgwick and Jackson* BCE (B)
ALIEN DUST $2.50 *Smithers* (C)
°THE SPACE-BORN 35¢ *Ace Double* pa

Tucker, Wilson
TIME BOMB $1.15 *Doubleday* BCE
WILD TALENT 5s6d *Sidgwick and Jackson* BCE (B)

van Lhin, Eric (Should be Erik. Pseudonym of Lester del Rey)
°POLICE YOUR PLANET $2.50 *Avalon*
POLICE YOUR PLANET $2.75 *Ryerson* (C)

van Vogt, A(lfred) E(lton)
°EMPIRE OF THE ATOM $3.00 *Shasta*
°THE PAWNS OF NULL-A 35¢ *Ace Double* pa

Vance, Jack
°TO LIVE FOREVER 35¢ *Ballantine* pa

To Live Forever $2.75 *Ballantine*

Verne, Jules

°Journey to the Center of the Earth, translated by Willis T. Bradley 35¢ *Ace Single* pa

Journey to the Center of the Earth, Bradley trans. $2.95 *Wyn*

Journey to the Center of the Earth 2s *Scottie* (B) pa

°Jules Verne, Master of Science Fiction 12s6d *Sidgwick and Jackson* (B)

The Short Stories of, edited by I. O. Evans 12s6d *Sidgwick and Jackson* (B)

Vidal, Gore

°Visit to a Small Planet and Other Television Plays $3.50 *Little, Brown*

———& ed

°Best Television Plays 35¢ *Ballantine* pa (Contains *Visit to a Small Planet*)

Viereck, George Sylvester & Eldridge, Paul

My First Two Thousand Years 35¢ *Crest (Fawcett)* pa

Waldo, Edward Hamilton (See Theodore Sturgeon, pseudonym. See Frederick R. Ewing, pseudonym, in *List Three*.)

Wallop, Douglass & Abbott, George

°Damn Yankees /The Year the Yankees Lost the Pennant/ $2.95 *Random House*

Walter, W. Grey

The Curve of the Snowflake /Further Outlook/ $3.75 *Norton*

°Further Outlook 12s6d *Duckworth* (B)

Ward, Arthur Sarsfield (See Sax Rohmer, pseudonym)

Wellard, John

Night in Babylon 4s *Macmillan* (B)

Wells, H. G.

Wheels of Chance & the Time Machine 6s *Dent* (B) New Edition

The World Set Free 6s6d *Collins* (B) New Edition

Wheatley, Dennis

The Black Magic Omnibus 21s *Hutchinson* (B) /Containing *The Devil Rides Out, Strange Conflict, To the Devil-A Daughter*/

The Devil Rides Out 8s6d *Hutchinson* (B)

The Hunting of Toby Jugg 7s6d *Hutchinson* (B)

The Ka of Gifford Hilary 16s *Hutchinson* (B)

Sixty Days to Live 8s6d *Hutchinson* (B)

Star of Ill-Omen 8s6d *Hutchinson* (B)

They Found Atlantis 2s *Arrow:Hutchinson* (B) pa

To the Devil-A Daughter 3s6d *Arrow:Hutchinson* (B) pa

Wibberley, Leonard (Francis)

°McGillicuddy McGotham $2.75 *Little, Brown*

Wilde, Oscar

The Picture of Dorian Gray 35¢ *Dell* pa New Edition

Wilding, Philip

°Shadow Over the Earth J 9s6d *Hennel Locke* (B)

Shadow Over the Earth J $3.50 *Philosophical Library*

Williams, David

°Agent for the West 13s6d *Cape* (B)

Williams, Jay & Abrashkin, Raymond
°DANNY DUNN AND THE ANTI-GRAVITY PAINT   J $2.50   *Whittlesey*

Williams, Nick Boddie
°ATOM CURTAIN   35¢   *Ace Double*   pa

Williamson, Jack & Gunn, James E.
   STAR BRIDGE   35¢   *Ace Single*   pa
————& Pohl, Frederik
°UNDERSEA FLEET   J $2.75   *Gnome*

Wollheim, Donald A.
°ONE AGAINST THE MOON   J $2.75   *World*
————& ed
°THE END OF THE WORLD   25¢   *Ace Single*   pa

Wylie, Philip
°THE ANSWER $1.50   *Rinehart*
   THE ANSWER $1.65   *Doubleday*   (Best-in-Books)
   TOMORROW!   35¢   *Popular Library*   pa

Wyndham, John   (Pseudonym of John Beynon Harris)
°THE SEEDS OF TIME   12s6d   *Michael Joseph*   (B)
   THE SEEDS OF TIME $3.00   *Collins*   (C)
°TALES OF GOOSEFLESH AND LAUGHTER   35¢   *Ballantine*   pa
   TALES OF GOOSEFLESH AND LAUGHTER $2.75   *Ballantine*
————& Golding, William & Peake, Mervyn
°SOMETIME, NEVER   12s6d   *Eyre & Spottiswoode*   (B)

Yelnick, Claude
°THE TREMBLING TOWER   10s6d   *Museum Press*   (B)

Youd, Christopher S.   (See John Christopher, pseudonym)

Zuber, Stanley
°THE GOLDEN PROMISE $3.00   *Pageant*

LIST TWO

January 1, 1957 through December 31, 1957

Adler, Allen A.
°MACH I $3.00   *Farrar, Straus & Cudahy*
   MACH I $3.75   *Ambassador*   (C)

Aichinger, Ilse
°THE BOUND MAN AND OTHER STORIES $2.75   *Noonday*

Aldiss, Brian W.
°SPACE, TIME AND NATHANIEL   12s6d   *Faber & Faber*   (B)
   SPACE, TIME AND NATHANIEL $2.75   *British Book Service*   (Import)

Anderson, Poul
   STAR WAYS   35¢   *Ace Double*   pa
————& Dickson, Gordon R.
°EARTHMAN'S BURDEN $3.00   *Gnome*

Appleton, Victor, II   (Group pseudonym)
°TOM SWIFT ON THE PHANTOM SATELLITE   J $1.00   *Grosset & Dunlap*

Armstrong, Anthony
°THE STRANGE CASE OF MR. PELHAM $2.95   *Doubleday*
   THE STRANGE CASE OF MR. PELHAM $3.50   *Doubleday*   (C)

Burnett, Whit & Burnett, Hallie   eds
　*19 Tales of Terror   35¢   *Bantam*   pa

Campbell, John W., Jr.   ed
　Astounding Tales of Space and Time   (excerpts from the Astounding
　　Science Fiction Anthology)   35¢   *Berkley*   pa

Carr, John Dickson
　*Fire, Burn! $3.50   *Harper*

Castle, Jeffery Lloyd
　*Vanguard to Venus $3.00   *Dodd, Mead*
　Vanguard to Venus $3.50   *Dodd, Mead*   (C)
　Vanguard to Venus $1.15   *Doubleday*   BCE

Christopher, John   (Pseudonym of Christopher S. Youd)
　No Blade of Grass   /The Death of Grass/ $2.95   *Simon & Schuster*

Clarke, Arthur C(harles)
　The City and the Stars   35¢   *Signet*   pa
　The City and the Stars   3s6d   *Corgi*   (B)   pa
　*The Deep Range $3.95   *Harcourt, Brace*
　The Deep Range $4.50   *Longmans, Green*   (C)
　The Deep Range   13s6d   *Muller*   (B)
　*Tales from the White Hart   35¢   *Ballantine*   pa
　Tales from the White Hart $2.75   *Ballantine*

Clement, Hal   (Pseudonym of Harry Clement Stubbs)
　*Cycle of Fire   35¢   *Ballantine*   pa
　Cycle of Fire $2.75   *Ballantine*
　From Outer Space   /Needle/   35¢   *Avon*   pa

Clifton, Mark & Riley, Frank
　*They'd Rather Be Right $3.00   *Gnome*

Coates, Robert M.
　*The Hour After Westerly and Other Stories $3.50   *Harcourt, Brace*

Coblentz, Stanton A.
　*Hidden World $2.75   *Avalon*
　Hidden World $3.00   *Ryerson*   (C)

Cole, Burt
　*SUBI: The Volcano $3.75   *Macmillan*

Collier, John
　Fancies and Goodnights   50¢   *Bantam*   pa   New Edition
　His Monkey Wife $3.75   *Doubleday*
　His Monkey Wife $4.25   *Doubleday*   (C)

Congdon, Don   ed
　*Stories for the Dead of Night   35¢   *Dell 1st Editions*   pa

Conklin, (Edward) Groff   ed
　A Treasury of Science Fiction   (excerpts from)   35¢   *Berkley*   pa
　Big Book of Science Fiction   (excerpts from)   35¢   *Berkley*   pa
　*Thunder and Roses, by Theodore Sturgeon   12s6d   *Michael Joseph*
　　(B)
　———& Conklin, Lucy   eds
　The Supernatural Reader   16s   *Cassell*   (B)

Conklin, Lucy (Mrs. Groff Conklin) & Conklin, Groff   eds
　The Supernatural Reader   16s   *Cassell*   (B)

Conquest, R.
　World of Difference   6s6d   *Ward, Lock*   (B)   New Edition

de Camp, L(yon) Sprague
  °SOLOMON'S STONE $2.75 *Avalon*
  SOLOMON'S STONE $3.00 *Ryerson* (C)
——————& Nyberg, Bjorn
  °THE RETURN OF CONAN $3.00 *Gnome*

Derleth, August ed
  BEACHHEADS IN SPACE (excerpts from) 35¢ *Berkley* pa
——————& Lovecraft, H. P.
  °THE SURVIVOR AND OTHERS $3.00 *Arkham*

Dick, Philip K(endrick)
  °THE COSMIC PUPPETS 35¢ *Ace Double* pa
  °EYE IN THE SKY 35¢ *Ace Single* pa
  °THE VARIABLE MAN AND OTHER STORIES 35¢ *Ace Single* pa

Dickson, Gordon R. & Anderson, Poul
  °EARTHMAN'S BURDEN $3.00 *Gnome*

Dikty, T. E. ed
  5 TALES FROM TOMORROW 35¢ *Crest* (*Fawcett*) pa

Dinensen, Isak
  °LAST TALES $4.00 *Random*
  WINTER'S TALES 35¢ *Dell* pa

Duncan, David
  °OCCAM'S RAZOR 35¢ *Ballantine* pa
  OCCAM'S RAZOR $2.75 *Ballantine*

Eager, Edward
  °MAGIC BY THE LAKE J $2.95 *Harcourt, Brace*

Elam, Richard M. ed
  °TEEN-AGE SUPER SCIENCE STORIES J $2.75 *Lantern Press*
  TEEN-AGE SUPER SCIENCE STORIES J $2.85 *Lantern Press* Library Edition
  °YOUNG READERS SCIENCE FICTION STORIES J $2.50 *Lantern Press*
  YOUNG READERS SCIENCE FICTION STORIES J $2.85 *Lantern Press*
    Library Edition

Eliott, E. C.
  °KEMLO AND THE END OF TIME J 6s *Nelson* (B)

Evans, I. O. ed
  JULES VERNE, MASTER OF SCIENCE FICTION $3.00 *Rinehart*
  JULES VERNE, MASTER OF SCIENCE FICTION $3.50 *Ambassador* (C)

Fallaw, L. M.
  °THE UGGLIANS $3.00 *Philosophical Library*

Farmer, Philip José
  °THE GREEN ODYSSEY 35¢ *Ballantine* pa
  THE GREEN ODYSSEY $2.75 *Ballantine*

Finney, Jack
  °THE THIRD LEVEL $3.00 *Rinehart*
  THE THIRD LEVEL $3.25 *Clark, Irwin* (C)
  THE THIRD LEVEL $1.15 *Doubleday* BCE

Fleming, Ian
  TOO HOT TO HANDLE /Moonraker/ 35¢ *Pocket Perma* pa

Frank, Pat
  FORBIDDEN AREA 35¢ *Bantam* pa
  MR. ADAM 2s *Panther* (B) pa
  SEVEN DAYS TO NEVER /Forbidden Area/ 15s *Constable* (B)

French, Paul (Pseudonym of Isaac Asimov)
  °LUCKY STARR AND THE MOONS OF JUPITER J $2.75 *Doubleday*

Gallico, Paul
  °THOMASINA $3.95 *Doubleday*
  THOMASINA $4.50 *Doubleday* (C)

Gallun, Raymond Z.
  °PEOPLE MINUS X $3.00 *Simon & Schuster*

Gardner, Martin & Nye, Russel B.
  °THE WIZARD OF OZ AND WHO HE WAS $3.75 *Michigan State University Press*

Garrett, Randall (See Robert Randall, pseudonym in collaboration with Robert Silverberg.)

Garver, Ronald G.
  °SAUCER PEOPLE $3.00 *Meador*

Gayle, Henry K. (Harold)
  °SPAWN OF THE VORTEX $3.00 *Comet*

Greenberg, Martin ed
  MEN AGAINST THE STARS (excerpts from) 35¢ *Pyramid* pa

Godwin, Tom
  °THE SURVIVORS $3.00 *Gnome*

Golding, William, Wyndham, John & Peake, Mervyn
  SOMETIME, NEVER 35¢ *Ballantine* pa
  SOMETIME, NEVER $2.75 *Ballantine*

Goodrich, Charles
  °THE GENESIS OF NAM $2.00 *Dorrance*

Gordon, Rex (Pseudonym of S. B. Hough)
  FIRST ON MARS /No Man Friday/ 35¢ *Ace Single* pa

Grinnell, David
  °ACROSS TIME $2.75 *Avalon*
  ACROSS TIME $3.00 *Ryerson* (C)

Gunn, James E.
  THIS FORTRESS WORLD 35¢ *Ace Double* pa

Hamilton, Edmond
  CITY AT WORLD'S END 35¢ *Crest* (*Fawcett*) pa

Harris, John Beynon (See John Wyndham, pseudonym)

Healy, Raymond J. McComas, J. Francis eds
  FAMOUS SCIENCE FICTION STORIES /Adventures in Time and Space/
    $2.95 *Modern Library* (*Random*)

Heinlein, Robert A.
  °THE DOOR INTO SUMMER $2.95 *Doubleday*
  THE DOOR INTO SUMMER $3.50 *Doubleday* (C)
  TIME FOR THE STARS J $1.15 *Doubleday* BCE
  °CITIZEN OF THE GALAXY J $2.95 *Scribner's*
  CITIZEN OF THE GALAXY J $3.25 *Saunders* (C)
  DOUBLE STAR 35¢ *Signet* pa
——& ed
  TOMORROW, THE STARS $2.95 *Doubleday* New Edition
  TOMORROW, THE STARS $3.50 *Doubleday* (C) New Edition

Herbert, Frank
  21ST CENTURY SUB /Dragon in the Sea/ 35¢ *Avon* pa

Hitchcock, Alfred   ed
  °STORIES THEY WOULDN'T LET ME DO ON TV $3.95   *Simon & Schuster*
Hough, S. B.   (See Rex Gordon, pseudonym)
Hubbard, L. Ron
  °FEAR   35¢   *Galaxy Novels*   pa
Jackson, Shirley
  LIZZIE   /The Bird's Nest/   35¢   *Signet*   pa
Jenkins, Will F.   (See Murray Leinster, pseudonym)
Judd, Cyril   (Pseudonym of Judith Merril and C. M. Kornbluth in collaboration.)
  GUNNER CADE   35¢   *Ace Double*   pa
Kornbluth, C. M.   (See Cyril Judd, pseudonym in collaboration with Judith Merril.)
La Farge, Oliver
  °A PAUSE IN THE DESERT $3.50   *Houghton Mifflin*
Leiber, Fritz
  °DESTINY TIMES THREE   35¢   *Galaxy Novels*   pa
  °TWO SOUGHT ADVENTURE $3.00   *Gnome*
Leinster, Murray   (Pseudonym of Will F. Jenkins)
  °CITY ON THE MOON $2.75   *Avalon*
  CITY ON THE MOON $3.00   *Ryerson*   (C)
  °COLONIAL SURVEY $3.00   *Gnome*
  OPERATION: OUTER SPACE   35¢   *Signet*   pa
  OPERATION: OUTER SPACE   10s6d   *Grayson & Grayson*   (B)
  OPERATION: OUTER SPACE $3.75   *Nelson*   (C)
  THE PLANET EXPLORER   /Colonial Survey/   35¢   *Avon*   pa
Leslie, Shane
  °SHANE LESLIE'S GHOST BOOK $3.00   *Sheed & Ward*
Lewis, C. S.
  °THE LAST BATTLE   J $2.75   *Macmillan*
  PERELANDRA   35¢   *Avon*   pa   New Edition
  °TILL WE HAVE FACES $4.50   *Harcourt, Brace*
Long, Charles
  °THE INFINITE BRAIN $2.75   *Avalon*
  THE INFINITE BRAIN $3.00   *Ryerson*   (C)
Long, Frank Belknap
  °SPACE STATION #1   35¢   *Ace Double*   pa
Lovecraft, H. P. & Derleth, August
  °THE SURVIVOR AND OTHERS $3.00   *Arkham*
McComas, J. Francis & Healy, Raymond J.   eds
  FAMOUS SCIENCE FICTION STORIES   /Adventures in Time and Space/ $2.95   *Modern Library* (*Random*)
McGuire, John J. & Piper, H. Beam
  °CRISIS IN 2140   35¢   *Ace Double*   pa
McIlwain, David   (See Charles Eric Maine, pseudonym)
MacLaren, Bernard
  °DAY OF MISJUDGMENT   15s   *Gollancz*   (B)
Maine, Charles Eric   (Pseudonym of David McIlwain)
  °HIGH VACUUM   35¢   *Ballantine*   pa
  HIGH VACUUM $2.75   *Ballantine*

*THE ISOTOPE MAN   11s6d   *Hodder and Stoughton*   (B)
THE ISOTOPE MAN $3.00   *Lippincott*
THE ISOTOPE MAN $3.50   *Longmans, Green*   (C)
THE ISOTOPE MAN $1.15   *Doubleday*   BCE

Mantley, John
THE 27th DAY $3.50   *Dutton*
THE 27th DAY $4.00   *Smithers*   (C)
THE 27th DAY $1.15   *Doubleday*   BCE
THE 27th DAY   5s6d   *Sidgwick and Jackson*   BCE   (B)

Matheson, Richard
*THE SHORES OF SPACE   35¢   *Bantam*   pa

Mead, Harold
*MARY'S COUNTRY   13s6d   *Michael Joseph*   (B)

Merril, Judith   (See also Cyril Judd, pseudonym in collaboration with C. M.
Kornbluth.)   ed
*SF THE YEAR'S GREATEST SCIENCE-FICTION AND FANTASY   *Second Series*
35¢   *Dell 1st Editions*   pa
SF THE YEAR'S GREATEST SCIENCE-FICTION AND FANTASY   *Second Series*
$3.95   *Gnome*

Merritt, A(braham)
THE FACE IN THE ABYSS   35¢   *Avon*   pa   New Edition
THE METAL MONSTER   35¢   *Avon*   pa   New Edition
SEVEN FOOTPRINTS TO SATAN   35¢   *Avon*   pa   New Edition
THE SHIP OF ISHTAR   35¢   *Avon*   pa   New Edition

Michael, Maurice   translator
BACH AND THE HEAVENLY CHOIR, by Johannes Rüber $3.00   *World*

Moore, C. L.   (Mrs. Henry Kuttner)
*DOOMSDAY MORNING $2.95   *Doubleday*
DOOMSDAY MORNING $3.50   *Doubleday*   (C)

Norris, Kathleen
*THROUGH A GLASS DARKLY $3.75   *Doubleday*
THROUGH A GLASS DARKLY $4.25   *Doubleday*   (C)

North, Andrew   (Pseudonym of Alice Mary Norton)
SARGASSO OF SPACE   35¢   *Ace Double*   pa

Norton, Alice Mary   (See Andrew North and Andre Norton, pseudonyms)

Norton, Andre   (Pseudonym of Alice Mary Norton)
*SEA SIEGE   J $3.00   *Harcourt*
*STAR BORN   J $2.75   *World*
STAR BORN   J $3.25   *Nelson*   (C)

Nyberg, Bjorn & de Camp, L. Sprague
*THE RETURN OF CONAN $3.00   *Gnome*

Nye, Russel B. & Gardner, Martin
*THE WIZARD OF OZ AND WHO HE WAS $3.75   *Michigan State University
Press*

Obruchev, V. A.
PLUTONIA   15s   *Lawrence & Wishart*   (B)

O'Connor, Edwin
*BENJY: A FEROCIOUS FAIRY TALE   /NOT J/ $4.00   *Atlantic-Little,
Brown*

Oliver, Chad
*THE WINDS OF TIME $2.95   *Doubleday*

THE WINDS OF TIME $3.50 *Doubleday* (C)
THE WINDS OF TIME $1.15 *Doubleday* BCE
Peake, Mervyn, Golding, William & Wyndham, John
  SOMETIME, NEVER 35¢ *Ballantine* pa
  SOMETIME, NEVER $2.75 *Ballantine*
Piper, H. Beam & McGuire, John J.
  °CRISIS IN 2140 35¢ *Ace Double* pa
Poe, Edgar Allan
  THE PORTABLE EDGAR ALLAN POE $1.45 *Viking* pa
Pohl, Frederik
  °THE CASE AGAINST TOMORROW 35¢ *Ballantine* pa
  °SLAVE SHIP 35¢ *Ballantine* pa
  SLAVE SHIP $2.75 *Ballantine*
  SLAVE SHIP $3.25 *T. Allen* (C)
——— & Williamson, Jack
  °UNDERSEA CITY J $2.75 *Gnome*
Pratt, Fletcher
  DOUBLE JEOPARDY 35¢ *Galaxy Novels* pa
Quinn, James L. & Wulff, Eve P. eds
  °THE FIRST WORLD OF IF 50¢ *Quinn* pa
Rand, Ayn
  °ATLAS SHRUGGED $6.95 *Random*
Randall, Robert (Pseudonym of Randall Garrett and Robert Silverberg in
    collaboration.)
  °THE SHROUDED PLANET $3.00 *Gnome*
Ray, René
  °THE STRANGE WORLD OF PLANET X 10s6d *Herbert Jenkins* (B)
  THE STRANGE WORLD OF PLANET X $2.25 *Smithers* (C)
Rember, W. A.
  °EIGHTEEN VISITS TO MARS $5.00 *Vantage*
Reynolds, Mack & Brown, Fredric eds
  SCIENCE-FICTION CARNIVAL (excerpts from) 35¢ *Bantam* pa
Rhodes, Denys
  °THE EIGHTH PLAGUE 13s6d *Longmans, Green* (B)
Riley, Frank & Clifton, Mark
  °THEY'D RATHER BE RIGHT $3.00 *Gnome*
Robinson, Frank M.
  THE POWER 35¢ *Bantam* pa
  THE POWER 11s6d *Eyre & Spottiswoode* (B)
Rohmer, Sax (Pseudonym of Arthur Sarsfield Ward)
  °RE-ENTER FU-MANCHU 35¢ *Gold Medal* (*Fawcett*) pa
Russell, Eric Frank
  MEN, MARTIANS AND MACHINES 2s6d *Corgi* (B) pa
  THREE TO CONQUER 12s6d *Dobson* (B)
  THREE TO CONQUER 35¢ *Ace Double* pa
  °WASP $2.75 *Avalon*
  WASP $3.00 *Ryerson* (C)
Rüber, Johannes
  BACH AND THE HEAVENLY CHOIR, translated by Maurice Michael $3.00
    World

Sandoz, Maurice
    FANTASTIC MEMORIES $2.00 *Doubleday*
    FANTASTIC MEMORIES $2.50 *Doubleday* BCE
Savage R.
    WHEN THE MOON DIED 6s6d *Ward, Lock* (B) New Edition
Sheckley, Robert
    °PILGRIMAGE TO EARTH 35¢ *Bantam* pa
Shelley, Mary W.
    FRANKENSTEIN 35¢ *Pyramid* pa
Shute, Nevil
    IN THE WET 35¢ *Pocket Perma* pa
    °ON THE BEACH $3.95 *Morrow*
Silverberg, Robert (See also Robert Randall, pseudonym in collaboration
    with Randall Garrett.)
    °MASTER OF LIFE AND DEATH 35¢ *Ace Double* pa
    °THE 13th IMMORTAL 35¢ *Ace Double* pa
Simak, Clifford D.
    STRANGERS IN THE UNIVERSE 35¢ *Berkley* pa
    STRANGERS IN THE UNIVERSE $1.15 *Doubleday* BCE
    STRANGERS IN THE UNIVERSE $4.00 *Musson* (C)
Slesar, Henry
    °20 MILLION MILES TO EARTH 35¢ *Amazing Novels* pa
Smith, George O(liver)
    SPACE PLAGUE /Highways in Hiding/ 35¢ *Avon* pa
    °TROUBLED STAR $2.75 *Avalon*
    TROUBLED STAR $3.00 *Ryerson* (C)
    HELLFLOWER 35¢ *Pyramid* pa
Smith, Thorne
    THE NIGHT LIFE OF THE GODS 2s6d *Penguin* (B) pa
    TOPPER TAKES A TRIP 2s6d *Penguin* (B) pa
Sohl, Jerry
    °THE TIME DISSOLVER 35¢ *Avon* pa
Stevens, William Oliver
    UNBIDDEN GUESTS $3.50 *Dodd, Mead*
Stoker, Bram
    DRACULA 35¢ *Pocket Perma* pa
Stubbs, Harry Clement (See Hal Clement, pseudonym)
Sturgeon, Theodore (Pseudonym of Edward Hamilton Waldo. See also
    Frederick R. Ewing, pseudonym in *List Three*.)
    THE SYNTHETIC MAN /The Dreaming Jewels/ 35¢ *Pyramid* pa
    °THUNDER AND ROSES, edited by Groff Conklin 12s6d *Michael Joseph* (B)
Taine, John (Pseudonym of Eric Temple Bell)
    G.O.G. 666 6s6d *Rich & Cowan* (B) New Edition
Temple, William F.
    MARTIN MAGNUS ON MARS $1.85 *Saunders* (C)
Thurber, James
    °THE WONDERFUL O $3.50 *Simon & Schuster*
Todd, Ruthven
    °SPACE CAT MEETS MARS J $2.25 *Scribner's*
Trevor, M.
    OTHER SIDE OF THE MOON $3.00 *Sheed & Ward*

Tubb, E. C.
    ALIEN DUST $2.75   *Avalon*
    ALIEN DUST $3.00   *Ryerson* (C)

Tucker, Wilson
    TOMORROW PLUS X /Time Bomb/ 35¢ *Avon* pa

van Vogt, A(lfred) E(lton)
    EMPIRE OF THE ATOM $1.15 *Doubleday* BCE
    EMPIRE OF THE ATOM 35¢ *Ace Double* pa
    °THE MIND CAGE $3.50 *Simon & Schuster*

Vance, Jack
    °BIG PLANET $2.75 *Avalon*
    BIG PLANET $3.00 *Ryerson* (C)

Verne, Jules
    JULES VERNE, MASTER OF SCIENCE FICTION, ed by I. O. Evans $3.00
      Rinehart
    JULES VERNE, MASTER OF SCIENCE FICTION, ed by I. O. Evans $3.50
      Ambassador (C)
    THE MYSTERIOUS ISLAND J $1.75 *World* (Rainbow Classics)
    OFF ON A COMET /Hector Servadac/ 35¢ *Ace Single* pa

Waldo, Edward Hamilton (See Theodore Sturgeon, pseudonym. See Frederick R. Ewing, pseudonym, in *List Three*.)

Walker, W. Grey
    FURTHER OUTLOOK 5s6d *Sidgwick & Jackson* BCE (B)

Walters, Hugh
    °BLAST OFF AT WOOMERA J 12s6d *Faber & Faber* (B)

Ward, Arthur Sarsfield (See Sax Rohmer, pseudonym)

Wellman, Manly Wade
    °TWICE IN TIME $2.75 *Avalon*
    TWICE IN TIME $3.00 *Ryerson* (C)

Wells, H. G.
    THE INVISIBLE MAN 35¢ *Pocket Books* pa
    THE TIME MACHINE 25¢ *Berkley* pa

White, James
    °THE SECRET VISITORS 35¢ *Ace Double* pa

White, T. H.
    °THE MASTER $3.50 *Putnam*

Whitehill, Joseph
    °ABLE BAKER AND OTHERS $3.75 *Atlantic-Little, Brown*

Wibberly, Leonard (Francis)
    °TAKE ME TO YOUR PRESIDENT $3.50 *Putnam*

Williams, Jay
    °THE WITCHES $3.50 *Random*

Williams, Robert Moore
    °DOOMSDAY EVE 35¢ *Ace Double* pa

Williamson, Jack & Pohl, Frederik
    °UNDERSEA CITY J $2.75 *Gnome*

Wilson, Richard
    °THOSE IDIOTS FROM EARTH 35¢ *Ballantine* pa

Wollheim, Donald A. ed
    °THE EARTH IN PERIL 35¢ *Ace Double* pa

Wright, Lan
  °WHO SPEAKS OF CONQUEST? 35¢ *Ace Double* pa
Wulff, Eve P. & Quinn, James L. eds
  °THE FIRST WORLD OF IF 50¢ *Quinn* pa
Wyckoff, Nicholas E.
  °THE BRAINTREE MISSION $3.50 *Macmillan*
Wyndham, John (Pseudonym of John Beynon Harris)
  °MIDWICH CUCKOOS 13s6d *Michael Joseph* (B)
———& Golding, William & Peake, Mervyn
  SOMETIME, NEVER 35¢ *Ballantine* pa
  SOMETIME, NEVER $2.75 *Ballantine*
Youd, Christopher S. (See John Christopher, pseudonym)

LIST THREE

RELATED, ASSOCIATIONAL AND NON-FICTION WORKS

Addams, Charles
  NIGHT CRAWLERS $3.95 *Simon & Schuster*
Asimov, Isaac
  INSIDE THE ATOM J $2.75 *Abelard-Schuman*
  ONLY A TRILLION J $3.50 *Abelard-Schuman*
———& Boyd, William C.
  RACES AND PEOPLE J $2.75 *Abelard-Schuman*
Barker, Gray
  THEY KNEW TOO MUCH ABOUT FLYING SAUCERS $3.50 *University Books*
Beller, William & Bergaust, Erik
  SATELLITE! $3.95 *Hanover House* (*Doubleday*)
  SATELLITE! $4.50 *Doubleday* (C)
  SATELLITE! $1.15 *Doubleday* BCE
  SATELLITE! 35¢ *Bantam* pa
Bergaust, Erik, & Beller, William
  SATELLITE! $3.95 *Hanover House* (*Doubleday*)
  SATELLITE! $4.50 *Doubleday* (C)
  SATELLITE! $1.15 *Doubleday* BCE
  SATELLITE! 35¢ *Bantam* pa
Bernstein, Morey
  THE SEARCH FOR BRIDEY MURPHY $3.75 *Doubleday*
———See also Kline, Milton V.
Bonestell, Chesley & Ley, Willy & von Braun, Wernher
  THE EXPLORATION OF MARS $4.95 *Viking*
  THE EXPLORATION OF MARS 25s *Sidgwick and Jackson* (B)
Boyd, William C. & Asimov, Isaac
  RACES AND PEOPLE J $2.75 *Abelard-Schuman*
Bradbury, Ray
  DANDELION WINE $3.95 *Doubleday*
  DANDELION WINE $4.25 *Doubleday* (C)
Brand, Max (See Frederick Faust, pseudonym)

Burgess, Eric
    AN INTRODUCTION TO ROCKETS AND SPACE FLIGHT 12s6d *Hodder & Stoughton* (B)
Capp, Al
    BALD IGGLE $1.00 *Simon & Schuster* pa
Clarke, Arthur C(harles)
    GOING INTO SPACE 75¢ *Trend* pa
    THE MAKING OF A MOON $3.95 *Harper*
Cohn, Victor
    1999 OUR HOPEFUL FUTURE $3.75 *Bobbs-Merrill*
Day, Bradford M. ed
    THE EDGAR RICE BURROUGHS BIBLIOGRAPHY 50¢ *Day* pa
    THE TALBOT MUNDY BIBLIOGRAPHY 50¢ *Day* pa
Dean, Abner
    WHAT AM I DOING HERE? 25¢ *Signet* pa
del Rey, Lester
    ROCKETS THROUGH SPACE J $3.95 *Winston*
Derleth, August
    AUGUST DERLETH: THIRTY YEARS OF WRITING, 1926–1956 gratis *Arkham*
Dingwall, Eric J. & Langdon-Davies, John
    THE UNKNOWN—IS IT NEARER? 35¢ *Signet* pa
Edwin, Ronald
    CLOCK WITHOUT HANDS 10s6d *Sidgwick and Jackson* (B)
    CLOCK WITHOUT HANDS $2.95 *Falcon's Wing Press*
Ernst, Morris L.
    UTOPIA 1976 $3.50 *Rinehart*
Ewing, Frederick R. (Pseudonym of Edward Hamilton Waldo. See also pseudonym Theodore Sturgeon in *List One* and *List Two*.)
    I, LIBERTINE 35¢ *Ballantine* pa /Hoax novel created by demand of New York's *Night People* radio program./
Faust, Frederick
    THE NOTEBOOKS AND POEMS OF "MAX BRAND", ed by John Schoolcraft $6.00 *Dodd, Mead*
Fortune Magazine, eds of
    THE FABULOUS FUTURE $3.50 *Dutton*
Freas, Frank Kelly
    A PORTFOLIO $1.50 *Advent*
Gaines, William M. ed
    UTTERLY MAD 35¢ *Ballantine* pa
Gallant, Roy A.
    EXPLORING MARS J $2.00 *Garden City (Doubleday)*
Gardner, Martin
    FADS AND FALLACIES IN THE NAME OF SCIENCE $1.50 *Dover* pa
Gartmann, Heinz
    THE MEN BEHIND THE SPACE ROCKETS $3.95 *McKay*
    THE MEN BEHIND THE SPACE ROCKETS 18s *Weidenfeld & Nicolson* (B)
Gaul, Albro
    THE COMPLETE BOOK OF SPACE TRAVEL $4.95 *World*
Gibbons, Gavin
    THE COMING OF THE SPACESHIPS 13s6d *Neville Spearman* (B)

Girvan, Waveney
  FLYING SAUCERS AND COMMON SENSE $3.00   *Citadel*

Goodwin, Harold Leland
  THE SCIENCE BOOK OF SPACE TRAVEL   /revised/   35¢   *Pocket Cardinal*   pa

Greenberg, Martin   ed
  COMING ATTRACTIONS $3.50   *Gnome*

Guieu, Jimmy
  FLYING SAUCERS COME FROM ANOTHER WORLD   12s6d   *Hutchinson*   (B)

Jessup, M. K.
  THE UFO AND THE BIBLE $2.50   *Citadel*
  THE UFO ANNUAL $4.95   *Citadel*

Kelly, Walt
  THE POGO SUNDAY BOOK $1.00   *Simon & Schuster*   pa
  POSITIVELY POGO $1.00   *Simon & Schuster*   pa

Kline, Milton V.   ed
  A SCIENTIFIC REPORT ON "THE SEARCH FOR BRIDEY MURPHY" $3.50   *Messner*
  ———See also Bernstein, Morey

Knight, Damon
  IN SEARCH OF WONDER: Essays on Modern Science Fiction $4.00   *Advent*

Langdon-Davies, John & Dingwall, Eric J.
  THE UNKNOWN—IS IT NEARER?   35¢   *Signet*   pa

Levitt, I. M.
  A SPACE TRAVELER'S GUIDE TO MARS $3.50   *Holt*

Ley, Willy
  ENGINEERS' DREAMS   15s   *Phoenix House*   (B)
  ROCKETS, MISSILES AND SPACE TRAVEL $6.75   *Viking*   New Edition
  ———& Bonestell, Chesley & von Braun, Wernher
  THE EXPLORATION OF MARS $4.95   *Viking*
  THE EXPLORATION OF MARS   25s   *Sidgwick and Jackson*   (B)

Linder, Robert
  THE FIFTY-MINUTE HOUR   35¢   *Bantam*   pa

Mallan, Lloyd
  MEN, ROCKETS AND SPACE RATS $5.95   *Messner*
  SECRETS OF SPACE FLIGHT   75¢   *Fawcett*   pa
  SECRETS OF SPACE FLIGHT $2.00   *Arco*

May, Julian   (Mrs. T. E. Dikty)
  THERE'S ADVENTURE IN ATOMIC ENERGY   J $2.50   *Popular Mechanics*
  THERE'S ADVENTURE IN CHEMISTRY   J $2.50   *Popular Mechanics*
  THERE'S ADVENTURE IN ELECTRONICS   J $2.50   *Popular Mechanics*

Moore, Patrick A.
  EARTH SATELLITES $2.95   *Norton*
  GUIDE TO MARS $2.75   *Macmillan*
  THE PLANET VENUS $3.00   *Macmillan*
  SCIENCE AND FICTION   10s6d   *Harrap*   (B)

Michel, Aime
  THE TRUTH ABOUT FLYING SAUCERS $3.95   *Criterion*

Miller, R. DeWitt
  FORGOTTEN MYSTERIES $3.00   *Citadel*
  YOU DO TAKE IT WITH YOU $3.50   *Citadel*